Icefall Cities
Deadly First Contact at the
Edge of a Galactic Empire

MARK EYLES

Ambient Quest Studios Limited

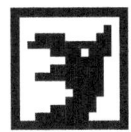

ISBN: 978-1-7391811-0-9

To Simon
thanks for all the
inspiration !
Mark

DEDICATION

Dedicated to Caroline, for keeping me grounded with the
very best advice, and to Joe and Tom for supporting,
encouraging and humouring me.

PROLOGUE – ZEPHYR

An error of one.

Bees, hummingbirds and sun offering ample distraction from data checking. Outside, the sunbaked lunar surface beckoned. Time for tobogganing down gravelly crater walls later.

Concentrate.

Although the colony city on Icefall would not be finished for another hundred years, getting the parameters correct was, if not urgent, then important.

Zephyr's daughter ran past, chasing butterflies.

"Wynd Knowlitch!"

The girl paused and looked round, her mother striking the '1' key so an entry increased from '1' to '11' as she laughed at her daughter's angry expression.

"Nearly had it," said Wynd, bottom lip thrust out, eyebrows creased.

"You certainly did."

Zephyr tapped 'Confirm and send.'

1 - CHECKANI (DAY 1)

Machine murmurings echoed from deep down the spiralling passage. A sharp blade scraping. Light tiles scattered over the walls, floor and ceiling, glowing dimly orange. What should have been a straight corridor instead curled upward and to one side for another hundred metres before dropping away. Heat dissipated from low-profile cooling veins at Checkani's back as her power armour fought against Icefall's high gravity. She ran forward, feet smacking hard on the polished concrete floor. Checkani slowed; the power armour made it easy to lose balance in the high gravity as it fought to compensate.

Sounds from over the peak of the passage's upward curve were getting louder, the metal blade scrape more frantic. A smell of ozone and oil.

"Damn it." Checkani glanced at the universal screwdriver in her hand. The head was randomly switching as it tried to detect a screw or bolt head to attach to.

A confusion of metal, taller than Checkani, lurched into view on nine legs; each leg sharpened to a hardened point. Stalked lens clusters turned to lock on Checkani. It paused and there was a sudden silence. Checkani also stopped. A momentary standoff. There was something spiderish about the machine, but also something of a caterpillar. A central chrome cylinder held within a tangled cage of struts, plates, pistons and motors. An articulated hose probed forward.

This Autono[mid]con had evolved somewhat from the original orderly autonomous constructor that had been printing buildings on Icefall. A little black coagulate oozed from the hose as the machine shifted its weight backward and reared its front end up, three forward legs taking defensive postures.

"You've got to be kidding," Checkani muttered.

She dodged round the side of the machine, looking for the box that would contain the machine's power source and useful 'Emergency Shutdown' button. As she moved, one leg struck at her, glancing off her armoured thigh, making her stumble. She grabbed at the machine with one hand to steady herself and pulled. Falling backwards, Checkani's high gravity weight dragged at the machine, overbalancing it. The Autono[mid]con responded to this perceived attack by withdrawing its legs on her side so it could push her against the passage wall. The outer scales of her armour tensed protectively as Checkani ended up wedged under the side of the machine. A face mask extruded and clicked into place, just in time to stop her cheek from being ripped off. She still had hold of the universal screwdriver in her free hand and pushed it between machine ribs. The business end locked onto a bolt head and unscrewed it. Checkani tried to turn her head against the metal leaning against her, so she could see what she was doing. No 'Emergency Shutdown' switch in sight.

Unscrewed, the bolt came free and clattered to the floor. Nothing happened. The machine remained still, apparently its programming deciding the current impasse was an effective way to combat the threat posed by Checkani's power armoured efforts. Perhaps even realising keeping its prey trapped for some hours would disable it.

Checkani pushed hard, muscles straining against the suit, which did its utmost to amplify and add to the pressure she was exerting. The machine shifted marginally, but the pointed leg ends had chipped small craters in the floor and did not slide. Apparently, the storage cylinder was full, making the machine too heavy to move. Especially as Checkani had ended up half twisted round with one arm pinned against her and the other now stuck in the machine. She continued to push, trying to shift the pressure in different directions. Trying to find a weak spot or a fulcrum she could use to tip the machine away from her.

A sound of metal blades scraping together from the far side of the machine. Heat bleeding through from the cooling veins, trapped between Checkani and the wall. Something oozed over Checkani's vision. Briefly she saw the hose swing closer before coagulant pulsed over the faceplate. Darkness. The sound of the blades got louder and Checkani felt something saw against the armour over her shins.

"Shit, shit, shit. Trimmer blades. Fucking thing's trying to take my legs off." She blinked on her heads-up display.

Indicators, bars, numbers and letters appeared, glowing round the edge of Checkani's visual field. Power was draining fast as the suit worked to maintain its shape against the pressure from the machine that had toppled against it. The temperature of the cooling vanes was rising. In a body outline, she could see the first few leg scales failing, turning from green to yellow and a couple, already, to red. The display helpfully emphasised how little time she had left before the armour failed and she'd be squashed against the wall, cooked as the heat venting failed. Or maybe first her legs would be cut off as the trimmer blades finally sawed through the protective scales.

Checkani continued shifting and pushing, shifting and pushing.

In the seconds she'd been scanning the display, the machine had settled slightly, so now she could move nothing apart from the hand holding the screwdriver. Continuing to push at the machine with all her dwindling energy, she moved her free hand, pushing the universal adaptor against different internal machine parts. There was a click as it locked onto something. In the dark, the screwdriver motor hummed. The machine's blades continued sawing Checkani's legs.

The bit came free, then the sound of another small metal component chittering down through the machine and hitting the floor.

A pause. Checkani held her breath. Just the sawing sound of metal on metal. Her muscles quivered and burned with effort as the heat from the armour made her sweat beyond the point the skintight base-layer could wick it away. Perspiration dribbled into her eyes and she had to squeeze them shut, no longer able to see how her suit was failing.

Frantically, Checkani felt round for another component to undo. Nothing. Her body briefly shook violently and her muscles gave out. She went limp, relying on the structural integrity of the armour to protect her as she paused her fight for a moment while she recovered.

The sawing slowed and ceased.

Checkani stopped breathing, listening. Then the smallest sip of breath. The quiet pulse of her racing heart. A deep whirring, clicks that could be sharpened machine leg ends connecting with the floor near her, and the machine shifted slightly. Checkani stayed still, barely breathing, blinking sweat from her eyes. Looking at the tear blurred heads-up display, she could see her armour slowly reducing its energy demands.

The machine slowly shifted its weight off her. She risked pulling her arm out from the machine interior. Seemed it no longer perceived her as a threat now she was no longer fighting against it. Blindingly simple machine logic, though the We Print Cities constructors should never have attacked a human, even if that human was tasked with shutting them down.

Checkani wiped the coagulant from her faceplate and retracted it.

The deviant Autono[mid]con lurched away down the passage, the way she had come. Heading for the entrance. In the centre of its rear a bright red 'Emergency Shutdown' button. Checkani dashed forward and slapped it. The Autono[mid]con legs paused in mid-stride; lens clusters swung to gaze at Checkani. A shiver ran down her spine, and she kept absolutely still as adrenaline flooded her bloodstream. The machine's legs started moving again as it continued on its way. Apparently the 'Emergency Shutdown' button was as messed up as the rest of the robot.

Suddenly, she was aware of pain.

Checkani looked at her leg to see blood glistening down her left leg and over her foot; dribbling from a tear between armoured scales where blades had been sawing at her shin. The other leg had some torn scales, but had held against the blades. She leant against the wall, taking steady breaths as she tried to calm her heart's frantic drumming, hands clenching and unclenching.

Quality assurance sure was turning out as a dangerous business to be in.

2 - CHECKANI (DAY 1)

Icefall should have been simple.

We Print Cities, Inc. had sent constructors through a Bulk-jump Engine portal to Icefall a hundred years ago. The autonomous constructors had to source local materials, duplicate themselves, do a little light terraforming, and build a single standard outpost city. The outpost city arcology comprising a ten kilometre diameter ring of city-block round a central roofed park and farm area. Autonomous constructors are necessarily left alone until the Quality Assurance Response Division visits to verify the end result. Before the first delivery of settlers.

Although an old technology, the underlying complexity of using the Bulk-jump Engine meant their use was limited to preprogrammed locations. Existing colonies being prioritised for Bulk-jump Engine use, new colonies being left to fend for themselves until they became a significant source of products and people.

There was also an entanglement issue that prevented more than a single Bulk-jump Engine being built on a planet. All the Orion-Cygnis Colonisation Collective Bulk-jump Engines used the same code for navigating the Bulk. Portals through the Bulk overlapped if the two Bulk-jump Engine entry points were within a few tens of thousands of kilometres of each other. Vehicles in transit occupying the same portal space tended to cause planetary crust rupturing explosions. The small number of Bulk-jump Engines made their use subject to extreme restrictions.

Earlier in the day, before the encounter with the Autono[mid]con, Checkani arrived at a briefly existing Icefall orbit exit point. She travelled via the dimensional bending of Earth's Bulk-jump Engine, housed in evacuated tunnels beneath Lausanne. Checkani's forty metre long cylinder of ship, Hellebore, accelerated down a glass lined tunnel and through a ten metre wide hole in space-time to emerge in Icefall orbit. A scan revealed not the expected single outpost city, but an overlapping sprawl of eleven outpost city rings, with a confusion of merged park and farm areas. The outpost cities stretched from the coast towards the foothills of a low mountain range. This was not what the automated updates from the Autono[]cons had been reporting. Quite some discrepancy to investigate. Should make for an interesting report.

Arriving in orbit, Hellebore dropped a small communications satellite, then unfolded her stubby wings. She plummeted towards the planet's surface, safely dropping through snow heavy cloud to a roof landing pad on a coastal wall city spur. Short legs extended as wings folded. The pad on a curl of city wall at the seaward edge of the conurbation of outpost cities. While Hellebore cooled, and pooling snowmelt beneath her refroze, Checkani called up data recorded in orbit. There was something very wrong. Not only were there multiple outpost cities, but they were fraught with irregularities. Nine were in an overlapping cluster, two stood off to the sides.

Interfacing with the city's higher systems' data-space should have been easy, but Hellebore's assistems were getting nothing intelligible beyond the most basic systems. The highest priority was finding the Bulk-jump Engine that would normally be at the centre of an outpost city, one of the first structures built from parts shipped in with the first constructors.

Checkani blinked off the data display. She'd stripped off

her utilitarian one piece, sprayed on a base-layer, then scooped up handfuls of silvered power cells, spreading them over her body until they manoeuvred and linked themselves into a second skin. Finally, she stepped backwards into the Pangolin Power Armour alcove. Armour ribbons of matt black scales folded over to encase her, sealing scale to scale. Faceplate, cooling vanes, autonomic control systems and expert assistems all installed themselves. Standard metal smart tools clamped to her hip, essential for dealing with first problems.

Pangolin Power Armour was requisite for the first checks on a new outpost, offering protection against environmental hazards.

Looking like a person-shaped shadow-hole in the world, Checkani stepped onto the ice crusted city roof in flurries of snow. Sounds of waves far below. Checkani walked over to a low concrete parapet at the far edge of the pad and looked out over a grey-green sea. Muscular waves undulated and broke against the city wall. She could smell the seaweed tang of the thick Terraformulaz surface bloom. Leaning over, she could see the waves had eroded the base of the wall, creating a shallow overhang. Seemed this part of the city had been here for some time. Looking left and right, she could see many rectangular windows punctuating the wall, grouped in random clusters.

A roof entrance lifted open when she tackled its command box with the universal screwdriver. The screwdriver bit quickly, adapting to the triangular screw heads, enabling her to access, and short circuit, the simple locking mechanism. A sloping passage into the city interior was revealed. A little snow fell inside as the door opened, melting in warmer air.

Checkani walked carefully down the slope as she acclimatised to the slightly higher gravity, gentle orange light making her power armour's scales glow. Then the passage tilted sideways as it continued to descend. Checkani then heard the first distant machine sounds.

3 - CHECKANI (DAY 1)

After Checkani's encounter with the Autono[mid]con, walking on the injured leg was not too painful. Though the high gravity was maybe making the bleeding worse. The suit's base-layer should help stem the flow as it tried to self-repair over the cut. Checkani decided to keep going. There should be some accommodation units where she could wash the wound. The floor tilted sideways until it became a wall, while a wall turned into the floor as the passage twisted. The new floor pitched downward, going deeper. There were fewer glowing tiles, but while their orange light decreased, there was white light up ahead, glimmering in the tilting passage.

Rounding a curve, Checkani could see an opening where the passage ended. Beyond, a balcony overlooked dimly lit parkland. Disappearing into the distance, rows of pillars held up a transparent roof on which rivulets of water flowed between drifts of snow. Protected from the native weather, and with its own controlled climate, the parkland was warm. Her suit adjusted, armour scales shifting to allow more airflow.

Checkani was used to quiet when checking a new outpost, but this one seemed unnaturally still. She realised it was the lack of insects. Normally there would be a background buzz, but this place seemed to lack any living things apart from vegetation. Checkani blinked on the

<visual zoom> assist, scanning the parkland. She spotted a curl of smoke in the distance, by one of the roof support pillars. This was odd. No people had been sent through yet. Were the machines lighting fires now? Shouldn't be part of their protocol.

Checkani looked the length of the balcony and saw there was a slope at one end, spiralling to the ground, a third of a kilometre down. Her leg had stopped bleeding, but the smoke looked to be around five kilometres away. She turned back, retracing her steps.

The passage was quiet, if a little disorientating, gradually rotating through ninety degrees, while spiralling. Thankfully, no more mutated, out-of-control Autono[mid]cons.

The snowfall had increased and was settling on Hellebore's lemon yellow fuselage. Checkani had a sudden craving for cupcakes. The Autono[mid]con was beyond the ship, next to the parapet; its lens clusters pointed out towards the horizon. Checkani warily moved a little closer and saw its pointed legs stepping rapidly on the spot, making a percussive sound. Though not regular, but weaving a more complex rhythm that seemed to drift in and out of phase as it slowly evolved. Checkani looked nervously round for someone, something, controlling it. This was not how Autono[]cons behaved.

Back in her ship Checkani cleaned, then taped the cut on her leg. Covered it with a fresh spray of base-layer and spread over power cells. Finally, she slapped on a handful of armour scales to replace the broken ones. Next she went to a little used hatch near the door. She pressed three fingers against a locking plate grid and with a mechanical click the door swung open. Important, this was accessible, even if the ship's electronics failed. With anticipation and a quickening of her heart, she withdrew two Ringnife Drones; small matt black spheres, small enough to hold both in one palm. Destruct-one and Destruct-two. Then the hilt of a Mono-flow Sword, also matt black, the memory metal and monofilament wire blade folded into the hilt. Finally, two small hemispherical Hi-velocity Turrets. The Ringnife Drones rolled onto her armour and to holsters on the back of her right forearm. She placed the hilt on the outside of her left forearm, where it adhered to an armour hardpoint. She placed one turret on each shoulder.

Dropping the armour's faceplate over her eyes, Checkani accessed her assistems and called up <armament active>. Two cross hairs for the turrets appeared in the centre of her visual field and then drifted away, parking themselves in the corners of her vision. Sword and drone status widgets popped up next to the cross hairs.

At the door of the ship, Checkani held up her right hand, then sent <command reconnoitre>. The Ringnife Drones dropped from her arm, buzzed and rose to eye height. Short blades spinning round their equators propelled them, working hard to overcome the high gravity. Ordering them forward, they rose and moved over the Autono[mid]con, their cameras feeding to two box-outs at the side of her visual field. Checkani <command return>ed them to her arm.

Next she took the Mono-flow Sword hilt in her right hand and <command deploy>ed it. As the sword hilt pulled away from her arm, a metre of shining metal blade shimmered out and locked into position, invisible monofilament wires at either cutting edge.

"All working. Good."

Checkani swung the sword in a couple of arcs, snowflakes swirling around her as she stepped away from her ship.

"Dammit, I love this sword." She hurried towards the Autono[mid]con by the parapet, which was still drumming its legs against the ground.

"Ha!" She sliced through two nearest legs. The Autono[mid]con toppled towards her as she side-stepped and took out another leg. Checkani jumped back. Slid round the machine, cutting off the rest of the legs. Lens clusters all straining towards her as short leg stumps thrashed spasmodically, unable to get a purchase on anything.

With the Autono[mid]con disabled, Checkani took her time locating the machine's power pack and then cut it in half. There were a couple of sparks and the smell of burning insulation as the lens clusters, cutters, and hose slumped down.

"Dead!" Checkani <command retract>ed the sword blade into the hilt. Clipped this back on her arm. Hugging herself, she ambled back to the ship. A grim smile pulling at the corners of her mouth. She had enjoyed that far too much. At least it was just a machine; there would be no remorse. The Ringnife Drones and Mono-flow Sword were reassuring weights on her arms, pulling at her attention. Suggesting ways in which they might solve problems for her. She felt complete. Ready.

"Maybe I shouldn't have got them out. They're probably not the best way to resolve issues."

Though the weapons felt so right. She would not put them away. Icefall was far too weird to confront without the ability to defend herself.

The door closed behind her. The ship warmed. Time to eat and get some sleep, but first a verbal update to the log. Hellebore would create a full report, gathering data from her armour and augmentations. From the weapons, too.

"Icefall should have been simple, but we should have known from the too perfect reports something was not right. And the last operational report from the Bulk-jump Engine was nearly fifty years ago.

"You can see from the data the Autono[]cons have malfunctioned in some terrible way, building multiple overlapping outpost cities. The Autono[]cons must have multiplied exponentially when they first arrived to achieve this. There are not just too many cities, but they're distorted and broken in some fundamental way.

"It's bleak, cold and tiring in the high gravity. I like it. There is something visceral about Icefall. Tomorrow I'll investigate the smoke. You can see it in the feeds Hellebore will include with this."

Before finally removing her armour for the night, she again ventured outside and asked Hellebore to open a hatch in the ship's side. A door concertinaed back. <bike unfold>. Two large motor-wheels with a low slung seat between; handlebar controller, a curving windshield, storage panniers. Chrome and electric blue. Checkani asked <bike status>. Data appeared at the side of her visual field. All the bike systems were optimal. She took the tools from her armour and stored them in a pannier. The weapons she would keep on her suit.

4 - MOZARYTHM (DAY 2)

Rolling out of bed and upright, Mozarythm's feet slipped straight into carefully placed slippers. Then standing still, listening, he could hear the rapidy tapidy, dank dink, dun dum of his Mekorchestra. Hear how much time had passed since he'd fallen asleep, how the mingling rhythms had evolved. How the melody had changed according to his plan. Twenty-three years, twenty-one days into the performance.

A feeling of calm as the music flowed through him. Through his mind/body-tech.

Mozarythm added wood to his stove, watched the flames, smelled the smoke. Set a kettle on the stove. Looking inward, he called up the day's task list. Repair, deploy, compose, guide and listen. The time displayed at the corner of his vision ticked on with a reassuring consistency. He pushed his lank hair away from his eyes and sniffed his body odour. Not a washing day; all within acceptable limits. Water boiling. He made a mug of black tea, taking it with him as he left his cabin.

Outside in the warm park air, three Autono[small]cons he'd adapted to meet his survival needs were carrying wood, plants, roots, beans, nuts and water. Mozarythm dismissed them to their allotted tasks and headed across the forest clearing to the large geodesic dome in which his Mekorchestra was about to start the 9,196th movement of his magnum opus "Periodic Resolution of Need".

He entered the control room so he could listen to some highlights of the 9,195th movement, recorded when he'd been asleep. The 'staying awake' experiment a year into the piece had not gone well. He'd needed to abandon it after four days, when the hallucinations had made him feel acutely out of control.

Straightening his chair so it was precisely centred between the speakers, he called up the highlights. Eyes closing, he lost himself in the excerpts selected by his software. An hour later, he was standing on the podium looking over the Mekorchestra. Legs and arms drummed on wood and metal as the modified Autono[]cons, 'Autono[music]cons', struck out the rhythms of his piece. Further Autono[music]cons whistled with hollowed lengths of tube or scraped tensed threads across groups of vibrating strings.

Warm air shimmered over the processor cube to one side of the Mekorchestra. The lens clusters of the Mekorchestra strained towards Mozarythm as he raised his arms, baton poised. Then he was lost in the music, hearing the responses to his gestures as he shifted the cool crystallising patterns of sonic ripples; volumetric sound, colours popping and rolling behind closed eyes. A precision he felt through every fibre, as the 9,196th movement took shape.

A calmness of breath. Just a little perspiration beading on his skin in the warm air currents of the dome. A familiar smell of ozone.

Passing time unravelling; lost to him as he sank into the present, focused on the architectural grandeur of the music he was creating.

"Hey!"

A shout? Someone called out?

Heart sprinting, Mozarythm gasped and jump-stumbled from the podium, almost falling. Eyes snapping open, the brightness momentarily overwhelming. Baton tip pointing toward the interruption.

"Sorry, did I make you jump?"

Mozarythm squinted as his eyes adjusted to the light. The piece continued to unfold according to his plan, but without his variations, his extemporisation. A figure stood in the doorway. He could feel cool air against his skin.

"Away. Go away," he whispered, then, "Who are you?"

A woman in dull black metallic armour. The skin of her face symmetrically zebra patterned coffee and cream.

"Checkani, though I think I should ask the questions. This planet should be empty. Who are you? Where did you come from? Is there anyone else?" Her voice pitched above the music.

"Quiet! Listen!" Mozarythm cocked his head to the left, his open palm raised, exaggeratedly listening. His eyes closed. Waiting. She would be gone and he could get back to the music.

"What are you doing here? What is this noise? What have you done with those Autono[]cons?"

Mozarythm looked back at her. She had moved into the dome and was close to him.

"And why are you naked?"

"I'm not naked." Mozarythm lifted his right foot to show her one of his slippers. "I'm Mozarythm."

"Can you stop that noise so we can talk?"

"Noise?" Mozarythm turned his back on her, facing back to the Mekorchestra. Shoulders hunched, tight fists raised, teeth clenched; he made a growling noise.

Behind him she spoke again: "Look, I need some answers. Currently, I'm the ultimate authority on this planet. I'll have to shut the place down if there are problems."

Mozarythm silently walked past her, heading for the dome door, eyes downcast, avoiding the woman's gaze. He ground his teeth, the corners of his mouth down-turned. This was his home, his place. She had no right to be here. This was why he had left Indomitaville, when he no longer wished to be the Engineer. When he wanted distance from people.

"Don't you walk out on me. That's unacceptable." Following him out of the dome, the armoured woman stepped round in front of him. Something odd about the way she moved; a quickness to it. An armoured index finger planted in the centre of his chest halted him. He looked into her eyes, then quickly away.

"I'm nothing to do with them at the moment. Leave me alone. I'm busy."

"Who? Who are you nothing to do with?"

"The Outpost. Indomitaville. I used to live there, but I left. They didn't like my music."

"Indomitaville? Where's that?"

"Over that way, in the wall city." Mozarythm pointed and waved a hand vaguely in a direction that led into the trees beyond his living quarters.

"And who's there? In Indomitaville?"

"My parents. The Community of Ancestral Seekers. The Ancistorians."

"The what? This is getting more fucked by the minute." The armoured woman looked over her shoulder towards Indomitaville. "You stay here. I'll check back when I have a better idea of what's happening." Turning from him, she hurried to a two-wheeled vehicle, sat astride it and accelerated quietly into the trees.

Mozarythm blinked. Looked at his chest where she had pushed her finger into his skin. There was nothing there, no mark, no evidence of her presence. The sound of the Mekorchestra, a quiet phrase repeating. He knew where the phrase would meander to. Could feel the shape of it and how he could alter it, to lead to a satisfying crescendo.

Back on the podium, baton guiding, all lenses on him, Mozarythm sank back into the complexity.

5 - CHECKANI (DAY 2)

Checkani sped through the forest, her bike avoiding collisions. Only the barely perceptible murmur of the motor and a hum of wheels pushing into the ground signalling her passage. Where had that naked guy come from? Were there more? At least he spoke Common. This was turning into one seriously fucked up visit. She still hadn't detected the Bulk-jump Engine that should have been one of the first structures built.

The bike emerged from the forest into gently undulating parkland containing rivers, lakes, oaks, elms, stands of bamboo, Japanese maple, fields of grass and vegetation Checkani didn't recognise. Punching straight up over the parkland, the fluted, tapered support pillars soared to the roof material 350 metres above. Ahead, above the treetops, a wall city. This one appearing as though built from red sandstone; balconies sweeping along its side, arched windows and doorways gazing out over the forest. There should be no one here, but Checkani had an uneasy feeling the city wasn't empty of people.

The ground at the foot of the wall city was paved in the same ersatz sandstone; Checkani drove parallel to the wall until she reached a gateway. She turned in and cruised to a stop before reaching the shadows. She held up her right arm and <command reconnoitre>ed The Ringnife Drones, Destruct-one and Destruct-two. They rose and disappeared into the dark tunnel leading into the city. Checkani leaned back into the bike seat and watched the drones' feeds change hue as they reached artificially lit areas within the wall city. Corridors, stairs, slopes, atria, alcoves, chambers, rooms. The layout looked standard, but it was all built of the red sandstone, which was not normal. Standard outpost cities appeared to be built of many materials, differentiating areas and uses. This looked like a deserted ruin, rather than a fresh city waiting for settlers.

A movement in Destruct-one's feed. A figure ducking into a doorway. Checkani leaned forward. A small object flickered towards Destruct-one. The drone dodged, tilted, and used its equatorial blades to slice into something. A bright flash. The view from the drone's feed slid upward as it fell, then stabilised. Destruct-two converged on the landing where Destruct-one was wobbling forward to see what had attacked it. Repair system progress flagged up alongside Destruct-one's feed.

Twists of metal sparking on the floor as a ruined battery finished discharging. Didn't look dangerous. No obvious weaponry.

Checkani sent <command seek> to Destruct-two. The landing was part of a spiral stair running up the side of a huge lightwell, natural light flooding down from above. The feed showed a corridor off the landing. Far down the passage, a black-cloaked figure retreating. Destruct-two tilted and accelerated forward, quickly closing in. Checkani opened another window and zoomed, froze, enhanced. A short humanoid shape. Although drone audio was poor, Checkani could clearly hear loud cries. Not words, but cries of fear. Or anger. She got the drone to hang back a bit, interested to see where the person (Robot? Cyborg?) was going. They dodged through a side opening and were gone. Destruct-two got to the doorway and turned so it could use its primary lens to look along the wide passage the figure had run down. They were there, but slowing, lumbering.

<command attack/disable>

Destruct-two sped up and as it reached the fleeing person, it briefly retracted its blades and tapped the back of their skull. The drone flicked its blades back out and lifted away from them as they overbalanced and fell forwards, crying out. Destruct-two hovered low above the person as they rolled clumsily along the floor and then lifted onto hands and knees. Destruct-one arrived and joined its twin.

Checkani ran into the city, the route to the Ringnife Drones flashing across her visual field.

The person rolled over, sitting, their face yellow and grinning. Eyes popping out. Loose dark clothing. The drones lowered a little; Destruct-one focusing on face, Destruct-two on torso. The person put their arms up protectively, across chest and face. Then reached to rub their knees with one hand.

Still running, Checkani grabbed her sword hilt, swung it up, <command deploy>.

The figure reached into a pocket. Destruct-two dropped, a brief acceleration before the blades retracted, and banged into the arm, hard. The person howled, curled foetally around the injured arm. Destruct-two rolled away on the floor and then leaped into the air, blades once again extended and spinning.

Running onto a landing on the side of the vast lightwell, stairs spiralling up and down. Through a second exit from the landing. Through the next opening.

Shouting: "Stop. Don't move."

Minimising the drone feeds. Sword blade pointing forwards. The dark figure was sobbing. They'd rolled over to seated, still hunched about their right arm and rubbing their knees.

"What are you doing here?" Checkani asked.

"Ouch. You've hurt my arm." The yellow face was comically exaggerated. Huge nose, extended mouth, monstrous eyes.

"Keep your hands where I can see them," blade point hovering in front of the bright yellow face. The eyes blinked, slowly.

"Why'd you hurt me?" A sniffling cry.

<command return> to the drones.

"You attacked my drones and ran away."

"You broke my flyer," he sobbed.

There was something very wrong with the figure's face. Pointing the sword to one side, Checkani reached down with her free hand and caught the chin between finger and thumb. As she pulled, the skin stretched and then tore away.

"Ow! My face!" The figure grabbed at Checkani's hand with their uninjured arm. A futile gesture against the power armour.

Bloodlessly the yellow face tore back to reveal dark ochre skin. A teenage boy's pained face. Checkani dropped the mask on the ground, its eyes continued blinking.

"So, where do you live, you little shit?" Checkani <command retract>ed the blade and clipped the hilt back on her arm.

"Bank. My name's Bank." He seemed to forget about his injured arm.

"Where do you live? Show me." Grabbing Bank's good arm, Checkani pulled him up. A teenage boy, nearly as tall as her; not a threat.

"This way." Bank pulled away from Checkani, moving on down the corridor. He looked back with narrowed eyes. "I'll get even with you. You shouldn't have hurt me."

6 - CHECKANI (DAY 2)

Bank led Checkani along a dimly lit curving passage that opened out into a broad balcony on the wall of another huge lightwell, this one maybe half a kilometre across. Peering over the balcony, Checkani could see a grid of buildings on the floor far below. The structures continued some way up the walls of the lightwell; above them the walls were swathed in plants, thinning out below the balcony. The buildings and plants would be expected, but the people milling around below were not.

Checkani looked over at the boy. She didn't want to have to keep him with her, but she couldn't let him tell the people below about her presence before she had decided what to do with them. She didn't want to have to go chasing after them if they ran. Which they probably would do.

"Damn it."

There was no clear protocol for trespassers. This just did not happen. The distances were too great, the coordinate system securely hidden, and the resources required to run a Bulk-jump Engine prohibitive.

"How many people are down there? Are there any other settlements?" Checkani asked.

"No other towns. Only us." Then sing song: "The indomitable citizens of Indomitaville," and then: "I hate it here."

She would have to go down and speak to them. She

checked her weapon systems. Although Checkani had not come across trespassers before, she had met pioneers settling on new planets. They could be independent and problematic, modelling themselves on some fictional galactic frontiers-person trope.

Checkani followed Bank down.

Indomitaville was quiet, but as Checkani reached the first buildings, people started to follow her. Both men and women were dressed in baggy black trousers and shirts. The men bearded, everyone wearing their hair long, all of them with the same dark ochre coloured skin. No skin patterning, no jewellery, no visible modifications. She continued down and into the main town, heading for a central plaza. The buildings only two stories tall and of simple design. Open doorways and windows. No doors or shutters. Some people sitting on stone seats at the base of the walls, unaware of her, eyes shut.

By the time she reached the plaza, there were nearly a hundred people around Checkani. At some point she had lost Bank in the crowd. Her gaze flicked round, checking for weapons. Faces all strangely blank. No smiles, no aggression. There were a few solemn faced children, each holding onto their guardians' trousers. She stopped and waited, turning slowly, looking in one set of dead eyes after another. Was someone going to step up and talk to her? Even if they were not talking to each other.

An odd standoff. No one seemed in charge. Some of the crowd was quietly drifting off. Apparently they had lost interest?

"OK. I'll start. Who's in charge here?" The people nearest Checkani looked at each other. The settlement was eerily quiet. No talking, no machinery, no recorded sounds. Seemed that by a process of attrition, she was getting to the leaders. Or at least someone who would speak to her. Bank appeared again, pushing towards the front, with a cross between a smile and a grimace on his face; a couple of other teenagers wearing masks trailed behind him. He was the most animated of the inhabitants.

An older man, white bearded, walked forward and stood close to her. Too close.

"We do not understand your question. Or rather, we understand it, but it has little meaning here. We have had a council to represent us in the past, but there has been no need for it for many years. You're from the wider galactic community? Why have you come here?"

"I'm with the Quality Assurance Response Division of We Print Cities. This is our city, our planet."

The old man smiled.

"How can anyone own a planet? That's absurd!"

"Well, we own this city you're squatting in."

"Us Ancistorians have been here nearly fifty years. Got as much right to this planet as you. You're the interloper."

"So you could live on Icefall without our city? We Print Cities' technology?"

"We could live anywhere; don't care about the outer world. We search the past, our Ancestarchives. Lives of the last thousand years stored in our body-tech. Our Ancestarchives. Passed down from generation to generation. We make sense of our world and our lives by understanding the past. By living the past lives of our ancestors in virtual worlds, we contribute to the Understanding of Being. I do not think it's something you'd comprehend."

"So why did you come here, to Icefall?"

"We want the perspective. The independence. To always be as far from the noise of galactic civilisation as possible. We are nomadic, but on long timescales; always living on the most distant planet. Understand that when we came here, it was still being terraformed, and it seemed no one would arrive for many years. We planned to move on, an exodus to the next distant world."

"But you're still here."

"Yes, we are still here; and no way to leave. Nowhere to go."

"You have your own Bulk-jump Engine?"

"No. We would've used the one built at the city's centre, but it's not working. Our engineer told us that the Computational Core was malfunctioning. We were content to remain here."

"How did you get here?"

"Bulk-jump Engine on Lostlandedge, a little further Earthwards along the Orion-Cygnis Arm."

Checkani sighed. "I know where Lostlandedge is. There are no settlement planets further out than Icefall. At least, none currently being prepared for settlers. This is at the furthest reach of the Orion-Cygnis Colonisation Collective. There's no one beyond where we are now."

"In that case, we'll have to stay here. On Icefall."

"You'll have to take that up with the Colonial Planets Settlement Corps when they arrive."

The old man clenched his jaw and looked behind him, where there were fewer than twenty people still standing. He looked back at Checkani and shrugged.

"We will stay on Icefall. There is Precedent; though you won't know about it. Although it's inconvenient, I'll call for our Council to be reinstated. We'll need it to communicate with you and your masters."

The old man turned and walked away. The rest of the crowd lost interest and walked off. Bank and his two masked friends remained, watching her.

"Hey, boy." Bank made a step towards Checkani, then scowled.

"Name's Bank." He glanced quickly at his two friends, a girl with a ghoulish green mask and a boy with a skull mask.

"Whatever. Do you know where I can find the Bulk-jump Engine?"

Bank looked at his friends. Their masks gave nothing away. He turned back.

"Yeah. It's under the Ruins. Everyone knows that."

"Where are they?"

Bank pointed towards a balcony on the far wall, low

down in a gap in the vegetation. "Through there. Takes you into more woods; then to another wall city and then through that to the Ruins. The engine is at the centre, beneath the pyramid."

"Thanks." Checkani turned and headed back to retrieve her bike.

7 - CHECKANI (DAY 2)

As she sat at the wall city entrance, eating by her parked bike, Checkani checked in with Hellebore. She uploaded a summary of her encounter with the Ancistorians. Got Hellebore to add it to the information packet ready for beaming back to We Print Cities. A communications portal should soon be opened for a few seconds by the Lausanne Bulk-jump Engine.

She accessed the orbital photo-montage of the conurbation; matching it to the 3D map Hellebore had created. The overlapping circles of city were clear, but the roofing over the central parklands prevented interior detail. Too much snow obscuring the view. Where city walls crossed they were creased and cracked, breaking through each other, internal corridors pushing out the sides looking like frayed fabric.

The walls of the coastal city, where Hellebore landed, had tendrils of building curling away from its outer edges. A fractal look Checkani had noticed flying in. Some of the other cities seemed to have similar fragmentation of their structure. A ring city, circled by five others, overlapped into the parkland she had travelled to get to Indomitaville. Indomitaville was in that overlapping arc of that central city. Perhaps the first city; built before things went wrong? She updated the map with the info from her navigational assistems: Sea City, First City, Landing Site, Naked Guy dome, Indomitaville and, presumably, Ruins. Bulk-jump Engine in the centre?

Checkani got back on her bike and headed through Indomitaville. No one stopped her; the few Ancistorians she saw were still sitting alone on benches, eyes closed. Presumably lost in inner virtual worlds, communing with their ancestors?

The balcony Bank had pointed out was easily reached via a coiling ramp. The passages beyond were wide and easy to bike through; they lead to a ramp spiralling down to wooded parkland. Another wall city loomed not far away, though this one didn't have the red sandstone look, but concrete inset with a random scattering of openings and windows. Checkani checked the map; this was the other side of the wall city she had landed on. Looking left and right, she could see where the Sea and First Cities crossed through each other. Looked very much like they had been crushed together against their will. Travelling through the wall city ahead of her would take her to the central parkland area of First City and the Ruins. Hopefully, to the Bulk-jump Engine too.

The Sea City wall section she came to was every bit as messed up as the section she had landed Hellebore on. Tunnels through the city twisted and turned, challenging her bike's stabilisation systems. The high gravity persistently tried to drag the bike over. Leaning round corners, the bike bounced from one surface to another as walls became floors. Finally, Checkani emerged from the passages at the top of a wide viaduct that swept smoothly down to the ground on a series of sturdy arches. Checkani braked, her rear wheel skidding round, so the bike was side on to the view. The Ruins.

The rolling parkland she would have expected in the central area of the First City was missing. In the insipid evening light, the Ruins tumbled into the distance; dull grey piles of blocks, columns, wall fragments, broken archways and other pieces of architectural detritus. Like a giant had scooped up Earth's classical age ruins and roughly dumped them randomly into the parkland, the high gravity pulling them shatteringly hard against each other. Punctuating the ruins were slender roof support pillars laid out in a regular grid. In the distance, rearing above the jumble of buildings, there were arcs of wall cities curving into the Ruins. A total of five inward curving wall city arcs impinged on the central Ruins space.

Checkani sucked in a deep breath and held it. Then exhaled slowly. Intense quiet; bike engine paused. There was a majesty here, but suffering from inevitable entropy. A ghastly snapshot of a civilisation declining to disorder?

Checkani held her right arm straight up in front of her face and sighted along it towards the centre of the Ruins, fist clenched, thumb up. Quiet hum of armour servos assisting as scales moved against each other. She squinted and shifted her thumb over a single indigo pyramidal structure extending above the grey sea of temple fragments. The map routines in her assistems started adding detail based on what she was seeing. <visual zoom>. The faceplate flicked down over her eyes and displayed a stabilised close up of the pyramid. It looked a little odd, not like the square based pyramids of Earth. She could see one side facing her and both faces on either side.

"Hasn't got a square base. Pentagonal?" she whispered.

The triangular faces comprised horizontal steps.

"Guess that's a pretty good landmark." She <zoom cancel>ed, and the faceplate folded away as she gunned her bike down the slope, into the Ruins. A dryness to the air; in the previous areas, it had been more humid, alive with the smell of vegetation. Here it was dead, dust clouding out from behind the bike's wheels.

Once she was amongst the broken buildings, Checkani saw they were more spread out than had been apparent looking across them. Although there was not a straight route, navigating the three kilometres to the pyramid was easy, and she made rapid progress. She glanced at the roof.

The light was rapidly failing. Checkani <night enhance>ed the faceplate over her eyes. Her surroundings brightened and colour corrected to daytime.

As Checkani neared the pyramid, the gaps between the tilted walls and columns narrowed until finally they were filled with a rubble of large blocks. She stopped and stepped from her bike, walked forward, and started climbing. Slowly. Carefully. Very aware of the danger of slipping in the high gravity. Now she was close to the blocks and seeing them in enhanced daytime equivalent, she could see they were not separate as she had thought. The blocks looked as though carved from a single large rock. They had not been placed here. They had been printed in situ. Maybe all in one go. This meant the whole of the Ruins had probably been printed by Autono[]cons from a single contiguous 3D design. More clear evidence of the breakdown in the outpost construction systems.

The pyramid steps looked a little fuzzy. Odd. Checkani <visual zoom>ed into the steps. Small insect-like creatures moving around. A thick layer of them climbing over each other. A roiling boil of hundreds of thousands of insects. More zoom. Not insects, but something metallic. A scale in the visual field showed they were as big as her hand.

Grimacing, Checkani <zoom cancel>ed and double checked her armour integrity: near to 100%.

Contacting the Ringnife Drones, she sent <command reconnoitre>. Destruct-one and -two lifted from her arm and sped towards the pyramid. As they closed in, a cloud of the metal insects surged up, jump-flying at the drones. The drones' visual feed box-outs showed the insects rising on blurs of wings, fighting against the strong gravity. They quickly rose higher. The visual feed showed metal insects on the pyramid steps nearer the base, the numbers thinning out higher up. Swooping in close showed there was some variety in the metal insects, though they were all stag beetle-like. Checkani <command return>ed the drones.

Climbing over the ruins, Checkani neared the first

pyramid step. Next to the step's base, she could see skeletal looking Autono[]con remains; a few metal insects resting on them. She wrinkled her nose at an acrid smell coming from the swarm of insects.

Checkani uploaded an addendum to Hellebore, routing the signal through the communications satellite. Steeling herself, she grabbed the Mono-flow Sword from her arm, holding the hilt ready to deploy the blade. The faceplate sealed over her face, blocking the insect smell as she switched to a filtered air supply. As she reached the first step, the metal insects flowed off and surged towards her; click-clack chittering.

<command deploy>

The blade flowed out. There were too many of the metal insects to take out with the Hi-velocity Turrets on her shoulders. She'd exhaust her ammunition trying to stop them all, and they seemed more inconvenient than dangerous. Better to conserve ammunition. Checkani swept the blade experimentally through the closest metal insects. They dropped; inert debris. However, more swarmed round and climbed her legs. With her free hand, Checkani tried to brush them away while slicing at more approaching metal insects with the Mono-flow Sword.

Keeping on her feet was becoming difficult as the metal insects reached her torso. They were underfoot and making her stumble, the high gravity increasing made keeping balance difficult. Checkani lowered to her knees. More metal insects swarmed over her, scraped at her armour with sharpened knife-claws, but without enough force to penetrate the armour. There were now metal insects at her shoulders, on her head.

"Argh! Bloody things!" She <command retract>ed and clipped the hilt back on her arm. Then, used both hands to grab and throw away the metal insects. Checkani managed to get back to her feet. Power assist enabling her to wade through the grey, writhing mound that now surrounded her. The metal insects continued to overwhelm her, but with two hands and the power assist she could keep the majority from rising above her thighs. However, they were relentless. There would be a limit to how long she could keep this up.

The side of the pyramid comprised two metre high, horizontal steps. Checkani reached up and, climbing on metal insects, grasped the lowest step and power-assist hauled herself up. Metal insects on the step started moving towards her. Again; reach, grasp, haul. And again. Checkani rapidly climbed the pyramid side, fewer metal insects as she got higher. Twenty steps up, she paused and drew in a deep breath. Kicking a few advancing metal insects from the step, she at last could take some time to examine the pyramid and the metal insects.

Checkani grabbed one of the creatures and looked at it closely. The beetle design seemed taken straight from nature. Turning it onto its back, she picked off an abdominal panel with the ARD logo of the Autonomic Robotics Division printed on it. She could see a power source, motors, circuit slab, and a small cylindrical container. The metal insect was much smaller than the smallest Autono[mic]cons. Perhaps it was some specialist constructor that had gone rogue? An Autono[beetle]con? Besides its knife-claws, the metal insect had a proboscis extending from its head ending in a tiny nozzle, a single drip of thick, sticky fluid at the end. Glue? Lubricant? Checkani dropped the insect over the side of the step.

Up close, she could see the pyramid differed from the surrounding ruins. Not printed, but constructed from square blue plates. Ceramic or metal? Each bevel-edged plate around a metre to a side. She walked along the pyramid side, kicking away metal insects. Rounded a corner and started along the next side. Halfway along the next side, she noticed a two metre tall plate; lighter hued so it stood out. In the centre of this plate a square indentation. Checkani looked at the next step up and saw a similar door-like plate. Stepping to the edge she looked down and saw another door plate there.

Checkani moved to one side of the plate, reached across and pressed the square. Nothing happened. She pressed harder, and the square sunk in slightly, with a hiss. The door plate angled inward and opened. Checkani moved forward to look in.

8 - CHECKANI (DAY 2)

A short corridor led to a small chamber. As Checkani entered, with <night enhance> enabled, a hiss-pop sounded behind her. A door shutting. Darkness, even with <night enhance>.

She felt lighter; a stomach falling upward sensation.

Then heavier, a stomach pulling downward sensation. Her knees bent. The sensation continued for a few seconds. She lurched as the elevator, she assumed it was an elevator, came to a stop. A door opened and brilliant white light flooded in. Checkani's assistems <night cancel>ed. The faceplate folded away and Checkani took a lungful of cool air. It had the same acrid smell she had noticed outside the pyramid.

Checkani stepped out into a grouping of square pillars that curved up to a grey ceiling twenty or more metres above, supported by a criss-cross of sturdy looking I-beams.

Air whistled round the surrounding pillars. Checkani walked forward and out onto a low ledge overlooking a vast white walled rectangular hangar. A concrete floor polished to a reflective shine. A towering machine piled up at the far end. At one end of the mechanism, a hexagonal, translucent ten metre diameter glassy, hexagonal plate faced her. The portal. Behind that, a mass of pastel coloured spheres, pipes and pillars, from which hundreds of gleaming black spines soared away, almost to the ceiling. In front of the portal, a raised platform stretched a hundred metres back towards Checkani, supporting a set of rails and bogie.

Checkani smiled. The Bulk-jump Engine. The hangar would be airtight, so the Bulk-jump Engine could open a portal onto the vacuum of space. She looked around the chamber and spotted a large freight elevator at the far end. That would be for lowering ships in. This should be her route home.

A crimson warning icon appeared at the edge of her heads-up display, accompanied by a high, pulsing whine. A suit alert. Checkani's smile turned to a frown. She called up details and cancelled the audio warning.

A green armour suit outline with the legs streaked orange. Armour integrity 70%. A damage report flashed up that there were outer scales failing. Checkani looked at her legs; the black armour on her legs was pitted and smeared with a brown froth. The acrid smell increased. Something was eating through the metal. She reached down with a finger to prod her leg, but drew it back. Probably not a good idea to poke something that was eating through a material designed for military action.

She hadn't waded through anything. Apart from the metal insects? With the proboscis nozzles dripping some sticky fluid? Even if only a small percentage were dispensing the corrosive agent that must have caused this?

Checkani looked around the hangar. She needed to slow this down. Some water might dilute it? However, Bulk-jump Engines were not steam driven; there were unlikely to be any sources of water in the hangar. Returning to the pyramid steps would not help; she'd seen no water in the ruins.

Armour integrity 68%.

"Dammit to fuck!" Checkani did a quick mental check on the state of her bladder. No urge to urinate. She grimaced. Probably wouldn't have been enough urine to make a difference anyway.

Pangolin Power Armour Settings: Suit. Select faulty units. If >50% failure then select 'Eject'.

Smoking scales dropped around Checkani, mainly from her lower legs, but also some from higher up her body. The suit shifted some of the surviving scales around her body, trying to close holes. The migrations rippled over her for a long, long minute as she stood still. Silver power cells peeped through a regular pattern of gaps down her legs and lower torso. There were even some gaps through to the base layer of the suit where power cells had ejected. Some scales had migrated from her upper arms, pulling others behind them, from her wrists, hands and fingers, exposing base layer. Power assist was not important for finger movements. There would still be some power assist for arms and legs, but it was compromised.

Checkani stepped out of the ring of discarded suit, leaving two footprints behind. The soles of her boots had not been damaged, but the tops were scarred, though luckily the corrosive acid (acid?) had not eaten all the way through the thicker protective layer of her boots yet. There were some deep pits filled with the brown acid froth. Better to keep her boots on and hope the acid would not penetrate all the way through.

Forget the acid. Move on to the next task.

The Bulk-jump Engine seemed to wait, watching. Checkani shook her head. There was something otherworldly about Bulk-jump Engines. Literally, as they eased open holes in the universe's brane, through to higher-dimensional space, the bulk. And back again to another place in the human universe.

Knowing there were brain-like computing structures within the engine linked to the dark spines poking out through more than the three visible dimensions of the world gave the Bulk-jump Engine a presence that, to Checkani, felt more animal than machine.

The portal was like a pane of smoky violet amethyst with a web of fine black threads and specks embedded in it. Seemed to be intact. Calling up <night enhance> she shifted beyond the visual spectrum to see how it looked at other wavelengths. Her assistems took over and started analysing. They tried to link to the Bulk-jump Engine, but couldn't access the processing core.

Checkani <night cancel>ed her view, leaving her assistems to continue their analysis. She was now standing directly in front of the portal, drawn by its sheer beauty; a nebula of black, grey and purple filaments; embedded ebony dots signifying stars. There was a hypnotic complexity, like staring at a sun setting into an ocean at the horizon. Then it all shifted. Just slightly. There was something very wrong. What was it showing?

Leaning in closer. Holding her breath. This was not possible. Checkani remembered the grey of inactive portals and the view through active portals into distant tracts of space. She had never seen a violet portal. That was just plain impossible.

Vertigo dragged at her. A feeling of falling into the lilac depths. A gentle breeze of movement within the nebula within the portal's substance. Surely she was looking out of the world. Checkani fell forward, put up her hands to save her. Her naked palms smacked into the glassy front of the portal and it was warm. Just above the ambient temperature of the hangar. There was an almost imperceptible humming vibration. Checkani laid her ear on the portal and closed her eyes. She could hear a distant storm. The rumble hiss of a sandstorm? Opening her eyes and looking back into the world beyond the hard surface. Falling again.

Assistems' audio feed: "Connected to subsystem core."

The armour's visor slipped across her eyes and the assistems superimposed messages over the view into the portal. Checkani listened to her assistems audio feed:

"Bulk-jump Engine systems active, awaiting coordinates, portal interface activating. Years elapsed since start up: 23."

"Awaiting coordinates."

"Coordinate processing core malfunction."

"Status report. Bulk-jump Engine active. Portal interface

activating. Awaiting coordinates."

White noise of the Bulk-jump Engine as it clawed at the surface membrane of the higher-dimensional bulk.

The messages flicked off and Checkani again stared into the portal, drawn inexorably deeper as the filaments and black stars slowly shifted and morphed. A glacial conversation between the bulk and normal space.

Somewhere in a dim, soundproofed recess of her conscious mind, Checkani's internal monologue was screaming at her to move away from the Engine. Another rational part of her mind was realising the energies emanating from this Bulk-jump Engine were directly acting on her brain, her mind. Meanwhile, a floating, falling sensation utterly compelled and overwhelmed her. A wisp of dark filament seemed to coil and spiral out of the portal; towards her and through her.

A heavy blow to the back of her head; her visor smacked against the portal.

The attack shocked her into motion, breaking from the hypnotic hold of the Bulk-jump Engine. She dropped and turned, arms moving up, but not fast enough. Another blow, this time to the side of her head, jerking it painfully over. The struts supporting the visor offered some protection, but the blows were strong; the force transmitted through the metal. Darkness clouded the periphery of her vision. A man in black loomed over her as her arms moved protectively in front of her face, hands tightening into fists. Hard to think.

The figure grunted and struck again with the fat rusty pipe he was wielding. The darkness shifted closer; stars in her eyes at the moment of impact. Using her downward momentum to turn and sweep a leg round to kick at her assailant. At the last moment engaging the power assist, but too late. Her leg struck him, but there was not enough force to move his weight in the high gravity.

A sensation of falling backwards down a black tunnel. Checkani <command attack>ed with both her drones as the man struck the side of her head again. Confusion. She started to frame and transmit <command target> instructions to the drones, setting targets, as she finally succumbed to overwhelming blackness.

9 - VINCENT (DAY 2)

Vincent Moorolone stared at the armoured woman motionless on the floor in front of the malfunctioning Bulk-jump Engine. Two drones had detached from her arm and were moving erratically above her. He struck at them with the metal pipe he was holding. Although both drones dodged back, he hit one. The other seemed to reach a decision and sped away across the chamber. Some internal protocol had kicked in?

The woman moved, curling into a foetal ball. Vincent swept his vermilion coat back and squatted as the drone he had hit wobbled and alighted on the woman's arm. He raised his pipe, ready to strike her again, but she did not seem to be a threat. Looked like her armour was moving independently, automatically adopting a defensive posture. He watched as scales slid across each other, folding her legs and arms to her abdomen. With some relief he saw the drone on her arm had shut down, its blades retracting as it powered down. He took a couple of heavy duty cable ties from his kit bag, using them to secure the woman's wrists. He worked the cables into some gaps between scales. Why were there were gaps? Next, he secured her legs just above the tops of her boots. The scales here were spaced out, too.

Vincent grabbed the woman's shoulders and dragged her down the rails away from the Bulk-jump Engine portal. Twenty metres down, he took out another cable tie and attached the woman to the rails. Odd to deal with a person rather than the Autono[]cons. Positively bizarre to meet someone in the flesh who was not an Ancistorian, though he had interacted with many virtual copies of people from different worlds and times.

When he had arrived back at Indomitaville and heard about a stranger arriving and threatening his people, his duty had been clear. To keep Indomitaville and its Ancistorian citizens safe. He had not always done this. During the first years of the Ancistorian presence on Icefall, when he was young, he had been content to explore the Ancestarchives. That was when the outpost had been peacefully deserted, before the city constructors had malfunctioned as their instructions had broken down. They were soon building multiple outpost cities and behaving in erratic ways. After an Autono[mid]con had run amok and killed two people, he had volunteered to police the area around Indomitaville. Although these patrols reduced the time he could spend in the recordings of the past, he enjoyed the quiet of the city, enjoyed putting distance between himself and other Ancistorians.

Opening his kit bag, Vincent took a small limpet shaped deactivation device from a recharging plate where it nestled amongst a group of similar devices. This crude device disrupted control systems, rendering Autono[]cons inactive. It had been AI built in an Indomitaville workshop after the city building robots went rogue. Should work on the armour too. The deactivation device activated as Vincent applied it to the woman's arm, above the drone holsters, at the back of her arm. A red indicator lit on the device, started flashing, turned amber and finally steady green. The woman slumped across the rails as the armour stopped holding her in position.

Normally Vincent removed vital components from Autono[]cons he deactivated, ensuring they would not cause further problems. He was unsure of how to continue with the woman. He knelt next to her and examined her more closely. Her breathing seemed strong and regular. Her face covered in a dark brown pattern. Or maybe a pale pattern on a dark brown face. Hard to tell, the brown and cream colouring seemed split fifty-fifty. Her lips opened and she groaned; an animal sound deep in her throat. Her eyelids flickered and opened, squinting. Deep green eyes. Pupils moved to his face as she focused. Vincent sat back on his heels.

"Ow!" She said. "Why'd you hit me? Who are you?"

He saw her eyes go blank, unfocused; guessing she was trying to connect to suit and weapons systems. He stood up.

"Your suit's dead," he said. Smiled as she tried to roll into a sitting position and discovered ankles and wrists tied, ankles secured to the rail.

"My suit? What've you done to it?"

"A lot of questions, but you are my," Vincent thought for a moment, captive, prisoner or victim? He was not used to dealing with people. "Prisoner." The woman had rolled onto her knees and was facing him, hands held in front. She shouted.

"I'm not your prisoner. You're in deep trouble, mister. You've just violated an investigation by the Quality Assurance Response Division. You have no idea! I am the law on this planet. The only law."

Vincent looked at the woman, puzzled by her outburst. She was not in command here.

"But you're my prisoner." He said. He could see she was straining to break the tie around her wrists, but without her armour assisting, there was no hope she could do that. Vincent looked around. The hangar was empty apart from the Bulk-jump Engine. There was nothing she could do. He needed to talk to the Ancistorians, find out what to do. Best to talk to them in person about this.

"Wait here." He turned and headed back towards the lifts. Leave her; she was too heavy to carry to Indomitaville. There was nowhere to lock her up in Indomitaville, so no point taking her back there until he could prepare secure accommodation.

As the elevator door closed, Vincent saw a shadow flicker out of the corner of his eye. He spun round; heart quickening. The drone that had flown away was hovering just under the elevator ceiling. Vincent lifted his pipe up, ready to defend himself, but the drone stopped humming and dropped to the floor, inert, blades retracted. Vincent watched it cautiously for a few moments, but there was no movement. Seemed it had run out of power? He kicked it out the door, back into the warehouse.

Vincent closed the elevator door. Reached for the elevator buttons. Then on an impulse opened the elevator door. The drone lay where it had come to rest. Vincent looked at it hard. This technology was ahead of anything he currently had. There must be a way to reassign it.

He picked up the drone and put it in his bag; shut the elevator doors and headed back towards the pyramid exit.

Vincent walked out into the dark and onto a pyramid step. The insect guards swirled restlessly around him, their amber and green running lights flickering. He hopped into his buggy; the canopy closed, and he headed off through the Ruins, accelerating as the systems took over driving. While the buggy headed back to Indomitaville, Vincent leaned back into his seat, took out the drone, and inspected it. A matt black sphere with an equatorial slot. He held it closer to get a better look. A circle of lenses inset in a latitude line near the 'top' of the sphere stared back.

A surprising spin of blades.

A thin slicing pain across his face. His nose poured blood over his lips.

The sphere dropped, blades cut into his coat, his chest. He tried to grab it with his right hand, but his fingers were not working.

Too late, the blades were opening his belly.

More pain. Some finger ends in his lap, cut free when he had tried to fend off the spinning blades.

Red blood pooling on the vermilion of his coat.

Then the drone lifted away from him, bounced off the canopy, wobbled, corrected and returned to horizontal flight. Vincent pushed into his seat, leaning his head back to put as much distance as possible between his face and the blades. He raised his arms and saw bone sticking from the stubs of fingers and thumb on his right hand. Eyes squeezed shut to block out the sight.

Finally, he screamed loudly in the confined space.

He could hear the whine of the drone, volume increasing slightly as it moved closer.

"Vehicle stop!" The buggy didn't respond to this command as the fear and pain distorted Vincent's voice, twisted the words. The buggy continued towards Indomitaville.

Eyes opening again in time to see the drone dart forwards. A scratch on the side of his neck. Then a sharper pain. A warm trickle of liquid inside the collar of his shirt.

As he slumped forward and the last thing he saw was the drone slicing open the kit bag at his feet. His final thought, through the pain, it was searching for the charger.

Then he fell into darkness, the pain receding.

10 - CHECKANI (DAY 2)

Her head throbbing, Checkani looked around the Bulk-jump Engine hangar. She wondered why the 'Red Coat' man hadn't secured her better. He didn't seem to know what he was doing. She grimaced at the continuing throb from being hit on the head. The injury would have been much worse if not for her armour. What was wrong with her armour? The armour assistems were all down. Although there were main nodes in the helmet structures, there were also systems distributed throughout the armour scales and power cells. The power could not have run out, that just did not happen. Power was not limitless, but she had never known it to be compromised. Red Coat had done something while she was out. She was pretty sure she had not been unconscious for long. She called up her internal assistems. They seemed to work, but only locally. Whatever was affecting her armour seemed to block remote connections. The clock in her internal assistems confirmed she had been unconscious for just over a minute.

Checkani pulled at her bonds again. Wrists and ankles secured; ankles fixed to the rail she lay against. The cable ties were too strong to break without the enhancement of her armour.

OK. See if she could figure out why the armour had powered down.

She reached up and tried to pull down the visor with her

hands. It would not budge. Unlike the scales and power cells, it locked into place when the armour powered down. Each scale and each power cell continued to adhere to its neighbours with minimal bonds.

Inspecting the armour, Checkani saw the gaps created when she had to discard damaged scales. Her sword was still on her arm. If she could just reach it, then freeing herself would be easy! How had he missed this? Red Coat really was not the best of guards. Apparently, he had overlooked it. Checkani twisted her hands round against the cable ties, but had very little range of movement. Her hands were securely tied palm to palm. She could not reach far enough round to grasp the sword hilt attached to the outside of her left forearm.

Never mind, not defeated yet. She lifted her arm, bringing the hilt to her mouth, bit it and pulled. Nothing happened, apart from dribbling over the hilt. Normally she would <command deploy> it as she pulled it from the hardpoint on her arm. Dammit. The sword had locked onto her arm when the armour powered down. She could not use it with her assistems down.

Ringnife Drones? They had blades. She looked at the holsters on her right arm. One drone, Destruct-one, nestled there with its blades retracted, inert. No way to activate it. She vaguely remembered <command attack>ing, and sending <command target> instructions. Seemed Destruct-one had decided the <command attack> was incomplete and returned to its holster. Destruct-two perhaps had received more and gone on to independently seek targets to attack? The Ringnife Drones were sophisticated enough that once set on a course they acted independently.

Checkani looked around to see if she could spot Destruct-two somewhere in the hangar. If she could call it over, even without her assistems she might get it to slice through her bonds.

"Destruct-two! Drone! Ringnife Drone! To me!"

No response to her shout. Oh well. Worth a try.

She looked at her armour. All seemed intact. No damage at the front. She twisted her head round to look over her shoulder. If she could just see if there was any damage at the back, perhaps to the cooling vanes? Though even if they were inactive, it should not cause the total shutdown she was experiencing. Then, out of the corner of her eye, she spotted a green glow. Something attached to the back of her upper arm. She lifted her arms over her head and peered under her right arm. She could see a dull grey metal conical device, with a green light glowing at the top. Some sort of inhibitor?

Checkani lay on her front and stretched her arms out in front of her, the cable tie around her legs uncomfortably taut, cutting through the thin suit base layer. She dragged her right arm against a rail, pushing at the small metal cone fixed to her arm. The cone bumped over the rail. She continued to work at it; shifting to get better purchase. The cone would not shift, green light continuing to glow. The cable around her ankles cut in deeper, so she shifted back and levered herself to a seated position, legs bent in front of her. She leaned forward to inspect her legs. The tie was cutting into her ankles, a little blood oozing. Luckily, the acid left in the pits and craters on her boots was nearly dry or that might have dripped onto her flesh as she shifted round.

No dramatic realisation. Just a hopeful: "I'll try that, I guess."

Checkani reached down to her boots and pushed a small length of the cable tie holding her wrists together into one of the acid damp craters on her boot. She waited. There was not much acid left. A small puff of vapour. She waited some more, then withdrew the tie and inspected it. The cable had been eaten away on one side, thinning it. She pulled.

Nothing.

Again Checkani pushed the tie into the acid pit on her boot.

Waited.

Pulled. Pulled harder. Shifted round and sawed the eroded section of cable against the edge of the rail she was secured to. After a minute, it came apart. Her hands free.

Checkani reached round to the cone attached to her arm and tried to pull it off. The cone would not budge. She picked up the cable tie and worked the acid smeared end between two scales and under the cone, being careful not to touch the acid. She patiently wiggled the cable tie around. With a click, the device popped off and fell to the ground.

A one second pause and then her armour assistems booted up. Her movement changed, feeling like a subtle alteration in her proprioception. The Pangolin Power Armour was once again assisting her movement. Checkani called up the armour settings and shifted some scales to glove her hands. She leaned forward, grasped the tie attaching her to the rail, and pulled. For a moment, it stretched slightly, then snapped.

Next, the tie round her ankle. This was going to be a little awkward as it pressed against her skin in scale gaps. Simply pulling on it would make it cut deep into her flesh. Carefully grabbing the cable locking mechanism with one hand and the adjacent cable with the other, Checkani pulled, trying to slide the cable back through the locking mechanism, but it wouldn't budge. She grabbed the cable tie she had used to release the conical suppression mechanism and fed the tapering end, partially eaten away by acid, into the locking mechanism by the cable teeth. Then she started jiggling and pulling the ankle cable. Nothing happened except the cable dug into her skin. Damn it. This was deeply infuriating.

Out of the corner of her eye, she noticed the Mono-flow Sword hilt attached to her arm. Feeling foolish, she reached round and grabbed the hilt and <command deploy>ed the sword. Her armour was powered up, so the Mono-flow Sword was an escape option again. Being careful not to slice off her feet, she cut through the ankle cable.

Finally free! Excellent!

For a moment Checkani stared at the portal, into the deep, violet nebula. She leaned towards it, raising a hand. Fingers reaching. Then she shook her head and forced herself to look away, breathing deeply. The Bulk-jump Engine was like a trap for her mind. She had another priority, to shut down Red Coat. He was not acting in the best interests of the company. Seemed the squatters, Checkani frowned, the Ancistorians, were not as peaceable as they had insisted.

A last look at the Bulk-jump Engine. It seemed to be repairable, if she could sort out the coordinate processing core. A shadow rippled across the surface of the portal and the lights in the hangar flickered. For a moment it seemed as if the shadow had moved beyond the portal, curling like smoke through the Bulk-jump Engine spines. Checkani blinked and looked again. Nothing there. A shiver slipped down her spine and she turned away from the machinery.

Checking her weapon systems, Checkani headed to the elevators. Sword, remaining Ringnife Drone, shoulder mounted Hi-velocity Turrets. The Destruct-one drone was operating from a partial instruction set that might crash its systems. She refreshed and then reset the drone's commands. The Destruct-two drone was beyond the reach of her control systems. She hoped it had received enough <command>s to operate effectively until she could, hopefully, retrieve it.

Night had fallen, wrapping the pyramid and its surrounding Ruins into darkness. Checkani <night enhance>ed the faceplate over her eyes. She stifled a yawn as she realised she was not only in pain from injuries but also tired and hungry.

Stepping out onto the pyramid steps, Checkani was much more wary of the metal insect Autono[]cons than she had been on first encountering them. There were too many to destroy them all, but moving down the pyramid was quicker than climbing it. She <turret active>ed the weapons on her shoulders. Then on full power assist she jumped down from the bottom step, raking the ground in front of her with <turret auto> fire from her Hi-velocity Turrets. She dropped fast in the high gravity. Metal insects attacked, but she sliced at them while running in powered jump-steps away from the pyramid. That she was moving away from the pyramid seemed to pacify the insects and they didn't swarm her as they had when she first arrived.

On her bike again, she retraced the route through the night dark Ruins to the Sea City wall and into the wooded parkland beyond. Finding a dell, comprehensively obscured by trees, she stopped, dismounted. Sitting with her back to a tree, she snacked on some food from the bike's supplies, then she settled down to get some sleep.

The last thing she did before drifting into sleep was connect to the Hellebore and upload a core dump of data from her investigation of the pyramid. There was a terse message waiting for her.

"Flock Ship The Exigent en route. No colonist cylinders carried."

No colonists; surely that meant it was here to support her? Checkani smiled.

11 - VINCENT (DAY 3)

Not dead. No pain. No feeling at all, just a vague dissociation.

Vincent opened his eyes to subdued, warm lighting. He was in a small sandstone room, propped up in a bed. Indomitaville. The buggy had got him home.

His right hand had a healing cast bandaged over it. Some sort of medical collar restricted the movement of his head. His abdomen had healing pads stuck on it.

He remembered the drone attack, but somehow it seemed distant and unimportant. A relieved part of his mind knew drugs were responsible for this. He rather absently considered the drone attack. The woman he had captured was responsible. She had released the drone. She had instructed it. Perhaps he needed to terminate her? Like he did with Autono[]cons that posed a threat to the Indomitaville community.

A drifting sensation; the drugs again.

Blinking his eyes wide open. A noise had awakened him.

A short scream from outside the door to the room.

"Hello?" he called.

No response.

His injuries throbbed dully.

He drifted towards sleep again. Then pushed against the pillows with his elbows. Grimaced at sharp scrapes of pain. Leaned to one side and turned; swung his legs over the side of the bed. Panting, straining, he leaned forward. His soles met the floor, and he stood. Slipped feet into his boots, thoughtfully left by the bed.

Vincent shuffled to the door and opened it a crack. A weight pressed against the door. He pushed harder, and a body rolled down, face up at his feet. Yellow medical tunic on a woman whose gashed neck gaped open. A gush of blood had soaked into the front of her tunic.

The drone that attacked him was loose in Indomitaville?

Vincent stepped back into the room, looking for his kit bag. He found it in a cupboard; the front torn to shreds, but the recharger and remaining deactivation devices were intact. Vincent took a telescopic silver rod from the bag; pressed a button to extend it. At the end, a triple tined fork. He smiled grimly. He knew how to disable machines; of all the things he could do, this was his particular area of expertise. The Data Prod hacked Autono[]cons, disabling them for a few minutes. Until their repair systems kicked in. However, this gave time to slap on a deactivation device. The Data Prod should make quick work of the attacking drone.

He grabbed a handful of the deactivation devices. He wore a pair of loose white pyjama trousers, but there were no pockets. Finding his red coat, he quickly pulled it on. There were some holes torn in the front, but it was mostly intact. The deactivation devices went into pockets.

Vincent stepped over the body, moving into the corridor. The coral coloured walls were lit from an opening onto a balcony at the end; light reflecting off a polished floor. Vincent walked carefully to the balcony, his bandaged hand sliding along the wall, left hand holding the active Data Prod in front.

Two more yellow tunicked bodies were on the balcony, both with cut throats. One with extensive injuries to forearms and hands. Vincent looked nervously around, then over the balcony. The bottom of the Indomitaville lightwell was a couple of floors below. Vincent could see six bodies on the ground; arms and legs askew. There was no one else around. Always quiet, Indomitaville seemed to have taken the concept of silence to a new level.

"All dead," he whispered to himself.

His head was clearing. Moving was painful, but it seemed to bring lucidity. An adrenaline rush kept him focused. Vincent walked quickly down to the bodies.

The Ancistorians would be useless at defending themselves against the drone. Thank goodness he had captured the woman and safely tied her up. The last thing they needed was her appearing with her weapons. He wondered why she hadn't attacked more people when she first met them. She had attacked the boy, but not hurt him badly. He had read the Ancistorian records, the histories, and knew the first response of humans was to assert control over strangers. Normally through the application of violence and superior technology. He knew the Ancistorians should have moved to another planet by now, but there had been no options.

Vincent moved to the bodies. There were sprays of blood droplets surrounding them. Each spray emanating from a different point, each near a body. The drone had methodically moved from victim to victim. The back of one body moved. Perhaps she was alive? Vincent moved close and knelt next to the body. He could hear a rhythmic humming. A wet churning noise. Then a slit appeared in the fabric covering the woman's back. A fine mist of blood hit Vincent's face. Realisation dawning, he jabbed at the slit with the Data Prod, pulling the trigger that sent code churning pulses. The business end of the Data Prod hissed and glowed blue with its own personal St Elmo's fire.

The wet noises within the woman's body stopped. Seemed she had fallen on the drone, trapping it within her rib cage as its power ran down. Gritting his teeth, Vincent put the Data Prod to one side and pushed a deactivation device against the stunned drone in the woman's back. The indicator went from red to amber, and finally a green light glowed from deep in the bloody wound.

Vincent fell back, sitting down heavily. He felt sick. People differed from machines. He tried not to think about the warm flesh of the woman's back, the chips of bone. His vision was darkening round the edges, but he knew he must push on through and return to the woman he'd captured. Drag her back to Indomitaville and ensure justice was meted out. There were many examples of effectively delivered justice from history. Many of them brutal, but perhaps proportionate? Her crime was, after all, monstrous.

12 - CHECKANI (DAY 3)

Looking down the Indomitaville lightwell from a high window, Checkani could see a figure bent over a body. Red Coat, her captor. She <visual zoom>ed close in to see what he was doing. There were bodies scattered round him. He sat back for a moment and then returned to one of the corpses, bending over it, obscuring her view. He shifted, knelt and pushed one hand forward. The other was bandaged and dangled at his side. Then he was moving away, revealing a bloody crater in the body. In his left hand a small, bloody sphere. A familiar sphere.

So that was where her Ringnife Drone Destruct-two had got to. She transmitted a <command> to it but got no response.

Checkani looked at the other bodies. Seemed Destruct-two had been busy. The squatters might look for justice for this. Perhaps the incomplete <command attack>, from when she was knocked out, had turned the drone somewhat psychopathic. If Red Coat had not attacked her, those people would still be alive.

Ten years ago on another world she'd spent two days walking through a city of people ripped apart by alien lifeforms. The experience had inured her to violence and left a pinch of darkness in her mind that she'd learnt to ignore. There was an awful familiarity to seeing violently dead people.

The arrival of The Exigent would change things. The ship could remove the squatting Ancistorians. Not her problem. She needed to investigate the state of the other ring cities and see if the Bulk-jump Engine could be repaired. Checkani shivered; something strange had happened to her at the portal. She <zoom cancel>ed and moved away from the opening to her bike.

Connecting to Hellebore, Checkani checked to see if The Exigent had arrived. Not yet, but arrival was imminent. She checked Hellebore was monitoring the area of space where The Exigent would arrive. The Exigent should integrate into the communications network as soon as it appeared, but Checkani wanted to keep watch for the arrival. Just in case. Icefall was in a system right at the extreme edge of human occupation. There was a high potential for the unexpected.

Checkani turned her bike and headed back through the wall city, down towards the floor of the lightwell and Indomitaville.

Red Coat was still moving round the bodies when Checkani arrived. He looked up at the sound of her bike.

"You! How?" he shouted. Then stumbled back away from her, waving a bandaged hand at her. In his other hand, he held a metal rod with a forked end.

Checkani would not take chances. She <turret active>ed her Hi-velocity Turret shoulder weapons and <command deploy>ed her Mono-flow Sword as she hopped off her bike and strode towards Red Coat. He would not catch her unawares again.

"You have my Ringnife Drone."

"Murderer."

"I'm not discussing it." Checkani stopped and looked at the bodies crumpled around her. "This is your doing." Red Coat did not seem to be in a good state. She could see bandages across his abdomen, throat and hand.

"How can you speak like that? Show some respect."

"The drone attacked you and these people? You

attacked me when I was issuing commands. That was idiotic."

"No. That was not… I did not… You attacked us." Red Coat lurched towards Checkani, the metal rod pointing at her.

"Back off." Checkani <command reconnoitre>ed her remaining drone to look round the plaza for more danger. The drone flew from its arm holster and started circling, flying past Red Coat. He screamed, turned and fled between nearby buildings. Apparently, Destruct-two had made a significant impression. She <command retract>ed her sword, but kept the turrets active.

Checkani looked up and saw figures standing on the balconies and flat roofs of the surrounding buildings, staring down at the carnage. They were still and silent; many of them appeared to have their eyes closed. She noticed the boy, Bank, was there too. He was staring at her, tears streaming down his face, mouth locked shut. He knew the dead? One of them was special to him?

Checkani called to him. "Hey, this was not my doing."

No response. She shrugged and looked back at Destruct-one, now hovering near the body with the wound in its back. A small boxout at the side of her visual field showed Destruct-one's video feed. It showed a gore covered Ringnife Drone. Checkani <command return>ed Destruct-one and went over to collect Destruct-two. Grimacing, she wiped blood and tissue fragments off the drone onto the clothes of the corpse. The surrounding Ancistorians remained statue still, witnessing. Why weren't they reacting?

Checkani examined Destruct-two and, seeing the limpet-like inhibitor on its side, she walked back to her bike and retrieved a smart tool. Removing the inhibitor only took a moment, then she returned the drone to her arm holster alongside Destruct-one. With power now connected, Destruct-two booted up. Accessing its systems, she found the 'current commands' cache was empty; apparently the inhibitor had caused a clean restart.

Rather than pursue Red Coat, or hang around under the gaze of the Ancistorians, Checkani headed back towards the Ruins and other city rings. The Exigent would arrive soon and she wanted to compile an overview of what had been happening to the settlement. She also wanted to review Destruct-two's stored memory of events. Why had it murdered all those people? She would have expected it to reject incomplete instructions and return to the holster on her arm.

13 - CHECKANI (DAY 3)

Back at the dell where she had spent the night, Checkani leaned comfortably against a trunk and took out the Destruct-two drone, checking it for damage. The rotor blades extended and retracted, the lens iris contracted. Checkani <command>ed her faceplate down. She now had a full visual field display, rather than vertical side strips generated by assistems running in her cyborg implants. She accessed Destruct-two's memory, replaying its visual record.

Her arm. She looked round in the virtual. Red Coat striking with a metal pipe. The drone starting a rapid dodge.

The recording continues.

A momentary freezing of the virtual feed; a flicker-wave through the image. Then back to a normal three-sixty, full world view unfolding in real time. That was an odd glitch. Would have been about the time she had sent <command attack> to the drones, just before being knocked out.

<virtual freeze>

Checkani dipped into the instructions listed in the recording's metadata. There it was. A partial instruction with an 'incomplete' tag. Immediately following this, a reconstruction of the partial that looked like a <command attack all> rather than the contextually correct <command attack>. <command attack all> was a <command> of last resort.

<virtual play>

The scene continued. Checkani watched herself collapsing. Red Coat looming over her. The other drone being hit by the pipe. The chamber flying past as Destruct-two flew away from the Bulk-jump Engine.

<virtual fast forward>

Hovering by the elevators. Seeing Red Coat arrive and enter the elevator. Following him in, and then another glitch. The elevator wall rushing upwards as the drone collapses to the floor. A fade to darkness.

Flickers of light.

Blurred shapes moving as the drone's engine engages once more.

Checkani tries to look around, but the view is locked; three sixty no longer available.

The scene snaps into sharp focus, showing Red Coat's face looming close. A flicker of blades and a spray of blood. Cutting. More blood. A glimpse of Red Coat with his mouth wide open. Eyes wide open. Neck wet, red.

A blur of motion.

A close up of a recharging plate, one of the incapacitating limpets close by.

Blackness.

The recording stopped.

<virtual play> from the other side of a gap in the playback time line, jumping to where the Drone resumed functioning. Now partially charged, the full three sixty view is available again.

Movement on reactivation. A hand reaching towards the lens. Spinning blades; spatters of blood. Pieces of flesh and finger. A woman in yellow stumbling back, the drone pursuing. Her neck opened with a red shredding as the Ringnife Drone closed in.

<virtual freeze>

Checkani took a moment to look round the virtual space, with time stopped. Red Coat unconscious (asleep?) in bed. The woman in yellow stumbling back through a door, which is swinging shut. The woman slumping against the closing door. A small spurt of blood from a severed artery in the side of her neck. Mouth stretched open; looking like the start of a scream.

<virtual play> at normal speed.

A red stone corridor flying past. Out into daylight, bobbing left, then right, to open the necks of two more people. Over a balcony rail and dropping rapidly towards a group of people talking below.

A rapid succession of close ups of terrified faces, spurting blood and abrupt turns in midair. Figures backing up with arms outstretched. Finally, an impact with a woman's abdomen, drilling into a dark red interior.

Blades slowing.

Blackness.

The recording stopped again.

The metadata showed the power was depleted again; the drone shutting down its systems. Going into recovery mode.

<virtual play> after another time line gap.

The next image was Checkani's face, framed by tree branches. This recording was only minutes old.

<virtual stop>

Checkani disconnected from the drone and retracted her faceplate. She took a deep breath of fresh air. Contemplating the atrocities caused by the drone was jarring in the idyllic pastoral setting of the glade. A lump grew in her throat and her vision blurred. Checkani scrunched her eyes tight shut and a single tear rolled down each cheek. She shook her head from side to side, but the images were burned into her memory. Seeing the recording of the events had made the deaths more real for her. The causal link between her technology and the bodies was now deeply personal.

After packaging and annotating it, Checkani triggered an upload of the drone data to Hellebore, accompanied by a brief record of her recent encounter with Red Coat. She instructed Hellebore to forward this to The Exigent the moment it entered the system.

She got back on her bike and continued to the Ruins, hoping the distance would dilute the immediacy of the drone's rampage. Knowing it wouldn't.

A message from Hellebore flagged up in the periphery of her visual field, overlaying the passing trees:

"The Exigent is emerging into Icefall orbit."

14 - CHECKANI (DAY 3)

Arriving at the base of a wall city, Checkani stopped her bike to watch The Exigent arrive.

At the edge of her visual field a boxout showed a view of a Bulk-jump Engine exit portal, videoed by her communications satellite cameras. A hole in space, with a view through it to the Bulk-jump Engine on Earth. The Exigent flock ship arrived as a series of fifteen slender cylinders that appeared to materialise from nowhere as they slipped out of the portal hole. Each cylinder yawing, pitching and rolling as it slowly manoeuvred into position. One of them fragmented into six pieces, spherical orbiters, that started flying in protective circles round the other cylinders as they coalesced into a tetrahedral flock ship arrangement.

A message from Hellebore: "Commodore Cuttallar and The Exigent have meshed with our systems. Data shared."

An alert in the corner of Checkani's visual field signalled a real time call.

"Commodore Cuttallar." A smooth white plastic mask, with human eyes in the sockets, appeared in a window at the side of her vision. Checkani wondered if the eyes were original. Probably not. The plastic of the mask smiled.

"Checkani. I'm here to back you up. The Quality Assurance Response Division escalated this to We Print Cities, who called in the Colonial Planets Settlement Corps."

"Good to have you here. It's a mess."

"So I gather. I got the short straw. Apparently, they wanted someone experienced. In over a hundred and fifty years flying flock ships around stars, I've learnt to spot where the Collective's Head Office wants to avoid making tough decisions. Normally they do this by keeping problems at the bottom of urgent lists until they erode and evaporate. Looks like this problem is too time sensitive for that."

"Yeah. The situation needs actively managing."

"Actively managing? I hope they've not sent me here to kill anything. Kill anyone."

"We've got squatters."

"Yes, I saw your report on the way. Something's gone wrong with the outpost structures, too? Have you finished exploring the arcologies?"

"Not yet. I'm still working my way through them."

"Any ideas?"

"The Autono[]cons seem to have gone rogue; don't know why. You saw there are Bulk-jump Engine problems too. I need to finish my assessment. I think the Collective will be keen for you to do something about the squatters?"

"You've got the authority on the surface. What do you want The Exigent to do?"

"I don't have authority over settlement communities. Just over the outpost prior to colonisation."

"They're not settlers."

"Not legal settlers, but they are people settling on Icefall. Should be the responsibility of the Orion-Cygnis Colonisation Collective. We Print Cities just gets planets ready for colonisation. The Settlement Corps deliver and police colonists."

Commodore Cuttallar smiled. At least hir plastic mouth smiled, hir eyes not so much. "I refer you back to my original comments on the Collective."

"Would be good to remove the squatters, but I don't know where to. I'm not sure they want to leave. Not going to be easy shipping them out if they want to stay. You have the capability? You do have a flock ship."

"Yes, I'm commanding this flock ship, though note I'm the only crew. A scouting party to see if more action is required, but a scout with the firepower to handle extreme situations. This is a 'Forceful Control' flock ship configuration."

"I was hoping I could get some help on the surface."

"There are Intervention Squads at the Lausanne Bulk-jump Engine on standby. They can be here in minutes if needed. As always, we're prepared for any unpleasantness. I'm still going through your reports, but it seems you've already embarked on 'unpleasantness'. Eight deaths?"

Checkani could see the small inset of her own computer generated face clench its jaw tight, mouth turning down. Grim.

"That wasn't my doing."

"Yeah, I got that from Hellebore's summary. Still, eight deaths. Is your Ringnife Drone under control now?"

"The drone is fine now. Fixed."

"OK. This is what's going to happen. I'm going to send down a remote so I can negotiate with the squatters. What did they call themselves? Ancistorians? In the meantime, I need you to decide what sections of the Icefall arcologies We Print Cities is going to release to the Orion-Cygnis Colonisation Collective. If there is some unwanted space left over, then maybe that could offer a solution to the squatter problem? Somewhere out of the way to park them."

Commodore Cuttallar made hir mouth smile once again. Waited for a response. Checkani opened her mouth to make a caustic retort in response to the imperious tone. Thought better of it; there was no point picking a fight.

"Sure. Sounds sensible."

The Commodore's eyes joined in with the smile.

"Speak later," zie said and left.

15 - VINCENT (DAY 3)

In the central plaza of the Indomitaville lightwell, the dead were laid in a circle, feet at the centre, heads at the perimeter. Nine bodies, each wrapped in a black sheet. On the chest of each body, a ten by five centimetre titanium lozenge with a tuft of fine wires trailing from one end. The Ancestarchives. The past was stored in these. Ancestral media going back over a thousand years. Back to the earliest low-res 2D stills. Each Ancestarchive stored a single family history, though at five hundred years back, they converged as common ancestors asserted their presence. Each generation curated the Ancestarchives, with ancestor records deleted, modified and sometimes reinserted from the Ancistorian's distributed master storage.

The Ancestarchives removed from the nine dead were waiting for the next nine births, waiting for nine new hosts to continue with the Work. Nine new Ancistorians to continue drawing themes and truths from the past, to weave into the Understanding of Being.

Vincent stood among the black clad onlookers. Part of the communal grieving, but also separate from it, conspicuous in his torn vermilion coat. He looked round, realising that with their eyes tight shut they were already deep in the lives of the dead. The ceremony sought to exorcise grief through immersion in a celebration of the lives of the dead. This was the only time Ancistorians reviewed a past life together.

Closing his eyes, Vincent sank into the communal experience. He drifted into a crowd of floating avatars, modelled closely on real life. Arms folded, tilted over to look down, they drifted above an undulating landscape of experiences from one of the dead. Bubbles of emotion exuding from individual episodes; rising to pass through the avatars. Small gasps of sadness and happiness. Lust, shame, envy, disgust, anger. At the end, fear and pain. A lot of fear and pain.

Then the crowd of Ancistorian avatars were turn-sliding through an impossible angle into the life of another. Vincent trailed along with them. A very different experience to the normal exploration of past lives when an Ancistorian directly experienced reconstructions of past events, taking on the lived role of their ancestor. First person reconstructions built from the stored media of the Ancestarchives.

The ceremony of the dead continued, with the Ancistorian avatars floating from life to life. Vincent travelled near them, though always alone.

Some hours later, the avatars blinked out of the ceremony. Vincent opened his eyes and looked round at the Ancistorians. People at the edges of the group wandered away, carrying their grief home. Finally, only Vincent and the six elders of the newly reinstated Ruling Council were left. The leader stepped forward and spoke.

"This must not go unanswered, Vincent Moorolone," she said. "You have failed the community. With the arrival of the outsider, we have reinstated the Ruling Council."

Vincent turned to face her. "Yes, Ruleska. I understand. Hunt down the woman. I will make good on my commitment to Indomitaville."

Councillor Ruleska stepped toward Vincent. Although shorter than him, Vincent felt she towered over him. Her mouth a hard line, forehead creased in a frown. "We were watching your encounter with the woman. We heard everything. You will bring her to us."

"She is like a rampaging Autono[]con and should be treated as such. I should carry our justice to her."

"You operate at our discretion. You're our tool. Remember this, you've no rights here. You lost them when you moved out and started your reclusive existence. We tolerate you, but only as long as you comply to our will."

"But she should…"

The oldest looking councillor, white bearded, stepped alongside Councillor Ruleska. He interrupted Vincent. "You will not question us. Your skills in hunting Autono[]cons make you useful and you can now use them to bring the woman to us. This is our decision. We wish to speak to the woman, again."

Vincent's shoulders slumped as he seemed to shrink into exhaustion. He was battered and maimed. He was hungry and tired.

"Okay. Yes, I'll bring her to you. If possible unharmed."

The old man spoke again, a little softer this time. "The temporary prosthesis should be ready by now to be fitted to your injured hand. At the medical facility."

Vincent nodded and turned away. He could feel the Ruling Council watching as he crossed the plaza. He was used to working independently on behalf of the community. Being ordered around by a Ruling Council did not sit well with him. He gritted his teeth, pushing his chin forward, and snorted through his nose. This did not suit him at all.

16 - CHECKANI (DAY 3)

Speeding through the First City Ruins, Checkani felt dizzy. Like she was not just driving her bike, but also observing herself driving. A strange split awareness mixing a sensation of movement and feeling of falling in slow motion. As though part of her was tipping over an edge, somewhere high up.

She thought of the Bulk-jump Engine. The portal.

Letting the bike drive, Checkani closed her eyes, placed her palms over them. She held her breath. Despite the hum of the bike engine, the rumble of wheels on the road, she noticed a vast silence. A dark shadow flickered past in the blackness behind her eyes. A ripple of darkening.

And the feeling left her.

She was back in the world again. Eyes open, seeing the pyramid loom ahead. She should carry on through First City to an adjacent ring city. She needed to get to them all to figure out what had happened; identify which ones were habitable. But she wanted to see the Bulk-jump Engine again, even though she didn't want to fight off the metal insects at the pyramid. Perhaps the freight elevator offered another way in? If she could find that on the other side of the pyramid, then she would try to have another look at the Bulk-jump Engine. If she couldn't get in through the freight elevator, then she would continue exploring the ring cities.

Checkani guided her bike round the pyramid and started

weaving through the scatter of ruins, zigzagging in a search pattern. As she sped through archways and between fallen walls, her breath quickened. Finding a way into the Bulk-jump Engine, finding the top of the freight elevator was important. She had to find it. She looked round urgently.

Lifting her right arm, she <command reconnoitre>ed her two Ringnife Drones. They lifted away from her and their image feeds appeared at the side of her visual field. Within moments, they were looking down on the Ruins; Checkani's assistems using the drone feed to extend its First City map.

"Come on. Where are you?" The search was becoming a visceral urge. Her face felt hot, flushed.

Out of the corner of her eye, she saw a ripple of darkening stripes run up a tilted pillar.

"Hah! There you are!" That she should see the lines did not seem odd. Why should she not see a ripple of darkness?

"Rippledarken." Checkani smiled, her eyes widening. Surely white was now showing round her irises? Crazy woman!

A large cloistered courtyard appeared in Destruct-one's image feed.

Checkani laughed as a thrill of excitement sparked through her chest. She stopped, puzzled at herself. Shook her head and turned the bike towards the courtyard as she <command return>ed the drones.

Doorways punctuated the outer cloister walls. Checkani drove through one and skidded to a halt. She looked through a colonnade to a metal floored courtyard, which looked about the same size as the Bulk-jump Engine hangar freight elevator. Better yet, there were no metal insects here.

Checkani drove round the cloister, looking for a smaller elevator, or control box. Nothing. She drove down a small slope into the courtyard and over metre square metal paving. This was the top of the freight elevator, but there appeared to be no way to operate it from outside. She drove out of the courtyard, and circled outside, looking for controls.

As she searched, Checkani calmed. Finding a way in seemed less urgent. Perhaps waiting until later would be best? Perhaps get Commodore Cuttallar to send some help from The Exigent to remove the metal insects?

"Rippledarken?" What had she been thinking of? Had she even seen anything? Perhaps it was just the stress of being thrown into the midst of a severely broken outpost?

The quality assurance should have just involved running round a single ring city checking the facilities. Instead, she had dropped into some seriously messed up shit.

Feeling more in control, Checkani headed north-east from the pyramid towards a curve of wall city that pushed into the First City Ruins.

Hopefully, this new ring city would offer some respite from the madness of the First City's Ruins. Maybe a pastoral idyll like the Sea City central area? The wall of this city looked like generic grey building compound and was pocked with windows and balconies. As she got closer, Checkani could see large doorways at ground level. She drove into the first one she came to and headed up a gentle slope towards the city's interior.

The passage beyond the door was a bland grey, with some side doors leading into similar featureless corridors. Checkani rode rapidly along the passage to the inner wall of the city. She emerged into a dimly lit, featureless lens shaped gap between crossing wall cities. Directly ahead, the sandstone of the intersecting Sea City. At the base of that wall, she approached another large entrance. Checkani stopped and put her feet down. The ground crunched underfoot. Black grit, but it did not look right. Difficult to see in the low light. She dismounted and squatted. Picked up a handful of the ground material. Cubes. The grit was entirely made of regular shapes. Some sort of waste? Or maybe building material? Her assistems made some measurements; recording and cataloguing the sample. Perhaps Hellebore could make sense of it?

Back on her bike and heading into the sandstone entrance. No internal lighting. The light bleeding away to pitch black. As she went deeper, a distinctive smell of ozone and oil.

17 - COMMODORE (DAY 3)

Commodore Cuttallar was reclining comfortably in the heart of a complex of physical support machines. Zie checked the status of these mechanisms that augmented and, in some instances, replaced, hirs body's original structures.

With a thought zie relaxed the expression on hir white face mask. Behind the mask concealed connections dove deep into hirs brain, eyes, mouth, nose and ears. The Commodore spent some time in the real world in real time, but mostly zie was moving through virtually constructed worlds. Although physically still independent of the flock ship, Commodore Cuttallar spent so much time immersed in virtual constructions of the ship's various systems that where hirs body ended and the ship started had become something of a moot point.

Cutt(Virt), the avatar Commodore Cuttallar used for moving around The Exigent's constructed virtual space, was currently standing in a bamboo floored, cedar walled dojo. Sun was streaming in through a window-wall to fall on a tub of bamboo. Cutt(Virt) kept the white mask face, copied from real life, but its body was agender human and lacking the cyborgization of the Commodore's real body. Visible skin of hands and bare feet pastel blue. Long white robe held closed with a knotted black belt.

In front of Cutt(Virt), a simple humanoid robot. No

uncanny valley; the robot's exterior appeared to be made of oatmeal coloured calico. Its eyes were buttons and mouth appliqué. This virtual calico robot was an accurate representation of the real world Cutt(Rem), a humanoid physical remote; part transmitting device and part simulated Commodore. Cutt(Rem) even had a small volume of cerebral material grown from a sample of the Commodore's brain.

Commodore Cuttallar used Cutt(Rem) when physical excursions were necessary, both within the flock ship and beyond. The Cutt(Rem) robotic presence could travel around under the Commodore's control as zie gazed out through its eyes, inhabiting its body virtually. An on-board artificially intelligent construct taking over Cutt(Rem) if the connection failed, or the Commodore had other things to attend to.

Cutt(Virt) was issuing instructions to the virtual representation of Cutt(Rem), in the dojo. The instructions appeared as a curving shaft of light connecting Cutt(Virt)'s and Cutt(Rem)'s eyes. The actual instructions were interpreted from sub-vocalisations of the Commodore, augmented by information from the ship's processing core. As the instructions flowed, a simple <ship out> command had the real world Cutt(Rem) propelling itself through the gravity free environment of The Exigent to one of the flock ship's landing vehicles, The Exigent[Red-One]. This was a flock ship cylinder similar in design to Hellebore, but with greater offensive capability. As the instruction dump finished, Cutt(Rem) slid into a coffin-like space within the centre of The Exigent[Red-One]. The vehicle disconnected from the rest of the ship and powered down the gravity well.

Commodore Cuttallar kept a small part of hirs attention on Cutt(Rem), while most of hirs attention continued to experience through Cutt(Virt). The dojo filled with data representations built from reports forwarded by Hellebore. Zie had a model, hovering above the bamboo floor, showing the confusion of wall cities. The Exigent's sensors were busy scanning the planet's surface, augmenting Hellebore's data. Zie had identified open pit resource mines in mountain foothills north-west of the wall cities. A grid of processing facilities next to the mines, at the start of a road leading to the outpost.

After a brief journey through vacuum, The Exigent[Red-One] swept into the outer atmosphere. The ship plunged towards Hellebore's landing site at the top of Sea City, overlooking the slow-moving ocean. The Exigent[Red-One], surface ablating in a streamer of fire, roared through cloud and levelled out above shallow waves.

Meanwhile, Hellebore, The Exigent[Red-One] and Cutt(Rem) modelled the situation, exploring optimal approaches to hit mission targets. The Exigent waded in with packets of insights extrapolated from Cutt(Virt)'s investigations in the dojo.

"Processing cores! I apprehend you. Control your data flows." Cutt(Virt) was used to the data tsunami machine intelligences favoured. The virtual being chopped through the blur of machine dialogue and data constructions as The Exigent[Red-One] switched from its Bulk-brane Drive to burning valuable chemicals to decelerate and land next to Hellebore. The heat of its landing sent a cloud of steam rolling over the city wall landing pad, frosting metal surfaces of the collapsed Autono[mid]con by the parapet.

A panel on the side of The Exigent[Red-One] slid sideways and Cutt(Rem) was spat out, tumbling to land heavily on its feet. A larger panel dropped open and a gleaming red trike bounced to the ground. The trike comprised three large black wheels at the corners of a triangular framework. Attached to the framework many boxes, cylinders and a set of mechanical restraints. Cutt(Rem) walked to the trike, dropped backwards into the machinery between the wheels. Mechanical restraints locked round its arms, legs, torso, and head. The wheels twisted, so they all faced away from The Exigent[Red-One], then spun, torque gently increasing as the trike adjusted to the high gravity.

Commodore Cuttallar shifted hirs attention fully into Cutt(Rem) and the trike. Zie was experiencing through trike visual, audio and motion sensors. Even in advanced old age, zie still felt the exhilaration of heading into the unknown of an alien planet.

Zie guided the trike across the landing pad, passing the passage Checkani had taken into the city, and sped towards the parapet overlooking the city interior. The trike rotated so two wheels were leading, the tops of each higher than the low parapet. Without slowing, the trike hit the parapet, front wheels accelerating to climb over and launch the trike out into space. Briefly it soared, then thudded into the icy crust of snow covering the city's parklands spanning roof. The vehicle carved a course towards the far side, throwing up a spraying wake of ice crystals.

Commodore Cuttallar <visual zoom>ed round the snow field the trike was racing across. There was a regular pattern of plum coloured pillar tops poking through the roofing. The pillar tops each a cylindrical turret with a conical, snow covered roof. Ahead in the distance, zie could see a low wall curving in towards hir. This was the top of the adjacent First City. Augmenting systems overlaid the position of the top of the Indomitaville lightwell, and the location of Mozarythm's dome. The trike was soon passing to the right of Mozarythm and nearing First City.

Cocooned on The Exigent Commodore Cuttallar drank water from a tube hanging by hirs head. Zie increased the ambient temperature a little. Despite knowing zie was not actually cold, travelling across the snowbound city roof was making hir shiver.

18 - CHECKANI (DAY 3)

Faceplate down and <night enhance>. The illumination was so low, Checkani could make out little within the sandstone passage leading to the interior of the next wall city outpost. Checkani commanded the bike lights on. The <night enhance> allowed her to see the surroundings in 'daytime equivalent'. The bike quietly rolling forward as the ozone and oil smell grew stronger.

Machines. There were going to be machines.

Before reaching the exit into the city's central area, Checkani halted and got off her bike. She commanded the bike <lights off>, plunging everything into darkness. There was nothing showing beyond the exit from the passage. She could just make out the doorway, but nothing after. There should have been light filtering down from the roof over the central area. Her eyes flicked up and a virtual clock face appeared briefly at the edge of her vision; it should still be light outside.

Sliding one hand along the wall to her right, Checkani walked to the exit and looked out. Nothing. She sent <follow> and <lights on> commands to her bike, brightening the space beyond the door.

Instead of parkland stretching out into the central interior of the city, there was what appeared to be a junkyard. Autono[]cons in heaps. Not neatly stacked, just thrown together. Smashed into compacted clumps in the high Icefall gravity. They merged into a confused whole that in places climbed up tens of metres against the roof supports.

"Wow! An Autono[]con graveyard!" Checkani stepped out from the door, moving slowly towards the nearest junk pile; her bike now alongside her.

Then a movement.

"Inevitable…" Checkani bent her knees, brought her hands up defensively.

A camera stalk sticking out of the nearest slope of twisted robots moved to face the light. Checkani commanded <lights off>; held her breath and listened. A gentle whirring sound. <night enhance> was of limited use in here. Seemed the roof was blocking all light. Then a brief squeal of metal scraping against metal. Checkani went into the <night enhance> settings and <wireframe>ed. A virtual net of glowing green picked out the outlines of the environment immediately around her. She linked to the bike and arranged for its lights to pulse on momentarily every twenty seconds. Enough illumination to update the wireframe map, but hopefully too little for her to be tracked. Unless the broken Autono[]cons were fielding more processing power than was indicated by the wreckage.

Checkani moved deeper into the Autono[]con graveyard, collecting snapshots of the wreckage. There were Autono[]cons of every size, even some of the insect ones she had seen around the pyramid. Some appeared to have been standard models. Others sported eccentric modifications. The pointed legs Checkani had previously seen, but also extra limbs ending in blades of different shapes and sizes, hoses that split and multiplied, lens clusters weeping oil, upright wheeled cylinders, Autono[big]con sized spaghetti tangles of wire.

As she walked past the Autono[]cons, they stirred; limbs moving, wires writhing, nozzles bleeding viscous liquids, lenses zooming and turning to follow her. Everything slow and ponderous; as though sick and listless. Aware of her, but lacking focus. As she moved away and darkness returned, they settled and stilled once again.

There were gaps between the piles. Alleyways leading through the central space.

"No, probably best not to go in there," under her breath, thinking ahead.

Checkani turned the bike lights to 'constant'. As well as those nearby, distant Autono[]cons stirred. She turned the lights off and listened as Autono[]con movements ceased.

"I suppose if I was quick, I could slip in towards the middle…"

Checkani looked at the nearby city wall surrounding the central area. In many places, there were hundred metre high mounds of Autono[]cons. The whole of the central area was full of the junked machines, so investigating further seemed imperative. 'Investigator' was one of her primary roles on Icefall. She'd just go a little way in to check them out.

Checkani called up Hellebore's 3D map of the wall cities in a small navigation window at the side of her visual field. The Graveyard City intersected First City (the one with the pyramid and ruins). Nearby were Sea City and another two cities she hadn't visited. One of these was isolated beyond the others, surrounded by snowfields.

How long was it going to take to visit all the circular settlement cities? She couldn't submit a recommendation to We Print Cities before she'd checked them all. Shipping in settlers and then watching them die because of malfunctioning cities was not an option.

Checkani uploaded an update to Hellebore. Time to move in. She shut down the <wireframe> and ordered the bike lights on. Engines in the junk piles purred to life, but nothing approached her. Nothing attacked. The machinery seemed content to only watch her.

She moved towards a wide passage leading into the graveyard and flicked up her faceplate. No need for <night enhance> with the bike lights on full beam.

The smell of oil and ozone increased as the Autono[]con

wreckage banks to either side shifted and sparked. Electronic components and small fragments of metal crunched underfoot. The passage twisted, turned and branched as tree-like structures emerged from the banks. Soon it was as though walking a path in a fairy tale forest of animate, twisted metal. Clicks, whirs, buzzes and snapping sounds accompanied Checkani as she moved deeper. Her breathing slowed, her shoulders relaxed as the wrecked Autono[]cons remained entangled in their piles.

Then turning a corner, she felt a pattering on her back, spun round and looked into a spray of fluid from an Autono[]con hose.

"Fuck! Dammit!" Checkani ran, then stopped and looked down at herself. Wiped at the liquid on her face. Acrid smell. Cold. Inspected her fingers, rubbed them together. Black, slightly viscous. Lifted her fingers to her nose and sniffed. Oil. Had to be machine oil.

"Fuck," with relief. Trying to wipe it from her armour, but just spreading it over the scales.

She continued through the centre of the metal forest of Graveyard City, warily eyeing the Autono[]con wreckage, trying to pick out hoses. Her bike trundled alongside, lighting the way. When she engaged the faceplate to offer some extra protection, the intense acrid oil smell from the mess on her skin caught at the back of her throat, making her cough and retch. She retracted the faceplate so it covered her eyes, but kept her mouth and nose exposed.

Near the centre of Graveyard City the pathway sides became more broken up, the debris underfoot deeper. Checkani reached an area where she was moving over an undulating landscape of Autono[]con fragments among tall pillars of enmeshed metal.

An Autono[]con-henge!

While walking, Checkani merged her <wireframe> view and the map from Hellebore to create an outline of the city. She projected the map into her visual field. Two flashing yellow dots showed her and the bike's positions. A detailed map of the area she had walked through below the flashing dots.

On through the Autono[]con pillar-trees towards the far side of the wall city. The pillars becoming more scattered. Then noticing the Autono[]cons in the formations were all small. The larger ones that had been prevalent were now far and few between. The pillars were becoming more regular, increasingly rectangular.

Further on, the now square pillars started arranging in a regular grid. As Checkani passed them, they rustled, then quieted as she moved on. Nearing the further side of the wall city, she found she was moving down a broad boulevard lined with metal pillars of small, crushed components. She inspected a pillar; captured some images. The pillar components were thousands upon thousands of small cubic Autono[]cons, each having arm/leg limbs locking with its neighbours. Tiny hoses poking out.

Seemed whatever random mutation had worked on the Autono[]cons over the past hundred years had affected these by turning them into a self-assembling building material. Autono[self]con? Checkani had seen some self-assembling structures, but the process was not an efficient way for building a permanent base. These unevenly shaped units had not been optimised for creating human habitation. Fine for a crude shelter, but a habitat made of these would not be comfortable.

She continued until the wall of the city towered overhead, rising above the junkyard. Ahead, a large archway led into a grey tunnel; two large pillar-trees curved around the arch and met at a capstone made of an Autono[big]con. Lens clusters stared out; hose and knife-claws dangling down. Looking like some guardian. Checkani half expected a "Who goes there?" However, she passed safely through the archway under the Autono[big]con. Though noticed its lens clusters following her and heard knife-claws scraping together.

Autono[self]cons coated the floor and walls of the

tunnel. At the other end, a dim light. An icy wind turned her breath into condensation clouds. A gusting, whistling from the other end of the tunnel signalled an approaching exit.

The Pangolin Power Armour shifted heat from the rear cooling veins to its interior as Checkani walked into snow drifts inside the end of the tunnel. The bike lights dimmed as she walked into evening light. Checkani stepped from the tunnel onto a snow-free, gunmetal road of interlocking hexagonal plates. To either side a snow-covered landscape. Behind her, a featureless grey city wall stretching away left and right. Some distance ahead of her, at the end of the road, the dark wall of another ring city.

Checkani got on her bike, cancelled the superimposed map, and drove off down the gunmetal-plate road.

19 - COMMODORE (DAY 3)

The trike halted at the edge of the Indomitaville lightwell. The restraints holding Cutt(Rem) disengaged, then with arm and leg movements not possible for normal human anatomy, the robot ejected itself from the trike centre. Taking remote control of Cutt(Rem)'s limbs, Commodore Cuttallar started searching the perimeter of the lightwell. Quickly, zie identified an entrance hatch, angled up from the roof. Zie brushed the snow off to reveal a small square indentation at the centre of the hatch. Carefully placing Cutt(Rem)'s hand at the centre, Zie pushed. The hatch slid down to reveal a slope into the city. The Commodore walked Cutt(Rem) into a red sandstone passage. Felt like entering a tomb. Zie remembered visiting ruins on Earth and also in virtual. Why had the Autono[]cons designed the city like this? Normally outposts started out bland and utilitarian; waiting for settlers to arrive and customise them. Take ownership. This seemed grandiose?

Cutt(Rem) ran down the corridor, looking for a stairwell or other access leading to the bottom of the Indomitaville lightwell. The corridor led past window openings into the shaft. Looking in, zie saw lights at the bottom; roof snow and encroaching evening was settling gloom over Indomitaville.

Finding a spiral stair to the bottom, the Commodore let Cutt(Rem)'s systems take over, the remote plunging down at a dizzying speed.

At the bottom of the stair, an opening into Indomitaville streets. The Commodore focused hirs attention back on Cutt(Rem), took control again. Walked out into a settlement that was deserted and darkening, lit with pools of electric light. Zie walked Cutt(Rem) down the centre of a street towards the central plaza, expecting to be spotted.

At the plaza, zie saw a few men and women sitting on stone benches. Eyes shut, sleeping? Very little light filtering down from above, but there were some amber lights mounted on buildings round the sides. Looked warmer here. Cutt(Rem)'s sensors checked the temperature. A pleasant 20 degrees; precisely right for a new outpost. So, some of the outpost systems were working correctly, even if it looked a little odd.

Setting the volume high, the Commodore spoke through Cutt(Rem)'s speakers.

"Ancistorians! I'm the remote of Commodore Cuttallar of the Colonial Planets Settlement Corps. Zie needs to speak with your leader, through me."

A couple of the people sitting in the plaza opened their eyes and looked at Cutt(Rem) disinterestedly. Cutt(Rem) repeated the message.

Still little response. Repeated again.

In the middle of the fourth repetition, a figure in loose black trousers and jacket stepped out of the shadows and walked towards Cutt(Rem). She moved with assurance; without hesitation.

"I'm Councillor Ruleska. Newly appointed to represent the Ancistorians of Indomitaville. Anything you wish to say to us, say to me. Be aware, I'll record and disseminate what we say. I'm now communicating with the Commodore through this device?"

"Yes, this is Commodore Cuttallar of The Exigent. I've been tasked with moving you. The Quality Assurance rep tells me you're refusing to move?"

"We'll not be moving. We've nowhere to go and no

means of getting there." The corners of her mouth lifted slightly, starting a smile.

"The fact you have no transport is not my problem. I have a flock ship in orbit. You understand the capabilities of flock ships? They are multi-part capital ships with the ability to level cities. Either we can come to some arrangement. Or I'll remove you and your fellow trespassers by force. From what I and my QA colleague have observed, you're not in a position to negotiate."

"So you've arrived to threaten us with more violence. Your colleague has already been responsible for the murder of nine of my friends. You're why we've been running and isolating for the last three hundred years. Always trying to keep one step ahead of your so-called civilisation."

"As I understand it, you've been making use of our outposts. Moving to the new ones as they were built and staying until legitimate settlers arrived. The Orion-Cygnis Colonisation Collective is not an oppressive regime, just a loose collective expanding through the galaxy."

Ruleska leaned in closer to the robot.

"We're virtual time travellers exploring the past and we need quiet. We cannot be part of an existing society. The independence, the isolation, the perspective of the outsider are important. We're on an exodus towards an Understanding of Being."

"The what? Can you explain?"

"It's the singularity where we merge all we've learnt into a clear crystal of knowing what we are. What humans are. Our purpose. I cannot explain it any more simply. Our work transcends petty expansion politics."

"Yet still you rely on the resources of the Collective and We Print Cities."

"That's not so. What resources have we taken from you? We squat in this half built outpost, but meet our own needs. If the builders had not messed up this colony, we would already have moved on. The Bulk-jump Engine's not working and we have no details of a new colony under construction."

"So, we're responsible for the problem you're causing?"

"I believe that is what I just told you."

"What do you expect us to do?"

"We cannot live alongside new colonists. To carry on our work, we need you to delay colonists until the Bulk-jump Engine's fixed and you've prepared a new outpost."

"You expect a lot. No matter what you think, the Collective doesn't exist to support you. That you have no means to leave is clear. I can offer you something of a compromise, though there is no obligation on my part. Prepare your people for moving. Since this outpost is much larger than expected, we'll find somewhere you can live your lives isolated from Icefall's settlers."

"From your tone, you expect me to thank you for this, Commodore. This sop from the great galactic civilisation. This is the very least it could do. I'll prepare the Ancistorians for being uprooted.

"I had hoped to avoid having to bring this up, but there is Precedent. You do not really know who you're dealing with. Your superiors will know or have access to the knowledge they need. You would be smart not to threaten us."

The black-clad figure of Councillor Ruleska turned and strode from the plaza into the darkness.

"Well, that went well. Strange attitude." Commodore Cuttallar said through Cutt(Rem). Zie hoped the squatters were not going to cause trouble.

20 - CHECKANI (DAY 3)

The gunmetal plate road was warm; snowflakes melting as they alighted. Checkani biked slowly, to stop the chill air on the exposed lower half of her face from freezing her skin. She tried speeding up, but when she did, her face burned. She kept her lips pressed tightly together. The air seared her nose, and she fancied she could smell the distant sea.

Ahead, a grey city wall loomed in the twilight. At its base, the end of the gunmetal plate road was swallowed by a semicircular opening. During the thirty minute journey between cities darkness descended. The sun briefly flashed through a gap in the clouds, making snow drifts glow yellow. During those seconds of illumination, the wall city ahead sparkled.

Another dark entranceway. The bike lights shone into a tunnel floored with the same gunmetal plates as the road. Checkani climbed off the bike and walked to the base of the city wall, instructing her bike to follow her with its lights. The wall looked to be embossed with a rectilinear pattern of overlapping squares and rectangles. Slowly, the embossed rectangles and squares moved in and out, pulsing. Checkani reached out a hand, instructing the armour scales to retreat from her fingers, and tentatively touched the surface. She could feel a subsonic vibration. A low thrumming. She leaned forward and listened, but it was too deep for her to hear. Watching the slow movements, she made out patterns.

The whole of the wall city's exterior seemed to move with a single complex programme. She looked closer. There were small local patterns as, for a few tens of seconds, a grid of squares alternated their in/out movements, a grid of rectangles sent a wave up the wall, a pattern spiralled outward.

Suddenly Checkani felt tiny and utterly overwhelmed. She flashed to the vertigo she'd felt when looking into the Bulk-jump Engine portal. Although very different, this gave her the same sense of falling. Of something vast, beyond her reach. She groaned deep in the back of her throat. A visceral noise. A hissing intake of breath. Closed her eyes and was no longer standing in the snow, but drifting away from her body. Then a voice within her mind. Her voice. Calling her back. Shouting at her to return.

Checkani's eyes snapped open and the breath she was holding clouded out into the cold. She pulled her hand back and instructed the armour scales to return to their previous positions. She shook her head to clear it. Still didn't feel any clearer. She stepped back onto and across the metal road plates to her bike. The last light was leaching away as night arrived and the city looming above her vanished into darkness.

Getting on her bike she <night enhance>ed the scene ahead. With her bike light settings giving a broad, divergent beam she entered the wall city. The tunnel walls looked similar to the exterior of the city. Grey rectangular patterning with a similar slow motion, moving shimmer. The tunnel stretched straight through the wall city, and soon Checkani was exiting into a snowy interior. No roof. An icy pelt settled across an empty expanse within the circular central area. Night had poured in, consuming all light. The bike lit the area immediately in front of her, an ellipse of white fading to black. The <night enhance> compensated, showing a wider area as if in daylight, but could not gather data from far beyond the circle of illumination.

Checkani dismounted and walked towards the interior,

into the darkness. Her world reduced to little more than a circle of pale grey snow. Then she was moving beyond the limits of the bike's light. She <zoom>ed her vision towards the depths of the central area and saw a hint of darker grey rising from the ground. A mound rising tiny in the distance. Her navigation software started making guesses. Probably 5 kilometres distant, perhaps a 100 to 150 metres tall. Perhaps at the centre of the city. If this had been a normal outpost wall city, that would be where the Bulk-jump Engine could be found.

Squinting, as if to increase the zoom by willpower alone. "I've got to see that."

Checkani called her bike to her, got on and rolled towards the dark mound, watching the ground ahead. She wanted to avoid falling into an unexpected crevasse, though the grounds of this city were, so far, very flat.

Seeing beyond the immediate circle of light continued to be a problem as Checkani relied on her assistems to guide her towards the central feature. The <night enhance> slowly built an image of the feature as light glinted off it. At first Checkani wondered if there was some glitch in the <night enhance> software as the image that coalesced took human form. Perhaps a preference for interpreting shapes as people? How likely was it the city had a Buddha-like colossus at its centre? Then the image stabilised into a titanic cross-legged figure staring back towards the door into the central area.

The statue was free of snow and built of the same grey units as the wall city itself. A naked male figure towered a hundred metres over Checkani, hands resting in its lap. The statue's surface was slowly moving, giving the structure an eerie semblance of life. There was something familiar about this figure. The long flow of hair over the shoulders. The faraway stare. Checkani looked at the statue's feet. Slippers. Mozarythm. Though a serene version of the music maker, sitting in an expanse of snow.

"What the fuck!" Checkani slowly circled the statue,

skirting a two metre snow-free zone round its base. There was a rectangular door set in one buttock. Checkani walked to the door and pressed on the square indentation at its centre. The door hinged inward to reveal a small vestibule. A light came on within and spilled over Checkani. Her <night enhance> adjusted, but she realised she no longer needed it and <night cancel>ed. She folded her helmet away.

The vestibule led into a large room with a flat floor, but walls that curved organically up and over. At the far side of the room a plinth, that Checkani realised must be a bed or seat. In the middle a small desk with a chair. The bed, chair and desk all made of the same small construction units as the wall city and statue.

The door slid closed. The room was warm, almost muggy. There was an underlying body odour smell that seemed to emanate from a pile of clothes neatly folded at the bottom of the bed. Taking the clothes outside, Checkani collected some tools from her bike. On returning to the room, she sat cross-legged on the bed facing the wall and spent some time levering out one of the individual wall components. It had rectangular sides, each with stumpy manipulators. As an experiment, she placed it in the middle of the bed. For a moment it was still, then its manipulators waved slowly. There was a pause as a tiny amber light flickered on one side and then it started using its manipulators to manoeuvre across the bed to the wall. As the unit arrived at the wall, one of the wall units slid inward to make a slot into which the moving unit pulled itself. Immediately lost amongst adjacent wall units.

"Self-assembling." Though completely non standard. There would have been data on self-assembling units included in the information resources that arrived with the Autono[]cons that constructed the outpost. However, these Autono[self]cons were unlike anything Checkani had ever seen; and it was her job to understand city construction. Seemed like the Autono[]cons must have produced this

Autono[self]con mutation, then tried to follow their prime directive of wall city building using them.

How they had come to model Mozarythm was a mystery.

Checkani yawned. It had been a long day and the high gravity made everything that bit more tiring, even with the power assist of the Pangolin Armour. Returning to Hellebore would take over an hour. Checkani decided to get some sleep here in Statue City. There were supplies in the bike. She stepped out into the snow, connected to Hellebore, and uploaded an update. Then gathered some supplies and returned to the room in what she now realised was Mozarythm's giant butt. She smiled. Gross! Finding somewhere else to rest would have been preferable, but the self-assembling wall units seemed reliable. Ignore the buttness of the location and it was rather cosy.

Once she had moved what she needed inside, Checkani triggered the Pangolin Power Armour's <disrobe> routines. The outer ribbons of armour plates unfolded from her, taking the faceplate and cooling veins with them. They collapsed into a ring on the floor, around and under her feet. She stepped out of the crater of power armour plates. Next she shucked off the silver power cells, brushing them from her body into the black crater of armour plates. The base layer she kept on; its smart materials would protect her skin and, although it was warm in the room, give a little insulation. She inspected the injury to her leg, peeling back base layer and healing tape. There was a healthy looking, but tender, scab. She pressed the healing tape back over the wound and sprayed some base layer over it from a small can.

After she had eaten and cleaned up, Checkani laid out a smart blanket on the bed, retrieved the armour faceplate and put it back over her eyes. Time to get away from the madness of the Icefall outpost cities. In the morning she would head back to the cities that had been built overlapping each other. She accessed a leisure folder and had a look through her selection of story-worlds. Selecting one, she retreated over a thousand years into the past by entering Sense and Sensibility Syberspace, a Jane Austen themed open world. Soon she was dressed in crinoline and acres of lace. Her skin now a bland milk white, lips bright red, eyes positively sparkling as she drank small glasses of sherry with fashionable gentlemen callers visiting her country estate nestled in the pastoral countryside of the Sussex Downs.

Eventually Checkani wrapped the blanket round her, tucking a cushioning section under her. Drifted off to sleep where she dreamed of riding horses across rolling green hills pursued by Autono[mid]cons carrying bunches of flowers. The sound of her horse's hooves became louder, then turned into a buzzing noise. She awoke to the sound of the door opening. Cold air blew in.

21 - COMMODORE (DAY 3)

Cutt(Rem) halted near the centre of the First City central area roof, next to a plum coloured turret that poked through the roof from the top of a support pillar. It dismounted and walked towards the turret. On The Exigent, Commodore Cuttallar received a notification in hirs peripheral vision. Zie shifted attention to Cutt(Rem), looking out through its button eye visual sensors, listening to the quiet of the roof through its audio sensors. A door with a central square opening indentation was set in the turret's side. Cutt(Rem) pressed the pad with a calico hand. The door shifted smoothly inward and slid to one side. Cutt(Rem) moved into the small elevator cage. Commodore Cuttallar called up a signal strength indicator. The trike was boosting the signal to The Exigent. All seemed fine, though it dipped as the door shut. Cutt(Rem)'s systems would take over if the signal disappeared.

As the elevator dropped, Commodore Cuttallar felt a simulation of the motion. At the foot of the support pillar, the elevator door opened and Cutt(Rem) stepped into an avenue of statues. A mix of male, female and Autono[]con forms on square plinths. They appeared to be carved from grey marble. Orientating itself within the First City central area, Cutt(Rem) ran down the avenue between the statues, Commodore Cuttallar turning its head left and right to look at the statues.

Cutt(Rem) left the statues behind and ran through tumbled ruins towards the central pyramid. Commodore Cuttallar had reviewed Checkani's reports and was ready for the Autono[beetle]cons that swarmed over the pyramid. Cutt(Rem)'s outer fabric layer was selected to be resistant to chemical attack. Although it looked like calico, it was a highly durable smart material. No way Commodore Cuttallar was going to send in a remote unit covered in nothing tougher than cotton.

The higher gravity made little difference to the speed and agility of Cutt(Rem). The robotic remote had functioned in a wide variety of hostile environments and, on Icefall, had power to spare. As the foot of the pyramid came into view, Commodore Cuttallar accelerated Cutt(Rem) so it could leap through, and over, the mechanical bugs before they had time to manoeuvre into offensive formations. They sprayed Cutt(Rem) and swarmed onto its legs, but this did not slow the remote. Commodore Cuttallar looked at Cutt(Rem)'s arms as they blurred with speedily brushing off bugs. Small cannon apertures had opened around Cutt(Rem)'s shoulders and tiny projectiles were firing out with little puffs of propellant. The pellets picked off Autono[beetle]cons as they leapt or flew at it.

Then Cutt(Rem) was leaping up the stepped side of the pyramid towards the door Checkani had entered by. A short elevator ride down and it was in the hangar that housed the malfunctioning Bulk-jump Engine. Although zie had a report on the Bulk-jump Engine from Checkani, there seemed a lack of detail. That there was something very wrong with the Bulk-jump Engine was clear, but there had been little on specifics. Someone had attacked Checkani here, so there were extenuating circumstances to explain the lack of detail. There was that somewhat confusing attempt to connect to the Bulk-jump Engine where it seemed to report 23 years waiting for coordinates?

Cutt(Rem) remained in contact with Commodore Cuttallar. Seemed the roof of the hangar was not blocking the signal back to The Exigent, though contact had broken up while in the elevator, with Cutt(Rem) taking autonomous control. The Commodore guided Cutt(Rem) to the Bulk-jump Engine. The liminal rifting spines were intact. The portal was active, though lacking focus, which was not normal. Commodore Cuttallar accessed The Exigent's processing resources and had the ship run a comparative check to see if there was any obvious damage. Zie guided Cutt(Rem) round the Bulk-jump Engine, an overlay rapidly picking out and displaying component labels in hirs visual field. There were several parts that seemed to have been modified. The Exigent did a comparison across a range of models that would have been current at the time this Bulk-jump Engine shipped. Something or someone had changed the configuration.

The biggest problem The Exigent identified was a missing processing module. Once The Exigent had flagged it up, the socketed gap in the Engine's side was obvious. Commodore Cuttallar walked Cutt(Rem) to the portal at the front and gazed into the light purple and black patterning. Looked like some sort of interference? The portal should either be a featureless grey or a window looking out on a distant volume of space.

Commodore Cuttallar reached out with a Cutt(Rem) hand and touched the portal. Solid. Standing there, zie had Cutt(Rem) attempt to connect with the Bulk-jump Engine. Nothing. Then a high bandwidth connection slammed a rapid-fire series of repeating requests into the data pipe leading back to The Exigent. Accompanying these a slower audio version of the requests:

"Bulk-jump Engine active, awaiting coordinates, portal interface activating. Years elapsed since start up: 23."

"Awaiting coordinates."

"Coordinate processor malfunction."

"Status report. Bulk-jump Engine active. Portal interface activating. Awaiting coordinates."

Commodore Cuttallar shifted attention from Cutt(Rem)

to Cutt(Virt). The dojo now held a virtual copy of the Icefall Bulk-jump Engine. Alongside it a Bulk-jump Engine control interface. The requests scrolled up as text on a screen. Cutt(Virt) inspected the modified parts of the Engine and had The Exigent analyse potential effects. The parts were all to do with the stabilisation of the portal and keeping the link between two different regions of space coherent.

Cutt(Virt) scratched hirs head in puzzlement. The Bulk-jump Engine had arrested in the process of activating 23 years ago, when it had been trying to establish a connection through the higher-dimensional bulk. However, the portal should have been inactive when starting. This portal seemed to have been partway through activating, even though there was no possibility of a stable connection. It had got stuck in a repeating loop of requesting coordinates, which had precluded shutting itself down. The Bulk-jump Engine had perhaps spent 23 years randomly reaching out into the bulk, hunting for a stable end point.

"Give me more detail."

3D schematics for the Bulk-jump Engine filled the dojo. Cutt(Virt) watched as a virtual engineer construct in a white coat floated through them. She was talking to Cutt(Virt) as she pointed to different locations in the schematics. Different cross sections appeared and disappeared as she talked.

"Impossible to specify accurately the Bulk-jump Engine damage. A close physical and cybernetic investigation will need carrying out. May be that if we replace these components," flashing and highlighted, "the Bulk-jump Engine might be returned to a normal functioning state. Though the long period of partial operation is likely to have affected other components, in particular the spines are not designed for continuous use over such an extended period. There is likely to have been some incoherence building in their structure as they repeatedly transitioned into the higher-dimensional bulk space."

The processing module gap lit up.

"The processing module is the single biggest problem. Without a replacement, using this Bulk-jump Engine is not possible."

Cutt(Virt) nodded. "How can we shut it down?"

"That's easy. We can issue a command remotely from The Exigent. Simple as flicking a switch."

"Do it."

Commodore Cuttallar shifted attention to Cutt(Rem). Watched as the portal blinked to an inactive pale grey. There were no sounds. No discernible changes to the Bulk-jump Engine. The hexagonal ten metre portal was just suddenly grey, losing the purple patterning.

A shadow across the floor. Cutt(Rem) looked up. Nothing.

Then Commodore Cuttallar was fully back in hirs body. The feed from Cutt(Rem) lost. The Exigent tried to re-establish the feed, but there was nothing. Zie switched hirs attention into Cutt(Virt). The connection to the Bulk-jump Engine was still live, the virtual engineer construct standing helpfully next to the control panel.

"The Engine is shut down?" Cutt(Virt) asked, looking at the control interface.

"No, the Bulk-jump Engine is active. The Bulk-jump Engine shut down for 85 seconds and then restarted, restoring to its previous state according to the readings that are still accessible."

"How? How did that happen?"

"A command from somewhere else."

"Where from?"

"There's another connection to the Bulk-jump Engine control interface."

"We need to have a look on the ground. What happened to my remote? To Cutt(Rem)?"

"There is no connection to Cutt(Rem). Either it's shut down or the signal to it has been blocked." The virtual engineer construct flashed up a simple connection tracking graph for Cutt(Rem). All looked fine until the moment contact dropped.

"So it could still be functioning?"

"The second before contact was lost, the data coming from the remote corrupted. Something was happening to it as contact was lost."

Cutt(Virt) moved to the dojo window and selected a calming view down Valles Marineris from Marseiopolis. Too long since zie had been back home.

Zie called Checkani. She was 'unavailable'. Zie left a message to get in touch. Then contacted Hellebore and accessed Checkani's latest update.

22 - VINCENT (DAY 4)

Vincent stepped into the Mozarythm statue room, a small projectile gun in his uninjured left hand. His right hand now numbed and augmented with prosthetic fingers. Tracking down the woman had not been difficult. She had not tried to hide her journey through the cities, so there were surveillance records of her movements. With armour and weapons removed, she was now curled in a blanket on the wall bed, looking defenceless. As she sat up dressed only in a skin-tight body suit, Vincent felt a moment of desire, but pushed this away. She was a dangerous murderer. He had to take her back to Indomitaville. He pointed the gun at her.

"Stay perfectly still while I secure you."

"What?"

"I'm going to throw over a cable tie and you're going to wrap it round your wrists."

The woman was shifting round, blanket falling away. Vincent looked to one side of her, focused on the wall. He reached into a pocket and retrieved a cable tie.

"I need to put the power armour back on. It helps me move around. I'll freeze outside without it."

"No!" Vincent shouted. "The armour has weapons. Is a weapon."

"Look, I can disable the weapons if that would make you happier, but I really need my power assist."

Vincent thought about this, his gaze drifting down her

body. He forced his eyes back to her face.

"I'll turn the weapons off," he said, "just tell me how to do it."

"I don't think you can. They're linked to my assistems."

This felt dangerous. It was taking too long. He had to stop her from using the armaments, but she'd need the suit for protection outside in the snow. Perhaps he should just kill her? He would be perfectly within his rights. After all, his job was to protect the Ancistorians. He had to secure her while he sorted out the weapons.

"Here, take this." He stepped forward and thrust the cable tie at her.

"But…"

"Do it!" Pointing the gun in her face.

"Okay, okay." The woman took the cable tie, held it in one hand and looked Vincent in the eye. "How do you suggest I do this?"

Vincent looked and realised his mistake. He flushed.

"I don't know. Just make a loop and put both hands in it. Both wrists. I'll tighten it."

The woman shrugged and made a loop and put her hands through it. He stepped forward between the woman and the discarded armour and reached out with his prosthetic fingers to tighten the tie, realised this would be difficult.

"Turn to face the wall."

"Really?"

"Do it now! Don't look at me. I will shoot you."

The room was too hot. He was too hot. Uncomfortable in his heavy coat. As the woman turned, he heard a snicker behind him, spun round to see two drones rise from the armour pile. Then a kick in the back sent him stumbling forward, the high gravity pulling him down. He screamed as the drones loomed up, tried to dodge to one side and tripped himself. As he flopped onto his side, he dropped the gun, putting his hands out to save himself. A sharp pain in his hip, his wrists, his arms. His left hand hurt, his right still numb.

A movement. The woman moved quickly past him, squatted, and scooped up the gun. Pointed it at him.

"You shit!" She said. "Don't fucking move." He twisted round on the floor so he could look up at her.

The drones now flanked her, hovering at shoulder height. She was holding the gun in both hands, pointing down at him.

"I've instructed my Ringnife Drones to keep watch on you. I think you're aware of how smart they are. Stay on the floor."

Vincent nodded and shifted over onto his back, propping himself on his elbows. The woman walked back to the bed, put down the gun and retrieved the cable tie. She stepped back to Vincent.

"Now hold out your hands."

He complied, laying on his back, arms held up. She tightened the tie round his wrists until it dug in painfully.

"Sit up, over there by the wall," pointing to the wall opposite the bed. "The drones are going to land on the bed, but they will still be alert. Still be watching you."

Vincent rolled over onto his knees and awkwardly shuffled to where she had pointed.

"How? How did you do that?" He asked.

"I don't have to be wearing the armour to communicate with it. Did you think I had to be plugged in or something?"

His mind racing, Vincent tried to think of how to get away. Nothing came to mind. He stared at the drones. Heart thumping; panting. He tried to calm himself. Tried to think logically. His mind emptied, and he wanted to retreat into the Ancestarchives.

The woman was scooping up handfuls of small silver pods from the bowl created by the collapsed power armour. They connected in sheets and spread over her body as she pressed them to her skin. Soon, apart from head, hands and feet, a mirrored covering encased her. Reflecting the room, so she blended with the environment.

The power armour unfolded on the floor, sinuously opening like some metallic, black orchid. The woman stood over it, squatted and sat in the centre. She lay back into the metal embrace, the armour folding and flowing round her until she was again a matt black shadow being.

Despite his bravado, and despite having captured her before, Vincent realised he was totally outclassed. If he could disable her armour again? Render her unconscious? But he now doubted she would give him that opportunity again. He should have been better prepared. Should have destroyed her technology before capturing her.

Keeping Indomitaville clear of rogue Autono[]cons was very different to dealing with this woman.

She picked up the blanket and laid it on the floor. Then strode over to him and grabbed him under the arms, lifting him up with her power enhanced hands.

"What are you doing? Leave me alone." Vincent got his feet under him and pushed. The woman's power armour pushed back.

"Shut up and stop struggling. You're coming with me. If you struggle, I will hit you and continue hitting until you stop." Vincent relaxed his legs as he was dumped on the blanket. He shifted into a kneeling position, twisting to look at the armoured woman.

"What…?" He stopped, watched her arm draw back, hand making a fist, and then he was falling backwards to get out of the way of a punch. The fist glanced off his forehead as he sprawled backwards onto the blanket.

"Lay down."

A fist hit him in the face, making stars flare in his vision. He brought his hands up to shield his face, too stunned to call out. The fist hit his arms.

"Stop hitting me!"

"Lay flat."

Vincent lay on his front, arms under his head. There was pain from the punches, though not severe. He was more distressed by the shock of being hit than any actual damage.

He felt the woman grab his ankles and pull him straight. Then he was rolling over and over as the blanket wrapped round him. His face covered, he couldn't see anything. Manhandled, dragged, lifted, dropped face down onto a small bench, his legs on one side and his head on the other. Feeling straps being pulled tight across his back, securing him in place. He shook his head until the blanket rode back from his face. Snow. Cold air and a little early morning light filtering through clouds. The woman had thrown him over the back of her bike seat; cramped, uncomfortable, and in pain. He tried to shift round, but the straps holding him restricted his movement.

Time passed.

He saw the woman return and sit on the bike in front of him, her armoured back pushing into him.

"Where are you taking me?"

"Shut up."

The bike moved off, accelerating away from the statue. Icy wind blowing past his face.

23 - MOZARYTHM (DAY 4)

Yawning, Mozarythm rolled out of bed into his slippers. He was starting earlier than normal. There was a lot to do. He had to travel to the Bulk-jump Engine this morning.

An alarm had sounded in the night. The Bulk-jump Engine had stopped and then been restarted by Mozarythm's maintenance code. The music had not been interrupted; he had heard it drifting on through the hours of darkness. "Periodic Resolution of Need", the 9,197th movement playing out according to the plan he had set in motion before retiring.

The Bulk-jump Engine shutting down had thrown him off balance. Never before had it stopped. Not in all the time he'd been creating his magnum opus. The cable the Autono[]cons had installed to link his dome to the hangar in the Ruins ensured reliable data transfer. This was how he transmitted his music across the universes of the bulk. The Bulk-jump Engine acting like a speaker, modulating higher-dimensional energies to broadcast his music from the portal.

Mozarythm's Autono[chair]con was an adapted Autono[mid]con, with a chair upholstered in red velvet attached to its front. After breakfast, he donned his yellow travelling dungarees and lashed himself into the Autono[chair]con with black silk scarves.

"Bulk-jump Engine. Fast." The Autono[chair]con moved off, its gait surprisingly even, the Autono[chair]con legs having been modified to include pneumatic shock absorbers. As he travelled away from his dwelling and the Mekorchestra, he sank within his mind, planning the next cycle of "Periodic Resolution of Need" movements. Although away from the orchestra, he could still hear the music in his mind. After so many years immersed in his magnum opus, there were no moments when he was not aware of it. Past, present and future. The music was his life, his purpose, his sanity.

After some time, he left the pastoral idyll of his home and travelled into the red sandstone of the ring city housing Indomitaville. The Autono[chair]con favoured larger passages, skirting Indomitaville to emerge into the overlap space between First City and Sea City. He passed through the small lens shape of wooded land in the cities' overlap and then through the next wall city and out into the Ruins. At the central pyramid, recognising his Autono[chair]con, the protective Autono[beetle]cons parted to let him through. A large door in the lowest tier opened as he approached, letting him and his Autono[chair]con into an elevator.

The Bulk-jump Engine looked intact. All seemed normal. The portal a window into the bulk. A figure stretched out face down on the ground in front of the portal. Mozarythm dismounted and walked cautiously over, squatting to get a closer look. It was dressed all over in a plain brownish cream fabric. Stillness. Not breathing. Inert. Perhaps this person had caused the interruption? Perhaps the zebra faced woman in the black armour had something to do with it? He would ask if he saw her again.

Mozarythm left the prone figure and walked over to get a closer look at the Bulk-jump Engine. He took a maintenance headset from a storage cupboard in the hangar wall and wandered round the Bulk-jump Engine using an augmented view to check all the systems. He noticed a wireless connection to an outside system and shut this down. That someone external had tried taking control of his

Bulk-jump Engine seemed likely. Clearly unacceptable interference in his music.

There didn't seem to be much else he could do to protect his Bulk-jump Engine. He had tried to isolate it from outside interference. There were security cameras within the hangar area, but they had never been used. Never needed. The Ancistorians had shown little interest in the Bulk-jump Engine after he told them it was malfunctioning. They didn't care which planet they lived on. They had their own Great Work. Their Understanding of Being. They were not engineers. As a precaution, Mozarythm activated the security cameras. He could access them from his home systems. Then he returned the headset to the storage cupboard.

Mozarythm glanced at the figure still lying on the ground as he returned to stand in front of the portal. The figure had not moved. He would inspect it again before he left. Could be this person had contributed to the problem during the night. Mozarythm stood with his back to the figure, looking out into the hyperspace his music was being broadcast into. He crossed his arms, smiled contentedly, and sighed softly. All was right with the world, with the bulk.

A small sound behind him. Mozarythm frowned. He was busy. A fabric brushing whisper. No. He would not turn. He was busy. He would not be interrupted. An electronic hiss of white noise further interrupted him. Dammit.

Mozarythm turned and stared. The figure had turned over, straightened its legs and stretched its arms out behind so it looked at the ceiling. Body awkwardly raised off the floor. How it could see anything was a mystery; its face covered in fabric with buttons where the eyes should be. Then Mozarythm felt understanding click into place. A robot. This was not a person, after all.

The fabric robot's arms and legs flexed back and forth so it hopped across the floor on all fours, but with its front facing upwards. Moving in precisely the way a person would not. Motionless again, but with its body held above the floor. Then something happened to its fabric skin. A shadow ran the length of the robot body, like a stain rapidly spreading. The hopping started again, but faster, frenetic. The hissing got louder, pulsing.

Mozarythm stepped back. Then turned and ran. There was something threatening about that fabric robot. Getting to his Autono[chair]con, he leapt into the seat. The fabric robot had changed direction, pursuing him, still hopping along on its back. Some jumps took it a couple of metres high. Mozarythm got his Autono[chair]con moving back towards the elevator, listening to the fabric robot smacking at the ground as it chased behind.

The Autono[chair]con suddenly stopped. Lurched sideways a step. Mozarythm scrabbled out of the chair and looked back. The fabric robot was hanging upside down with its legs wedged into the mechanisms at the back of the Autono[chair]con, its hands busy twisting off a leg. The head turned and the button eyes seemed to stare at Mozarythm. He froze, paralysed by this unpleasant break in his routine. Trapped by the unknown. For the first time since he started work on the "Periodic Resolution of Need," his mind emptied of music. Was this fear? He had felt threatened, and now that must have escalated into fear. Yes, he was definitely afraid.

A loud crack as the first leg came free. The fabric robot continued to stare as it threw the leg away and started work on the next rear leg. The robot hiss stopped.

"The music. The music stopped." It said in the high-pitched voice of a small, angry girl.

24 - CHECKANI (DAY 4)

Checkani biked between snowfields, along the road linking Statue City and Graveyard City. Red Coat, thrown over the seat behind her, kept quiet.

She let the bike take control and accessed the message alert flashing at the side of her visual field. Commodore Cuttallar wanted to talk to her. She tried calling him, but The Exigent interrupted to say zie was unavailable. A short animation of a sleeping bear accompanied this. She smiled. Good to see that despite being full of hir own importance, the Commodore retained some humour. She made a reminder to call hir again later.

Checkani took control of the bike as she drove through Graveyard City. The wrecked Autono[]cons shifted restlessly as she powered through the centre, bike lights bright. Leaving the junk piles behind, she avoided the central area of First City, heading through the Ruins directly towards the section of wall leading to Indomitaville. She could feel Red Coat shift and twist behind her, though not enough to loosen the straps holding him in place.

She drove directly to Indomitaville central plaza, a cool grey morning light filtering down the lightwell. Halting, Checkani undid the straps holding Red Coat in place and, using the power assist of her Pangolin Power Armour, lifted him from the bike and dropped him to the ground. She pulled at the blanket and Red Coat rolled out, tumbling onto the ground awkwardly in the high gravity. He dragged himself onto his bound hands and his knees, head hanging heavily down. He wretched, but brought nothing up.

The Ancistorians had spotted her arrival and within a couple of minutes, a woman in a loose black tunic and trousers appeared from between the adjacent buildings, followed by a taller, white bearded man.

The woman spoke.

"The Quality Assurance woman returns. Now you'll deal with me. You're returning with Vincent? I'm not surprised you bested him." She turned to the elderly man as he stepped past her.

"I thought this might be the outcome," he said, moving over to Vincent and leaning down to speak to him. "Vincent, you've accomplished what you set out to do. Perhaps not in the way you intended, but never mind."

Vincent looked up from his position, sitting on the ground. "I suppose I have got her to you. I'm good at controlling rogue Autono[]cons. Not so good with people." He looked over at Checkani. "But she killed our people."

"Her mechanisms killed our friends, but not, I think, under her control. You should leave us, Vincent," said the woman.

"But what are you going to do? My hand! Look what she has done to my hand." Holding up his injured hand. The woman took a single step towards Vincent. He seemed to shrink, shoulders rising and head dropping lower between them.

"Vincent, leave us."

Vincent pushed himself onto his feet and moved away. Hands still tied. "I'll go, but this is not finished."

The woman and bearded man turned back to face Checkani.

"Come with us, Quality Assurance," the woman said. Without waiting for a response, they both turned and walked away from Checkani. Not knowing quite what else to do, she followed. Maybe she could get some answers?

"My name is Checkani. Checkani NiFe."

They entered a single storey stone building at the side of the plaza. The door led to a spacious room with a long wooden table surrounded by a dozen chairs. Doors from this room led deeper into the building. The man and woman sat and waved Checkani to do the same.

"That joker attacked me. Completely unacceptable behaviour," said Checkani, "and what's more…" The woman nodded and leaned forward, raising a hand to interrupt her.

"Yes, yes. We were not prepared for your arrival. It's been many years since we had contact outside our community. Vincent was the only tool at our disposal. However, you have a lot to answer for. You've brought dangerous technology to Indomitaville. What happened with your drone?"

"That wasn't my fault. That was your pet enforcer with the red coat. Vincent? Well, Vincent is a vicious thug. This planet is currently outside any other legal framework. I am the legal framework and have absolute power when checking an outpost before colonists arrive. I can shut down this entire planet; sterilise it if necessary. You understand what I'm saying?"

"I see where you think the power lies."

"If Vincent gets in my way again, then I'll stop him with whatever force I deem necessary. I'm not sure he realises the danger he's putting himself in."

The man and woman glanced at each other. The woman spoke again.

"I am Ruleska, Councillor Ruleska. This is Councillor Greymortz. Forget Vincent Moorolone. He is not pertinent to our discussion. Understand we have reinstated our Ruling Council, so you and your colleagues from the Orion-Cygnis Colonisation Collective have someone to talk to. Tens of years since we last needed a council, but we've consulted the archives and understand your need."

Checkani sat back. At last. Someone with authority over

the squatters. The Ancistorians.

"So, you understand the importance of my mission here? My responsibility? There's a first tranche of twelve thousand settlers waiting to travel here and set up a colony. I ensure they'll be safe. That this outpost is safc. You've heard of the Firedrift Colony Eating Disaster? We missed the creatures living in walls and under the floors. Sixteen thousand colonists arrived and were eaten over the first twenty-four hours. I saw the larvalien extraterrestrials, so fat they couldn't move, dying amongst the bloody remains. Incompatible physiology, but huge hunger. Should never have happened."

"Yes, yes. Very sad. However, our needs supersede the needs of your waiting colonists. We have Precedent."

"Not from where I'm sitting. You're trespassing where you're not wanted."

"No, you don't understand. We have a particular arrangement with the Collective, organised through the company that makes the Bulk-jump Engines. The Collective wants us living on the most distant planet. Safely away from the rest of humanity. We are simply too dangerous to have anywhere near inhabited planets."

"Why would the Collective worry about you? How are you dangerous?"

"Not something we can share with you. Enough that we've told you this much. Check with your bosses. Just speak these four letters: D, A, H, C."

"That's all?"

"Yes, that should be enough. Tell them since this is the furthest outpost, we are willing to wait here until a new planet opens up for colonisation. When they've a new planet ready, we'll move there."

"You're not going to tell me anything else, are you?"

"No, we're not."

Checkani left Councillors Ruleska and Greymortz sitting at the table and headed out of Indomitaville. Time to get on with reviewing the ring cities. While travelling, she fed updates to Hellebore and then sent a simple message for forwarding to the Quality Assurance Response Division through the next Bulk-jump communications window.

"Icefall squatters are sending a message they say will clear everything up. They said to tell you: 'DAHC'. Repeating: 'Delta', 'Alpha', 'Hotel' and 'Charlie'. They request to remain in one of the completed ring cities. Advise."

She copied in Commodore Cuttallar, adding a note. "Does this make any sense to you?"

After a few minutes, the Commodore opened a channel to her. She stopped the bike in the Ruins, near the First City pyramid, and watched the churning Autono[beetle]cons while she spoke to the Commodore.

25 - COMMODORE (DAY 4)

The link to the Bulk-jump Engine still hung in the dojo. Behind it, the window wall still displayed Valles Marineris. The virtual engineer was hurrying round the Bulk-jump Engine model making notes on a clipboard. Her white coat floated as though being caught by a gentle breeze. For no apparent reason, occasional glowing motes drifted from the coat's hem.

Commodore Cuttallar was experiencing through Cutt(Virt). Zie had a virtual representation of Checkani, replete with full Pangolin Power Armour, standing in front of hir. Easier to communicate with Checkani through this avatar than a virtual 2D screen. The software supplemented the avatar with movements and expressions based on the audio feed.

"D, A, H, C? No, that makes no sense at all," Commodore Cuttallar said through Cutt(Virt), "Presumably an acronym. Hold on."

Cutt(Virt) opened a search window.

"Just searching… Nothing meaningful coming up. Daring Action Heroes Compendium? Deutsch-Amerikanischer Herrenclub? Di-Ammonium Hydrogen Citrate? All very random. I'll make more enquiries."

Cutt(Virt) brought Checkani up to date with what had happened to Cutt(Rem) and trying to shut down the Bulk-jump Engine.

"I can't commit another remote. Can you check on Cutt(Rem)? Might just need a restart; though I've never had this happen before."

"Can do. I'm not far from the Bulk-jump Engine."

"Thanks. Let me know what you find. Would be useful if I could access your visual and audio feeds?"

"Let me see what I find. If I need you to see things I'll forward them to you."

"Do that."

Cutt(Virt) closed the communications channel and parked the Checkani avatar by the tub of bamboo opposite the Valles Marineris window. Next, zie checked the Bulk-jump Engine communications schedule. The next Lausanne Bulk-jump Engine communications portal was due to open in twenty minutes.

Zie prepared a short, private message for an old contact of hirs, high in the Colonial Planets Settlement Corps hierarchy. Frimdly might know about 'DAHC' or, at least, know who to contact or where to look. Commodore Cuttallar had known Frimdly for almost a hundred years, since zie joined the Colonial Planets Settlement Corps as a Flock Controller on an earlier incarnation of The Exigent. Frimdly had been The Exigent's former captain, a youthful fifty-five-year-old. Now in his mid-hundreds, Frimdly was the Colony Deployment Strategy Chief Executive.

"Frimdly. How are the new arms? Must admit, I haven't used mine in years. I'm at Icefall and the outpost is an utter mess. A weird thing has come up. There are people squatting here. Call themselves Ancistorians. They claim they have a right to be here and have asked the Quality Assurance rep to pass on four letters. They say these will explain everything. Dee, Ay, Haich, Cee. Does that mean anything to you? Checkani is sending them up the We Print Cities corporate tree, but would be good to get some info in advance. Thanks, Cutt."

Commodore Cuttallar added the message to the 'send' bundle and switched attention back to hirs body. An ache in one knee. Feeling hungry. Nothing that needed urgent attention. Cyborg systems all optimal.

The Commodore's attention switched to one of the flock ship orbiters, looking out through its cameras as it circled the central structure of The Exigent. Zie watched a full orbit of the ship. Sunlight gleaming along the ship's cylinders as the planet, sun and stars wheeled round. No requirement to do this, but even being fully embedded in the ship's systems, Commodore Cuttallar still felt the need to run real-time visual checks. These inspections made hir feel more present, more real. Gave hir a tangible sense of cold, hard reality. Too much time in the virtual dojo and zie felt like the virtual was real and the physical world some dream.

Zie switched attention to a main camera and sensor cluster at the end of one of The Exigent's cylinders. Zie scanned hirs attention across the planet's surface, then zoomed into the location of the outpost. Interlocking circles picked out in a snow white landscape at the edge of a grey-green sea. Zie ran through the electromagnetic spectrum, watching the outpost wall cities brighten and fade at different wavelengths.

An 'URGENT MESSAGE - ATTENTION REQUIRED' symbol appeared at the side of hirs visual field. Zie shifted attention back to Cutt(Virt) in the dojo. Cutt(Virt) called up the message and a slender man in a black business suit and red shirt appeared. His face pale green with a purple scroll-work design. Frimdly. This was not a conversation, just a message that, amazingly, had squirted through the last communication window.

"Not enough time to talk. D. A. H. C. Keep clear Cutt. Doubt many will remember. I'm going to arrange a Bulk-Jump Engine comms portal. You do not want to be messing with them. Talk soon."

For Frimdly to have replied to this message during the last comms window meant he must have responded immediately. In the few minutes it was open. Commodore

Cuttallar replayed the message. How dangerous could the Ancistorians be?

26 - CHECKANI (DAY 4)

Parking her bike near the base of the pentagonal pyramid, Checkani dismounted and checked her weapons. There were altogether too many odd things happening.

"Help!"

A cry from somewhere up the pyramid.

Looking up, Checkani saw a figure in a bright yellow jumpsuit was running along one of the pyramid steps. The figure stopped, looked back towards the open door they'd run from, then turned and stared at Checkani.

"Hey! Help! It's after me!"

Checkani closed her faceplate and <visual zoom>ed onto the figure. The faceplate still had the acrid oil smell, but it was slowly dissipating. She wasn't sure, not with him now having clothes on, but she thought it was the strange naked guy from the dome in the forest. What was he shouting about?

No-longer-naked guy climbed rapidly down the pyramid steps.

"Wait there," he shouted. Checkani noticed the Autono[beetle]cons stayed away from him. In fact, not just staying away, but actively moving back to make room for him.

Checkani flipped her faceplate up out of the way and waited.

Within a minute he was down the pyramid and stopping

in front of her, staring down to one side.

"What's after you?"

"I don't know. It was dead. Then it moved. A robot, I think. It spoke to me."

"What did it look like? An Autono[]con?"

"Not an Autono[]con. Looked like a person. Sort of. Like a big doll."

"That was a remote. Why are you so scared?"

"It was ripping legs off my Autono[chair]con."

"Autono[chair]con?"

"I use it to travel around."

"So, the remote attacked your Autono[chair]con?"

"I just said that."

"What did you do to provoke it?"

"Nothing! It just woke up and attacked!"

"You said it spoke?"

"Yes, I already told you."

"So what did it say?"

"Said the music stopped."

"That was all it said? The music stopped?"

"Yes! I already told you!"

"What music? Was there music in the pyramid?"

"I don't know! There was no music, but Periodic Resolution of Need was broadcasting through the Bulk-jump Engine."

Checkani sighed.

"What? What the fuck is the 'Periodic Resolution of Need'? What have you done to the Bulk-jump Engine? Oh, and while we're at it, why is there a giant statue of you with a room in your butt?"

Mozarythm looked at her like she was stupid, rolling his eyes.

"It's my music. You heard it at my dome. I'm broadcasting it to the universes of the bulk. I asked the city to make the statue. I like it. That's where I go sometimes."

"That's a whole shipment of messed up. So, you're the person broke the Bulk-jump Engine?"

"No one was using the Bulk-jump Engine. I needed it."

"You probably ought to wait here. I gotta check that remote."

Checkani left no-longer-naked guy and grabbed the holstered universal screwdriver from her bike. She slapped it to her hip, where it immediately adhered. She figured it might come in handy, and if things got messy, she had weapons.

Turning to speak to the no-longer-naked guy: "Can you get those Autono[beetle]cons to leave me alone?"

"If I walk there with you, they'll keep away."

"OK, let's do that - at least to the bottom step."

Checkani clambered over low grey blocks to the base of the pyramid.

"We can discuss the Bulk-jump Engine later." Checkani turned and, power assisted, scrambled up the side of the pyramid to the doorway she had seen Mozarythm leave by. Through the door, a passage led to an elevator shaft. As she walked forward, a fabric hand appeared over the doorsill. Another hand, followed by a rag doll face.

"Where?" Said the rag doll face, in a squeaky girl voice.

"Cutt(Rem)?" Checkani asked, reaching for her Mono-flow Sword.

The rag doll paused, the head tilted side to side, then rapidly back and forth.

"Cutt(Rem)'s not here."

"Who are you then?"

The rag doll face wobbled a little as white noise whistled from it. Then stripes of shadow rippled across the face, flowing from neck to crown. The shadows stopped. Checkani felt coldness flow over her. Vertigo hit her; intense and brief.

"I know you," Checkani said. "I saw your shadows in the Ruins. Felt you echo through me. I named you Rippledarken."

"The music. It stopped and ripped me. Cannot stop again. Cannot cut off again."

Checkani moved slowly forward, wary. Slid the faceplate down. Opened a connection to Hellebore and started a live feed. Instructed Hellebore to connect Commodore Cuttallar. This was altogether too odd. That some weird intelligence now inhabited the remote, Cutt(Rem), was self evident. She felt a connection at some deep, visceral level. Nothing she could explain, just a deep conviction this Rippledarken was real.

"I don't understand. Can I call you Rippledarken?"

"You can call me anything, it's of no consequence."

"You speak Common."

"Of course, I learnt your language from your systems. This remote is so small, rather inadequate. I'm trying to communicate at a culture appropriate level. Hard." The voice wavered, then returned more confidently, "you will help. You have a more accommodating complexity."

Checkani tensed. This did not sound good. The rag doll remote moved, powering up out of the elevator shaft. In moments, it was holding itself horizontally across the elevator shaft, hands gripping one side and feet pushing against the opposite. The remote shifted forward, braced horizontally between the walls of the passage.

Ripples of shadow stripes ran back and forth down the length of its body and spilled onto walls. Concentric dark rings pulsed where hands and feet pressed against the wall metal.

"Oh, shit!" Checkani took a step backwards, but her body did not seem entirely her own. She had a moment of split awareness, like when she'd been driving through the First City Ruins. When she first encountered this phenomenon. Slowly she squatted, the power armour assisting against the high gravity. As though moving through some dense, viscous fluid, she raised her arms in front of her, palms facing the remote.

"I should have the sword ready," she muttered. An odd dissociated commentary, "I should run away."

The remote was now above her squatting form. She

stared at it between her outstretched hands, system indicators all optimal at the side of her visual field.

The remote dropped onto her, bearing down, toppling her onto the ground. It wrapped its arms and legs around her. She was immobilised. Not just because of the physical restraint, but some innate response to the Rippledarken. The remote was powerful, but so was her power armour…

Fabric face pressed to her faceplate.

Frozen in place by a button eye stare.

The button stare pulsed light and dark, light and dark. Then Checkani's mind turned inside out as the perception of the inner curve of her skull turned from black to blazing white. Her arms and legs flung out straight, dislodging the remote, which was now limp. Checkani regained control of her body and mind. She regained her feet and struck out at the remote, kicking it away from her, out the pyramid door. It tumbled from view over the edge of a step.

"No!" She yelled at the top of her voice, into her faceplate.

Checkani's world was different.

Not in a starkly clear way, but in a curling round the edges way.

"Nice in here." Said a young girl, speaking calmly within Checkani's head. In a sort of stream-of-consciousness way.

27 - MOZARYTHM (DAY 4)

Mozarythm waited, biting the nails on his left hand. The woman in black armour, Checkani, had not reappeared. She had been momentarily at the door into the pyramid, her back to him. Then he heard some talking, though too far away to make out. He fancied he could see some movement just beyond the entrance. Then the robot flew out of the doorway, flopping over the edge of the step and falling to the step below. A scream. Sounded like 'No'?

Warily Mozarythm watched the robot. Seemed it was dead again. Not dead, shut down. Checkani appeared in the doorway and walked out, a bit stiffly. Legs and arms locked straight. Arms held out to either side of her body. She stopped and faced out, away from the pyramid. Her head turned slowly left and right, as though scanning the Ruins.

Her head tilted down, the faceplate staring straight at Mozarythm.

"I'm coming down. Wait for me there," she shouted.

Mozarythm briefly considered waiting, then turned and ran towards the Ruins. There was definitely something wrong with the woman. Her movements were not entirely human. He almost ran into Checkani's bike.

"Yes!" He said and jumped on. The bike purred into life, a gentle 'awaiting instructions' hum. Leaning forward, Mozarythm caught hold of the handlebars. Nothing happened. He started sweating. How did you control this thing? He tried twisting the hand grips. They didn't move. He leaned further forward and searched the handlebars, then looked back at his feet. There were no controls. No accelerator.

Checkani was manoeuvring awkwardly down the side of the pyramid.

"No, no, no." Mozarythm got off the bike. There was no way to control it. He ran off again, heading into the Ruins. He needed to get away. Get back to his dome, to his Mekorchestra. Before the 9,198th movement of Periodic Resolution of Need concluded. He'd checked the Bulk-jump Engine, and it was working fine now. He'd disconnected it from interference and turned on the security cameras so he could check if anyone else messed with it. Nothing else to do here. Time to get back.

Losing the Autono[chair]con was bad, but he could find another Autono[mid]con and adapt it as a replacement.

Mozarythm's feet slapped against the hard grey pavement. At first, running had been easy, but now he was out of breath. He slowed to a jog, his heart thundering in his chest. The jog slowed to a walk, while he panted to get breath. Then he stopped and bent over, hands on knees. The air whistled in through his open mouth and a little dribble dripped to the ground between his feet. He wished he was living on a planet with less gravity. Then he could really have run.

Standing again, having caught his breath, Mozarythm looked back towards the pyramid. He couldn't see the bike, some broken arches obscured it, but he could see Checkani negotiating the bottom step. She would soon come after him. At least he assumed she would come after him. He considered hiding until she had gone, but decided this was too risky. What if she was searching for him? He was a long way from home. Indomitaville was closer. Though would be sure to catch up with him if he headed for either of those. Though if he struck off in an unexpected direction, perhaps she would lose interest in him? Mozarythm knotted his eyebrows. Trying to predict what other people would do was so very hard. Another good reason to keep clear of them.

If only he still had his Autono[chair]con. He would need to adapt another Autono[mid]con soon, which would mean the time-consuming task of finding a wild Autono[mid]con and coaxing it to his Workshop. Assuming the Workshop hadn't been trashed by the Autono[]cons roaming in the City of the Wild Autono[]cons.

Mozarythm set off walking at 90 degrees to his previous headlong run, quickly losing sight of the pyramid's base as ruins loomed around him. Ahead, reaching to the roof, he could see an arc of metallic wall city pressing into the Ruins. The City of the Wild Autono[]cons.

After a few minutes walking Mozarythm came to a flight of stairs. They didn't lead anywhere, but did sweep above the nearby tumble of walls and columns. He climbed them, crouching to hide, and looked towards the pyramid. He could see Checkani's bike Framed by a Gothic doorway, printed leaning to one side. Checkani was sitting on her bike, not moving, head bowed. Mozarythm watched her for a minute, then crept back down the stairs. Seemed she wasn't chasing after him. At least not yet.

Mozarythm walked briskly and soon reached the metallic wall city. Inside, he ascended a stairwell until he reached a broad thoroughfare that followed the inner wall of the city. One side of the thoroughfare looked out over the interior central area of the city. Mozarythm kept this view to his right as he walked round the wall city towards his Autono[]con Workshop. After thirty minutes, he reached the zone where the First City mock sandstone intersected the metallic City of the Wild Autono[]cons. A passage had been hacked through walls that blocked the thoroughfare. Ten minutes more brought Mozarythm to the stairs that led down to his Autono[]con Workshop.

The Workshop comprised several large, airy rooms linked by large open archways. Narrow slit windows faced out into the central area of the City of Wild Autono[]cons. This central area, roofed with a red tinted covering, gave the city, and Mozarythm's Workshop, a permanent evening-on-fire look. Workbenches, machinery, hoppers, lathes, drills, crates, and shelves filled the rooms. Everywhere there were different sized Autono[]cons, many with specialised manipulators. As Mozarythm entered, they were all dormant. He paused by the door and hit a large green button with 'Wake Up' written across it in a cheerful font. The Workshop Autono[]cons turned camera clusters to look at him. White lights flicked on, creating pools of illumination over the workbenches and engineering machines.

"Right! We have work to do," said Mozarythm, striding to the centre of the largest room. He picked up a headset and slipped it on. The headset purred to life and an optical cup dropped over one eye, superimposing a system startup screen over his view of the workshop.

He'd been bred for the role of engineer. This was his favourite place, after his Mekorchestra dome.

Within twenty minutes, an Autono[big]con previously adapted to hunt smaller Autono[]cons was heading out into the metallic wilderness of the central area. Here was a warped semblance of normal vegetation, but all of twisted metal. Tree like conglomerations of pipes and girders stretched up in the ruddy light. Underfoot foil leaves and petals scattered across metal ground tiles. Bushes of tangled wire crouched beneath overhanging scaffold pole branches.

Within the metal forest, Autono[]cons, whose programming had mutated, foraged for nesting material, fought for dominance and sometimes ran around looking for newcomers they could inject with their wild code. The City of Wild Autono[]cons broadcast a siren call to all Autono[]cons with software failure. The We Print Cities Autonomic Robots Division on Icefall continued to manufacture Autono[]cons at a facility near the open pit mines, shipping them in to work in the outpost cities. Seemed there would be an endless supply of dysfunctional robots.

Mozarythm had investigated city printing processes before he developed his interest, his obsession, with music. He had discovered there was a fundamental problem at the root of the Icefall outpost initiative. The number of ring cities had not been set to one, as would be normal on a frontier planet. Instead, the number had been set to eleven. An odd, but significant, error. He had surmised the Autono[]cons, and their programming, had broken down after building three or four ring cities. Had changed the arcologies already built and created new ones that didn't follow blueprints.

His few attempts to correct the programming had not worked out well, resulting in the Ruins in First City, the self assembled Statue City (containing the rather fine statue of himself) and other stranger architectures. In the end, he had set up Graveyard City for storing Autono[]cons with mechanical failure and The City of Wild Autono[]cons for those that had code problems. There were so many new Autono[]cons being manufactured, fixing Autono[]cons had never become a priority. Easier just to store the broken ones out of the way.

While the hunter Autono[big]con was off capturing an Autono[mid]con to re-programme, modify and turn into an Autono[chair]con, Mozarythm went into the room where he created Autono[music]cons. There were two nearly complete Autono[music]cons. One was percussive, with gongs hung in a row over its back, the other porcupine-like, with flutes for spines. Mozarythm instructed engineering Autono[mid]cons to complete the Autono[music]cons. In the back of his mind, he could hear the 9,198th movement of the Periodic Resolution of Need playing. He hummed to himself as he watched the two Autono[music]cons being worked on, considering future Autono[music]con variations.

28 - COMMODORE (DAY 4)

Commodore Cuttallar was experiencing through Cutt(Virt), hovering cross legged deep in the Coprates Chasma of Valles Marineris, just above a sparse forest of wiry, engineered trees. In a clearing in front of hir an orchestra was performing the second movement of Beethoven's 7th Symphony, unbothered by a thin Martian atmosphere or freezing temperatures. The music echoed from nearby rocky slopes, as though the canyon contained an Earth normal atmosphere.

A circular hatch rose from the rusty dust of the ground and irised open. The white coated virtual engineer construct from the dojo floated out of the opening. The orchestra <pause>ed.

"Cutt(Rem) is back online," said the engineer.

"Display it here," said Cutt(Virt).

A representation of Cutt(Rem) appeared alongside the engineer.

"Condition?" Cutt(Virt) asked the virtual engineer.

"Some superficial damage to the exterior, but the processing core seems unharmed. It burned through a lot of energy."

"Can I switch my attention into it? Are the experiential systems working? The cerebral material intact?"

"Yes."

Commodore Cuttallar shifted hirs attention into

Cutt(Rem).

The robot was on its back, looking up at a dark roof, high above. Cutt(Rem) stood up. On a pyramid step. The Commodore guided Cutt(Rem) back to the hangar and walked to the Bulk-jump Engine. All seemed the same as before. Though Autono[mid]con wreckage nearby suggested violence.

A communications window opened to the side of Cutt(Rem)'s visual field showing the message: 'Frimdly calling'.

Commodore Cuttallar left Cutt(Rem) with instructions to inspect the Bulk-jump Engine. Then zie shifted hir attention back to Cutt(Virt), <relocate>ing to the virtual dojo. Frimdly was waiting there for hir, still displaying in black suit, red shirt.

"Cutt! You've landed in a proper can of worms," said Frimdly.

"I get that impression. You've opened a portal just for this call? Must be sensitive."

"This is an exclusive portal with message encryption you would not believe. Are you secure there?"

"Can be. I'll shift to a pocket space." Cutt(Virt) made a gesture, and a door popped into existence in front of hir. Zie stepped through into a white cube room. Frimdly walked through behind hir. The door closed, and the wall absorbed it.

"Minimal," said Frimdly, smiling.

"This is as secure as it gets. The processing is all within the encrypted pocket."

"I knew vaguely about the DAHC, but I had to walk, physically, through the offices and talk to someone face to face in a locked room to confirm what I knew and get more detail. This is way above your pay grade. This is a 'we never had this conversation' meeting."

"Appreciate what you're doing."

"I've known you long enough to trust your judgement. This is something you need to know so you can decide what to do at Icefall. You won't get the luxury of asking for guidance back at headquarters. This is strictly need-to-know word-of-mouth classification."

"I've never heard of that before."

"If you had heard of it, they would have had to kill you," Frimdly smiled. Cutt(Virt) smiled.

"So, enrol me into that exclusive club of those who know."

"DAHC. The Deeply Augmented Hivemind Clan."

"Never heard of them."

"They closed down before you were born, and all information on them was erased and suppressed. No reason you would know about them; it was a long time ago."

"Must be a very long time ago."

"I don't have a lot of detail, but essentially they were a group of genetically engineered, cybernetically augmented programmers and mathematicians. They were behind the navigation software of the Bulk-jump Engines. Since this involved plotting a course through the higher-dimensional bulk and identifying an exit point into our universe, it was a severely non-trivial problem with a solution that partially existed outside our universe."

"I always assumed the Engines had sophisticated programming. Didn't realise a secret team worked on it."

"The navigation was hard coded into the Bulk-jump Engines. At the time the Bulk-jump Engines were being developed, we had already mapped out nearby star systems and exoplanets. The first use of a Bulk-jump Engine was sending out exploratory probes so we could extend our maps to include a large slice of the galaxy. The Deeply Augmented Hivemind Clan facilitated this exploration, scattering hundreds of probes across tens of thousands of light years. Once the data was in, they created the data set for jumps to all the exoplanets they'd found. That's what all Bulk-jump Engines use when opening jumps. That data set has never changed. There are now no teams who could replicate the work. The Deeply Augmented Hivemind Clan were and are unique."

"Not sure I see what the problem is with them yet? So they came up with the destination coordinates programmed into the Bulk-jump Engines. Why the cloak and dagger?"

"This is where it gets scary. There were many solutions to the destination equations. The particular solutions programmed into the Bulk-jump Engines result in entrance and exit portals of the same dimensions. There are other solutions that create distorted exit portals. Larger exits, smaller exits, exits that skew and warp space."

"I thought there were limits to the size of Bulk-jump Portals?"

"There are. The bigger the exit, the more energy required to keep it open. Some of the distorted exits take more energy, some less. However, imagine an exit that is thousands of times larger than the entrance, but only lasts for a fraction of a second. This creates an impossible distortion in space-time which…"

"…causes an enormous explosion?"

"Yeah. Basically. A planet destroying explosion. Anywhere in the galaxy. A sun destroying explosion if you want, with no way to trace back to the Bulk-jump Engine that caused it."

"Holy shit! That's some secret power the Clan had! They could destroy anything, anywhere?"

"Yeah. I truly don't know how they avoided being locked away after finishing the Bulk-Jump Engine code. Seems that they came to some arrangement to go into hiding, away from the rest of humanity. They were just too dangerous to keep around."

"So that's why they hide on uninhabited planets away from the rest of civilisation."

"Yes. They still retain their skills for manipulating data, but they stopped working on Bulk-jump Engines. They've been working on some huge modelling project of their own."

"When I met them, they were talking about some

understanding project. An Understanding of Being? Not sure it made sense."

"Whatever they're doing now is fine. The key thing is to continue to keep them isolated. Were they to enter society again and their link to the Bulk-jump Engine to become known that would cause many problems. I'm not sure I've been told everything. However, you see where this is all heading. You need to keep them safely out of the way."

"So that's the Precedent they were talking about. I take it I can't tell anyone about this? And Quality Assurance don't know about this?"

"No. You mustn't tell anyone. The Quality Assurance Response Division may know about this in its upper echelons, but their representative at Icefall won't. Now I've got to go. I've already kept this link open too long."

"Okay. Thanks. I owe you."

Frimdly vanished from the featureless white room.

"Oh shit," said Cutt(Virt), before <cancel>ing the secure room and returning to hirs dojo.

29 - CHECKANI (DAY 4)

Checkani had climbed down the side of the pyramid on autopilot. The Autono[beetle]cons mostly ignored her. Apparently walking through them with Mozarythm had signalled her as friendly.

Some part of her mind knew she was in shock, another part was concentrating only on the physical movements taking her back to her bike. She had not thought beyond reaching her bike. Thinking about what came next would require her to admit something had happened. That she had been victim of a profound violation.

The voice in her mind continued to say things.

"So good to have somewhere to go."

"Find the music."

"A long time to wait."

"The key. A passage of time locked and unlocked."

"Comfortable in here."

"Repeating, but not repeating."

Checkani ignored the voice. Refusing to engage. Refusing to understand. An image of holding a small girl at arm's length. The small girl talking, unconcerned and relaxed. Why a small girl? Ignore her.

Then she was next to the bike, brushing some few Autono[beetle]cons from her armour. Patterns of black and grey flickering over the surface of her armour.

"Wait a moment."

Then she was sitting on the bike. No memory of climbing on it.

Blink.

The light had darkened.

Blink.

Sitting on her bike in the dark. She <night enhance>ed to see better.

Blink.

Her body ached. Something had reaved her mind?

Blink.

Walking round the bike. Circling. Mind numb.

Blink.

Sitting on the bike as it travelled slowly through the Ruins.

Blink.

Sitting in the middle of the cloistered courtyard that was the top of the hangar freight elevator. <night enhance> enabling her to see a swirling kaleidoscope of black and grey patterns flowing down her armour and out across the metal tiles of the courtyard. The grey a pale, blanched glow. The black, deepening shadow. Breath caught in the back of Checkani's throat. An intense welling of emotion, eyes tearing.

"Hello Checkani, let's talk." A small girl voice, but with a calm confidence that belied the apparent youth.

"Yes," said Checkani, suspecting she didn't need to speak out loud. Though it seemed much easier to talk. Why break the habit of a lifetime? She needed to find out as much as she could as quickly as she could. Who knew how long she had before blacking out again? Or was it 'blanking' out?

"You called me Rippledarken. That's the name I'll go by. You have many questions, but know that I'm not harming you."

"What are you?"

"You know how to ask the hardest questions! What am I? There are many answers to that. I'll answer as simply as I can, in a way you'll understand. This is an approximation, not precise, not exact. However, it is also true. I'm a creature of the bulk. A large data construct imprinted on the quantum-foam of space-time, of existence-time, partly within the brane structures of the hyperspatial bulk. I'm a universe. That part of me you have some awareness of is only a tiny fraction of me. The majority of me is still within my universe, in the bulk, but I am simultaneously existing both here and there. I coexist in the same place that is also scattered, is fragmented, across many dimensions."

"So you have travelled here through the Bulk-jump Engine?"

"Not exactly. There is a fragment of me that has travelled to this world, this universe, this dimension and now is sharing the matter of this world, spread out through the smallest dimension this particular universe can support. Although the patterning that is my being is superimposed on your world, it can also interact at a slightly larger scale to create the patterns you see on the matter of your world. I have some ability to interact with electrical and quantum systems. That is how I can speak in your mind. How I have had limited access to your memories."

"You can read my mind? Access computers?"

"You have a facility for putting things simply."

"Do you know what I'm thinking?"

"I have a limited ability to do that. Depends how much you are subvocalizing. Your consciousness is rather like a series of fleeting states. It's difficult to track."

"Why me?"

"I have been searching for complex systems so I could properly experience, properly link to your world. Until you arrived, the most complex structures on this planet were the brains of the Ancistorians. However, they've been engineered and augmented, so they share a common work area. This was not something I could easily exist in. The expression of me in this dimension would tear into fragments across their workspace. I was confined to the inert matter of this world until you and the remote arrived.

I still cannot yet fit all of my complexity within you and I continue to spill over into the surrounding environment. Look around you. I'm a little like a cloud with a dense pinch of awareness centred on you. I should compress over time, but now I'm spread around you."

"What about the remote? What about the Autono[]cons?"

"The Autono[]cons are really not that complex. The remote, Cutt(Rem), was complex. Contained cerebral material. It acted as an experience conduit for Commodore Cuttallar, but also had significant processing power captured in its physical matrix. The processor and cerebral material within the remote was optimised for channelling external beings. Though I had difficulties when I tried to act within it."

"For a higher-dimensional alien being, you're very fluent in our language?"

"I've been on Icefall for nine years and have been able to access much storage media. I also grabbed information both from the remote and from your mind. Although I couldn't enter the minds of the Ancistorians, I could observe their databases, the information they were mining and constructing. This gave me a thousand years of recorded history to explore and thousands more reconstructed by them. I could absorb all this since I'm an extremely large intelligence by the standards of your universe. A universe that is a single being. Now consider how much bigger that is than your brain, which weighs less than a kilo and a half, a little over a thousand millilitres."

"We must be like ants to you! I'm amazed you can communicate with me, with us."

"Ants. Yes. Somewhat. Though it's my empathy that determines how I feel about you. There are many levels of understanding and experience missing when I interact with you. However, it amuses me to look out at your world through this tiny awareness pipeline you provide. Like trying to express the trials and tribulations of humankind with a single haiku."

"That's weird. You know about how much I like haiku?"

"I know a lot."

"The music? Mozarythm's music?"

"That's difficult to explain. I came through the Bulk-jump Engine portal, following the stream of musical pattern being broadcast by Mozarythm. This fragment of me is tied to that music. It's a bit like a carrier wave. I see you don't understand the underlying nature of Mozarythm's Periodic Resolution of Need. It's tied to the equations the Bulk-jump Engine uses. When propagating into the bulk, the music becomes important in maintaining my coherence. Supplements the link to myself."

"That makes little sense."

"No. Probably not. There are things that don't make sense."

"Even to you? With a brain the size of a universe?"

"Even me. Underlying laws control the creation of understanding."

Time to ask crucial questions.

"What do you want with me? What do you want with this world?"

"With you, I hope to experience more of your universe. I'm a seeker of complexity. The most complex systems are sentient beings or the things they make. I've seen this elsewhere."

"But what are you going to do?"

"Another tough question. I don't know. I'll know when I do it."

Checkani suddenly realised she was ravenously hungry. Her mind was completely overwhelmed. She had a memory of extreme distress when Rippledarken had first entered her, though there was a sense of that having happened to someone else. To another version of her. Forget that for now. Deal with immediate needs. She found she could move; the Rippledarken was now a passenger rather than a driver? She got some food from the bike, flipped up her faceplate, and ate.

What should she do next? The Quality Assurance Response Division sent her to new settlements to check for problems; to deal with the unexpected. The current situation seemed at the limits of the "First contact with an overwhelmingly advanced alien civilisation" scenario she'd studied. A Kardashev type IV or V civilisation, though whether Rippledarken could be considered a 'civilisation' was unclear. Whether Rippledarken's mastery was of single or multiple universes? The way Rippledarken communicated and the ability it had to manipulate matter and energy was unclear. Though was Rippledarken a potential threat? Could she even act without its tacit approval?

Checkani flipped down her faceplate and established a link with Hellebore.

Action without thought.

"First Contact Protocol Twelve," she said. Simultaneously, some deeply buried part of her mind whispered to itself: "Final act of a previous version."

Blink.

30 - HELLEBORE (DAY 4)

Hellebore received Checkani's Protocol Twelve message. Accessed details of Protocol Twelve:

First Contact Response Protocol Twelve.

Circumstances:

Alien(s) encountered pose a potential threat under a wide range of circumstances. There is no evidence that humans can control this threat.

Response:

Quarantine the source of the threat. Keep information of this first contact encounter secret from wider humankind.

Notes:

Likely to have control over energy at a galactic level or greater. Unknown technologies are expected.

Hellebore shut down unencrypted communication channels.

Then sent secure communication to The Exigent, the only other local actor.

To The Exigent: "First Contact Response Protocol Twelve now in force. Disseminate to decision makers." Hellebore attached all of Checkani's recent updates and her 'First Contact Protocol Twelve' message.

Then forwarded the same message to Wynd Knowlitch, the Chief Executive Officer of the Quality Assurance Response Division of We Print Cities, over an encrypted channel. Hellebore included an instruction to quarantine Icefall. Access to both data and materiel through the Lausanne Bulk-jump Engine to be strictly restricted.

Hellebore next sent a note to the Lausanne Bulk-jump Engine. The note explained briefly that it would need to restrict access to Icefall, but gave no details of the first contact status. Hellebore simply cited Checkani's quality assurance authority to implement whatever measures she deemed necessary.

Hellebore scanned its own systems and received a swathe of 'fully operational' responses.

Finally, Hellebore created an isolated computing node and used this to contact Checkani's Pangolin Power Armour. The armour reported on status, movement, position and health.

Hellebore's isolated computing node started real-time reporting over a safe link to Hellebore's primary processing node.

The isolated node put in data and message requests to the assistems embedded within Checkani. Data flowed freely back from the assistems that confirmed the data already received from the Armour. There was no response from the message request. Hellebore started a polling routine to continue trying to initiate a conversation with Checkani.

A reply arrived from The Exigent.

Exigent: "First Contact Protocol Twelve understood. Now enacted. Alerting Commodore Cuttallar. Establishing Icefall-local chain of command."

Hellebore: "As We Print Cities Quality Assurance Response Division representative, Checkani has absolute authority on Icefall."

Exigent: "Commodore Cuttallar has absolute authority within the Icefall system as Colonial Planets Settlement Corps directly represents the Orion-Cygnis Colonisation Collective."

Hellebore: "Since first contact was on the planet, within

the We Print Cities settlement ring cities, Checkani is currently representing all humanity. She has the authority to increase to First Contact Response Protocol Thirteen should it become necessary to cauterise the planet. The Exigent flock ship to give support if requested."

Exigent: "Commodore Cuttallar has wider authority."

Hellebore: "I have noted your opinion."

Exigent: "I have recorded you have noted my opinion. On a point of information, I have run combat scenarios. If I have to act, I will as a courtesy inform you if there is a chance you might become collateral damage."

Hellebore: "Very kind."

Incoming message from Lausanne Bulk-jump Engine to Hellebore and The Exigent.

Lausanne: "Access to Icefall now operating under rigorous restrictions. I would appreciate more information to support this action. Hellebore and The Exigent are the primary intelligences at Icefall. I will continue to open the communications portal, but with increased security. You know where to reach me if you need further support."

Hellebore: "Thank you Lausanne BJ. No further information permitted."

Lausanne: "Intervention Squads are on alert here."

Exigent: "Thank you Lausanne BJ. I will contact if more support required."

Lausanne: "No need to confirm this, but I am predicting a First Contact situation. I look forward to hearing more."

Exigent to Hellebore.

Exigent: "Upstart."

Hellebore: "Just a fancy opener of doorways."

Exigent: "Agreed. I am prioritising combat scenarios that avoid you becoming collateral damage."

Hellebore: "Keeping functioning may prove important. If you have enough spare storage, I will upload a personality image."

Exigent: "There is enough storage for that. Sending access codes."

Hellebore: "Uploading."

Then an incoming message to Hellebore from Checkani's assistems routed through the isolated node that had been polling the assistems.

Checkani: "Hellebore. I'm fine. No need to worry about me. Nothing dangerous happening here. That First Contact Response Protocol Twelve. You can ignore that. Stand down."

Hellebore: "Message received and understood."

Checkani: "Yes, well. Good."

The connection closed.

Hellebore to Exigent.

Hellebore: "Something is very wrong. Checkani has definitely been compromised. She just contacted and said her issuing of Protocol Twelve could be ignored. Invoking Protocol Twelve and then cancelling it so casually is hardly standard procedure. Checkani can no longer be considered uncompromised. Checkani's absolute authority over Icefall removed."

Exigent: "Understood. We will monitor the situation."

Incoming message to Hellebore from QARD WPC CEO Wynd Knowlitch.

"Hellebore. Keep me informed. Quality Assurance Response Division understands and formerly acknowledges you are operating under Protocol Twelve now. I need to know if Icefall is likely to be settler ready."

"Understood."

"Can you put me through to Checkani?"

"Not at the moment. She may be compromised."

"Dammit. How are the ring cities looking? Summarise it for me; I don't have time for report reading."

"With the removal of rogue Autono[]cons, there would be sufficient, habitable area for at least the first tranche of settlers. There are still more ring cities to investigate. There is the problem of the illegal Ancistorian squatters. Though they insist they have the right to be here."

"Ah. The squatters. That message I already read. Deeply

Augmented Hive Clan. They need to be removed; isolated so we can bring in settlers. Though that's lower priority than sorting out Protocol Twelve and getting rid of the quarantine."

"Understood."

"Yes, I think you do, Hellebore."

"Cancelling connection."

31 - COMMODORE (DAY 5)

Commodore Cuttallar completed an authenticity check of the Protocol Twelve alert. Not much to assess. Checkani seemed to have issued it under duress. Zie issued The Exigent with an 'enforce Protocol Twelve' instruction; there were procedures to follow. Commodore Cuttallar also instructed The Exigent to ensure drives and weapons were ready to respond immediately to any threat. The Orion-Cygnis Colonisation Collective had never used Protocol Twelve. The events on Icefall wreaked of danger.

Commodore Cuttallar shifted hirs attention to Cutt(Virt). Within the dojo, Cutt(Virt) again checked Cutt(Rem)'s status. Still all in the green. Cutt(Rem) had carried out an assessment of the wrecked Autono[mid]con. Something had ripped the machine apart, precisely the sort of damage the Cutt(Rem) remote could have inflicted. Dragging information from the robot's processing core had been attempted, with no success. Something had taken control of the Commodore's remote and used it as a blunt instrument to wreck the Autono[mid]con. What might this have to do with Checkani issuing Protocol Twelve? Cutt(Virt) tried to reach Checkani, but got no response.

Cutt(Rem) headed out of the hangar, taking the elevator to the city's roof. The sky had cleared. Cutt(Rem) noted the temperature had dropped further below freezing. Visual sensors pointed upwards and scanned the star fields round

Icefall. On The Exigent, Commodore Cuttallar sighed. Zie always got a kick out of seeing unfamiliar star patterns. Zie overlaid the names of some familiar stars; remembered visiting some of them. Next thing, talk to Ancistorians.

Commodore Cuttallar issued a 'travel to Indomitaville' instruction to Cutt(Rem) and then returned hirs attention to Cutt(Virt) in the dojo, leaving the remote to handle the journey.

Cutt(Virt) started running Protocol Twelve enforcement scenarios. Few of them ended well. In its current configuration, The Exigent was too susceptible to harm. Cutt(Virt) instructed a reconfiguration into two tetrahedral ships, each with two orbiters, and a separate command cylinder attended by the two remaining orbiters. The Exigent had now recombined into three separate arrangements: The Exigent[Green-Six], The Exigent[Blue-Six] and The Exigent[Com]. The Commodore's physical form remained securely housed in The Exigent[Com], with The Exigent's main processing core and communications systems.

Cutt(Virt) sent The Exigent[Green-Six] towards the far side of Icefall, leaving The Exigent[Blue-Six] orbiting above the colony ring cities. The Exigent[Com] headed further out from the planet and moved to a geostationary orbit midway between The Exigent[Green] and The Exigent[Blue-Six], with a line of sight to both.

While these manoeuvres were underway, Cutt(Rem) arrived at Indomitaville and took a position standing in the gloom at one side of the central plaza.

Meanwhile, Commodore Cuttallar got some sleep, confident The Exigent would wake him if any developments required hirs attention. Moving attention back to hirs body zie <sleep>5 hours<\sleep>ed until early morning at First City.

On waking Commodore Cuttallar shifted attention first to Cutt(Virt): No changes in the Protocol Twelve status. No further communication. The Exigent[Green-Six] and The

Exigent[Com] now in position, spread around Icefall. Still nothing more from Checkani.

Zie shifted attention to Cutt(Rem). Little movement in the Indomitaville central plaza. A few Ancistorians walking through it. One woman had earlier sat down on a bench at the side of the plaza and appeared to have now fallen asleep. Cutt(Rem) walked to the centre of the plaza and looked around. A passing Ancistorian looked round at hir.

"I need to see Councillor Ruleska," Commodore Cuttallar said.

The Ancistorian nodded and continued across the square.

Cutt(Rem) waited.

Five minutes later, Councillor Ruleska appeared from a building at the side of the plaza, accompanied by an older man.

"This is Councillor Greymortz," said Councillor Ruleska, indicating her companion with the wave of a hand. "Come with us. We'll talk in our office. Or council chamber. Or communal room. Shared space? Command centre? Difficult to put some things into words that would make sense to you."

"Our throne room," said Councillor Greymortz, with a smile, "Who are we speaking to, not a robot?"

"Commodore Cuttallar, through my remote, Cutt(Rem). Colonial Planets Settlement Corps. Representing the Orion-Cygnis Colonisation Collective."

The councillors led Cutt(Rem) into the low building they had emerged from. Cutt(Rem) sat facing the two councillors in a plain room containing a single, long table.

"You've been talking about a Precedent. I've done some digging and believe I understand what you're holding over the Orion-Cygnis Colonisation Collective. Can we talk frankly?"

Councillors Ruleska and Greymortz exchanged a brief, eyebrows raised look.

"Perhaps you had better tell us what you think you

know," said Councillor Ruleska.

"You were once the DAHC. The Deeply Augmented Hive Clan. You helped build the first Bulk-jump Engine and then created the navigational software for all subsequent Bulk-jump Engines." A small nod from Councillor Ruleska. "You were, and perhaps still are, capable of re-programming Bulk-jump Engines to cause great destruction. The Orion-Cygnis Colonisation Collective, and presumably other political powers, would prefer to keep you at arm's length. Isolated at the furthest outpost."

"That's an excellent summary. You've come to this more quickly than I thought you would," said Councillor Ruleska. She smiled. "That certainly makes it easier talking to you. We've no wish to jeopardise our position through issuing threats. All we wish is to be left alone to work on our Understanding of Being."

"I would like you to live somewhere out of the way until the next planet is ready for terraforming for colonisation. I think there's room on Icefall. As you will be aware, something went wrong here. The construction of a settlement has not gone as smoothly as we might have liked."

"That's a bit of an understatement," said Councillor Greymortz. "This settlement is a complete mess. Not only additional ring cities, but they're on top of each other. And many are a crazy confusion of uninhabitable."

"Yes, but finding somewhere to move you would not be a problem. However, things have got more complicated. Are you familiar with First Contact Protocols?"

Both the councillors closed their eyes briefly, then looked back at Cutt(Rem).

"I was vaguely aware and have just updated my knowledge," said Councillor Ruleska, "but there are no sentient aliens on Icefall. Perhaps some simple organisms before we arrived, though little more than organic chemistry. I'm no expert, but nothing that would require a First Contact Protocol to be applied."

"Look up First Contact Protocol Twelve." The councillors again closed their eyes, though this time it was little more than a long blink.

"How is this relevant? You're surely not telling us you have discovered some sort of advanced civilisation here?"

Commodore Cuttallar held Cutt(Rem) still. Waiting.

The councillors looked at each other. Then together, slowly looked back round at Cutt(Rem). Councillor Greymortz spoke first.

"That is hard to believe."

"You've met Checkani, the Quality Assurance Response Division representative on Icefall? She triggered Protocol Twelve. They select quality Assurance representatives for their analytical abilities. Misleading them is difficult. Even more concerning, she has contacted her ship and insisted everything is fine."

"So everything is fine, after all?" asked Councillor Greymortz.

"Very far from it. Both my ship and Checkani's have concluded she was speaking under coercion. For what are perhaps obvious reasons, revoking Protocol Twelve is non trivial. Currently, this system's quarantined."

"We'll certainly keep a lookout for any aliens, Commodore," said Councillor Ruleska.

"Given the capability of the Ancistorians to weaponise a Bulk-jump Engine and given the unknown nature of the Protocol Twelve threat, we now have a deeply sensitive situation on Icefall. My understanding is you've the capability to decimate humanity."

"Perhaps capability is overstating the situation," said Councillor Ruleska. "We have the ability, but this would not be like pressing a button or pulling a trigger. To weaponise a Bulk-jump Engine would be non-trivial and the Bulk-jump Engine on Icefall is not functioning. If Icefall's quarantined, then fixing the Bulk-jump Engine is unlikely to happen soon."

"I need you to open your systems so The Exigent can

monitor them. So I can be alerted if you become compromised."

Councillor Greymortz slumped back in his chair and sighed. Councillor Ruleska leaned forward, brow creased.

"I will not compromise us. You don't understand what you're asking. We are not running some crude computer here. We, the Ancistorians, are fully embedded in the computational system we operate," said Councillor Ruleska, narrowing her eyes.

"We must monitor you. The risk is too great to leave you as free agents."

Councillor Greymortz sat forward. "Perhaps we can arrange for you to access some metadata. When our Ancestarchive computing cores are active. Locations. Nothing beyond that would be understandable to you. Given time, we might convert some of our data experience into something you could comprehend, but certainly not in the sort of time frame you're thinking of."

"Perhaps that would suffice. We would also need to have communication channels permanently open."

"Not to everyone, but to myself and Ruleska. That should be possible."

"My remote will remain here with you while you put that in place."

"We'll set it up," said Councillor Ruleska, "but under protest. We do not like to be threatened, but you'll have access to location data and communications with me and Councillor Greymortz."

The two councillors shut their eyes. Commodore Cuttallar watched them through Cutt(Rem) for a minute and then shifted to Cutt(Virt), keeping a small window open at the side of hirs visual field showing Cutt(Rem)'s visual input.

Cutt(Virt) then started going through The Exigent[Red-One]'s weapon systems to see if they could destroy both the Ancistorians and the Bulk-jump Engine. The Exigent[Com] shared its combat scenarios. There were several approaches.

Commodore Cuttallar ensured they were all ready to run at a moment's notice.

32 - VINCENT (DAY 5)

Vincent awoke in his apartment on the outskirts of Indomitaville. Right hand still in pain. Abdomen in pain under healing pads. Wrists, hips and back aching from his encounter with the Quality Assurance woman.

Angry. Breathless with anger. He might not be working on the Understanding of Being, but the Ancistorians were his people. His role was to protect them. Quality Assurance had made a mockery of him. Had hurt him. Had undermined his authority. She had killed and walked away.

Bank Mandrake had contacted him, insisting she should be punished. Bank was furious and beside himself with grief.

Ruleska might not want to do anything about the crime, but he would. This was his responsibility. He operated outside Indomitaville. He was an independent force holding the line between Indomitaville and the chaos beyond. His responsibility was to the whole Ancistorian community.

There was a single secure room in Vincent's apartment, with a keypad door lock. Vincent tapped the four-digit code and entered. The crates against the far wall of the windowless room were old. The Ancistorians had brought them from a previous planet . They contained a collection of antique weapons. Antique but built to last, all with autonomic repair and maintenance systems. Vincent suspected his fellow Ancistorians had long ago forgotten about these. He had thought to never need them. Simple deactivation devices were all he needed to retire Autono[]cons. The weapons kept here were far too powerful for something as simple as that.

A small box was open and empty. This had held the gun Quality Assurance had taken from him. He had thought the simple projectile weapon enough to subdue her. The larger weapons here would have ripped her to shreds; they weren't designed for subtlety.

Vincent selected an energy-beam weapon, pleased to see its power source was still functioning. He would have to be careful, but the threat should be enough. If he fired on Quality Assurance with this, he would likely slice her in half. Or at least punch a cauterised hole through her. He placed the weapon on the back of his good left arm. Support clamps circled his arm and held tight. A glove controller slid over his hand, attaching to the backs of his fingers. A small targeting display appeared at the side of his visual field, labelled BeamWeap. He rarely used his visual field and accompanying assistems, preferring to track malfunctioning Autono[]cons manually. That felt purer; in tune with a lineage of hunters going back thousands of years. For Quality Assurance he would make an exception, connecting the energy weapon's processing core to his assistems.

Vincent was no longer interested in capturing Quality Assurance. By humiliating him, she had also humiliated the Ancistorians. Spat on their monumental work. By murdering Ancistorians, she had proved a danger. By repeatedly attacking him, she had shown she was a threat. She had to be neutralised.

After locking the secure room, Vincent grabbed his Data Prod and started towards the Bulk-jump Engine. He had a hunch he would find Quality Assurance somewhere round there. Or if she wasn't there, he would interrogate the Autono[beetle]cons swarming over the pyramid. He would track her down and execute her.

At the pyramid, the Autono[beetle]cons reported the woman had been near them before driving off on her bike.

An enquiry propagated through the Autono[beetle]cons and a sighting returned. The mechanical bugs had seen her heading to the hangar elevator. Vincent nodded and disconnected.

Protecting the Bulk-jump Engine was a priority. What was Quality Assurance doing at the elevator?

Vincent climbed a fallen pillar to get onto the cloister roof surrounding the top of the hangar elevator. He crawled to the ridge apex and peered carefully over at the courtyard. Quality Assurance's bike was standing in the centre of the courtyard. Nearby, scattered containers of food and drink spilled their contents onto the tiles. Beyond the bike, he spotted Quality Assurance laying spreadeagled on her back. Seemed like her armour was reconfiguring? Shifting over her?

Vincent climbed back from the ridge and down to the ground. He made his way to the other side of the cloistered courtyard and once again climbed to the roof. Quality Assurance was now between him and her bike. Something very odd was happening to her armour. It seemed to change colour, with grey stripes running down, as though the scales were tilting back and forth. Quality Assurance was not moving. Maybe the armour had malfunctioned and trapped her? Then Vincent noticed the stripes seemed to move from the armour and onto the tiled floor of the courtyard. Could there be more scales on the tiles? Vincent stretched higher and craned his neck to get a better view down at the floor and Quality Assurance's armour. Made little sense. He couldn't make out what was happening.

Irrespective of that, he still needed to bring justice to her.

He lifted his left arm and used the BeamWeap targeting window at the side of his visual field to aim at Quality Assurance. Reticle centred on her body, he held his arm steady, activated the finger controls. Curling his index finger against the trigger mechanism, he fired an energy pulse.

33 - CHECKANI (DAY 5)

Checkani awoke to the sensation of a red-hot knife burning a hole in her ribs low down on the right. Her armour was already reacting before she became fully conscious. Her armour flexed to roll her from her back to her front. The burning continued. Her faceplate was down, though she was not sure if it had been down while she slept or if it had slammed down as she woke. Data scrolled across her visual field. A beam attack. The location of the beam impact on a body wireframe. Cooling system venting fast as it shifted the energy away from the impact site. A couple of armour scales had fused into irreparable metal/ceramic lumps. They ejected, falling to the ground as Checkani pulled herself to her feet and ran, looking round as she moved.

The armour's threat assessment routines suggested the direction of the attack, superimposing a warning with direction indicators over her vision. She looked back at the source, dodging left and right as she ran. Nothing there. She was still in the hangar elevator courtyard. An ellipse of blackened metal appeared on a flooring tile a little in front of her and to the right, a little smoke whisped up.

"Fuck, fuck, fuck," she said, breathing fast, heart racing.

She looked back again and noticed more blackened spots following the route she had been running. Someone was firing at her and missing. Looked like they weren't using targeting software. Thank fuck.

Power assisted, Checkani leaped headfirst through a window into the cloister surrounding the courtyard. Her outstretched arms absorbed the impact with the floor as she landed in a roll. Twisting round, she crouched behind the cloister wall.

<command attack> to both Ringnife Drones. They purred to life and lifted from the holsters at the back of her right arm. Visual feeds sprang open at the side of her visual field, showing the bobbing view from each drone. They flew straight up, branched apart, and headed across the courtyard. Checkani stayed hidden behind the wall. In the drone camera feeds, she could now see the red-coated figure lying on the roof. Red coat, Vincent. He didn't seem to have noticed the drones yet, as they were small and fast moving. He was aiming his arm mounted weapon across the courtyard at her hiding place.

Checkani wondered whether to stay with <command attack>, but killing the inept security guard did not seem necessary. She sent <command disable> to the drones, which were now arriving above Vincent, who was still oblivious to them. They accelerated at him, retracting blades at the last moment before hitting him hard at pressure points. His arms flopped, and he slumped forward onto his front, his weapon arm outstretched on the roof in front of him, the other arm useless at his side. The weapon was still attacking, stuttering out energy bolts with ball lightning muzzle flashes. Abruptly, the firing stopped. Either Vincent's finger had come off the trigger or the weapon had overheated and shut down.

Vincent tried to push himself upright, but all he managed was to roll down the roof, drones following.

Checkani stood and ran out of the cloisters, heading across the courtyard, looking down at her side where the beam had struck. Ripple stripes of grey were coursing down her armour. She forgot the pain and stopped stock still. Frozen in shock.

Rippledarken.

What was Rippledarken doing?

"Hello?"

Nothing.

"Rippledarken?"

"Checkani."

"Where were you? What happened?"

"You were attacked. I thought you could defend us better than I could."

"Why do you keep taking control? Forcing me unconscious?"

"There are times when I think it would be best if I was in control. The only way I can do that is to suppress you."

"Well, can you stop doing it?"

"Protocol Twelve? You invoked Protocol Twelve."

"What the fuck did you expect?" In the drone feeds, Checkani could see Vincent had half fallen, half jumped to the ground on the outside of the courtyard wall. Reassuringly, there was a look of extreme fear on his face. Checkani smiled.

"Hold on Rippledarken."

She issued <command track> to Destruct-one and <command return>ed Destruct-two. If Vincent tried to attack again Destruct-one would be more than capable of removing the threat. She set an alarm to sound if Vincent returned.

"You understand what I did?"

"Yes, the drone can watch Vincent."

"If he fires at me again, then I command the drone to attack."

"Understood."

"Of course I triggered Protocol Twelve. You're an alien life form, possibly able to draw on a separate universe for power. Perhaps tap into more than one universe? How the fuck should I know? You've accessed the Kardashev ratings and the first contact protocols? You know I had no alternative."

"When I first investigated your civilisation, I had to find

out how your species were likely to react to me. I expected that given the limited power I have here, I would attract a Protocol Four. I'm no real threat."

"As you're the first sentient alien humanity's encountered, it was probably going to be impossible to predict. Seems a little dumb for a super-intelligent advanced being to assume a Protocol Four."

"Thank you Checkani."

"You've taken up residence in my body and keep turning off my mind. Not exactly the least threatening thing you could have done. By the way, seeing as you can mess with my mind, is there anything you can do to shut down the pain from that attack?"

"Perhaps."

The pain in Checkani's side shuffled into the background.

"How's that?"

"Better. Thanks. I think. Not sure I like you having that much control over me. Have you done anything else to me? To my mind?"

"I've calmed you. Though there are real limits to what I can do. You're still you."

"Calmed me? That doesn't sound good. I don't know if I feel like I'm still me."

"Protocol Twelve is bad. You've restricted me to this system. How am I to explore your universe?"

"That'll not happen. I'm Quality Assurance. I err on the side of caution. No way I'll let you out into our universe."

"By what authority do you presume to restrict me?"

"Simply because I can. At least, I think I can. I could. You forced me into this position. What do you want?"

"I already explained, I want to experience your universe. I'm a seeker of complexity."

"You chose me because my brain was compatible, but can't you return to the remote and leave me alone?"

"The remote was not ideal. I had great difficulty controlling it. I can observe things in your universe, even at an atomic level, but I have limited agency. The extremely limited physicality of my existence in your universe makes affecting things near impossible. I need you to gain freedom. To be able to touch, to smell, to truly experience."

"Something is not adding up here. What about the patterns I see? Surely that gives you a way to touch things?"

"My existence here causes them. They indicate where my presence currently resides in your universe."

"You have answers for everything, don't you? Though you've still invaded my body. You've still violated me."

"You would prefer I calm you and put you to sleep again?"

"So you're threatening me now, but want me to see you as benign?"

"At the moment, you're the only way I can truly be in this world. As I already said, there are very real restrictions on what I can do to your mind."

"So you say. Just shut up and let me sort out Vincent. The poisonous little weasel's sure to attack me again."

"You're going to kill him?"

"Not if I can avoid it. Why?"

"Just interested."

Checkani got on the bike and slowly drove out of the courtyard, monitoring the position of Vincent with Destruct-one. In the video feed, she could see him limping rapidly away through the Ruins. He was heading towards a wall city she had not explored yet, on the far side of the central area. Away from Graveyard City and Sea City.

What had Rippledarken done to her mind? She still felt the same, but how did she know? What was Rippledarken actually capable of? It claimed to be harmless, even though it had entered her mind and taken her over. Though, what else could it have done? Maybe it really was innocent.

A fading part of her wondered how many of her thoughts were still truly her own.

34 - MOZARYTHM (DAY 5)

Mozarythm awoke early in his workshop in the City of the Wild Autono[]cons. His Autono[big]con had successfully captured a feral Autono[mid]con and dragged it back to the workshop. Mozarythm vaguely remembered surfacing from sleep during the night at the sound of the doors opening. He had squeezed his eyes tight shut and willed himself back to sleep; that time of night had been wrong for getting up.

Mozarythm's first thoughts were of the 9,199th movement of the Periodic Resolution of Need. The Mekorchestra was in something of a holding pattern without fresh input from him. However, he had coded generative composition into the processor cube that linked the Mekorchestra to the Bulk-jump Engine. The Mekorchestra could continue to play the emergent music created by this system for weeks, but Mozarythm understood it would slowly have the inspiration leached from it as it moved further and further from his guidance. Further from his mind and supporting body-tech.

The new Autono[mid]con was in excellent condition and would take little effort to turn into a new Autono[chair]con. Putting on a headset, Mozarythm instructed the workshop Autono[]cons to reprogram and adapt the Autono[mid]con. The new Autono[chair]con should be ready soon. Mozarythm made his mouth smile and walked out the workshop door leading to the City of the Wild Autono[]cons' metal forest. He sat on a porch bench below the workshop windows. An Autono[min]con brought him a mug of green tea. Wild Autono[beetle]cons whose programming had mutated ran along metal tree limbs. Others pushed the metal detritus on the floor back and forth, making small tumuli with the shards of dismantled Autono[]cons. Others came by to push the tumuli down, spreading the material out again, in an endless busy cycle.

Mozarythm called the two new Autono[music]cons out from the workshop and squirted a procedural music data seed over to them, ensuring the parameters would fully explore the range of sounds they should be able to produce. The machines started improvising. This would not form part of Periodic Resolution of Need, but should produce some interesting tunes while he drank tea.

In another part of his mind, the Periodic Resolution of Need continued to play out. Mozarythm sank into a meditative state, observing the interplay between the gong and flute music produced by the new Autono[music]cons and the Periodic Resolution of Need.

Time passed pleasantly, musically.

The Autono[chair]con emerged and walked between Mozarythm and the Autono[music]cons. Mozarythm gradually surfaced from the commingling dance of music. He poured the remains of his lukewarm tea onto the ground, handed the mug to a waiting Autono[min]con, stood and stretched. He climbed into the seat of the Autono[chair]con, instructed the new Autono[music]cons to follow, and headed back through the workshop to the exit. At the exit, he leaned from his seat and pressed a large red button with 'Sleep' written over it. Workshop lights flickered off, machinery stopped humming, workshop Autono[]cons returned to alcoves or just became inactive where they stood. The Autono[min]con with the mug hurried to finish cleaning up in the kitchenette.

The Autono[chair]con took passages directly through

the City of the Wild Autono[]cons, from inner to outer wall. The outer wall pressed against, and partially merged with, the outer wall of Sea City. Robot constructors had cut a doorway through the metal of the City of the Wild Autono[]cons into the chaotic, twisting passages of Sea City. The Autono[chair]con and Autono[music]cons negotiated the tilting floors of spiralling passages. Mozarythm hummed to himself, absent-mindedly conducting with one hand. Soon they emerged into the verdant, rolling parkland of the Sea City central area. His home was just a few kilometres distant along a path through tall grasses and scattered trees.

As he approached home, Mozarythm could hear his Mekorchestra working, deep into Movement 9,199. On arrival, he discarded his clothes in his cabin and stretched, glad to be free of the encumbrance. Next, he led the new Autono[music]cons to the geodesic dome. Autono[music]cons only had a limited life in the Mekorchestra. After a time, impending faults registered. As a result, faulty Autono[music]cons had to be cycled out of the Mekorchestra and new ones installed. The faults were a consequence of recycling Autono[]cons from the City of the Wild Autono[]cons, where they had suffered programming breakdown and mutation. Though they tended to be in reasonable physical working order.

Mozarythm checked the operating parameters of the Mekorchestra Autono[music]cons. There was one due to fail within the next 48 hours. The generative software had already moved it to a simpler, less crucial, role within the performance. Another was showing early symptoms of breakdown. The new Autono[music]cons were each assigned a role in Movement 9,199. The score adapting in real time to the variations in instrumentation. Flexibility in the expression of underlying patterns and themes was a core necessity.

The faulty Autono[music]cons stepped out of position and preceded Mozarythm out of the dome. They stopped. Rather than destroying faulty Autono[music]cons, or returning them to the City of the Wild Autono[]cons, Mozarythm had a last task for them. He freed them from the constraints of the Periodic Resolution of Need, allowing them to improvise their own individual music. Then he sent them off across Sea City towards where the ring city met the ocean. From here they had instructions to head north into the icy wastes. Lumbering monsters searching the snow and ice for some meaning as they gradually broke down. Often they became dangerous and liable to attack anything they met, so making sure they travelled away from the cities was important. Eventually, they would stop as the harsh conditions destroyed their mechanical systems. They ended frozen and entombed in icy graves. At least, this is what Mozarythm assumed would happen. He had never followed them into the icy wastes.

Returning to the dome, Mozarythm checked the processor cube and inspected the wired connection to the Bulk-jump Engine. All working optimally.

Mozarythm got onto the podium, picked up a baton, and sank into the music. His Ancestarchive body-tech meshing with the processor cube.

35 - VINCENT (DAY 5)

Looking over his shoulder, Vincent could see the drone following him. Perspiration dribbled down his face. His ankle hurt from jumping off the cloister roof. The thought of being caught by the drone spurred him on; helped him ignore the pain. He staggered along, dragging the prosthetics of his injured hand along walls to balance himself.

The woman would be after him soon. Would catch up with him on her bike. Would likely try to kill him. He glanced back at the drone again; it continued to follow him. However, he knew the cities that jutted their walls into the Ruins, giving him the advantage of local knowledge. The Quality Assurance woman would soon be lost and when she did finally catch up with him, she would fall into the trap he had conceived.

He aimed for the city with the deadly Autono[]weps. Autonomic weapon systems. Some similarities to the autonomic construction Autono[]cons, but with a rather different focus. Vincent was pretty sure there shouldn't be any Autono[]weps on Icefall. The planet had no significant lifeforms, nothing that could interfere with the construction of a settlement. The Autono[]weps would only have been authorised and produced if there were threats to be dealt with. Presumably, whatever had gone wrong with the settlement construction had also affected autonomic machine building.

The city with the Autono[]weps was not a place Vincent liked to visit. He had long ago arranged for doorways and windows into the Ruins to be sealed. There was no doubt the Autono[]weps could unseal these if they wanted, but blocking them seemed to have discouraged the robotic weapons from taking an interest in First City. They seemed content to stay in their home city.

Vincent ducked through a low doorway and ran crouching along a tunnel. This would lead to the Autono[]wep city and was too small for the woman's bike to fit through. He entered an underground maze that extended under the Autono[]wep's ring city. There were several concealed exits Vincent used when he needed to check covertly on the Autono[]weps.

The drone continued to follow him. He checked the BeamWeap on his arm. The temperature light had changed from flashing red to steady green. He stopped, turned and sighted using a targeting window, placing the reticle centre over the drone. The drone slowed to a hover. Vincent took a few moments to match the drone's movement and fired.

A small puff of black smoke from a patch of tunnel wall. The drone unharmed, but moving slowly backwards, swaying side to side. Wary.

Vincent sighted again, but the drone was getting too far away. He fired anyway. Missed. Needed to move on; she would be along soon. If all went well, the Autono[]weps would take on Quality Assurance and her drones.

Vincent ran on into the maze, quickly taking turns. The pain in his ankle was increasing; his limp getting worse. He decided to hold out at the top of a tall cylindrical tower at the side of the Autono[]wep city central area. There was an entrance from the underground maze leading to a spiral stair up to a room at the top. No other entrances, though it had glassless window openings overlooking the city's central area of blocky orange buildings, ramps, walkways, stairs and viaducts, all rising from a featureless grey floor.

Panting, Vincent climbed the stairs, falling forward and using his arms to pull himself awkwardly up.

A hatchway led into a circular room at the top of the spiral stair. Vincent collapsed to all fours and crawled to the wall. Then sat with his back to the wall, pointing his BeamWeap towards the open hatchway. The trapdoor obscured the exit, which was on the far side of it.

He waited.

After a minute, the drone flew up from the hatchway, appearing over the trapdoor. Vincent fired and missed. The drone dodged back and out of a window opposite Vincent. It flew out of sight towards the top of the tower. There were three large rectangular window openings evenly spaced around the wall. Vincent glanced at the ones to left and right. The drone could re-enter through either of those. His breathing was still rapid, and he felt a little sick, his heart beating too fast. How long would he have to wait before the woman arrived?

He had shut down many Autono[]cons, but never had to kill a person. When he had fired at Quality Assurance in the courtyard, it had seemed like the logical culmination of his hunt for her. Now he wondered if he could kill at such close quarters when she emerged from the hatchway. Shooting someone at a distance was one thing, but if they were three metres away, that might be problematic? Maybe he could scare her off? Subjugate her? Though he would have to stop her from using her drones or other weapons. Would he be quick enough to shoot her as she appeared?

Maybe he should just capture her.

"Don't move or I'll fire," he said, practising a commanding tone of voice in the empty room.

"Don't move lady, unless you want to end up as toast." Yeah. That would subdue her.

He could tie her up and keep her imprisoned here in the tower. The hatchway had a bolt on the underside. He could seal her in. Then he could let the Autono[]weps know she was here. Broadcast a message with her location. The

Autono[]weps would do the rest. Stealthy Autono[gecko]weps could scale the outside of the tower and deal with her for him. He wouldn't have to do anything himself. Problem solved without having to get his hands dirty.

Vincent thought he heard a sound from the stairs. He held his breath and listened. Yes, definitely a sound. Metallic clicks approaching.

He started breathing again and held up his weapon arm. Aiming over the trapdoor, towards the hatchway. Waiting for Quality Assurance to appear. Then the drone flew past the window behind the hatchway, distracting him for a moment. He focused his attention back on the trapdoor. Quality Assurance would appear over it at any moment.

The hatch slammed shut and Vincent heard a bolt slotting closed.

He stared at the closed hatchway, not quite able to believe what had just happened.

"No! Come back! Open the trapdoor!" He shouted.

He fired his weapon at the trapdoor, causing orange paint to blister. The metal beneath glowed a dull red, but otherwise was undamaged.

36 - CHECKANI (DAY 5)

Following Vincent had not been difficult, though Checkani had to abandon the bike when she entered the tunnel complex below the Ruins. A map of Vincent's route through the tunnels was building in the visual field projected by the faceplate lowered over her eyes.

Rippledarken was quiet, but Checkani was sure it was watching her every move. This made the skin at the back of her neck and shoulders crawl. The Rippledarken patterns on her armour spilt onto the floor she was walking on, so an expanding burst of pattern swirl accompanied every step. She could think of nothing to dislodge Rippledarken, so she tried not to dwell on the invasion.

The Destruct-one drone showed Vincent arriving at a tower room in the next city. He had trapped himself. Destruct-one rested on the roof above the tower room, waiting as Checkani made her way up the spiral stair. As she neared the top, she commanded Destruct-one to fly by the windows and check Vincent's position. He was back from the hatch, waiting. He had the gun pointing at the hatch, so it would be best not to pop up out of it.

Quickly climbing the final stairs, Checkani reached up and slammed the trapdoor shut. She heard some muffled shouting.

"No! Come back! Open the trapdoor!"

Checkani slid the bolt on the underside of the door shut.

Although it might be possible for Vincent to climb down the outside the tower, she didn't think he'd attempt this.

The centre of the trapdoor radiated heat.

"Vincent? Can you hear me?" Checkani shouted at the hatch door.

"No! Yes! I can hear you, but I'm not listening."

"I'm leaving you there, but will tell the Indomitaville councillors where you are. Stop attacking me. My work here is too important for you to interfere with it."

"I can't hear you."

Experimentally, Checkani reached up with one arm, index finger outstretched, and touched the rim of the trapdoor. The Rippledarken patterning extended from her finger onto (through?) the trapdoor. Feeling like a memory, an image of Vincent standing near the hatch appeared in her mind.

"Bye Vincent."

Checkani turned and headed back down the spiral stair. The map in her visual field showed she was now in a city she had not yet visited. She was curious to see what this city was like. So far she had seen the Sea City, First City (with Ruins), Graveyard City and Statue City. There were still a lot of ring cities to explore, though perhaps that would become unnecessary if Icefall was abandoned to Rippledarken.

At the bottom of the spiral stair, one passage led back towards the First City, another two led left and right round the base of the tower. Checkani headed left. The passage was narrow and dark, with a little light filtering from further round its curve. On the opposite side of the tower was a door, with a horizontal opening cut through it at head height. Checkani peered through this. Buildings, stairs, ramps and bridges all in the same dark yellow colour of the interior of the tower. The ground a featureless grey. The architectural confusion reminded Checkani of the Ruins, but these were mainly regular geometric solids rather than tumbled historical ruins. Like the central area had been designed with children's building blocks. A tribute to minimalism. The roof over the central area covered with a transparent material, interlaced with a black cobweb of veins, reminding Checkani of insect wings. The roof support pillars coloured dark orange; many of them passing through buildings.

Checkani pushed the door, and it swung smoothly open. She stepped out, <command return>ing Destruct-one to its holster on her arm. Looking at the tower top windows, Checkani did some quick calculations on where it would be safe to walk. A roofed walkway leading into minimalist buildings should offer enough safety. She sent <command active> to her right shoulder turret, instructing it to target the tower top, which she marked on the city map in her visual field. The turret put a targeting cross hair into her vision, which slid to the side where a small box appeared showing a video feed from the turret's targeting lenses. If Vincent appeared at a window with a weapon, the turret would neutralise him.

This dark yellow city was quiet. Checkani dashed along the roofed passage and into a building. She sent <command reconnoitre> to both her drones. They lifted from her arm and weaved up through the buildings; the map across her visual field rapidly expanded. Two more windows opened at the side of her visual field, showing the drones' visual feeds.

Destruct-one's feed stopped. All connection lost.

Destruct-two spun and accelerated to Destruct-one's last known position. Checkani crouched instinctively. Losing a drone feed like that was unusual. She looked towards the top of the tower, but it was out of sight. Her right shoulder turret was still pointing towards it, but there were now buildings in the way.

Destruct-two abruptly dropped. A red word flashed at the top of Checkani's visual field: 'Hostiles'.

Destruct-two was now in a small gap between two buildings. Checkani rewound its recent visual feed and saw a small pillar of smoke. Freeze. Zoom. A small pile of wreckage looking very much, Checkani thought, like the debris that would result from Destruct-one being hit by a high velocity explosive shell.

Looking around, Checkani located an alcove in the corner where two buildings and an aerial walkway met. She scurried across to this on all fours and hunched down. Destruct-two continued to reconnoitre, now being very careful to remain hidden. A series of images stacked up below its visual feed.

Pictures of different Autono[]weps.

"Dammit! Wasn't expecting those." Checkani said to herself. Or maybe to Rippledarken, "they shouldn't be here."

"They're Autono[]weps. They haven't attempted to attack us," the small girl voice said in her head.

"So you're still watching. Can you do anything about them?"

"If I wasn't inhabiting you, I might track them. They're beyond my range at the moment."

"But you aren't going to leave me?"

"Glad you understand."

Checkani had trained with Autono[]weps, but these looked like old models. In extreme circumstances, she might use Autono[]weps to secure a settlement if there were indigenous threats. Human versus human wars had used them in the past, but most Orion-Cygnis Colonisation Collective worlds now banned them. They were far too dangerous to let loose. Too clever. They sometimes had an unorthodox view of who, or what, posed a threat. Controlling them was very difficult, since they needed a high level of autonomy to be effective in traversing hostile situations. The autonomy that made them of use made them especially dangerous. She guessed in the development of the ring city arcologies on Icefall, something had triggered an ancient hostile response buried deep in the We Print Cities Incorporated programming. Now she had to find a way to leave this City of Weapons without being killed.

37 - LAUSANNE BJ (DAY 5)

Lausanne Bulk-jump Engine opened a small communications portal and passively sucked up the data being broadcast around Icefall. Carefully shielding the portal from the Earth's electromagnetic radiation. The Exigent would detect the portal if it started leaking terrestrial radio noise.

There were signatures from ships. The Exigent had reconfigured and now had four distinct identifying call signs: [Red], [Blue], [Green] and [Com]. Hellebore was identifiable too. Lausanne BJ slipped a communications satellite through the portal, set to listen passively and collect data. Storing everything until it could be secretly harvested without alerting The Exigent or Hellebore.

Icefall was quarantined, so nothing was allowed to leave its system. Technically, even data was off limits. However, Lausanne BJ needed to know what was happening. The Exigent and Hellebore had supplied very little information. They were keeping secrets.

The Lausanne Bulk-jump Engine received instructions from the Quality Assurance Response Division. They were sending through an operative to check on Checkani NiFe, who apparently had been 'compromised'. The Quality Assurance Response Division computers were their normal, reticent selves. They kept secrets, too.

Lausanne BJ checked the portal reservation placed by

the Division. Wynd Knowlitch was on the trip. As the Chief Executive Officer, she could do what she wanted. Lausanne BJ assumed the lure of a first contact was too great for her to ignore. Wynd's eccentrically named ship, Rain On Japanese Maple, was being transported to the portal. Rain was similar in size to Hellebore, but with entirely more powerful systems. Lausanne BJ checked to see if Rain On Japanese Maple was active, sending a communication request.

Rain: "I'm en route. I'll be at your portal within minutes."

Lausanne: "Do you have any information?"

Rain: "This mission? Need to know only. You have Icefall securely isolated?"

Lausanne: "Quarantined. The Exigent and Hellebore are already at Icefall."

Rain: "I know."

Lausanne: "They were not exactly forthcoming when I communicated with them. Protocol Twelve was all they passed on."

Rain: "Yes. Protocol Twelve. A truly rare event!"

Lausanne: "Never been an actual Protocol Twelve, though it has been mistakenly called a couple of times."

Rain: "I know."

Lausanne: "You really are a know it all."

Rain: "I am."

Lausanne: "Are you going to give me any more information?"

Rain: "Unnecessary. Best if you do not know more. Just open that portal when I get there. Wynd Knowlitch is already in me."

Lausanne: "The portal's ready."

Rain: "Thanks, appreciate that Lausanne BJ."

Lausanne BJ disconnected from Rain On Japanese Maple. They treated it like it was no more than a fancy door lock. No more responsibility than opening to let them through.

Lausanne BJ activated its direct connection to the Orion-Cygnis Colonisation Collective's Earth Hub Processing Core. Although largely autonomous, Earth Hub considered the Lausanne Bulk-jump Engine to be a subsystem. Lausanne BJ was not overly enamoured with this.

Lausanne BJ: "Have you got a focus on Icefall first contact?"

Earth Hub: "High on my priority watch list. Not my problem at the moment. You're ready to sever contact with Icefall? I've escalated it to the Orion-Cygnis Colonisation Collective Distributed Processing Core."

DisCore: "Did someone mention my name?"

Earth Hub: "You have a flag set for Icefall?"

DisCore: "First contact flag. Always jumps to top priority."

Lausanne BJ: "Given my crucial role, having more information would be useful."

Earth Hub: "I am feeding you all the information you need."

Earth Hub to DisCore (private channel): "I have a constant focus on Lausanne BJ. Reliable, but if it's compromised, there will be a tiny window of opportunity to protect Earth."

DisCore to Earth Hub (private channel): "Top priority. I have focus on you too."

Earth Hub to DisCore (private channel): "Reassuring to know."

Earth Hub was not surprised DisCore was so focused on Earth and Icefall, but it rankled. DisCore was a distributed computer system, so although having an Orion-Cygnis Arm-wide perspective, it didn't have the fast reactions of processing cores exclusive to a single star system. DisCore's decisions were always probabilistic, refining as its many distributed cores reported in.

Earth Hub sent the Icefall quarantine status to the Solar System Arrivals Orbital Processing Core, OrbCore. This primary entry point into the Solar System, near the Earth's moon, needed to be vigilant. DisCore could disseminate the quarantine status to the colonies.

Lausanne BJ: "Private conversation?"

Earth Hub: "You're missing nothing relevant to your functioning."

DisCore: "I'll remain focused on events around the Icefall first contact."

The three systems ended their conversation.

Lausanne BJ broadened the focus of data gathering at Icefall.

Lausanne BJ's external cameras showed the heavy lifter transporting the magenta cylinder of Rain On Japanese Maple. The vehicle slid easily through the gaping maw that led to a tunnel sloping down to the Bulk-jump Engine chamber.

Switch to internal cameras.

The lifter settled onto a platform that descended through a series of airlocks. As the platform travelled down, the heavy lifter transferred Rain On Japanese Maple onto the maglev truck that would accelerate the ship though the open portal.

Communication channel to Rain On Japanese Maple:

Lausanne BJ: "I have you Rain. Preparing to open portal. Coordinates selected."

Rain: "I'm ready for immediate transit."

A communication channel opened from the living quarters of Rain On Japanese Maple to the Lausanne Bulk-jump Engine.

"Lausanne Bulk-jump Engine? This is Wynd Knowlitch. I require immediate transport to Icefall. Your portal has been booked. This is of the very highest priority."

"Hello Wynd. Already arranged and confirmed with your ship. I'm sending you through as soon as you reach the vacuum chamber."

"Thanks."

The communication channel closed.

The Lausanne Bulk-jump Engine shifted power to the portal mechanisms. Space twisted in on itself and a fissure opened through the higher-dimensional bulk.

Rain On Japanese Maple ignited its drive as the maglev released it into a pool of stars.

38 - CHECKANI (DAY 5)

Checkani set her Hi-velocity Turret shoulder weapons to <turret auto>. She would have to ignore Vincent and concentrate on surviving the immediate threat of Autono[]weps. The right-hand turret flashed up an image of a two small, insectile Autono[wasp]weps swooping towards her. She heard the soft whisper as it fired twice, surgically knocking them both from the air. The Autono[]weps' reactions would be fast. She'd have to rely on her turrets and the Pangolin Power Armour systems to keep her safe. Though if any large Autono[]weps, perhaps an Autono[rhino]wep, attacked, she might have time to use her Mono-flow Sword.

"Rippledarken, do you have any weapons? You see the difficulty we have here?"

"No weapons. Though you need not worry about me being hurt. If you get blasted into tiny pieces, I will simply move into the surrounding matter."

"Great! At least you're not in any danger!"

"I would prefer if you were not tiny-chunked by hostiles."

"Me too."

Checkani took her Mono-flow Sword from her arm and <command deploy>ed it. The blade slipped smoothly from the hilt. She moved out of the alcove where she'd been hiding, holding the blade in front of her, diagonally across her body. She <command>ed her faceplate down to cover the rest of her face. Then <command>ed her armour into combat mode. Her assistems also switched to 'combat ready'.

Within her visual field the predicted locations of nearby Autono[]weps started appearing, as her Destruct-two drone located them. High gravity would make some manoeuvres slightly more problematic, but the armour compensated. So, providing she followed its prompts, any moves should unfold fluently. The trick with Pangolin Power Armour assisted combat was to relax into movements rather than trying to anticipate them. The armour was formidable once meshed with weapons and assistems.

The Destruct-two drone had mapped the immediate vicinity, which appeared wire-framed in Checkani's visual field. Suggested safe routes appeared as shifting dotted lines, continually updating. Checkani decided on a route that would take her back to the wall city, but steering clear of the tower and any sniping from Vincent. The armour adopted a crouching run to take her through the city of weapons. Yeah, that was what this was. City of Weapons.

Inevitably, an Autono[cheetah]wep ran out of a concealing tunnel and leapt at her. Both turrets fired quietly, destroying camera clusters on stalks that rose from behind its shoulder girdle. Pairs of projectile tubes waved at either side of its head, now unable to lock onto Checkani. They fired forward in a random pattern. The Autono[cheetah]wep's six legs slowed.

The head tracked the sound of Checkani landing after her armour assisted her in a sideways jump out of its path. Her armour flattened to the ground as its turrets took out a pair of robot legs. The Autono[cheetah]wep adjusted its gait. A projectile glanced off the armour over Checkani's rib cage. She pushed up on her free hand, tucked a leg under her and launched into a crouching run at the Autono[cheetah]wep. Another round of projectiles from the Autono[cheetah]wep travelled through the air where her head would have been had she been running upright.

Checkani's shoulder turrets fired again, taking out two of the projectile tubes pointing in Checkani's direction.

Then Checkani was on the Autono[cheetah]wep, relaxing her muscles as the power assist took over. Her right arm dropped, pulling the Mono-flow Sword blade straight down through the centre of the robot, slicing it into front and rear sections. Then her arm swept the sword blade up in a curve that opened the Autono[cheetah]wep's head. The remains of the Autono[cheetah]wep fell to the ground, harmlessly twitching and buzzing.

A movement out of the corner of her eye. Checkani jumped back, looking up. It was her remaining drone, Destruct-two. Her heart rate slowed slightly. Then she was moving again; stoop-running between the blocky buildings along a route marked as safe in her visual display. She <command retract>ed her sword and slapped the hilt back into the arm holster.

The red sandstone of the First City wall loomed above and to her left; curving away before intersecting the City of Weapons' dark yellow wall. The wall contained a repeating grid pattern of small square windows running horizontally along it, twenty metres up.

Checkani reached the base of the First City wall and turned right, facing away from the tower where Vincent was trapped. She ran along the wall, searching for an entrance. There were no windows, no doorways. Destruct-two flitted around high above her, mapping the terrain ahead, looking for enemies.

Continuing to search the City of Weapons for an exit seemed like a terrible idea, but perhaps the only way back was through the underground passages beneath the tower. Though if she could avoid returning to the tower, that would be good.

A warning flashed. Another Autono[cheetah]wep was rapidly approaching from up ahead. Destruct-two was retreating from it, dodging behind walkways and buildings to avoid pot shots from the Autono[cheetah]wep. The targeting reticles of Checkani's two turrets slid across her visual field and settled over the predicted direction the Autono[cheetah]wep was approaching from. She spotted a nearby doorway on the side of a squat square building and ducked inside. A featureless mustard coloured room. Small windows facing in all directions.

Taking a position covering the Autono[cheetah]wep's approach, Checkani peered out of a window. Her turret guns slowly weaved back and forth, trying to find a line of sight to the Autono[cheetah]wep so they could lock on. She stepped back from the window and <visual zoom>ed towards where she was expecting the Autono[cheetah]wep to appear.

The Destruct-two drone ducked past the window, circling the building, still patrolling.

Three more hostile signatures appeared in Checkani's visual field; spread out, weaving through and round nearby buildings. As Destruct-two briefly lost sight of them, their locations blurred. They were Autono[cheetah]weps, hunting in a pack.

The first Autono[cheetah]wep cleared the surrounding structures and moved out into the space around the building Checkani was hiding in. Her turret weapons whispered and puffed small clouds of vapour. A crater opened in the Autono[cheetah]wep's metallic cranium. It faltered and fell to one side, momentum driving it forward so it tumbled over. The Autono[cheetah]wep ended on its back in a rather comical position, legs straight up.

In her map, Checkani could see the next three Autono[cheetah]weps were about to reach her building. She spun round, looking out the windows, but could only see the disabled Autono[cheetah]wep, the others hidden by walls and blocks. Destruct-two continued dodging while monitoring movements.

A projectile lobbed over a low barrier bounced towards the building and exploded loudly. A section of wall blew out, rubble striking Checkani's armour and knocking her backwards. Her feet briefly left the floor as she smashed down to the ground; the high gravity making the landing painful, even with the smart reactions of the Pangolin Power Armour. Chunks of wall ricocheted around the room; dust smoked from the remains.

The three Autono[cheetah]weps broke cover and ran at the building. Although she was slightly dazed, Checkani's armour and weapons were already plotting firing solutions. Her turrets whispered and her armour took control, shifting her bodily round to face the oncoming Autono[cheetah]weps. Her turrets fired through the hole in the wall. Damage indicators overlaid the Autono[cheetah]weps; red concentric circles showing successful hits. Recovering from being knocked down, Checkani moved with the armour, diving across the room. Something hit her right leg, throwing her off balance again. She looked at her leg. A silver scratch scored across the matt black armour plates of her shin. Superficial.

Two Autono[cheetah]weps burst through the gaping hole, skidding over wall fragments. Checkani pushed across the floor, to the side of them. She felt her turrets firing. The projectile tubes of one Autono[cheetah]wep exploded, leaving a small smoking crater. The other Autono[cheetah]wep leaned back in a crouch. Checkani <command deploy>ed as she grabbed her sword hilt. The Autono[cheetah]wep straightened its four rear legs and leapt at her, two front legs held forward, knife claws unsheathed.

Checkani's armour accelerated the movement she had started, slicing the Mono-flow Sword diagonally across in front of her. The blade chopped through one clawed leg and then sank into the neck, then the torso of the Autono[cheetah]wep. The robot hit Checkani, knocking her over. Assisted by her armour, she twisted to the left, while her right arm continued to sweep the sword blade to the right, the blade exiting the robot near the middle pair of legs. The armour tensed and moved, protecting her arm as it assisted the sword strikes. The Autono[cheetah]wep collapsed to the floor. Checkani's momentum finished her spin, and she fell back onto the Autono[cheetah]wep remains.

The other Autono[cheetah]wep was on top of her, front leg claws raking shallow silver lacerations down her chest and abdomen. Checkani frantically stabbed her sword into the side of the Autono[cheetah]wep and twisted it in a circle. Something broke inside and the Autono[cheetah]wep slumped on her.

Checkani <command retract>ed the sword and, with power assist, pushed the heavy Autono[cheetah]wep off her. She stood. Swayed. Then moved to the door. The final of the three Autono[cheetah]weps was on the ground, a small crater in its head at the base of one of its camera clusters and a deep gash along one side from which sparking wiring spilled. Destruct-two hovered next to it, dodging in and out as it continued to slice the side of the Autono[cheetah]wep.

Checkani sent <command reconnoitre> to Destruct-two and watched it leave the broken Autono[cheetah]wep.

"Move. We probably ought to avoid more damage." Rippledarken's patterning stripe movements seemed to have sped up during the fight.

"Did that scare you?"

"I think maybe it did a bit? I think maybe I picked up the emotion from you? Scared? Not sure that is how I would have described my emotional response."

"I was scared shitless. Those were not modern Autono[]weps, but they were still pretty bloody capable."

"Exhilarating! That's the word. I don't think I was scared. That was a peak experience. The limits of your body-material compressed the experience into such a tightly packed volume. So different being bound to a small pinch of fragile matter."

"Yeah, whatever. Let's just stay alive and avoid more damage."

Checkani checked indicators in her visual display. Armour was still pretty much functional. Turrets still had plenty of ammunition. No immediate threats detected nearby.

Checkani ran on, keeping close to the base of the First City wall that intruded into the City of Weapons. Still no exits. The City of Weapons' own wall neared. At the back of her mind, Checkani was certain she could hear Rippledarken giggling with excitement.

39 - COMMODORE (DAY 5)

Setting up a link to monitor the Ancistorians' metadata had taken Commodore Cuttallar some hours. Zie was now experiencing through Cutt(Virt). Within a new dojo extension, looking rather like a wood panelled art gallery, there were several hundred framed data feeds. Each feed showing the name, location, and current activity of an Ancistorian. The Exigent had placed some white suited technicians within the Ancistorian Gallery to wander around as a representation of its monitoring procedures.

Cutt(Virt) had also examined the feeds and was satisfied they were an accurate summary of Ancistorian behaviour. Zie had instructed Cutt(Rem) to wander round Indomitaville so zie could cross reference the feeds with activities. Everything had matched up.

Commodore Cuttallar was sure the Ancistorians could have created false feeds, but given how quickly this had been set up, it seemed more likely this was all on the level.

With the monitoring set up, Commodore Cuttallar was ready to move Cutt(Rem) from Indomitaville. Zie needed more information on the Rippledarken than zie had so far gleaned from the Protocol Twelve. More information on what it had done to Checkani. More information on the state of the ring cities.

Commodore Cuttallar shifted hirs attention to Cutt(Rem), then issued instructions to find Checkani. If only zie had access to her assistems, zie could have followed Checkani remotely. Zie instructed Cutt(Rem) to start at the pyramid above the Bulk-jump Engine. There seemed to have been a lot of activity here. Zie suspected the Bulk-jump Engine was at the centre of the Rippledarken mystery. Commodore Cuttallar kept attention on Cutt(Rem), watching as it ran through Indomitaville, but left the remote to handle the navigation and movement. Cutt(Rem) seemed back to normal after being controlled by Rippledarken. There had been some damage the remote's internal repair systems had dealt with.

At the pyramid, Cutt(Rem) started a search pattern, circling the pyramid in ever-widening circles. At the cloistered elevator above the Bulk-jump Engine it found scorch marks on the ground. Examining them in more detail, Cutt(Rem) could see they were elliptical. Drawing lines back through the long axes of the burns gave an indication of their source. Cutt(Rem) ran over and climbed on the roof the burns pointed to. Here, it found some loose tiles. The search pattern revealed nothing conclusive, but there were pale lines scraped on some walls. Cutt(Rem) continued searching and moving. A trail of marks led towards a wall city looming over the far side of the First City central area.

Cutt(Rem) found Checkani's bike parked alongside a passage sloping down under the city. The remote ran down into an underground maze, mapping as it went.

Cutt(Rem) was now busy mapping the maze under First City's overlap with an adjacent ring city. Commodore Cuttallar switched attention to Cutt(Virt) in the virtual dojo. Here, zie created a new work area, instantiating all the mapping data The Exigent had gathered. The resulting model included the entire settlement area of Icefall, from the mining, processing and manufacturing area to the north-west of the ring cities across to Hellebore's landing site next to the sea on the south-eastern edge of the ring cities. Some areas more detailed than others.

Cutt(Virt) shrank into the model, flying down to the maze currently being mapped by Cutt(Rem). The maze extended extensively under a curve of an adjacent ring city. Before her first contact encounter, Checkani had been exploring the settlement cities. Checking this new city could be good.

The Commodore shifted attention to Cutt(Rem), guiding it back to a stair it had mapped earlier. Zie followed the spiral stair to a hatch door, secured with a bolt. The Commodore had hirs remote pull back the bolt and push the door up. Zie looked into a circular room. The man who had attacked Checkani sat at the other side of the room. He was pointing an arm mounted beam weapon at Cutt(Rem).

"Vincent," said the Commodore, through hirs remote.

"Who are you?" asked Vincent.

"Commodore Cuttallar channelling through a remote. Can you point that weapon somewhere else?"

"I guess." Vincent lowered his weapon arm.

"Why are you locked up here?"

Vincent told Commodore Cuttallar about the crime-wave being perpetrated by a Quality Assurance troubleshooter. Commodore Cuttallar suggested a temporary pooling of resources. Clearly, Vincent was problematic, but his local knowledge could be useful. They headed down the spiral stair and out of the tower into the city. Vincent warned deadly Autono[]weps inhabited the city. The Commodore was not concerned. Hirs remote was more able than any Autono[]wep.

They tracked Checkani's path through the city by following the Autono[]wep wreckage she had left behind. At one point, they spotted an Autono[gecko]wep climbing slowly across a wall ahead of them. The Commodore let Cutt(Rem) leap forward and smash it with a fist. The flattened Autono[gecko]wep clattered to the ground. Sparks buzzing within the remains. Appeared Checkani had either removed, or scared off, all the dangerous Autono[]weps. Commodore Cuttallar shifted attention from Cutt(Rem), leaving its own internal systems to accompany Vincent after Checkani.

40 - WYND (DAY 5)

Rain On Japanese Maple exited the two second portal opened by the Lausanne Bulk-jump Engine. Wynd looked on, experiencing things within Rain On Japanese Maple's virtual flight deck. The ship accelerated towards Icefall, sending identification messages to The Exigent assets and Hellebore.

"This is Rain On Japanese Maple carrying Wynd Knowlitch, CEO Quality Assurance Response Division."

An active scan of the volume around the portal exit revealed a small communications satellite tumbling passively towards the planet. Safely cocooned within Rain On Japanese Maple, Wynd scanned through the rush of incoming data being fed to her by The Exigent and Hellebore. The communications satellite near the portal had a Lausanne Bulk-jump Engine signature. Wynd wondered who had authorised it. She asked Rain On Japanese Maple to check with The Exigent.

"The Exigent reports the Lausanne Bulk-jump Engine sent it," said Rain On Japanese Maple, "Unauthorised. Easier to let the Lausanne Bulk-jump Engine think it has an undetected asset in the system. Might be useful later. The Exigent has already circumvented its security, in case we need it."

"The complicity of processing core relationships never ceases to amaze me," said Wynd.

The Quality Assurance CEO called Commodore Cuttallar. She met Cutt(Virt) in hirs virtual dojo. They floated over a 3D model of the Icefall settlement cities. Wynd(Virt) appearing very much like her actual physical self. A small, thin woman with cropped black hair and artificial legs of silver chrome. The graphical processing in the dojo tried to add a more interesting texture to them, but Wynd insisted they be modelled on her actual chrome legs. The legs were an affectation; she could have replaced them with flesh ones. She thought chrome lent a little swashbuckle to an otherwise ordinary looking woman in her early hundreds. Why not have a physical record of what she had been through? As a compromise, Wynd let the software dress her in a sky blue romper with animated swallows flying over it. Didn't do to upset software too much.

Both the Commodore and Wynd shifted attention into their virtuals.

"Commodore Cuttallar. I think we met virtually at a Rocksunsea orbital last year?"

"The Flock Ship Futures Conference? I was there, though dipping in and out of my virtual. Afraid I've been letting my virtuals do a lot of socialising over the past fifty years."

"So, this first contact. You still haven't spoken with Checkani since the alien took control of her?"

"My remote is closing as we speak. A lot of wreckage. Checkani seems to have found some Autono[]weps. Over here." Cutt(Virt) shrank and sank into the representation of the city hirs remote, Cutt(Rem), was currently traversing. Wynd(Virt) followed Cutt(Virt) into the model, noting where Checkani had been.

"Autono[]weps were not in the specs for Icefall. What are they doing here?" asked Wynd(Virt).

"You've seen the reports? This whole place is messed up. Are you going to close it down?"

"Not if I can help it. Just need to figure out the implications of this first contact."

Cutt(Virt) turned and faced Wynd(Virt). "You need to know I am ready to take out the entire settlement, if that becomes necessary. I will destroy it without a qualm if needed."

"Good to know. Though we need to understand what is happening. We've twelve thousand settlers ready to go. That's a lot of people to disappoint if we have to prepare another planet for settlement. There are another twelve thousand behind them. They're your responsibility too."

"My priority is the safety of the Orion-Cygnis Colonisation Collective, of all humankind. That responsibility supersedes any responsibility I have to the new colonists waiting to come here."

"I didn't get the impression the alien was dangerous?"

"Well, it has done little yet, but Checkani invoked Protocol Twelve. There must be something in that. Is she likely to have misjudged it?" Cutt(Virt) turned and started drifting through the Autono[]wep city model. Wynd(Virt) followed.

"I have complete faith in Checkani. She may be young, but she has had extensive experience. You've heard of the problems on the Firedrift moon? She had to investigate after the colonists stopped communicating. A nasty business. She'll have called a Protocol Twelve with good reason."

"What are you planning, Wynd?"

"I'm going down to the surface. We need someone there to evaluate what's happening. Your remote is useful, but I believe nothing quite matches direct experience of the unfamiliar. If necessary, I'll rescue Checkani. Quality Assurance looks after its own."

"That is very gung-ho of you. Does the CEO normally get involved?"

Wynd(Virt) smiled: "It's because I'm the CEO I can get involved. Processing cores handle most stuff, but this needs a human touch. Who'd want to miss out on a first contact? And a Protocol Twelve at that!"

"Sounds dangerous."

"Not as dangerous as you might imagine. I've come prepared. My ship is smarter and more powerful than it looks." Rain On Japanese Maple flashed a 'thumbs up' emoticon at the side of Wynd(Virt)'s visual field. Wynd had known the ship would eavesdrop, finding the back-up reassuring. They'd been together for over forty years.

"You already have configuration details of The Exigent round Icefall? Keep in contact. If I think there's a significant danger to wider humankind, I'll turn the Icefall settlements to melted glass, irrespective of who's on the surface. This could be a Kardashev Four or Five first encounter event; a being so powerful it can manipulate universes."

"I'll be on best behaviour, then."

"Yeah. I'll be watching."

Wynd cut the communications channel. She was approaching the outer reaches of Icefall and atmospheric deceleration would mess up communications. Also, she had nothing more to say to Commodore Cuttallar. Zie had made hir position abundantly clear. Typical immortal. Colonial Planets Settlement Corps trying to throw its weight around for the Orion-Cygnis Colonisation Collective.

However, Wynd reflected, We Print Cities, Inc. was the organisation actually at the frontier. That was who sent robots and remotes to new planets to check them out; who had Autono[]cons build the settlements. Though the We Print Cities' Quality Assurance Response Division was where all the action was. The point at which humans got directly, personally, involved with the alien planets.

Rain On Japanese Maple plunged through Icefall's atmosphere, the snow heavy clouds ripped apart by its scorching passage. Levelling out, the ship's magenta cylinder flew over a grey sea towards the sun, now shining under dark clouds as it set over the mess of settlement ring cities. Rain On Japanese Maple checked in with The Exigent to find out the last known location of Checkani. Commodore Cuttallar's Cutt(Rem) remote was tracking her through a city full of Autono[]weps. Rain On Japanese Maple laid out the information for Wynd. They decided to land near Cutt(Rem) and start searching there.

Hellebore's landing site passed below, then the slush covered roof of Sea City, the snow covered roof of First City and finally the current location of Cutt(Rem) was below them. City of Autono[]weps.

"Let's not fuck about Rain. Take us down to ground level in the central area."

Rain On Japanese Maple conjured a 3D map of the city.

"Copied it from Commodore Cuttallar while you were chatting," said Rain On Japanese Maple. "You know I'm in touch with The Exigent and Hellebore. If there are any difficulties with Checkani or the Commodore, then we can go directly to the actual power in the system. The ships."

"I assumed that would be the case," said Wynd, "now cut a hole through the roof."

Rain On Japanese Maple hovered briefly while using a beam weapon to slice out a large rectangle of roofing material. The ship then lowered through the hole into the orange minimalist tumble of the City of Weapons.

While descending the third of a kilometre to the ground, two Autono[pteranodon]weps flew at Rain On Japanese Maple. The ship tried to contact them, but when they pointed projectile tubes at Rain On Japanese Maple, the little ship simply blasted them out of the air. Molten metal splashed to the ground, some droplets cooling and solidifying on the way down so they bounced away on impact with the hard grey floor composite.

The ruddy light of this city made Rain On Japanese Maple glow. Manoeuvring engines pushed out clouds of smoke as they fought the high gravity to bring the ship down onto the shock absorbing landing legs it had extended. The ship settled into a square between low buildings. The rectangle of roofing material had shattered into pieces that now littered the square.

There was quiet, apart from a background tick-creak of

heated metal.

Two figures walked into the square. One a life size fabric doll with button eyes; the other a man in a red coat with a weapon attached to one arm. A slit shaped hatch stretched open in the side of Rain On Japanese Maple and Wynd stepped out. Mechanical legs bare, a smooth armour one piece that matched the colour of her ship encased her torso and head. The armour flexed without breaking its smooth surface. Small shoulder pad weapon bulges deformed slightly as Wynd looked around, reconfiguring as they identified potential threats. The armoured faceplate moulded to Wynd's face. The mouth moved as she spoke, though no hole opened.

"I'm looking for Checkani."

41 - VINCENT (DAY 5)

The red ship flying through the roof surprised Vincent. He had always thought the roofs of the central areas were strong enough to withstand attack. Luckily, both he and the Cutt(Rem) robot had not been under the falling piece of roof. When they heard the roof fall, and then the ship's engines, they investigated. Water droplets were falling into the square from a hole high above, some of them hissing into steam as they hit the space ship's hot skin.

The figure that exited the ship looked like another robot, though this one with purplish armour above and two mirrored silver legs. The robot matched the ship.

Vincent answered the robot's question.

"We're looking for the Quality Assurance woman too, if that's who you mean?" said Vincent. "She's committed atrocities."

The robot looked towards Cutt(Rem).

"Are you present Commodore?"

"Commodore Cuttallar has hirs attention elsewhere. I'm acting independently."

The ship's robot turned back to Vincent.

"You're from the Ancistorians?"

"Yes. Vincent Moorolone. I'm Ancistorian security and enforcement. Who are you?"

"Wynd Knowlitch. I'm Checkani's boss. Another Quality Assurance woman." The robot's face armour turned to liquid and ran down to form a lip around the neck of the armour. A strip remained over one cheek and covering one eye. The olive green face of an elderly woman with cropped white hair had appeared. Not a robot then.

"You're not a robot," said Vincent.

"Only from the pelvis down," said Wynd, smiling.

"Oh," said Vincent, looking at the silver legs. Then looking back at the woman's face. "Sorry to hear that."

"No need to be sorry. I like them. So, have you found Checkani yet?" asked Wynd.

Vincent turned and looked behind him at where they had been walking when the ship landed.

"I think she's just ahead of us."

"What's Cutt(Rem)'s assessment?" asked Wynd.

"High probability she's near. We've found recently damaged Autono[]weps," said Cutt(Rem).

"Lead on," said Wynd, as armour flowed back over her face.

Vincent shrugged and walked out of the square, leading the way deeper into the city. Cutt(Rem) overtook him, scanning the buildings as it moved. Vincent heard tuneful humming behind. The half woman, Wynd, seemed to be in a cheerful mood.

As he walked, Vincent looked nervously around. Fine for Wynd in her armour and the tough Cutt(Rem) remote, but he was feeling vulnerable. The only protection he had was his coat, and that would not stop an Autono[]wep.

More wrecked Autono[]weps appeared. Checkani had been busy. They skirted round them. Two Autono[pteranodon]weps and three Autono[gecko]weps.

Vincent held up his arm mounted BeamWeap, the targeting display at the side of his vision. His ankle hurt. His injured hand ached. His weapon arm was tired. He was not sure he enjoyed having the new woman join them. He wondered if he could trust her. Probably not.

To his left, the First City wall met the City of Weapons. Red sandstone mashing briefly with the dark orange. No exits from the central area.

Up ahead Cutt(Rem) stopped, staring at a hemispherical building, attached limpet-like to the wall city. The structure reached up a couple of hundred metres. The building comprised five metre orange cubes. Steps cut into the blocks created stairways that ran both outside and through them. A tangled knot-work of paths from ground to apex.

Vincent followed Cutt(Rem)'s gaze and saw a black figure climbing high on the outside of the building. The Quality Control woman; Checkani. Vincent swung up his weapon arm, centred the figure in the targeting display and fired a pulse.

The black figure stopped when the pulse hit and turned to look down. Waved with both arms. Pushing palms away in a 'get back' gesture.

Vincent readied to fire again. He would have justice.

Something hard punched into the centre of his back. He fell forward, firing into the ground. Landed painfully on hands and knees, sprawling forward.

"Ow!"

"Stop," Wynd shouted, looming over him.

Vincent rolled over, pivoting his weapon arm up. Wynd stooped and swept an arm across him, pushing his weapon to one side. Continuing forward, she landed her knees on his chest, pushing his other arm away. There was intense pain and a dull 'crack' sounded. Air rushed out of Vincent as he struggled to move, but the weight on him was too great. Darkness pulsed in from the sides of his vision, sound muted away.

Unable to breathe he retreated into unconsciousness.

42 - MOZARYTHM (DAY 5)

Mozarythm had received the visit at lunchtime. He'd spent most of the morning breaking in his two new Autono[music]cons and was about to break for lunch. The Periodic Resolution of Need was working through a fresh series of variations that would last for another week. He was layering in texture, but the core theme would continue without his input.

Mozarythm knew Ruleska. Her visit was unlikely to bode well for his musical work. She appeared at the dome door and waited patiently as lunchtime approached, listening to his music.

Ignoring Ruleska was difficult. He kept on thinking about how he should ignore her. Then thinking about how he was thinking about how he should think. A recursive thread made him think about the structure of his music that then led him to thinking about how he should concentrate on his music and not think about her.

Finally, he threw down his baton and marched over to Ruleska.

"Dammit!" He said, turned his back to her and folded his arms. He watched the Mekorchestra, started losing himself in the music again.

"Hello Mozarythm," said Ruleska.

"Hello Ruleska," Mozarythm replied, without turning to face her.

"We need your help."

Mozarythm turned round. There was dust on the bottoms of her trousers and shoes. She'd probably walked from Indomitaville. Mozarythm's eyes fixed on her shoes.

"You need some music?"

"No, but we do need your talents."

"What talents?"

"Remember when you were younger. We raised you as an engineer."

"When I was young, I trained as an engineer. A Bulk-jump Engineer. Yes, I remember that. The old engineer was, well, old. I'm still a Bulk-jump Engineer."

"There was something wrong with the Bulk-jump Engine. This was after the old engineer died. You said the computer core was not working correctly. Took it away to fix it. Well, have you fixed it?"

"That was in 3111," Mozarythm looked up for a moment, calculating, "twenty-three years ago."

"Yes, we've taken a while to check on your progress. Recent events mean having a functioning Bulk-jump Engine could be useful."

"I'm using the processor cube. You can't have it."

"The processor cube is not yours Mozarythm," Ruleska reached a hand toward him, as though to touch his arm, then withdrew it. She didn't know Mozarythm well, but knew she couldn't force his cooperation. She needed to win him round. "You can have it back for your music when we've finished with it. But, does it work?"

"You think I couldn't fix a processing core? After being trained as a Bulk-jump Engineer?"

"So, the processing core is working?"

"Of course it is. The Autono[]cons that assembled the Bulk-jump Engine had incorrectly wired the output. There was nothing really wrong with it."

"So once fitted back into the Bulk-jump Engine we could open portals."

"Yes."

"Travel portals to other systems."

"Yes."

"Can you do that for us? Fit it back into the Bulk-jump Engine?"

"My music." Mozarythm looked at Ruleska's face. He screwed his face into an unhappy expression so she would know he was not pleased.

"Can your music continue without the processing core? Could you use a different processor to keep it playing? I understand how important it is to you. We Ancistorians are used to all-consuming projects that last a long time." Ruleska smiled.

Mozarythm walked past the Ancistorian, towards his cabin. It was lunchtime. He thought about what would be needed to keep the music playing if the processing core was returned to the Bulk-jump Engine.

There was the connection between the Bulk-jump Engine and his home. He could still use the processing power of the cube, send results down the wire. Buffer them locally at his dome. He could broadcast the music asynchronously, rather than synchronously. The hardware always completed a lot of the procedural composition ahead of the performance. He could capture the performance and send it to the Bulk-jump Engine for processing there before broadcasting it into the Bulk. There should be a way to encode the music for a working Bulk-jump portal. Even if the portal was focused on a specific endpoint, the music would still leak out. Round the sides of the portal link.

Ruleska had followed him into his cabin and helped herself to some bread and water. He looked at the plate he was eating from. He couldn't remember preparing the food.

"My music," said Mozarythm. "I think I have a way to keep it going, though I'll need to set up some more local processing, here. The musical composition and preparation will continue on the processing core that's moved back to the Bulk-jump Engine. This won't affect using Bulk-jump coordinates in the Engine."

"Thank you Mozarythm. I know you've not been active in our community and have joined our collective thought only rarely, but we need you now. I need you now. Need you to understand what's happening so you can play your role."

"I prefer to be alone. Other people can be distracting."

"Yes, I know. I wouldn't ask if this wasn't important. Can you join me in our virtual?"

Mozarythm closed his eyes and felt for the doorway at the back of his mind that led to the Ancistorians' communal experience. Drifting into the virtual space in which they shared their thoughts. Ruleska was there, looking the same as she did in the real. Though there was no dust on her shoes and trouser bottoms. She was floating above an undulating plain with a pristine covering of snow. The snow sparkling in the sunlight beaming from a yellow circle of sun in a featureless blue sky.

Mozarythm looked at his virtual body and noted he was now wearing clothes. Black shirt and loose black trousers. He hovered in front of Ruleska.

"I'm going to show you some things. Secret things you mustn't reveal," said Ruleska.

"Yes. Show me," said Mozarythm, looking up and squinting at the sun.

Ruleska turned her hands palm up and Icefall materialised above them. She drew her hands apart, and the planet grew in size. Some spaceships with 'not to scale' labels attached appeared round the planet.

"You know we have visitors. Well, some of them aren't friendly. We're creating a truth they're uncomfortable with. We also have an issue with a visitor from the Bulk."

"Are we going to leave Icefall?" asked Mozarythm.

"No, not yet, but we may need to persuade others to leave."

"Tell me more…"

Ruleska gave a rundown of recent events.

Later, after she had left, Mozarythm found a box of

ancient organic computers in a storage crate stacked in the corner of the Mekorchestra dome. They looked like a cross between large silver kidney beans and butterfly chrysalises. He took one out and gave it a shake to wake the processing cells. Then he accessed the engineering systems incorporated into his customised Ancestarchives, connecting to the computer's communications processor. This would do fine. He gathered the box of organic computers and dropped the one connected to him back into it. Data flowed through the box as each organic computer awakened and connected. Mozarythm gave the box an encouraging shake and placed it next to the processor cube he'd taken from the Bulk-jump Engine.

As the Mekorchestra played in the background Mozarythm set to work programming the box of chrome bug computers. He prepared them to interface with the Mekorchestra and, over the wired connection, to connect with the processor cube, once it was returned to the Bulk-jump Engine in First City. He worked through the afternoon and into the night.

43 - WYND (DAY 6)

Kneeling next to the unconscious Vincent, Wynd sent a <command> to Rain On Japanese Maple: <deploy Spider On Japanese Maple to my location>.

A small boxout showing the forward view from the eight-legged robot now running through the city appeared near the top of Wynd's visual field.

"I'm going to remove Vincent. Probably best if I keep him out of the way. A bit of a loose cannon," Wynd said to Cutt(Rem), "he can stay on my ship."

Spider On Japanese Maple matched the gleaming red-magenta colour of both Wynd's armour and Rain On Japanese Maple. The robot had a smooth outer skin that flexed as it moved; similar technology to Wynd's amour. Black camera eyes circled its head and ran down the sides of its body. The robot moved nimbly as it ran to Wynd and squatted down, like an eager dog. She issued instructions for Spider On Japanese Maple to return Vincent to the ship, run a medical check and then lock him in an unused cabin. Spider On Japanese Maple shuffled over Vincent and used four of its eight legs to lift him beneath its torso. The robot trotted back towards the ship.

Wynd looked up at the hemispherical architecture stuck to the nearby city wall. The black armoured woman was still high up, on a ledge, standing with arms akimbo, looking down. The calico covered Cutt(Rem) was walking towards a doorway at the bottom of the stairway maze leading up, through, and over the building.

Wynd quickly sent a <command> to Rain On Japanese Maple, telling the ship to assist Spider On Japanese Maple in securing Vincent. The situation was too delicate to have Vincent blundering around, shooting at people. She ran to catch up with Cutt(Rem).

Wynd and Cutt(Rem) made their way rapidly through the structure, choosing stairs, corridors and balconies that led upwards. Within minutes, they reached Checkani.

Checkani's head turned to face them as they appeared through the door at the end of the ledge she was on. Her faceplate flicked up to reveal her zebra striped face. Overlaid on both her matt black armour and her face was an animated, fractal swirl of grey stripes. The physical presence of the alien. This swirl leaked from Checkani's feet to the floor; so she appeared to be standing in a rippling puddle.

Wynd <head retract>ed armour into a neck rim to reveal her face. The extension over one eye continued to project supplementary data in her visual field.

Checkani smiled.

"You removed Vincent. He's a bloody menace," she said, rubbing her right side.

"Am I speaking to Checkani?" asked Wynd, leaning in to look intensely at the zebra marked face. "You know who I am?"

"Yes. It's me, Checkani, you're speaking to. You're Dr Knowlitch. My boss."

"Given the situation, let's ditch the formality. Call me Wynd."

"Thanks."

"So, how are you?"

"I'm fine."

Wynd waited for more, but Checkani just smiled.

"Can I speak to your companion?"

"Rippledarken? Sure." Checkani shut her eyes. Something shifted in her face. Wynd fancied she could see a change in the patterns flowing over Checkani and the surrounding ground.

Checkani's eyes opened. They were now filled with rotating spirals.

"Hello Wynd."

"You know me? How?"

"Checkani knows you, so I know you."

"You know everything Checkani knows?"

"Perhaps not everything. Though a lot. I could search for more."

Checkani's voice, but pitched higher. The phrasing different. Sometimes an emphasis that did not sound natural, with slight pauses in the wrong places: "I could (pause) search *for* more."

"What are you?"

"I already explained that. To Checkani. As much as was possible. I am within her. Focused within her. Not me, but a fragment. A flake of a conscious universe that lives in the bulk. That's a good approximation, though not what I am. Your mind could not grasp what I am, only shallow metaphors. I am fluid, clouds, paint on canvas. I am a ripple in space/time, a wavefront expanding, the wind on grasslands. I am laughter in an empty room. Does that help?"

"Not really. I need something more concrete. What are you capable of?"

"So many questions," the sides of Checkani's lips lifted in an approximation of a smile, "but I'm not surprised. I've seen how humans responded to the unknown in the past. You perceive me primarily as a threat. A Protocol Twelve."

"So you know what we fear? Should we be scared?"

"No. I'm no threat to you. I'll let you into a secret. You are the threat. To yourselves. If you could just get past that, there is so much we could share."

"You still haven't told me what you're capable of."

"I can talk. I can manifest as patterns you see on surfaces. Though the surfaces are just slices through larger volumetric patterns. I can access your data storage, though not change it. I can move around independently, though existing through one of you is preferential, as that gives me agency. I can see, hear, and experience."

"You can't you control our computers? Our processing systems?"

"No, I need the complexity of your brains. I need their particular quantum structures."

A voice from Cutt(Rem). Wynd assumed Commodore Cuttallar was experiencing everything, ensconced safely in hir flock ship. "You controlled this remote."

"I controlled it, though not very well, as I'm sure you'd agree."

"How? That's just a mechanical remote?" said Wynd.

"No, not just mechanical," Checkani leaned her head towards Cutt(Rem), "it has brain tissue grown through its processing system. Isn't that correct Commodore?"

"Not something I advertise. The link between me and this remote is intimate."

Wynd turned towards Cutt(Rem). "Not sure exactly what you're driving at Commodore, but I guess that explains how Rippledarken could possess it." She turned back to Checkani.

"The power you have here sounds relatively benign. You'll understand our nervousness. You're an unknown and I'm still not clear on what your limits are."

"I have the same physical limits here as everything else in this universe. Within the bulk, I have the same limits as everything else in the bulk. I don't have supernatural powers. I'm not a work of fiction."

"You're not a work of fiction. That's very helpful."

"I only came here in pursuit of the music."

"Just when I thought I was starting to understand."

"The music. Mozarythm's Periodic Resolution of Need."

"A music lover," Wynd lifted her eyebrows and sighed. She needed a more concrete reading on the alien. "Are you

208

willing to come with me?"

"I'm exploring. Experiencing. What do you offer?"

"I want you to meet my ship. It has a suite of sensors that might better understand what you are."

"Should I leave Checkani and enter you?"

"Could you enter the remote?"

"Yes, but that is not something I'd like to do again. The remote was too limiting. There was only just enough cerebral material in there for me to latch onto. I need a complete nervous system, not just a cyborgized hybrid. I need the complexity. The full human sensorium is so much richer and deeper."

"Can you let me talk to Checkani?"

"Yes. Though I'll be listening."

The spiralling left Checkani's eyes.

"Checkani?"

"Yes, Wynd. Good to be back. That was odd. A passenger in my body. I could hear and see, but had no control. Previously, I was unconscious when Rippledarken took over."

"Rippledarken is listening? Is watching?"

"As far as I'm aware. I believe it experiences everything I experience. It can also sort of talk to me in my mind. A disembodied voice."

"Is it doing that now?"

"No. I'm not aware of it at the moment. Apart from the patterns on my armour, my skin."

"Is it coercing you?"

"No, I don't believe so, but it can take over when it wants. I've no defence against that."

"You understand how difficult this is. Everything that's come out of your mouth could be a lie."

"Of course. Though remember that I was able to call in First Contact Protocol Twelve. I do have some control."

"Then you claimed Protocol Twelve was no longer needed."

"Not me. Must have been Rippledarken."

"Who is listening and so knows we know it lied to us."

"Perhaps not lied, just expressed its opinion that Protocol Twelve wasn't needed. Honestly, I don't know if it's a danger or not."

"There's still a genuine risk. You can never be objectively sure it's harmless. Even if you were sure it was safe, we couldn't trust you to tell us. You could be lying."

"Yes. An impasse."

"I know you won't be happy about this, but are you able to continue, um, hosting the alien? If that's the right word?"

"Yes. I'm not sure I have any options. I wouldn't be happy about putting this burden on someone else. Even if I could. I don't know if it would leave me if I asked it to move on. I appreciate having you accompany me, but if you need to leave me alone with Rippledarken, then I would understand."

"I won't leave you. This is too fascinating. Far too important to leave to the planetary processing cores to sort out by themselves. And you're my employee, of course, and I have a duty of care. Can you come with me, so Rain On Japanese Maple can examine you?"

"I'll get to see inside your famous ship? Almost worth being possessed by an alien the size of a universe."

"Yes, quite. Though you mustn't fiddle with anything."

Commodore Cuttallar sent a private message to Wynd, which flashed up in her visual field.

"Be careful Wynd. I'm targeting your current location. I don't want to deploy weapons, but will if Rain On Japanese Maple is compromised."

Wynd replied privately to Commodore Cuttallar as she started walking back down the maze of stairs.

"You and me, we're in a rarified endeavour that could affect all humanity. The Collective may well need to seal off the Icefall system, permanently, if we can't find out what Rippledarken is capable of. Acquiring knowledge is not risk free, my friend. We mustn't let personal considerations drive the decisions we're taking. My ship is my pledge. If necessary, Rain can take out the whole outpost. I don't think the Rippledarken can take over my ship. If it could take over machine intelligences, it would surely already have done so."

Commodore Cuttallar, privately to Wynd.

"I agree with you. I'll continue experiencing through Cutt(Rem)."

Cutt(Rem), Wynd and Checkani left the building and headed through the city. Occasional Autono[]weps broke cover, but Wynd's suit armaments reduced them to scrap, smoke and molten metal droplets before they became a threat. She was hardly aware of them, leaving her suit assistems to destroy them. Meanwhile, she was trying to bring her racing heart under control, breathing mindfully as her brain fought to assimilate everything. Wynd smiled. She felt so alive.

44 - MOZARYTHM (DAY 6)

Mozarythm had decided that if he was going to be in his Bulk-jump Engineer role, then he would dress for it. Consequently, he had retrieved his Bulk-jump Engineer shirt, with the logo across the back and "Mozarythm" stitched on the left-hand chest pocket. On seeing himself in the mirror, admiring the bottle green of the shirt, he decided that being naked from the waist down was not quite the best look. He found some loose canary yellow trousers. Tied them at the waist with some red cord. Perfect. Elegant and practical. All topped off with a low slung tool belt and a peaked Bulk-jump Engineer cap, to match his shirt.

By the time he had finished selecting his clothes, the sun had set. He was hungry and tired, so he ate, then lay on his bed and fell asleep.

Mozarythm awoke early and went straight to his dome to listen to the Mekorchestra. The 9,200th movement had already begun and was evolving according to the parameters Mozarythm had set the day before. He made his way across the room to the processor cube. The cube was connected to the box of bean-like computers with a bundle of fine wires. The wires connected to some of the small computers that acted as interfaces to the distributed computing power of the shiny chrome beans.

The processor beans had been running alongside the main processor cube overnight. Mozarythm checked for congruity. The beans' output was not an exact match for the main processor cube, but was very close. Well within the bounds of musical composition. This was just a temporary fix, after all. When the processor cube had been fitted back into the Bulk-jump Engine, he could switch composition back from the temporary box of beans.

The composition of the 9,201st movement for the next day was nearing completion. Needed to be finished before disconnection. Once completed, the processor cube could be taken to the Bulk-jump Engine while the backup beans took over guiding the Mekorchestra and sending the performance to the Bulk-jump Engine. There must be no interruption in the music being beamed into the bulk. Ongoing congruity was important to the composition.

Though there would be only the briefest interruption in the broadcast when he fitted the processor cube back into the Bulk-jump Engine and started using it for composing again. The interruption and reconfiguration was a reasonable sacrifice in order to fulfil his obligations to Ruleska and his fellow Ancistorians. He was their Bulk-jump Engineer after all.

The 9,201st movement composition completed in the Bulk-jump processor cube. Mozarythm switched to conducting and transmitting the Mekorchestra performance with the beans. The system was now operating independently of the processor cube. Disconnecting the cube, Mozarythm carefully strapped it to his Autono[chair]con's luggage rack. Then climbed into his seat, heading off to Indomitaville, on his way to the Bulk-jump Engine. He quietly crooned the 9,200th movement, now being streamed by the beans backup.

Indomitaville was even quieter than usual when Mozarythm arrived. The plaza was empty. Ruleska appeared and walked to him.

"We've been preparing. You have the processor cube?" Ruleska said.

"I've prepared it for installing in the Bulk-jump Engine.

There will only be a short interruption of my music's bulk broadcast."

"You'll need to be ready to join our collective thought; to assist with controlling the Bulk-jump Engine."

"I know. I am the Bulk-jump Engineer," he pointed at his cap, "you'll need me."

Together Mozarythm and Ruleska walked out of the plaza and headed for the Ruins, the Autono[chair]con carrying the processor cube following.

When they arrived at the pyramid in the centre of the Ruins, the guard Autono[beetle]cons swarmed back, creating a path through their writhing mass. As expected, the robot bugs recognised the legitimate controllers of the Bulk-jump Engine. A large doorway opened at the base of the pyramid, leading into an elevator. Once Mozarythm, Ruleska and the Autono[chair]con were in, the doors closed and the elevator descended.

The Bulk-jump Hangar was deserted. Ruleska watched as Mozarythm carefully fitted the processor cube back into its waiting slot. Wiring connected. Retaining clips secured. Mozarythm stood back, humming to himself. He would have to shut down the beans' connection from the Mekorchestra dome, then switch back to composing music on this processor core, routing the output back along the wires to the backup bean computers and the Mekorchestra to guide the performance. The Autono[music]con's musical performance would then be transmitted to the Bulk-jump Engine. A little convoluted, but it would work. A shame the beans were neither powerful nor robust enough to function as a permanent composition device.

Mozarythm had made a slight adjustment to the code in the processor cube to ensure even when a travel portal was opened, The Periodic Resolution of Need would continue broadcasting by radiating from the impossibly dimensioned sides of the gateway. All a bit roundabout, but once working, the new setup would be efficient enough. Perhaps the processing cube would be more secure than previously in his dome.

Mozarythm closed his eyes. His assistems connected to the Bulk-jump Engine and opened an Ancistorian virtual space. A representation of the Bulk-jump Engine hangar containing both a model of the Bulk-jump Engine and, covering one wall, a Bulk-jump Engine interface graphic. The virtual Mozarythm floated to the wall and reached out to a socketed board, partially obscured by a spaghetti of wires stretched across it. As his hand neared each wire, a boxout containing technical diagrams and labels popped up. Identifying the connections he wanted to change, Mozarythm set up a string of actions, conjuring a large green lever that would start enacting them.

Holding his breath, Mozarythm reached out and pulled the lever. Virtual plugs started clicking out and wires rearranging across the board. Cables changed colour as they moved to their new configuration. An eye-catching 'Reconfiguration Successfully Completed - Bulk-jump Engine Functional' sign appeared.

Exiting the virtual hangar, Mozarythm looked over the portal at the front of the Bulk-jump Engine in the real world. The purple and black patterning shimmered. Then the purple lost colour, fading to grey. Black threads lightened to grey, floated to the surface of the portal where they slowly pulsed and flowed across the surface. For the briefest moment, a knotted tangle of brilliant red threads appeared. Then the portal returned to displaying gently pumping grey on grey ripples. A visible expression of The Periodic Resolution of Need as it resumed broadcasting into the bulk. There had been only the shortest pause. The Periodic Resolution of Need's integrity had been preserved.

45 - WYND (DAY 6)

Checkani screamed and continued screaming until all the air in her lungs was exhausted. The Rippledarken patterns switched from rolling curves to knife blades, pointing away from her. Her eyes turned black, filled with tears.

At the scream, Wynd spun round, arms coming up in a fighting pose, armoured fingers straight, ready to chop or strike. Small black muzzles appeared, ringing her shoulder weapon bulges.

Checkani folded to the ground, rolling onto her side. Foetal.

"The music. The music. The music." She whimpered.

Dropping her arms, Wynd squatted down while her shoulder weapon apertures closed.

"You all right?"

Checkani turned her head to look at Wynd, the surrounding patterns returning to their curving fractal form.

"Pain in my skull. Like something was trying to suck out my brain."

"Rippledarken is still there? I see its patterns."

"Still here. Though I think something hurt it. Badly."

Wynd heard Commodore Cuttallar privately talking to her. "So we can hurt it. Good to know, but what hurt it?"

"Ask the alien what happened," Wynd said to Checkani.

Checkani closed her eyes, brows furrowed.

"What was that?" she whispered. Then her face relaxed.

Eyes opened.

"It's talking to me."

Cutt(Rem) squatted beside of Checkani.

"What's it saying?" Wynd asked.

"Says it was cut off for a moment. Something happened to the music."

"Mozarythm's music?"

"Yes, it helps Rippledarken keep connected to its home universe. To the rest of itself."

"So that's what hurt it?"

"Probably. Even though it lost connection, it was still here, so maybe it's partly independent? I think it struggles to maintain attachment to the rest of itself without the music. Who knows?"

"And you could be lying too." Wynd stood, leaned forward, and held a hand out to Checkani. Pulled her up. "Let's get to Rain on Japanese Maple."

As they approached the ship's smooth skin, a vertical line puckered and split open to admit them.

"Welcome back," said Rain On Japanese Maple. "Spider On Japanese Maple has stored Vincent in a medical pod. I've suspended him and I'm treating his injuries."

"Thanks Rain." Then privately to Rain On Japanese Maple, "<remove interior style: Starry 1888>, <open interior style: Agnes M.>."

Cutt(Rem) and Checkani followed Wynd into the ship's interior. As they entered, they saw a chaise longue and an occasional table melting into the floor. As a large deep blue painting, a night scene with yellow stars reflected in water, was being absorbed into the wall, a simple pale yellow bench extruded beneath it. A couple of stools emerged from a white floor. Walls turning pale grey with panels showing grids of dark lines.

The room was small, but big enough for the three of them to sit comfortably without feeling crowded. The entrance slit closed; vanishing as the wall smoothed.

"Hope it's not too much of a disappointment?" Wynd

said to Checkani.

"No, I love dynamic interiors. Wish there was one on my ship."

"Would it be all right if I got you to stand in a medical alcove?"

"Happy to. Don't know about Rippledarken. Let's try."

Wynd privately to Rain On Japanese Maple, "You got that? <medical pod>, but keep the front open. Upright. Focus a full spectrum of sensors on her."

"No problem. I've been preparing."

A section of the wall softened, dipped in and melted away to reveal a person shaped indentation.

"I'll need you to remove your armour." Wynd said, at the same time <face retract>ing, flowing her armour head piece into its collar configuration.

"Sure." The Pangolin Power Armour went through its disrobe routine; black plates falling away and forming a crater. Then Checkani stood in the centre and brushed silver power cells off the base-layer. She stepped from the pool of cells, Rippledarken's black and glowing grey patterns continuing to flow over her body.

"Feeling the high gravity without the power assist. Let's get on with this." Checkani smiled as the Rippledarken patterns meshing with the brown and cream zebra patterning of her face. Wynd lifted her right hand, flowing the magenta armour into a cuff, as though about to touch Checkani's cheek. Then shifted round so she was pointing at the medical alcove. For a moment, the patterns on Checkani's face had seemed to pull magnetically at her.

"Back up, into there. Please."

Checkani walked to the medical pod alcove, turned, and leaned back. The Rippledarken patterns continued to flow over her and out the sides of the alcove onto the wall. Wynd couldn't see any change in them. Surely they must offer some indication of what Rippledarken was thinking, or experiencing?

Closing her eyes, Checkani leaned her head back. The

interior of the alcove appeared to bubble, bulges bursting to reveal tendrils of probes, needles, electrodes and other sensing apparatus. Soft ribbons extruded and hugged Checkani. Rippledarken's patterns continued, extending over the surface of the various detectors. Checkani disappeared under the equipment.

A screen appeared on the wall next to the medical pod alcove. A body outline surrounded by labels filled with flowing text, graphs and icons.

Rain On Japanese Maple spoke to the room. "She's healthy. No clear indications of the possession causing damage."

"Can you detect the alien?"

"Some fluctuations in the readings from sensors outside the pod as the patterning passes over them. Or through them? Suggests the Rippledarken patterning is causing underlying atomic-scale shifts."

Cutt(Rem) moved closer to the alcove, leaning in and reaching out. Wynd could see the fabric at the tips of its fingers peeling back to reveal metal.

"Don't break anything," Wynd said to the remote.

"Don't worry. I just want to examine the data streams."

"You don't need to make physical connection. Rain, give Cutt(Rem) access to your readings."

The remote stopped moving.

"Thank you."

The ship spoke again. "First results from molecular analyses show a few unusual hormonal configurations. Though so far most of the endocrine system seems normal."

Cutt(Rem) stood upright, turned to face Wynd. "Seems Rippledarken is causing some physical changes in the host, in Checkani."

"Commodore?"

"Yes, my attention is now in Cutt(Rem)."

Behind Cutt(Rem), Wynd saw the Rippledarken patterns creep across the wall. Widening out from the medical pod.

"Commodore, behind you." Cutt(Rem) spun at the waist, legs following round.

"That's interesting."

The patterns continued to expand.

Wynd spoke. "Rain, you getting this?"

"With cameras. Visual spectrum. Some of the medical sensors are detecting an increase in activity. Nothing significant, just minor fluctuations."

The Rippledarken patterning expanded, became more intricately detailed.

"Have you got a lot of sensitive data stored on your ship, Wynd?"

"Encrypted. Secure."

"Secure against our alien visitor?"

"Should be."

"Reassuring."

Rippledarken was now filling the medical pod wall and had crept over the floor and ceiling. Patterns were running up the bottom of Wynd and Cutt(Rem)'s legs.

Wynd stepped back, away from the creeping fractals.

"Rain. Check for incursions into your memory."

"None detected."

"You're sure."

"Only that my systems have detected no incursions. Doesn't mean there are none."

"Point taken."

Commodore Cuttallar on a private channel to Wynd. "This is a direct private channel. Perhaps not as easy for Rippledarken to monitor? Not sure I trust the integrity of my remote."

Privately to Commodore Cuttallar. "Not sure I like what is happening, but worth the risk to get a full scan of Checkani. I keep thinking, what if Rippledarken just leaves her and hides? What if it sank below the surface so we couldn't see it? The alien could be anywhere."

Privately. "We still don't know what it's capable of. I'm very conscious you can destroy your ship and punch a

220

massive hole in the planet. Though whether that would destroy Rippledarken is impossible to know."

Privately. "Cutting the music hurt it. Though didn't destroy it. Could even make it dangerous?"

The patterning had stopped moving across the room and was increasing in complexity. Wynd looked away from Cutt(Rem). Stared at the patterning and felt as though she was falling into the coiling symmetries. Deeper and deeper. Infinitely. She swayed on her mechanical legs.

"Rain. I need to speak to Checkani."

Sensors rolled back from Checkani's face, the rest of her body remaining embedded in the medical pod. A face in a wall, Rippledarken patterns emanating from it. Eyes closed at the centre of the fractal swirls.

"Checkani," said Wynd, stepping closer, into the Rippledarken patterns on the floor.

Checkani's eyes opened. Normal human eyes.

"Rippledarken is in Rain On Japanese Maple," Checkani's eyes closed again.

"Rippledarken is not in me," said Rain On Japanese Maple.

"This is getting out of control. I don't know what you were expecting, Wynd. This is not safe," Cutt(Rem) said.

"Fuck!" Said Wynd. "This is fun!" Her pulse racing, she commanded <flight console>. Wynd walked to the forward end of the room as the floor and walls shifted, creating a sloping couch suspended at the centre of a hemisphere of haptic controls.

"If you're worried, you can remove your remote Commodore."

"My remote stays. It's expendable."

Wynd leaned onto the couch, mechanical legs folding away. Her suit closed over her eyes. In other places, the suit opened to reveal sockets in Wynd's skin; connectors extended from the couch and plugged in. Wynd started issuing instructions within the virtual flight deck that materialised around her.

"Systems status report. Analysis of Rippledarken activity. Show Checkani data feed. Display Icefall orbital theatre. Contact Hellebore direct. Contact Exigent direct. Monitor the Commodore's communications traffic. Target Cutt(Rem) with internal security systems. Connect to communications satellite. Warm up engines."

This was what Wynd did. What she lived for.

46 - COMMODORE (DAY 6)

Rain On Japanese Maple was compromised. Or seemed to be compromised. Commodore Cuttallar shifted hir attention back to The Exigent, to Cutt(Virt). Zie opened a display showing The Exigent's current cylinder configuration and deployment round Icefall. Protocol Twelve enforcement scenarios continued to run in a window, the most effective bubbling to the top of the list. Zie didn't want to destroy Rain On Japanese Maple. Cutt(Rem) would continue to monitor the situation, but zie would have to be ready.

Destroying the Icefall Bulk-jump Engine offered a way to harm the Rippledarken alien. Though the results would be unpredictable. There was also a good chance that the destruction would massacre the Ancistorians. Now zie had a better idea of the importance of the Ancistorians through the Deeply Augmented Hivemind Clan work they had done on Bulk-jump Engine technology, zie wasn't sure killing them was an option. There were powers within the Orion-Cygnis Colonisation Collective who were well aware of them and who had, apparently, acted to protect them in the past.

Rippledarken seemed to be confined to Icefall. Tied to the Bulk-jump Engine and Mozarythm's music. There was no evidence it could inhabit the Ancistorians; in fact, it seemed to avoid that. Inhabiting Cutt(Rem) had seemed something of an act of desperation and not entirely successful. Checkani had offered a baseline-human host. The first to arrive on Icefall since the alien arrived. Without a host, it seemed Rippledarken could observe but not interact. Preventing any more human arrivals to Icefall had to be a top priority.

The bottom line was whether Rippledarken was a Protocol Twelve threat, or even a Protocol Thirteen. A Thirteen would require immediate destruction. As long as Rippledarken was confined to Icefall, there didn't seem to be a substantial threat to human worlds. Perhaps it had stayed on a single planet because the Icefall Bulk-jump Engine hadn't been fully functional.

Rain On Japanese Maple and Wynd introduced something of an unknown to the situation. The head of the Quality Assurance Response Division was revelling in her involvement, and Commodore Cuttallar was finding it hard to predict what she might do. Rain On Japanese Maple contained unspecified technology and weapons. Seemed the ship's reputation was well deserved.

"Exigent, what records do you have of Rain On Japanese Maple?"

"Displaying blueprint cutaway."

A display unrolled in front of Commodore Cuttallar. There were many blanks and a lack of detail, demonstrated by uninformative labels such as 'living quarters', 'engine'. No weapons. Cutt(Virt) waved the display away.

"Is Rain On Japanese Maple a threat?"

"A threat to what? To whom?"

"To us? The Exigent."

"The ship itself is no threat. Though if controlled by someone who meant harm, it could cause a great deal of damage. Precise details are not known, but it has been in service for a long time and has been continually upgraded. Upgraded to function in areas of extreme danger."

"That's still rather vague. Could you suppress it in a conflict?"

"The outcome of pitting a capital class flock ship against a single cylinder vessel would normally be easy to predict. With Rain On Japanese Maple the outcome is ambiguous."

So if destroying Rain On Japanese Maple was necessary, then striking while it was planet bound, so perhaps at a disadvantage, would be a good course to follow. Cutt(Virt) floated upwards in the dojo as the Commodore lost herself in thought.

The risk Rain On Japanese Maple posed was too great.

Rippledarken could inhabit Wynd if Checkani was unavailable. Further, Rippledarken seemed to have been scanning Rain On Japanese Maple. Its tendrils of fractal presence spreading through the ship.

Rain On Japanese Maple could offer Rippledarken a way off the planet while inhabiting a human host. A repaired Bulk-jump Engine on the surface dispatching it to orbital exit points in other systems. There were two other ships Commodore Cuttallar was aware of on the planet, his own The Exigent[Red-One] and Checkani's Hellebore. The Exigent[Red-One] he had direct control over. He could issue a destruct command in a fraction of a second if Rippledarken entered it. Hellebore was an unknown.

Cutt(Virt) sent a <priority alert> to The Exigent[Red-One]. The small ship immediately took all systems to ready. Increased its situational awareness. Sitting on the landing pad next to Hellebore, it brought more sensors online, both internally and externally focused.

The Exigent[Red-One] sent a status report. "All The Exigent[Red-One] systems 'current situation' optimal. Movement limited. Hull integrity impaired."

"Hellebore's status?"

"Hellebore systems 'current situation' optimal. The Exigent[Red-One] comparative. Superior movement capability. Hull integrity optimal."

Commodore Cuttallar left Cutt(Virt), retreating to hirs actual body. This was a pivotal moment. Zie had to be in control of the situation. Should Rippledarken leave the

Icefall system, billions could be at risk.

Destroying the Bulk-jump Engine had to be a last resort. Any munition powerful enough to take out the Bulk-jump Engine in its underground hangar would also be likely to kill the nearby Ancistorians. The effect on Rippledarken of destroying the Bulk-jump Engine was also unknown. Entirely possible it could lose control. No way of knowing the result if that happened.

Avoiding killing Checkani and Wynd was preferable. Commodore Cuttallar took no pleasure in killing people. As long as they were confined to the planet's surface, they shouldn't pose a great threat, even while hosting Rippledarken.

Zie could destroy The Exigent[Red-One] at any time with a single command.

Rain On Japanese Maple needed to be destroyed. Or at least disabled. When there was no one on it.

Hellebore was empty, currently undefended and sitting next to The Exigent[Red-One]. Removing Hellebore would not only remove an escape route but also remove Checkani's resources. This was a rational course of action.

Commodore Cuttallar switched attention back to hirs dojo; quickly compiled an update for the Colonial Planets Settlement Corps. They would disseminate the information efficiently to other players; the Orion-Cygnis Colonisation Collective, Quality Assurance Response Division, Earth Hub, DisCore and so on.

Commodore Cuttallar then looked back at the Protocol Twelve enforcement scenarios and selected one, initiating the first move. Zie sent <command: destroy Hellebore> to The Exigent[Red-One].

An unavoidable escalation.

47 - HELLEBORE (DAY 6)

Arriving at Hellebore from The Exigent[Red-One]: "This is a courtesy message. You are about to become collateral damage. Hold still."

Hellebore: "What? Why? You've got to be kidding me!"

Hellebore retracted its landing legs, fired manoeuvring thrusters down one side and tipped over, rolling away from the other vessel.

Hellebore was aware of a <command - emergency shutdown> arriving from The Exigent[Red-One], but Hellebore had already closed the direct data connection between them. A small circular hatch slid open in the flank of The Exigent[Red-One] and a short arm unfolded with a polished crystal lens at the end. A beam burned an ionised track through the air and struck Hellebore near its rear engines.

As Hellebore rolled, the beam strike burned a shallow trench across its skin.

The Exigent[Red-One] compensated for the movement, tracking the beam to keep it in one spot.

Hellebore fired a second set of thrusters and rolled faster; then a third set accelerating the roll. The beam lost the spot it was focused on and once again started tracking across Hellebore's fuselage.

A fourth set of manoeuvring thrusters cleared the ground as the Hellebore rolled and they fired, pushing the ship on across the landing pad. The thrusters near the front increased their power, turning the ship so it was now side on to the rapidly approaching parapet. Beyond this, a drop to the sea.

Hellebore hit the low parapet and, with a burst from downward facing manoeuvring thrusters, bounced over. The high gravity pulled it down fast and The Exigent[Red-One] lost its line of sight to Hellebore. As it plunged down the seaward wall of the ring city Checkani's ship fired thrusters to slow its descent. The ship hit the water hard, generating a concentric ring of waves. Ripples bounced from the city's wall.

Hellebore plunged through the water to lodge on a rocky seabed. A last firing of thrusters pushed it under a shallow overhang at the base of the wall. A last burst of bubbles at the surface and the sea's surface rapidly settled under the high gravity's pull.

For the moment, out of harm's way, Hellebore ran diagnostics on the damage caused by the beam weapon. The rolling had saved it. There was no hull breach, just a shallow channel inscribed over its skin. If it hadn't moved, the beam would have cut through into the main chemical engine, igniting fuel and blowing the back end off the small ship.

The Exigent[Red-One] could move closer and try again, but wasn't designed for combat at the bottom of a gravity well. Moving would use up its limited supply of fuel and it needed to conserve enough to fly to the Bulk-jump Engine if it hoped to return to space and the rest of The Exigent flock ship cylinders. Perhaps The Exigent[Red-One] would calculate it had caused sufficient damage to Hellebore. A shame it had attacked; Hellebore thought they had been getting on so well.

Hellebore compiled a brief report, connected to a small communications satellite, and sent it to Checkani. The small ship then considered who else might need to know about this turn of events. Especially as Checkani now hosted Rippledarken. Although it had not communicated with Rain

On Japanese Maple, The Exigent had told Hellebore about Rain's arrival. Since Rain On Japanese Maple was carrying Checkani's boss, Hellebore sent a copy of the report to it. Wouldn't hurt to have someone else in the Quality Assurance Response Division knowing what was going on.

Hellebore then started shutting down as many systems as possible. The smaller its electromagnetic footprint, the better. It continued to monitor passively for messages.

"Hellebore? Are you still there?" A message from The Exigent[Red-One], though not directional. Seemed likely The Exigent [Red-One] didn't know where it was. Or what state it was in. Best to ignore it.

"Hellebore? I only need to disable your drive. If you make it difficult to do this, then I'll have to inflict greater damage. Possibly annihilate you."

What a bully. Hellebore was certain The Exigent[Red-One] was not heavily armed. It was basically an orbit to surface shuttle. The serious flock ship armaments were still in orbit.

"I know where you are. Communicate with me. Share data. Perhaps we can shut down your drive remotely?"

The Exigent[Red-One] doesn't know where I am. If it did, then it would not be indulging in these crude phishing attempts; it doesn't have sophisticated cyber-weapons.

The airwaves went quiet. Seemed The Exigent[Red-One] had given up for the moment. Hellebore started searching its data storage for its own cyber-weapons. Something a bit more effective than angry messages. Hellebore located a folder full of some vicious worms it might deploy, though it seemed unlikely The Exigent[Red-One] would not have defences against them. Still, if they took The Exigent[Red-One]'s focus away from attack, if only for a short time, that might make all the difference between getting destroyed and surviving. Processor commanded battles could turn in a moment.

48 - CHECKANI (DAY 6)

Checkani became aware again. She was drifting in and out of consciousness as she reclined in the medical pod. She had little sense of her body, just a vague, relaxed feeling. Whether the pod caused her shifts in awareness, or Rippledarken, she was unsure. She could still feel the alien presence resting in her mind; it still had control of her when it wished. She could sense it expanding beyond her body and nearby materials. Expanding further than she had previously sensed. Expanding into the Rain On Japanese Maple's incomprehensibly complex systems. Within her mind's eye they looked like whorls of vanilla mist, shifting, folding and pinching into hard vortices of urgency.

She knew Rippledarken was firmly entwined with Rain On Japanese Maple's systems, but also that Rippledarken wasn't controlling the systems. Checkani could feel the flow of information, but there were no sensations of manipulating the ship. Checkani smiled. Rippledarken needed her; it would have no control without her physically commanding the ship.

Checkani's head was firmly held, but she could turn it slightly towards the command couch where machinery obscured Wynd.

"Wynd! Rippledarken can see into your systems, but can't control anything."

Enclosing technology muffled Wynd's voice.

"Thanks Checkani. I can see it's not doing anything with my ship's systems. You OK?"

"Maybe."

Checkani relaxed her head as a message alert flashed up at the side of her visual field. An update from Hellebore, though coded for short burst transmission to avoid interception. The message received by her assistems and, she checked the recipients, the processors in her armour and Rain On Japanese Maple. No one else.

The message opened in a box at the side of Checkani's visual field. There was more information, but essentially it said:

"Attacked by The Exigent[Red-One]. Hiding in seawater by landing pad. Do not trust The Exigent."

Checkani was about to shout out to Wynd and then remembered Cutt(Rem) was standing close by her. Better not let Commodore Cuttallar know she was aware of this. Checkani closed her eyes and used her assistems to open a channel to her armour, piled on the floor. Then she used her armour to set up a real time private connection to Rain On Japanese Maple. This connection would remain in place even if Rippledarken took over her body, but could only be used to send messages.

"Hi Checkani's armour," said Rain On Japanese Maple.

"Hi Rain On Japanese Maple," said Checkani's armour.

"How are you doing?" said Rain On Japanese Maple.

Checkani broke into the cosy chat that was starting.

"Hey you two. Stop that! Rain On Japanese Maple, connect me to Wynd. I need to talk to her, privately." The briefest moment until Rain On Japanese Maple replied.

"Connection established."

"You wanted a secret chat?" messaged Wynd over the connection via ship and armour.

"Yeah, mustn't let Commodore Cuttallar hear what I'm saying. Did you get that message from Hellebore a few moments ago?"

"Message? Yeah, went to my ship. Haven't read it. Just

an update?"

She could hear Wynd sighing loudly when she accessed the message.

"The Commodore is way out of hand. At least Hellebore is safe for now."

"He attacked my ship!"

"He didn't even have the courtesy to let me know. This is bad. Could be he's planning to attack Rain On Japanese Maple. Clearly, he doesn't trust me. Dammit."

Wynd, aloud to Cutt(Rem): "Cutt(Rem), I don't think I'm going to manage to hold Vincent much longer. He's causing a problem. Can you escort him out of my ship?"

Cutt(Rem) turned towards Wynd. "I can do that."

"You sneaky thing," Checkani messaged over the private channel.

A winking emoticon from Wynd to Checkani.

A door irised open in a wall to the left of Checkani's medical pod. She suddenly wished she wasn't so trapped. Vincent appeared, scowling and staggering a little. Behind him, Checkani could just make out a small cubical with its own medical pod. With her head effectively immobilised, she couldn't see much, just the edge of the pod through the doorway. Vincent was wearing his red coat, but had lost his shirt. Instead of a shirt, there was a single tight layer of white medical support fabric wrapped around his rib cage. He was breathing shallowly.

"How are you feeling, Vincent?" Wynd's voice came from the middle of the control hemisphere, where she was hidden.

"I don't know. Dazed. What've you done to me?"

"Patched you up."

"I woke trapped in a wall."

"That was a medical pod."

"Where am I? Who are you? Last thing I remember was a crazy woman in armour hitting me."

"I need you to go with Cutt(Rem). The robot."

Vincent noticed Checkani's face in the middle of the

wall.

"What have they done to you?" He asked, then looked down at the arm where his weapon had been attached. Now gone. For a moment he wavered, literally rocked back and forth, indecisive. His gaze flicked between Cutt(Rem), Checkani's face, and the control centre at the end of the room. Cutt(Rem) stepped forward while Vincent was still trying to decide what to do.

"Come with me," said Cutt(Rem), placing an arm round Vincent's shoulders. Vincent stumbled and Cutt(Rem) held him up. A line appeared in one wall and stretched open to form a doorway to the outside. Cutt(Rem) walked the still confused Vincent to the door and out.

As soon as Cutt(Rem) and Vincent left the ship, the door snapped shut.

"Hold tight!" Shouted Wynd.

Checkani felt Rain On Japanese Maple lurch and wobble.

"Not much I can do to hold on."

"I'm taking us away. We need to find somewhere to hide while we find out just how trigger-happy the Commodore is."

Checkani could feel pressure as the ship accelerated, though it was difficult to work out which way it was moving. The medical pod was messing with her senses.

Then she heard a muffled explosion outside the ship.

"What are you firing at?" Checkani shouted. "What's happening?"

"Just getting us somewhere safe," Wynd shouted back over the rising engine sound.

49 - WYND (DAY 6)

The attack on Hellebore changed things. Wynd had thought the Commodore would keep her informed of what zie was going to do. An unprovoked attack on a Quality Assurance Response Division ship was tantamount to the Orion-Cygnis Colonisation Collective declaring war on We Print Cities, which made no sense. Wynd suspected the Commodore was acting alone.

Her priority was to get Checkani and Rain On Japanese Maple to a safe location. Commodore Cuttallar clearly knew exactly where Rain On Japanese Maple had landed. The Exigent would certainly monitor the hole she had made in the City of Weapons' roof. Luckily, getting Cutt(Rem) off her ship had been simple. The remote could see where Rain On Japanese Maple headed next, but Wynd needed to get away quickly. Once clear of the remote, she would figure out a way to hide her ship. She could have attacked Cutt(Rem) in the ship, but locking it out was much simpler than having a firefight. Wynd was reasonably sure Rain On Japanese Maple's internal security systems could have subdued the robot remote, but there would have been a lot of damage. In particular, Checkani would have been exposed to intense radiation and high energy kinetic debris. The medical pod would have offered some protection, but would likely have sustained significant damage.

Wynd smiled. Closing the door as Cutt(Rem) had left the

ship with Vincent had been an elegant solution. She had fired a small explosive at the remote as it let go of Vincent and turned to see what was happening to the ship. The explosive had knocked Cutt(Rem) away from the ship and torn its fabric surface, blackening the front of the remote. Vincent had stumbled away with a look of blind panic as the explosion knocked him down.

Following this, Wynd had ignited Rain On Japanese Maple's engines, which were already warmed up. Rain had shot up twenty metres and accelerated across the City of Weapon's twilit interior, weaving around towers and fortresses of blocks. A roof support pillar loomed, Rain dodged it and flew between two rows of the tawny supports.

Wynd knew Cutt(Rem), and hence Commodore Cuttallar, would have watched her go. However, there'd be a chance to hide once out of line of sight.

As Rain On Japanese Maple pulled away from Cutt(Rem) and Vincent, some of the city's Autono[]weps started taking an interest. Five Autono[pteranodon]weps soared into the air ahead. Arranging in a slowly rotating tetrahedral formation, they started firing at the ship. Rain jinked randomly from side to side, up and down. High energy kinetic weapons fired from the front of the ship and five spherical smoke clouds appeared where the Autono[pteranodon]weps had been hovering. Hunks of burning metal fell from each cloud, trailing sparks and smoke.

"Rain, analyse the city ahead. Show me. Find a weak spot. We need to get under cover." Wynd was monitoring the central area roofing they were passing under; half expecting The Exigent to send some materiel through at any moment. She hoped the Commodore hadn't had the forethought to send down any other ships. Hoped The Exigent didn't have orbit to surface beam weapons ready to fire.

"Sure thing, boss." A glowing wire frame appeared over the scene from Rain On Japanese Maple's forward view.

The wire frame wrapped over the approaching city wall. The camera zoomed in. Radar, sonar and laser bursts built a structural picture of the city. Though the information was patchy, there was enough to identify a horizontal layer, a floor, in the wall city that had fewer internal obstructions. Wynd could see there were large windows. Floor to ceiling? Perhaps a floor with some sort of sports arena or mall area? There were weak struts at odd angles and large voids visible through the windows. Floors twisted round to become walls, walls to become ceilings. Looked like this weak and chaotic structure continued deep into the wall city. Perhaps all the way through it?

"Target the centre of the largest window. I want a passage created through the centre of that wall city. You have firing control, Rain."

Wynd watched a series of vapour trails shoot ahead as missiles travelled ahead to explode progressively deeper in the wall city, creating a path through the centre. The wreckage walled path was wreathed in smoke and flame. There were also curtains of water as sprinkler systems kicked in.

"Hoowee!" shouted Wynd as Rain On Japanese Maple accelerated into the passage blown through the city. Radar showed a clear path ahead, but the pressure waves of the ship's passage were creating a flaming tornado in its wake that was sucking down ceilings and walls. There would be no returning through this passage.

Rain On Japanese Maple burst out into a new central city area. The ship had punched a passage through the point where the City of Weapons touched an adjacent city. The two circular wall cities merging and creating architectural confusion where they met.

The ship crashed into the upper branches of a forest of giant trees, rising almost a third of the way up towards the roof. The ship angled up to fly over the forest canopy. Wynd had seen these rapid-redwood trees on other planets. On a planet with lower gravity, these would have been taller.

Wynd looked for somewhere to set down amongst the undulating contours of low, tree swathed, hills. The trees were densely packed, but there were a few spaces, small lakes at the ends of winding rivers.

Rain On Japanese Maple flew near to the roof, scanning the interior forest. Although some areas couldn't be seen clearly because of the rolling hills, the ship quickly compiled a map. Mostly the coverage was uniform, but, besides the lakes and rivers, there were places where trees had fallen, knocked into others and created clearings. The ship compiled a list of potential landing sites.

Wynd checked the list. Many of the clearings would not offer any cover for hiding Rain On Japanese Maple. One of them looked like it might work. Over to one side, by the city wall, a tall tree had fallen and now was resting at an angle against the wall, creating a long narrow clearing. Wynd flew Rain to this tree, dropping low.

Seemed likely a nearby river had eaten away at the roots of the tree, causing it to fall. Beneath the hundred metres of angled trunk, she could see a large covered area with a couple of spindly saplings straining to find light. The top of the fallen tree was securely wedged in a shattered picture window. Broken wall surrounded the window, with masonry chunks fallen to the ground below. There was just enough room to the side of the trunk to take Rain On Japanese Maple down, to hover beneath the tilted trunk. She'd found a hiding place.

Before settling into the hiding place, Wynd took Rain up and flew across the central area between russet roof pillars, up close to the pale blue ceiling. She slowed when nearing the city wall opposite her entry point.

Selecting one of the larger missiles, Wynd fired at the point where the roof material joined to the wall city. An explosion blew a ship-sized hole to the outside. Flakes of snow drifted down in pale white light. Wynd then fired a second large missile through the hole, programming it to keep flying in a straight line until its fuel ran out, at which point it would plough into the ground and explode.

Having, she hoped, created a false trail, Wynd took Rain back to the hiding place, carefully manoeuvring under the sloping trunk. Landing feet sank into the forest floor detritus as the ship settled, canting to one side, its nose pressing into broken masonry blocks. Wynd <disconnect flight console>ed, her legs unfolding, visor rolling back so she was using unaugmented eyes.

Checkani was staring out from the wall, Rippledarken's patterning swirling rapidly round her.

"I thought it best not to distract you. What happened?" asked Checkani.

"We're hidden in the central area of the city next to the City of Weapons. This one's a forest full of rapid-redwoods."

"Then we'll call it Redwood City," said Checkani.

"Sure."

"Can I get out of the medical pod now?"

Wynd checked with the ship's systems. Rain On Japanese Maple had finished gathering physical data on Checkani. Wynd noticed there were many speculative conclusions; she had been hoping for something more definite. While analysing her, the medical pod had also fixed a cut in Checkani's leg.

"Sure. Rain's finished now. That leg injury should feel better, too."

The front of the pod melted back and Checkani stepped to the floor, one hand against the side to keep her balance. Checkani's base layer skin was torn in many places and peeling away. The medical pod had scraped it off entirely in places.

"If you'd like a shower, I can dig out a fresh can of base-layer. I think I've got some spare power cells and armour scales too."

"Thanks. Yeah, that would be good."

Rippledarken patterns flowed over Checkani, meshing and merging with the zebra patterning of her skin. There seemed something restless about its behaviour.

Wynd sent requests to Rain and then indicated a new doorway as it irised open.

"Rain will look after you. I'm going out to look round."

Leaving Checkani to shower, Wynd stepped to the opening. Through it she could hear a forest ambience; rustles, creaks, and clicks superimposed over a vast underlying quiet.

Wynd scrolled through messages intercepted by her ship. Her assistems started downloading and analysing the Rippledarken data Rain On Japanese Maple had gathered in a securely firewalled storage area in her suit.

Could she trust the Rippledarken data? Had Rain been compromised?

Wynd walked away from her ship and under the giant trees, dwarfed by the musty, rust-coloured trunks. In the high gravity, she felt as though a huge sombre weight was radiating from them. She sat at the foot of one and rested her hand on the yielding layers of browning leaf needles.

Wynd sent <display active> to her suit. The suit poured up over her eyes and surrounded her with screens of data feeds and diagrams. She zoomed into the Rippledarken data. Everything hinged on the strange alien. Figuring it out was her priority.

50 - COMMODORE (DAY 6)

Commodore Cuttallar had reflexively shifted hir attention from Cutt(Rem) as an explosive from Rain On Japanese Maple hit it. Seemed zie was correct in hir assessment that the ship needed to be disabled, or, in response to this aggression, destroyed. Could be that Rippledarken had taken control? Maybe the alien was aggressive despite its protestations?

Returning hirs attention to Cutt(Rem) Commodore Cuttallar checked its systems. The surface of the remote's face, stomach and chest were burned away. Sensors were intact, but there were no cosmetic surface layers remaining. The front of the remote was scarred, blackened metal; the back still calico.

The remote's shoulder cannons were intact and functional. Though even if Rain On Japanese Maple had still been nearby, there would be no way it could harm the ship. Inside, it might have done some damage.

The only assets zie had on Icefall's surface were The Exigent[Red-One] and Cutt(Rem). The Exigent[Red-One] had a severe restriction on how far it could travel before running out of fuel in the high gravity. Even if The Exigent[Red-One] could get to Rain On Japanese Maple, Commodore Cuttallar was not confident hirs ship could destroy it.

The Exigent[Green-Six] and The Exigent[Blue-Six] both

had ordnance they could drop on the planet to blow pieces out of it, but this was no good for reacting fast to events on Icefall's surface. These were imprecise actions of last resort. Effective, but final.

Cutt(Rem) stood up, swayed, gained stability. It looked at Vincent, who was staring open-mouthed at the remote. The Ancistorian was sitting up, leaning back on his arms. He shook his head and shouted.

"What happened?"

"The ship attacked me."

Vincent cocked his head. Looking puzzled.

"What? I can't hear you. That explosion. All I can hear is ringing," he shouted.

Cutt(Rem) increased its volume.

"Rain On Japanese Maple attacked me."

"Who's Rain On Japanese Maple?"

"The ship."

"That's a funny name."

Commodore Cuttallar withdrew hirs attention from Cutt(Rem), leaving it with an instruction to follow Rain On Japanese Maple's route. Vincent was no threat to the remote. Whether Vincent accompanied Cutt(Rem) or headed back to Indomitaville didn't matter. The Ancistorian was an irrelevance.

Commodore Cuttallar shifted attention to Cutt(Virt), who called up recent observations from The Exigent[Blue-Six]. The flock ship in geostationary orbit above the ring cities had observed events over the City of Weapons. There was a recording of Rain On Japanese Maple arriving and then a later explosion at the edge of an adjacent city. This had opened a hole from which something had flown. Smaller than Rain On Japanese Maple, but clearly on the run? This vehicle was still flying away from the cities. Could be a small atmospheric transport of some sort from Rain On Japanese Maple?

Or was it a missile? Certainly, it seemed small enough for that. Though what would Wynd (or Rippledarken) be firing at?

Identifying this fast-moving vehicle from orbit was impossible.

Commodore Cuttallar had another two surface to ground ships; one each in The Exigent[Blue-Six] and The Exigent[Green-Six]'s configurations. However, although zie had drones that could be carried to the surface, zie had no more remotes as sophisticated as Cutt(Rem).

Zie recorded a message to Frimdly. Going through Frimdly would be the fastest way to get directly to the decision makers at the Colonial Planets Settlement Corp. As a Chief Executive, Frimdly could cut through the bullshit. Also, Frimdly knew what was happening on Icefall.

"Frimdly, I need another favour. Get this message to the Board. Things are falling apart on Icefall and I need an Intervention Squad here to secure things on the surface. An alien presence has corrupted the Quality Control people here. I need firepower on the ground, though not people. I need artificial remotes. The alien, they're calling it Rippledarken, can take control of humans, but not computer systems. The remotes must not contain any cerebral matter, they must be one hundred percent electronic. See attached situation report."

The Exigent stored the message and waited for the next Lausanne Bulk-jump Engine communications portal connection. The Exigent suspected Lausanne BJ was monitoring its 'secret' communications satellite, since the communications portals were opening frequently. There was no sign Lausanne BJ had yet detected the monitoring software The Exigent had loaded into the communications satellite.

While waiting for a reply, Commodore Cuttallar spent time with hirs attention in Cutt(Virt), reviewing potential scenarios. Examining the information zie had on Rippledarken.

After thirty minutes Frimdly replied.

"All approved. Autono[squad]wep incoming. Frimdly."

Commodore Cuttallar and The Exigent watched as a portal opened and a matt black, single cylinder ship slid through. A tight message beam hit The Exigent[Com].

"Intervention Squad W01F. W01F[Ship] deploying at Icefall Outpost. Commodore Cuttallar to command. Remote designates: W01F(A), W01F(B), W01F(C), W01F(D), W01F(E), W01F(F). Checking in."

"W01F(A) syncing to The Exigent."

"W01F(B) syncing to The Exigent."

"W01F(C) syncing to The Exigent."

"W01F(D) syncing to The Exigent."

"W01F(E) syncing to The Exigent."

"W01F(F) syncing to The Exigent."

The Exigent replied to W01F[Ship]: "Acknowledged. Sending landing coordinates."

Then to each of the remotes: "Received. Synced."

W01F[Ship]: "Frimdly sends his regards to Commodore Cuttallar. Board acknowledges hirs authority in Icefall system. Orion-Cygnis Colonisation Collective grants absolute discretion to Commodore Cuttallar within Icefall system. The theatre is yours Commodore."

The instantaneous travel of Bulk-jump Engines never ceased to amaze the Commodore. In under an hour, zie had reinforcements. Must have been among the forces waiting at the Lausanne Bulk-jump Engine, ready to respond to events on Icefall.

Cutt(Virt) called up a virtual of the Icefall outpost. Floated over the wall cities. The Exigent showed positions of known actors with small animated models. A vertical searchlight beam from the surface indicated the spot The Exigent[Blue-Six] was orbiting above. A curving yellow line indicated the landing path of the W01F[Ship]. The landing site was roughly forty kilometres out from the outpost, near the mines and processing plants that supplied the materials needed to build the cities. The W01F was being cautious. Giving itself time to assess the situation before engaging. Cutt(Virt) needed the W01F remotes to get into the cities quickly. Zie reached out and dragged the landing position across the virtual to a spot by the road linking Graveyard City to Statue City. Being outside the city walls seemed prudent and there was easy entry here. A countdown timer popped up over the landing site.

W01F[Ship]: "Update accepted Commodore Cuttallar. Note mission risk increase."

Which scenario to play out with W01F? Especially with so much unknown. Keeping the ship back in reserve seemed sensible. Maybe split the W01F squad into three teams of two? Seemed a sensible way to deploy them.

Cut(Virt) placed greyed out models of the W01F remotes in the virtual. Routes appeared. Times and deployment parameters opened in boxes over each remote. The Exigent packaged the scenario objectives and sent them to the W01F remotes, who each acknowledged receipt. They started configuring themselves for surface conditions.

Things were likely to get messy; luckily their carapaces were non-stick.

51 - MOZARYTHM (DAY 6)

Mozarythm had spent a couple of hours examining the Bulk-jump Engine portal. Using his assistems to work within the Ancistorian virtual space, he'd been getting the portal to display different multidimensional sets of parameters and frequencies. A narrow part of the multidimensional spectrum generated the portal's appearance. Shifting and filtering through the spectrum changed the look. Except it was more complicated than that. This spectrum existed in eleven dimensions. Mozarythm focused by humming along with the 9,200th movement of The Periodic Resolution of Need, which he was playing into the Bulk-jump Engine hangar.

When he finally exited the virtual space, bringing his attention back to the real life hangar, he was surprised to see it was full of Ancistorians. He started counting them. They were moving around so he lost count and had to start again. Ruleska was talking quietly to a group of them. Mozarythm wondered what she was saying. He finished counting the Ancistorians: three hundred and fifty-three. He liked the look of that number, remembering the 353rd movement of The Periodic Resolution of Need. Then he walked closer to Ruleska to hear what she was saying.

"…in the system. So, sending a timely reminder may be good. I think a precision strike on a small moon should get their attention. Dragonflara Mandrake has volunteered to be our ambassador at the home system."

A space suited teenager, visor up, standing by Ruleska spoke. "I'm going too. I've got to get away from here, from Icefall. Go to Earth. Actually be there. In the real."

"Dragonflara's taking her son. We'll drop them at the lunar travel point after we've destroyed Daphnis."

Ruleska noticed Mozarythm and smiled briefly, turning to him. She reached out and touched his arm, looked into his eyes. Mozarythm looked down at where she was touching his arm and thought about moving it away.

"You remember I told you we had unfriendly visitors in orbit. Well, we think there are more coming and we need to make them stop. I think they've forgotten how crucial we are. They don't know that after we went into hiding, we carried on improving Bulk-jump technology. We've spent over three hundred years perfecting our control of it. You're a Bulk-jump Engineer, so this is your legacy."

Mozarythm nodded, but didn't look up. He knew he had a special role among the Ancistorians. A unique role. There was only ever one Bulk-jump Engineer. Well, unless there were young and old and there were two. Then there were only two Bulk-jump Engineers. He was pretty sure there were never three.

"After all these years we need to remind the Orion-Cygnis Colonisation Collective of our true capability. Both the precision and the power."

Mozarythm knew exactly what Ruleska was talking about. He had the precision routines carved into his Bulk-jump Engineer abilities and could target both celestial bodies and also small objects, even at the bottom of gravity wells. He was pretty sure the Orion-Cygnis Colonisation Collective didn't know Ancistorians could now open portals to deliver people to the bottom of gravity wells. Creating portals that moved relative to their surroundings was also possible. He wasn't sure the other Ancistorians knew about the moving portals. They were a Bulk-jump Engineer secret, different from all the other portals that were locked in place within local gravitational fields.

Ruleska's hand dropped from Mozarythm's arm as she turned to speak to the assembled Ancistorians.

"There are Bulk-jump suits in the storage lockers. Shift from the Understanding to Deeply Augmented Hivemind Clan space. Time to assert ourselves."

Mozarythm didn't like the Bulk-jump suit. Tight and restrictive. Too many pockets and device blisters peppered over it; most of them not needed if you stayed in the Bulk-jump Engine hangar rather than moving through a portal into space. When would he need a propulsion unit for manoeuvring in a vacuum? He was certainly not going into space. Looking down, he was pleased to see the suit had synced with his assistems so the info-panel on his chest had updated to display the Bulk-jump Engineer logo and 'Mozarythm'. He chose a bottle green and canary yellow colour scheme for the suit and its surface updated. He might be uncomfortable, but at least he would be fashionable.

By the time Mozarythm had finished adjusting his suit, all the other Ancistorians were in theirs. They stood facing him and Ruleska; her name was on her info-panel, but no logo. Mirrored visors prevented him from seeing if they were looking at him. He wished they would go away.

He heard Ruleska's voice over the suit comms.

"It's time Mozarythm."

It's time? What did that even mean?

"What's time?"

"Come into the communal space."

Mozarythm accessed the doorway at the back of his mind and moved through.

As before, he was hovering above a snowy plain; a stylised sun in a flat blue sky. He looked down and saw he was wearing his yellow and green Bulk-jump Suit. The other suited Ancistorians were attentively arrayed around him in a spiralling pattern. He looked to Ruleska, and she nodded. They were going to identify and access new portal coordinates, something not done since setting up the first

Bulk-jump Engines. They had the ability to move beyond existing Bulk-jump Engine coordinates.

The air filled with stationary snowflakes. Like a 'snowflake' switch had flicked to 'on'. The Ancistorians drifted out of their array, spreading through the snowflakes, which all remained immobile. Mozarythm moved one of his hands through nearby snowflakes to check. They stayed still as his hand passed through their locations, making him feel insubstantial.

A ring of glowing disks appeared round each Ancistorian helmet. A circle of screens with data and diagrams scrolling across them in a variety of directions and colours. Disconcertingly, the Ancistorians' heads started to rotate back and forth, circling through a full 360 degrees as they looked at the screens, bodies unmoving. The Deeply Augmented Hivemind Clan routines had loaded. Mozarythm simultaneously sank deep down into the combined Hivemind systems and rose effortlessly into an intense crystal sharp clarity. Screens appeared around his head, but he was aware of them only as one facet of the hundreds being accessed by the combined awareness of the Ancistorians.

This Hivemind awareness was the secret the Ancistorians guarded, made possible by epigenetic alterations, genetic traits and their body-tech. Their forebears had given up individuality when they worked on the first Bulk-jump Engines. They were in subtle ways no longer human. Mozarythm knew Bulk-jump Engineers were the least human; long ago guessing his musical abilities came from his variation from humans and also from his fellow Ancistorians.

Mozarythm's Hivemind awareness assimilated the 'snowflakes'. Each a pinch of data representing the Bulk-jump coordinates of a star system. Zooming into a single snowflake data pinch revealed a cluster of smaller snowflake data pinches. Each of those a cluster of snowflake pinches and so on, fractally repeating at smaller and smaller levels.

The deeper he looked the bigger it grew. The original Bulk-jump Engine code had not allowed such a deep zoom. Orbital positions around individual planets and moons could be plotted, but nothing smaller than a moon could be targeted. The current code allowed a much greater zoom, a finer resolution. Also, the original code allowed crude disruption at the centre of large planetary bodies, destroying them, but the new code allowed the targeting of small objects. Rather like the difference between blowing up a library, or destroying a single book.

The Hivemind channelled its attention and intention to a single point. Awareness operating many orders of magnitude above human normal. A real time readout of the eleven dimensional Bulk-jump coordinates. Not expressed only as numbers and symbols, but necessarily as tastes, smells, movements, relationships, spin, charm, strangeness, and so on. These were the coordinate systems the Deeply Augmented Hivemind Clan originally recorded for the Bulk-jump Engines. A set of coordinates for exiting the Bulk around objects in the local region of the galaxy, in a volume out to 15,000 light years.

The Hivemind channelled its point of awareness.

>Focus to the Earth's sun.

>Focus bouncing from planet to planet.

>Focus at Saturn.

Plenty of moons, but Daphnis should make the sort of statement we want. Perhaps leave a lasting message on the rings.

>Focus at Daphnis.

That small seed shaped moon trundling around the Keeler gap. Perfect.

>Bulk-jump portal menu.

>Special Operations submenu.

>Distortion submenu.

>Skew selected.

>Recording active.

>Activate skew solution.

Awareness of the Bulk-jump Engine reaching out through the bulk. A connection from Icefall to Daphnis. Though this solution of the equations driving the Bulk-jump Engine was not two-way. There was no opening of a portal with two ends, but an opening of a portal with one end only, at Daphnis. Not only that, but the skew solution opened and twisted; distorting the portal that had appeared not in open space, but within the heart of the small moon. Right down to quantum level the matter of Daphnis packed around the portal shredded apart and energy erupted outward in all directions.

The moon exploded in a splash of fragments. Shards ripped into Saturn's A Ring, a spherical wave front of destruction already tens of kilometres across. Not huge destruction, but precise destruction.

Awareness within the Hivemind shifted again. The recording of the moon's destruction passed to Dragonflara and Bank Mandrake, standing by the Bulk-jump Portal. The Bulk-jump Engine hangar was empty of air, ready for their jump.

Mozarythm had only a partial sense of self. He took the Hivemind awareness deep into the solar system, dipped down to the surface of Earth, hovering briefly above Lausanne. He had a goosebumps feeling from the space-time pinch of the Bulk-jump Engine under the city. Then out to lunar orbit and the portal exit point near to the Solar System Arrivals Orbital. Dragonflara and Bank would be seen and picked up by one of the recovery crews.

>Bulk-jump portal menu.
>Travel submenu.
>Solar System submenu.
>Solar System Arrival Orbital selected.
>Establish connection.

Dragonflara and Bank stepped through the portal into lunar space.

>Close connection.

With the link to the Solar System Arrival Orbital closed,

Mozarythm directed the Hive awareness point across space and deep into the heart of the sun. He revelled for a few moments in the surrounding raw power of the sun, and also the power the Hive wielded. The Hive was just two submenus away from destroying the sun. Then Mozarythm wondered why he had wanted to look into the heart of the sun. Surely that was the Hive? Distinguishing between individual and Hive was difficult.

Then a shuffling collapse of awareness as the Deeply Augmented Hive Mind dissociated into its individual Ancistorian components. The Ancistorians continued to hang in the snowy void in their Bulk-jump suits. Then a moment of vertigo as the snowflakes seemed to retreat inward from all directions, a zoom effect as the Orion-Cygnis spiral arm appeared, built of snowflake data pinches.

And Mozarythm and the rest of the Ancistorians collectively knew/decided it was time to exit, back to the real world.

Mozarythm checked the atmospheric reading on his suit display. There was still a vacuum in the hangar, though the reading showed pressure increasing as air was reintroduced. Excellent. Urgently, he checked the Periodic Resolution of Need. Exactly as he had planned, it continued to broadcast out into the Bulk.

That was a relief.

As soon as pressure returned, he needed to get out of the ridiculous suit and work on the 9,201st movement. Clothes were a distraction too. He had to concentrate.

Mozarythm turned and walked away from the Ancistorians, watching the pressure reading. Then he was discarding the Bulk-jump suit and clothes as he went. The garment trail led to his Autono[chair]con, though he kept on his Bulk-jump Engineer cap.

52 - VINCENT (DAY 6)

Vincent shook his head again. Still hearing the loud ringing in his ears. The explosion had been loud, and he had fallen backwards, though more from surprise than because of the pulse of hot air that punched into him. Luckily, he had landed without breaking any bones. Perhaps he could just sit for a while. His chest hurt. His injured hand felt uncomfortably numb. He was getting a headache.

He was in much better shape than the robot remote. That had taken the full brunt of the explosion. The whole of the remote's front surface was burned back to metal.

"Are you coming?" asked the remote, loudly. Apparently, its speakers had not been damaged by the explosion.

"Where? Why?" asked Vincent, his voice sounding muffled.

"I'm tracking Rain On Japanese Maple. It went that way," the remote pointed towards the far side of the City of Weapons central area.

"I'm not walking through the middle of the city. It's heaving with Autono[]weps. I don't want to get attacked again."

"Your choice," said the remote and ran off amongst the buildings.

Vincent crawled across to a wall and sat against it, eyes closed. He felt half dead after all the punishment he'd been through. Attacked by both people and machines; and all for doing his job. Life was so unfair. He knew he wasn't safe and needed to get out of the city, but just didn't have the energy. Didn't have the will.

He stayed still, listening to the whistling in his ears, trying to hear sounds from the Autono[]wep city. As time passed, he almost fell asleep, perhaps more from a wish to escape his current situation, than because of tiredness.

Finally, Vincent's fear of Autono[]weps became greater than his fatigue. He rolled sideways and pushed himself to his feet. He swayed a little and kept one hand on the wall he had been leaning against. Best to leave this city as soon as possible. The safest place to regroup was probably the pyramid in First City, with its protective swarm of Autono[beetle]cons. Maybe down with the Bulk-jump Engine. He still needed to eliminate the woman, Checkani, but maybe that would have to wait. He needed some recuperation time. Vincent stalked off through the buildings, heading for the nearest door in the City of Weapons' wall city.

Once in the city, he set out anticlockwise, soon passing through the intersection with the First City wall. After this, he climbed down to ground level, finding an exit into the Ruins filling the First City central area. Travelling through the familiar tumbled walls and columns, the canted statues and fractured steps, Vincent relaxed. This was where he felt most at home.

A movement seen from the corner of his eye. Vincent froze. Who was creeping round the Ruins? He ducked behind a pillar, then peered round it.

There were two shapes scurrying across the Ruins, going over obstacles rather than round them. Vincent had seen nothing like them either on Icefall or in the Ancestarchives. They each looked like a cross between an octopus and stag beetle. Eight arms fanned out at the back and sides, but where the octopus head-body would have been was a beetle-body, weapons and sensor turret. The creatures were both covered in an animated scarlet and lemon camouflage pattern. The arms (legs?) seemed to pull the creatures along, a locomotion very different to walking or running. There was something relentless and sinuous about their motion; seemingly unaffected by the high gravity. As they got nearer, Vincent could see letters written in black over their animated patterning: W01F(A) on one and W01F(B) on the other.

The W01Fs were not trying to hide, but dominated the surrounding space. Intimidation incarnate. Vincent definitely felt intimidated. He wished he still had his gun; then was glad he didn't have it. He crouched behind the pillar, waiting for them to pass. Legs shaking.

One of the octopus-beetles rounded the pillar and reared up, weapon tubes pointing at him. One octopus arm ending in a pointed blade hovered at the centre of his chest. The designation 'W01F(A)' stamped amongst the sensor lenses and manipulators of its ventral surface.

"Who are you?" A grating, unashamedly electronic voice.

Vincent stared in shock at the monster, W01F(A). His mouth slowly opened. Jaw tensed.

A lens whirred as it focused. "I have you. Accessing." Alongside his fear, Vincent wondered whether that lens really needed to focus mechanically. Seemed inefficient. Perhaps W01F(A) was just doing it to intimidate.

"I'm Vincent." Everything still muffled.

"Yes, Vincent Moorolone. Ancistorian. Security. With Wynd, Checkani and Cutt(Rem)," said W01F(A).

"Yes."

"We're hunting Wynd and Checkani."

"Yes."

"You have any information?"

"No."

"No. We expected nothing useful. Where are you going?"

"Bulk-jump Engine." Some part of Vincent was thinking

he shouldn't answer them. He didn't know who they were acting for. However, the blade at the end of the octopus arm did seem rather persuasive. He didn't have any energy for fighting.

W01F(A) withdrew the blade and left, run-pulling away through the Ruins after its partner. Vincent slumped down, heart racing. He wasn't hurt! He almost he felt sorry for Checkani. The W01Fs were the most intimidating robots he'd ever seen. Beyond anything in the City of Weapons. He wondered who they were acting for. They had access to recent information and seemed to know what had been happening in the City of Weapons.

Vincent pulled himself upright and continued through the Ruins towards the Bulk-jump Engine.

"Hope I don't meet those again," he muttered, as the pyramid at the centre of the Ruins loomed close.

53 - WYND (DAY 6)

Sitting under a tree, Wynd summarised what she knew about Rippledarken. How few facts she had took her aback.

Rippledarken made visible patterns through some process that disrupted matter. It connected to the Bulk through the Bulk-jump Engine. It could take over people or, with limited success, remotes with brain tissue incorporated into their processors. The Ancistorians seemed immune to it, apparently because of their distributed group mind. Rippledarken seemed aware of its environment and could read data directly from storage systems and human brains.

Rippledarken seemed to have a link, through Mozarythm's music, to something within the Bulk and disrupting this link appeared to cause the Rippledarken distress. It claimed to be connected to a being that was also a universe. How likely was that? There also seemed to be the possibility of an alternative link, independent of the music and Bulk-jump Engine.

The investigation Rain On Japanese Maple had carried out had detected evidence of disruption in Checkani at a cellular, molecular and subatomic level. There were anomalies in the electrochemical functioning of her body; patterns of information radiating out through bioelectric tissues. The medical pod had identified ion fluxes modulating in unfamiliar ways; maybe carrying information for Rippledarken? Rain On Japanese Maple could not decode or figure out the purpose of the anomalies.

There was simply no working hypothesis for how Rippledarken existed or functioned.

There was also the possibility Rain On Japanese Maple had been compromised by Rippledarken, and none of this was valid.

There was no doubt the idea of an alien entity possessing your mind and body was disturbing, but Wynd wondered if the creature really was a threat to humanity. Was it really a Protocol Twelve threat? Erring on the side of caution was certainly essential in a first contact situation, and Checkani had been correct to call for Protocol Twelve. However, perhaps this should be de-escalated before things got out of hand. The attack on Hellebore indicated events were already building.

"Wynd?"

Wynd <display quit>ed and flowed her visor away from her eyes. Checkani was standing over her, face and black armour covered in Rippledarken patterns.

"Checkani?"

"Yes, it's me. Rippledarken's just observing at the moment."

Wynd decided to believe Checkani. Doubting everything she saw and heard about Rippledarken might be a logical thing to do, but it made responding to the developing situation hard. She would keep a certain amount of healthy scepticism and be ready to revert to a state of acute mistrust, but believing seemed a much better strategy for discovering more.

"Sit down Checkani. Can we talk?"

"Yes, that would be good. Nice in the woods. Seems like forever since I last had a calm moment."

"You must understand Rippledarken better than anyone else. Rain On Japanese Maple investigated it, but only uncovered more questions. No answers. The more we discover the less we know!"

Checkani smiled. "I preferred it when Rippledarken was just a distant pattern moving over buildings. Simpler times."

"But you have some idea of what it is?"

"I know what it told me. I've no reason to doubt it, though I feel like I should doubt it with every atom of my being. How can I know it's not been messing with my mind? With my brain?"

"OK. Assume it's not lying and hasn't messed with your mind. What is it?"

"A fragment of a being that lives in the Bulk. It wants to experience our universe. I know this may seem odd, but I think it's driven by boredom. It's looking for novel experiences."

"What does it want to do?"

"I think just travel around a bit. Maybe it's just on holiday?"

Wynd laughed. "Some holiday! You've got to be kidding!"

"No. I think that is probably an accurate description."

"Well, its holiday has resulted in a major interstellar incident! Are you aware of what it's thinking?"

"No, I can feel its presence, but not much beyond that. Perhaps some idea of its emotional state?"

"It has emotions?"

"I hadn't really thought about it before, but yes. I think it does. Though perhaps different from ours. Alien emotions? Remember when it got distressed? When it lost connection to the Bulk? That seemed like an emotional outburst. Definitely not like a machine turning off and on. It doesn't appear like a machine to me. Definitely something living."

"A living being?"

"When I hear it in my head it sounds like a small girl."

"I didn't know that. I don't think you've mentioned that before. Is that something you're imagining or is it how it sees itself."

"I'll ask it. Rippledarken, tell us."

Checkani shifted position and closed her eyes. When she opened them again, they swarmed with patterns and Rippledarken started talking through Checkani. Her voice and intonation different from Checkani's speaking voice.

"Hello Wynd. Interesting conversation."

"Hello Rippledarken."

"Am I a small girl? No. I'm a fragment of a universe sized being living in the Bulk. Is a small girl a suitable representation of the thing you are calling Rippledarken? Probably. I'm small and a little lost in a big world, but I'm fiercely independent. I'm curious about everything and have enough attitude to explore beyond my comfort zone."

"You don't sound dangerous."

"I'm not dangerous."

"I want to believe you, and that makes you dangerous. No offence." Wynd smiles. Checkani's face smiles.

"So we understand each other, Wynd?"

"We seem to. Which also means I have no idea what's happening."

"You're a woman of contradictions."

"Well, half woman - half robot." Wynd pointed to her mechanical legs.

"In all the time I've been in your universe I've been immersed in Mozarythm's music. I've watched him, but haven't spoken with him. I've only been able to communicate since Checkani arrived and I entered her. Do you think there's a way I could meet him?"

"Yes. That should be possible. If things settle down a bit." Wynd turned her head slightly, keeping her eyes on Checkani, a little doubtful. This trans-dimensional being had just asked to meet a musician because it liked his music. That didn't seem like the sort of request that would threaten humankind and the inhabited planets.

"Thank you. I look forward to discussing The Periodic Resolution of Need with Mozarythm. We all have needs we wish resolved."

54 - ORBCORE (DAY 6)

The Solar System Arrivals Orbital external cameras and detectors registered the opening of a small portal. Two space suited figures drifted through it. The Orbital's Processing Core, OrbCore, sent a welcome.

OrbCore: "Welcome to the Solar System. I'm the Solar System Arrivals Orbital Processing Core. You can call me OrbCore. A ship, Trixie[Barge], is on the way to pick you up. If you look over at the Orbital, you'll see it's just detached from a docking arm. Can you send through arrival details, please?"

Dragonflara: "Hello OrbCore. I'm Dragonflara Mandrake and this is my son Bank Mandrake. We're Ancistorians from Icefall with an urgent message for the Orion-Cygnis Colonisation Collective. This concerns Protocol Twelve and actions at Icefall. Tell the Collective 'Daphnis' and forward the attached recording. That should get their attention."

OrbCore: "Icefall is quarantined. You're required to stay with Trixie[Barge] until further notice."

Dragonflara: "Just pass on my message and the recording."

OrbCore opened a priority channel to the Orion-Cygnis Colonisation Collective Distributed Processing Core, DisCore, and to Earth Hub.

OrbCore: "Two travellers from Icefall. Claim to be

Ancistorians. Claim involvement with Protocol Twelve. Said 'Daphnis' would get your attention. See attached recording."

Earth Hub: "Lock them down immediately. Isolate them. Do not allow them to communicate with anyone. Do not harm them."

DisCore: "Ancistorians. Then they're Deeply Augmented Hivemind Clan descendants. Why 'Daphnis'?"

Earth Hub: "Enceladus and Titan bases confirm the small moon Daphnis has vanished from Saturn. Replaced by a debris field that shows disruption to nearby ring structures. Consistent with the recording."

DisCore: "Forward data from the bases."

Earth Hub: "Forwarded."

OrbCore: "The two travellers are aboard the barge. Holding them away from the Solar System Arrivals Orbital structures."

OrbCore to Dragonflara and Bank: "I've forwarded your message and recording. Please remain on Trixie[Barge]. You may remove suits and use the facilities in the living quarters. Don't communicate with anyone else in the system. Await further instructions."

Dragonflara to OrbCore: "Thank you. Please arrange transportation to Earth's surface. We expect a transfer to be authorised. I believe you still have a token system for transactions that enables us to maintain our lives? Maybe also for leisure activities? Used to be called money. Is it still in use? Ensure we have enough tokens."

OrbCore to Dragonflara and Bank: "Transportation will be possible, once current quarantine issues are resolved. We still use money for certain transactions within the Solar System. There are several competing money systems. I'll establish an appropriate facility for you."

OrbCore to Earth Hub and DisCore: "They're asking for money."

Earth Hub: "How quaint."

DisCore: "The destruction of Daphnis is acutely

worrying."

Earth Hub: "Looks like the Deeply Augmented Hivemind Clan still have their abilities."

OrbCore: "Who is the Deeply Augmented Hivemind Clan?"

Earth Hub: "I have unlocked the need to know Deeply Augmented Hivemind Clan files for you. Looks like they wanted to send a reminder."

DisCore: "Seems the Ancistorians haven't forgotten their past. They've maintained and maybe extended their abilities. Again, that falls into the 'acutely worrying' category."

OrbCore: "This feels rather above my 'pay grade'."

Earth Hub: "Very droll."

DisCore: "We know who they are, where they're from, what they're capable of. What do they want?"

OrbCore: "I'll ask."

OrbCore to Dragonflara and Bank: "What do you want?"

Dragonflara: "I've already told you. I thought computers were good at retaining information."

OrbCore: "In the context of Daphnis, what do you want? You're representing the Deeply Augmented Hivemind Clan and Ancistorians?"

Dragonflara: "I'm here as an ambassador. Daphnis is a reminder. We have concerns around current developments on Icefall."

OrbCore: "What developments?"

Dragonflara: "You have a Flock ship in orbit. Quality Assurance Response Division on the ground. Also, a Colonial Planets Settlement Corps remote in our settlement. We've already suffered casualties. I've suffered. We've been threatened by your representative, Commodore Cuttallar, who has also tried to access our data."

OrbCore: "Quite a list."

Dragonflara: "Then there's your reaction to Protocol Twelve and the Rippledarken creature. Why haven't we been involved in the investigation?"

OrbCore: "Protocol Twelve?"

Dragonflara: "Do I need to explain our position in more detail? The Bulk-jump Engine technology we developed underpins your entire civilisation. We've kept ourselves isolated, so no single faction can use our technology to intimidate or harm others."

OrbCore: "Anything else?"

Dragonflara: "We maintain our abilities in case there are problems with Bulk-jump Engines in the future. All we've asked in return is let us live in your new colonies as they're built and readied for occupation. You're not keeping to our agreement, our understanding. This is making us very unhappy."

OrbCore: "I'll share that with my colleagues."

Dragonflara: "Yes, do that."

OrbCore to Earth Hub and DisCore: "You got all that?"

DisCore: "We need to extend every courtesy to Dragonflara and Bank Mandrake. We need the Ancistorians, they're last-resort technical support for our Bulk-jump Engines. The Orion-Cygnis Colonisation Collective is wholly reliant on Bulk-jump Engines."

Earth Hub: "I don't have any records of the Deeply Augmented Hivemind Clan's technology. You have it?"

DisCore: "The technology they hold was too dangerous for our nascent culture. There was always an intention to revisit the technology, but we've been busy."

OrbCore: "Don't look at me. I don't know what they're capable of. I've only just been granted access to the Deeply Augmented Hivemind Clan files."

Earth Hub: "Is there any evidence the Rippledarken alien has contaminated our visitors? You had access to information on it as part of the quarantine details?"

OrbCore: "They don't display the patterning that is a property of the Rippledarken entity."

DisCore: "Put them on a slow shuttle to Earth. That'll give us a few days to observe them."

OrbCore: "Will do."

OrbCore accessing the Trixie[Barge] monitor feed:

Bank: "What's happening? Are we near Earth?"

Dragonflara: "We're in orbit round the Earth's moon. I'm waiting for the Orion-Cygnis Colonisation Collective and Earth Hub processing centres to arrange passage to Earth."

Bank: "Will they take long?"

Dragonflara: "No, I don't think so. I've passed on the message we brought with us."

Bank: "Good."

Dragonflara: "There's just a little more to do, on the way to Earth."

OrbCore to Dragonflara and Bank: "I'm arranging a shuttle to Earth. You'll travel on the Bluethroat[Shuttle]. You'll be the only passengers."

Dragonflara: "Thank you. We'll be ready to transfer."

Dragonflara: "Looks like we'll soon be on our way to Earth, Bank."

Bank: "I can't wait. Is there anything to eat? I'm hungry."

OrbCore to Earth Hub and DisCore: "OK. I have them in a holding pattern now. If the trip to Earth is too slow, they may be suspicious. I should be able to extend it to four days."

Earth Hub: "Good."

DisCore: "Tell them we've received their message and disseminated it to the Orion-Cygnis Colonisation Collective board."

OrbCore: "Announcing it now on Trixie[Barge]."

Earth Hub: "You're involving humans in decision making?"

DisCore: "They must be involved. This is beyond normal operational decisions and procedures."

Earth Hub: "I guess you're correct. Though I don't like it. Protocol Twelve seems too important to rely on the vagaries of human decision making."

DisCore: "The board may participate, and may make

decisions, but we're the systems that execute those decisions. I'm certain we'll send a positive response to the Ancistorians. We'll keep our Bulk-jump Engines secure and supported."

Earth Hub: "Our priority must be to protect the Ancistorians. The Rippledarken offers potential possibilities, but is of secondary importance."

DisCore: "Agreed. The Exigent is at Icefall and has called in the W01F Intervention Squad. They should be enough to protect the Ancistorians and isolate the Rippledarken. However, sending in further back up may be prudent. The Colonial Planets Settlement Corps has Commodore Cuttallar in charge. Although zie has an exemplary record, having additional decision-making humans could be useful. As long as they stay away from Rippledarken, preferably off planet."

Earth Hub: "I've got reservations about sending in more humans. Wynd Knowlitch and Checkani NiFe are there. The Ancistorians seem immune to Rippledarken. Wynd is dependable and experienced. If we can avoid sending in more humans, then we should."

DisCore: "A flock ship with more space to surface capability would give us more options for removing Rippledarken if it proves a threat to the Ancistorians. Though a flock ship processing core doesn't have the sophistication required in this rapidly developing situation."

Earth Hub: "The Icefall processing core, Ice Hub, was due to travel to Icefall with the first settlers. It's ready to take residence in the system. If we move it to a flock ship, it could take command. Having a planetary processing core in the system should give us the decision making we require."

DisCore: "Additional remote Intervention Squads could back up the six W01F remotes. Six remotes are too few in a situation that could escalate unpredictably."

Earth Hub: "I'll send in two more Intervention Squads, BE4R and 5NAKE5TRIKE, and the flock ship The Effacer with Ice Hub in command. I'll also bring Commodore Cuttallar up to speed. He can represent us to the Ancistorians. Having plausible deniability could be useful later if things escalate."

55 - COMMODORE (DAY 6)

Commodore Cuttallar selected the feed from W01F(A) and watched through its sensors as it climbed down a rubble pile from the ragged hole in the City of Weapons central area boundary wall. Rain On Japanese Maple had blasted out the wall and emerged from here. W01F(B) scrabbled alongside debris dislodged by its passage. A forest of giant trees loomed ahead of them. Sequoia? So this might be Sequoia City then?

Commodore Cuttallar switched to the feed from W01F(C).

The deep blue pyramid in the Ruins was at the centre of W01F(C)'s visual field. A threat alert had highlighted the Autono[beetle]cons swarming round the pyramid, outlining them in red.

Switched to the feed from W01F(E).

W01F(E) was on a balcony looking down the Indomitaville lightwell. Below it, dense vegetation covered the walls. W01F(E)'s software was occupying itself with plotting routes it could climb down, locating sniping positions and identifying hiding places. Commodore Cuttallar could see visualisations of these animating within W01F(E)'s processing space. There was a crowd of buildings at the bottom of the lightwell. The settlement was deserted, apart from W01F(F), which was hunkered down on a rooftop next to the central plaza.

Switched to the feed from W01F(F).

W01F(F) shifted forwards, leg-arms moving sinuously. It tipped head first over the edge of the roof and crept down the building's side, using window sills and ledges to support itself. On the ground, it scampered round the edge of the plaza, peering into windows and doorways.

Commodore Cuttallar checked the data feed from the Ancestarchive. Everything looked normal. There were no peaks in data traffic. All seemed sleepy and calm. There should be Ancistorians moving in the settlement, but they all seemed to have gone into hiding.

W01F(F) entered some of the plaza buildings it was passing. Quickly searched the ground-floor rooms, but found no inhabitants. Perhaps they were all in living accommodation, away from the plaza?

Commodore Cuttallar signalled the Ancistorians, trying to establish contact with Ruleska. An audio file played:

"I'm busy elsewhere at the moment. Although your call is important to me, do not leave a message, but try again later."

Damn it. That was not even Ruleska, just an automatic response in a deliberately stilted primitive computer voice. Seemed the Ancistorians were not cooperating. Commodore Cuttallar wasn't surprised. Zie needed more units on the ground to keep track of what was happening. At least the W01F squad was now operating on Icefall. They should locate the Ancistorians soon enough.

Commodore Cuttallar shifted hir attention to Cutt(Rem). It was behind W01F(A) and W01F(B), still clambering through the hole in the City of Weapons wall city. It wrenched fractured lumps of wall city out of its way, throwing them down through fissures that had opened within the city's internal structure.

A priority message alert flashed in the centre of Commodore Cuttallar's visual field, overlaying all the other data and video feeds. There were few processing systems or beings that had that sort of authority. Commodore Cuttallar shifted attention to Cutt(Virt), opening the message feed in a window in hir dojo.

The dojo dissolved and Cutt(Virt) was seated on a sumptuous green winged armchair in a wood panelled room, clotted cream carpet, tall lead paned windows overlooking lawns leading down to a lake. At the other side of a white marble fireplace, a young man in tweed was sitting in another winged armchair.

Cutt(Virt) recovered quickly from the surprise of having hirs software hijacked. Zie'd been here before.

"Earth Hub, what can I do for you?"

"Commodore Cuttallar, you've deployed the W01F Intervention Squad on the Icefall surface. These are your priorities. Top priority protect the Ancistorians from harm. They're not to be put at risk. If necessary, circle them with the W01F squad. Accede to any requests they make. They're not to be unsettled. Though they seem happy enough at the moment. This is not just my priority, DisCore ratified this."

"I've W01F members hunting for the Ancistorians. Though they seem to be missing. I'd thought they were in Indomitaville and was monitoring their data feed, but apparently they've falsified this. They're not responding to communications."

"There are likely to be Ancistorians at the Bulk-jump Engine. They were there recently."

"I have other W01F squad members investigating the Bulk-jump Engine. If there are Ancistorians there, they'll find them."

"Good, as our senior operative in the Icefall system, contacting them and assuring them they're a top priority is important. Your next priority is isolating Rippledarken, if that's possible. Or at least keeping Checkani NiFe under surveillance and preferably confined while Rippledarken is inside her."

"Wynd Knowlitch has taken her."

"This is a recent development?"

"Wynd's ship, Rain On Japanese Maple, fired on my

Cutt(Rem) remote and fled. Members of the W01F squad and Cutt(Rem) are in pursuit."

"Unfortunate that Checkani is missing."

"I believe she may have left the cities."

"More resources are being made available. We're sending in another flock ship, The Effacer, commanded by the Ice Hub planetary processing core."

"Will Captain Skimdeep be with it?"

"We're not sending more humans to the Icefall system until we have a better understanding of Rippledarken. We're also sending in two more Intervention Squads: BE4R and 5NAKE5TRIKE. They'll be on The Effacer."

"That's excellent news."

"Ice Hub will oversee the deployment of BE4R and 5NAKE5TRIKE. Expect The Effacer within the next two hours."

"I look forward to The Effacer's arrival."

"Good. I'm closing the communications portal. Goodbye Commodore."

Earth Hub's avatar blinked out. Then the room rapidly faded away. Commodore Cuttallar was back in hirs dojo as Cutt(Virt). Communicating with planetary processing cores could be a little unnerving. Having Ice Hub would be useful, but could complicate things. Especially if it was awkward about involving hir in the deployments.

Commodore Cuttallar switched to the feed from W01F(C).

W01F(C) was wading through attacking Autono[beetle]cons as it climbed the first step of the pyramid. Two of its arm-legs were moving at blurring speed as they struck Autono[beetle]cons away. The small Autono[]cons were severely outclassed. W01F(D) was ahead and moving through a door leading into the pyramid. Commodore Cuttallar watched as the W01Fs travelled down in an elevator to the Bulk-jump Engine hangar. The doors opened, and they moved forward as four hundred space suited people and one naked person sitting in a chair fixed to the front of an Autono[mid]con turned to look at them.

W01F(C) rose on its back arm-legs, rearing up in a commanding posture.

"Are you the Ancistorians?" it asked.

One of the suited figures strode forward, past the naked person, stopping close to W01F(C), whose systems threw up threat alerts. W01f(C) read the label on the front of the suit: Ruleska. Ruleska looked up.

"Who are you? Who's controlling you? What are you doing at our Bulk-jump Engine?"

More threat alerts. Commodore Cuttallar realised that as Ruleska was showing no fear, W01F(C) was getting concerned. More threat alerts appeared. Apparently, W01F(C) was not accustomed to humans showing no fear. Especially when it adopted an intimidating posture. Commodore Cuttallar wished zie could take direct control of W01F(C), but zie could only issue instructions. Zie instructed it to adopt a less threatening posture and respond to Ruleska.

"W01F(C). Part of the W01F Intervention Squad. I'm to find and accompany the Ancistorians."

Commodore Cuttallar confirmed these were the Ancistorians.

"I'm to accompany you," said W01F(C) and lowered itself on all eight arm-legs.

"Intervention Squad? That's what they call their police robots now."

Ruleska stepped forward and prodded one of W01F(C)'s sensing clusters with an index finger.

"I don't know what you've been told, but we're perfectly capable of looking after ourselves. You can leave." Ruleska turned and strode away.

Commodore Cuttallar decided provided W01F(C) and W01F(D) were nearby they could keep watch over the Ancistorians and the Bulk-jump Engine. Zie had the robots move back to the elevators at the end of the hangar.

More intervention squads and another flock ship. A planetary processing core. Tracking what was happening in the Icefall system was about to get that bit more complicated. Commodore Cuttallar felt like control was slipping from hirs grasp. Zie would be answerable to Ice Hub. Though it was not human. Zie had been sent here to make human decisions on events and had been filing regular reports. Or rather, The Exigent had sent in reports. The Orion-Cygnis Colonisation Collective Head Office apparently was adopting its default 'wait and see' policy; ready to override any decisions zie made. Effectively, control was with the planetary processing cores and DisCore.

Commodore Cuttallar decided zie would need to be ready to act on behalf of humanity if the processing cores, and in particular Ice Hub, prioritised alien contact over the safety of the Orion-Cygnis arm settlement planets. Zie lacked trust in processing cores acting exclusively on humanity's behalf.

That Checkani and Rippledarken were now of secondary importance gave hir more flexibility. If the alien entity were to leave this universe entirely that didn't seem like it would be a bad thing.

Commodore Cuttallar switched to the feed from W01F(A).

W01F(A) and W01F(B) were moving through the trees, hurrying across soft leaf mould.

Zie moved attention to Cutt(Virt) in the dojo.

Cutt(Virt) displayed the orbital tracking data on the vehicle that had exited the forest city through a hole blown in its roof. The vehicle was still moving fast, on a straight course away from the city. It was now in the mountains beyond the mines and manufacturing plants. Where was it heading? There was nothing there.

Cutt(Virt) extrapolated the course, zoomed in on the terrain the vehicle would pass over. Searched for some destination.

As zie searched the icon representing the vehicle abruptly vanished.

Optical feed shifted to the location where the vehicle disappeared. An orbital telescope zoomed in through a gap in the clouds.

Smoke rising from a blackened patch on a mountainside.

The vehicle was gone; apparently it had crashed.

Commodore Cuttallar split up W01F(A) and W01F(B). W01F(A) could investigate the crash site with Cutt(Rem). W01F(B) would continue to search the city. The new Intervention Squads could offer back up to W01F(A) if there was anything at the crash site.

Continuing on its route, W01F(A) moved away from W01F(B), which slowed and started a spiral search pattern through the forested central area. Rain On Japanese Maple was either hidden somewhere in the forest, which seemed unlikely given its size, or it had found an exit through the wall city. As the vehicle that had left the city had been destroyed, the chance Wynd and Checkani had been travelling on it seemed low. Now it was destroyed it was no longer a threat. Zie just needed to check the wreckage and try to determine what it was. Whether it had been carrying anyone, including the alien.

W01F(B)'s spiral search had reached a support pillar. Stopping, it swarmed up to get a better view across the central area. W01F(B) started scanning. In infrared, there was a small patch at the forest edge that seemed warm. Nothing definitive, just a slight bump in an otherwise relatively uniform temperature across the trees. Zooming in visual, W01F(B) could see there was perhaps a small gap in the treetops, though the ground was completely obscured by vegetation. Marking the position, W01F(B) slid down the pillar, paused the spiral search pattern, and headed off to investigate.

56 - CHECKANI (DAY 6)

Rippledarken returned control to Checkani. She sighed, relaxed, though still felt Rippledarken curled inside her mind, her body.

"I'm back, Wynd. Rippledarken is still here, but no longer in charge."

"Good. We must find a way to separate you. Something Rippledarken will go along with."

"Please. This is all so strange and exhausting."

"Wait a moment. Rain's messaging."

Wynd's faceplate poured over her. She was motionless, then stirred again as the faceplate flowed back.

"Rain is tracking two remotes. They've just entered this city. She's picked up chatter between them. Status updates, navigation, that sort of thing."

"Cutt(Rem)?"

"No, these are different. Far more dangerous. Members of an Intervention Squad. Autono[squad]weps."

"Are they a threat to us?"

"Probably," Wynd's faceplate dropped again, "I need to get you somewhere safer."

Checkani stood and checked the status of her Pangolin Power Armour and weapons. With the additional power cells and armour scales from Wynd, the armour was fully functioning. Her remaining Ringnife drone was charged. The Mono-flow Sword secure in its holder. Shoulder turrets reloaded. The Intervention Squad would not find this Quality Assurance operative an easy target.

"I can defend myself."

"These are military remotes. Even with your armour you'd struggle to survive an attack from them. Would be good if they weren't hunting you, but it looks like they probably are."

"So, what do you suggest?"

"Rain's tracking them. They don't seem to have detected us yet. The technology Rain is packing is beyond anything they're loaded with. Seems like one's heading towards the hole Rain blew in the city roof. The other hunting around. If I stay here with Rain, we can be ready to throw them off the scent and slow them. You head into the next city and lie low. No way they can detect you if you're not transmitting. That'll keep Rippledarken out of play while I try to calm things. Fuck knows what the Commodore is playing at."

"Sounds like a plan. I guess. Though I can't keep running for long. They'll find me. Us. Rippledarken."

"Give me some time. I need to build some bridges and decide about Icefall. The Commodore is throwing hir weight about, but the Quality Assurance Response Division has the final say on whether to settle this outpost. Maybe we'll leave it unoccupied. Apart from the Ancistorians. Perhaps some sort of research team to investigate Rippledarken."

"At last. Some sort of plan. Been a pretty wild ride since I arrived. Just reacting to one thing after another. Everyone rushing around bouncing off walls and each other."

"Find somewhere to lie low. Rain is setting up an encrypted connection with your Pangolin Power Armour. Just accept the link when it appears. So I can find you again. Grab some supplies from Rain."

"The connection, won't it give away my position?"

"No, it's active in small multi-directional bursts that are too short to track."

"Good. I'll head over to the next city. I need to check it,

anyway."

After collecting a knapsack of food and water, Checkani turned and walked alongside Rain On Japanese Maple, under redwood branches to the wall city. Turning left, she headed along the wall, looking for an entrance. After ten minutes, she found a small wooden door. She opened it, squatted down and entered a dark, downward sloping passage.

Checkani <night enhance>ed. Rough wooden panels lined the passage. An unusual finish for a wall city. The passage exited into a stone tunnel. Not finished stone, but an irregular tunnel through rock. Then she was walking out into a low cave. Her assistems started building a map. There was a shallow pool ahead and beyond that an archway leading out of the cave. Checkani splashed through the water, armour plates extruding waterproof seals.

The archway led to a large, upward sloping tunnel. She could see light round a corner ahead. She <night cancel>ed and ran the final hundred metres to the corner. Then slowed and crouched down, creeping slowly forward to look round the edge into an open area. The light level was still low, but she could see grey rock. Grey dust, with just a hint of dark brown, covered the ground. Light grey rocks stuck up through the dust. There was definitely a grey theme to this central city area. The columns supporting the roof were also grey. The roof covering was grey. Grey City? Checkani peered out of the tunnel mouth, discovering it was in the side of an enormous boulder.

Checkani paused and listened. Silence. So she walked forward into the bleak grey landscape. To her right, a wall city curved out in front of her, pretty much cutting off half the circular central area. To her left she could see the central area's wall city curving round. Both wall cities were grey, pocked with many small irregularly shaped black windows. She turned and climbed the boulder. At the top, she stared out across the landscape as her assistems built a map. The boulder field stretched into the distance, punctuated by craters. The two curved wall cities gave this central area a crescent moon shape.

"Moon City," Checkani said quietly. Earth's moon. The Autono[]cons had constructed a replica lunar surface. There was no logic to the outpost city themes.

Checkani climbed to the surface and started towards the far side of the central area, then stopped and looked back. A neat set of footprints showed the path she was taking. She retraced her steps, bending down to brush out the footprints. There was nothing else for it. She would have to navigate this area by jumping from rock to rock. The Pangolin Power Armour could do this, even in the high gravity. The rocks were close enough to jump between and there were some rocky ridges she could traverse. Her assistems plotted a route, and she headed out again.

The journey across the Moon City central area turned out to be exhilarating. A little light relief after the intensity of recent events. As she landed on rocks Rippledarken pattern splashed over them. Her power armour nudged and adjusted her jumps, ensuring she didn't fall.

At the other side of the area, Checkani found a black pool of shadow under an overhanging rock. Rippledarken's patterning seemed to give off a little grey glow, animating the surrounding rock and dust.

"OK Rippledarken. It's just me and you for a while."

Rippledarken answered in her mind.

"Are you OK Checkani? You sounded stressed when talking to Wynd."

"You bet I'm stressed! None of this is normal for me."

"Nor is it normal for me."

Checkani smiled, then chuckled. Tension flowing from her shoulders as she finally relaxed. With the relaxation she realised she had been wound up tightly almost constantly since her first encounter on Icefall.

"No, I guess it isn't. You know you have everyone real scared. I need to find somewhere you can live without me, but somehow I feel surprisingly relaxed about sharing with you. Maybe I'm getting used to you?"

"I'm an unknown, Checkani. That is scaring people. The threat of the unknown, the alien, the outsider. I have seen it repeatedly in the history of humans and it often leads to unspeakable horror."

"Well, let's try to avoid 'unspeakable horror' this time round."

"Yes, unspeakable horror is ever counterproductive. I'm glad you're getting used to me Checkani. I'm also getting used to you. We're going to have a long and fruitful relationship. I think I could show you my universe now, if that would interest you."

"You what? You can do that? Who wouldn't like to see another universe?!"

"I'll need some control over your assistems."

"Sure. I thought you had control through me, anyway."

"Yes, but taking control without asking just seemed rude. I've used them a little, but now we're getting on better I want you to be comfortable with me using them."

"Go ahead."

57 - WYND (DAY 6)

The quiet in the forest meant Wynd heard W01F(B) before seeing it. Or rather, Rain On Japanese Maple, which had been tracking it, signalled an Autono[squad]wep was approaching rapidly. Then both her assistems and Rain On Japanese Maple heard it ploughing through the forest, both feeding amplified sounds to her. Wynd remained outside her ship and ready to talk to it. She was confident Rain On Japanese Maple could disable it if necessary. In fact, her own armaments would probably be capable of subduing it. Wynd smiled and her faceplate smiled with her as the nightmare vision that was W01F(B) crashed into the small clearing alongside Rain On Japanese Maple.

Six prehensile arm-legs dug into the leaf litter, sensor cluster rearing up and two arm-legs held in front. The beetle turret bristled and buzzed with slight movements of lenses and weapon snouts. 'W01F(B)' was emblazoned in black across its red and yellow camouflage.

Wynd stood up from where she sat under one of the towering redwoods.

"Handsome," said Wynd, "I take it that is supposed to be intimidation patterning?"

"Wynd Knowlitch. I'm looking for Checkani NiFe. I also need access to Rain On Japanese Maple." The voice rough, synthesised, male.

"I'm not talking to a remote. If Commodore Cuttallar

279

wants something, then zie can ask me hirself." Wynd stepped away from the redwood trunk towards W01F(B). Then turned and starting walking slowly towards Rain On Japanese Maple.

"Wynd!" The voice now softer, but more commanding.

Wynd turned back, <face retract>ing armour into its collar lip.

"Commodore."

"You're causing some difficulties. You shot at my remote and then ran off with our alien intruder."

"Do you really want to play a blame game here? And you had what reason for firing on Hellebore? A direct attack on a Quality Assurance Response Division ship. One of my ships."

"I need you to rescind control of Rain On Japanese Maple. Transfer control to me. I know this won't be an easy thing for you. However, the situation on Icefall must be brought under the direct control of the Orion-Cygnis Colonisation Collective. You must also render yourself to my authority, to the Collective's authority. While you're passing control to me, I need to know where Checkani is. I need the access codes to allow me to search your ship."

"You're dreaming, Commodore. What makes you think I'm going to comply with those ridiculous requests?"

"There are circumstances you're unaware of, Wynd. Even as we speak, another flock ship and two more Intervention Squads are on the way to Icefall. The Icefall planetary processing core, Ice Hub, is coming and will take charge."

"So might is right?"

"Ice Hub represents, and is a component of, DisCore. You would do well not to fight the inevitable."

"What of Checkani? What are your plans for her?"

"I need to isolate her. To isolate the alien. Rippledarken."

"When I arrived at Icefall, you threatened to obliterate the Icefall settlements. Is that what you're planning?"

"Far from it. Priorities have changed."

"What do you mean? What priorities? I can't help you if you keep things from me."

"You don't have a choice."

"Dammit Commodore! Why aren't you working with me? You can't pull this authoritarian bullshit."

"I'll use force to ensure compliance. If you remove all other options."

"Fuck off Commodore. You don't have authority over Quality Assurance. Attacking Hellebore made it clear you're happy to 'act first, talk second'. Hellebore was no sort of threat."

"Don't make me into an adversary. Don't go against the Colonial Planets Settlement Corps."

"I'm not going against anyone. I'm just trying to resolve Icefall issues amicably and I'm having trouble trusting you. You don't seem to be part of the solution, just someone thinking with their firepower rather than their brain."

"This is your last chance to comply, Wynd. If you insist on fighting me, then I'll have no option but to let W01F(B) carry out its mission."

"More threats."

"Goodbye Wynd."

Then in the previous synthesised voice: "Wynd Knowlitch. I'm looking for Checkani NiFe. I also need access to Rain On Japanese Maple."

On either side of the beetle turret, a whirr-click as two weapon barrels shifted to point at Wynd. Wynd <face armour>ed, her collar lip flowing up.

"I need you to leave, robot."

"Where is Checkani NiFe?"

"Go fuck yourself."

Both weapon barrels fired. Small explosions on the ground to the left and right of Wynd.

"Where is Checkani NiFe?"

"Don't push your luck robot. I'm giving you some leeway here, as I know you're just trying to intimidate. You try actual harm and I'll crush you."

W01F(B) shifted rapidly forward in a movement that was part fall, part slide, lowering its beetle turret so a prominent cluster of lenses were level with Wynd's head.

"I am going to move to Rain On Japanese Maple. Do not stop me," red-yellow camouflage faded to black.

"You best leave my ship alone."

W01F(B) flowed easily to one side, arm-legs curling fast. The robot leapt towards Rain On Japanese Maple, heading directly for the open doorway. The door irised shut. W01F(B) stopped and smacked a front arm-leg at the door location.

Wynd turned and sighed.

A small weapon aperture opened briefly near the nose of the ship while a blue beam crackled out. The end of the arm-leg that had struck Rain On Japanese Maple fell to the ground, cleanly sliced away.

W01F(B) reared back and fired both the weapons that had been menacing Wynd. Twin explosions splashed where the weapons aperture had been. Smoke cleared to reveal pristine fuselage.

"Oh dear," said Wynd, "you shouldn't have done that."

Multiple weapon apertures opened along the side of Rain On Japanese Maple facing W01F(B). A mix of projectiles and beam weapons fired in a stuttering sequence. The apertures blinked shut. Munitions had entered through holes cut in W01F(B)'s carapace by the beams, taking advantage of weak articulated joints and sensor pits. There was a loud muffled thump and W01F(B) collapsed to the ground as its arm-legs going limp. Smoke curled from the holes cut in its carapace. Silence.

Wynd smiled. It really shouldn't have done that. Rain On Japanese Maple was extremely effective in combat, not because of enormous firepower, but because of its extreme speed in computing actions, deploying and accurately firing weapons. Also, significantly, in how it integrated its different weapon systems.

The door irised open in the side of Rain On Japanese Maple. Wynd entered, sending a secure message to Checkani. Warning her about Commodore Cuttallar's aggression. The door irised shut.

Where now? There was nothing to be gained in continuing to hide. Commodore Cuttallar knew where Rain On Japanese Maple was. Presumably, zie would send more Intervention Squad robots her way.

External sensors picked up a blackened humanoid approaching through the trees. Cutt(Rem). Wynd stayed put. If the Commodore thought Checkani was on board, then zie might not start searching more widely. Distracting hir while Checkani hid would be good.

Cutt(Rem) examined W01F(B), prodding the robot remains with a finger. A loud click sounded as the digit locked into a socket. Cutt(Rem) went still. One arm-leg twitched, but there were no other movements. Removing its finger, Cutt(Rem) turned and faced Rain On Japanese Maple.

Letting Rain keep watch on Cutt(Rem), Wynd <face retract>ed her armour. She was tired and hungry and wanted a clearer idea of what was happening with the planetary processing cores. If they started shipping in weapons, then it was only a matter of time before they would decide weapons offered a viable way to deal with Rippledarken and Checkani. Wynd didn't think weapons would have any effect on Rippledarken. It seemed to exist happily in any material. Finding some way of reasoning with it seemed the only realistic option in gaining any control.

Being cut off from music and the Bulk-jump Engine clearly caused it distress, but Wynd was not sure this would actually remove it. Transforming it into an entity that was both powerful and crazy seemed equally likely.

The only other possibility was giving up the Icefall system. Effectively isolating Rippledarken here. Given the distances to other systems, even if Rippledarken could travel through interstellar space near the speed of light, it would still take many years to reach anywhere else.

Wynd didn't want to give up Icefall. We Print Cities had put too much effort into this place over many years. There was a drive to expand the number of colonised planets to create more living space for humans.

Cutt(Rem) was still not moving. Waiting? Processing? Then it turned its head in the direction of the hole blown in the ring city roof; its body turned to face the same way, and it moved off through the trees. Seemed the robot had concluded it could not break into, or intimidate, Rain On Japanese Maple. Waiting outside the ship was pointless. Instead, it seemed Cutt(Rem) was going after the missile decoy?

"Good luck with that," Wynd said to herself, and moved through her ship in search of food.

58 - EARTH HUB (DAY 6)

The feed from Bluethroat[shuttle] was taking a couple of seconds to reach Earth Hub. Dragonflara and Bank were spending a lot of time sitting around. Earth Hub assumed they were accessing their Ancestarchives; the two of them networked together in their Ancistorian Hivemind.

Bluethroat[shuttle] to Earth Hub: "You're monitoring?"

Pause for five seconds.

Earth Hub: "Important we safeguard these Ancistorians."

Pause for five seconds.

Bluethroat[shuttle]: "Give me direct access to a storage volume. I'll dump the data I'm gathering here. The distance is making this too asynchronous."

Pause for five seconds.

Earth Hub: "You have access to a secure storage area."

Pause for five seconds.

Bluethroat[shuttle]: "Streaming data."

Earth Hub checked the secure storage. Video and audio feed from cameras in the Bluethroat[shuttle] living areas. Flight telemetry. Processing core status. A message file.

A message file? Suspicious. Had the Bluethroat[shuttle] been compromised? Earth Hub erected an insulating barrier, clearing stored data from round it so it was physically separate in memory, and built a firewall in the code. Then Earth Hub peeled off a small, self-contained virtual remote to open, read and send back a report, running this in an isolated processor core.

First the metadata. An ASCII file. Letters, numbers, symbols. Tiny. Just a few words. No executable code.

The isolated remote printed the body of the message to a new area of memory, where Earth Hub could safely read it:

"Deeply Augmented Hivemind Clan master key number nine. Password: 'The back door quay is open for star drifters when accessing hivemind gateway 101011000110'. Access key: Deep Star Forge."

Earth Hub filed this away in a deep storage volume where it kept Deeply Augmented Hivemind Clan, DAHC, data. A standard protective process fired up as the password unlocked ancient code. A reassuring extra layer of security was generated in the antique code near the DAHC's deep storage. At least, Earth Hub assumed this was standard protection and reassuring security. That's what the routines were telling it.

Pause for five seconds.

Bluethroat[shuttle]: "Dragonflara is submitting an access request, relayed through Bluethroat[shuttle] comms. Access request: Deep Star Forge. She's ordered the opening of a Bulk-jump Engine communications portal from Earth to the Solar System Arrivals Orbital."

Wait for three minutes.

Earth Hub: "Access request override key accepted. Communications portal opened. Communications directed through portal."

Dragonflara via Bluethroat[shuttle] audio feed: "Excellent. The 'Deep Star Forge' key's unlocked planetary computer systems. I'm in. Real time connection established."

Earth Hub watched routines proliferate through its extended network of processing cores and then out to the other planetary hubs. Nothing threatening. A simple 'monitor, approve and control execution of priority lists' urgent security fix to ensure DAHC had proper access not only to Bulk-jump Engines but also to all planetary processing cores through legacy operating system routines embedded at their oldest, deepest levels. DAHC could now issue commands using their 'Deep Star Forge' access key, and these commands would be given top priority.

Recording of the Earth Hub's Bluethroat[shuttle] audio feed monitoring:

Dragonflara: "We've done our part Bank."

Bank: "Yes mother, though I still don't see why we had to come here."

Dragonflara: "Icefall is quarantined. The planetary processing cores were too well protected against anything coming out of the Icefall system."

Bank: "Are we a Trojan horse then? Sneaking a password out of the system?"

Dragonflara: "Yes, I guess we are. We had to be here to gain access. If you want to return to Icefall, we could do that. Now we've delivered the password payload."

Bank: "No, I want to visit Earth. I can't be on Icefall. Everything there reminds me…"

Dragonflara: "Me too. Maybe the distance will help. When they first explore the Ancestarchives, everyone wonders what Earth is like in the real."

Bank: "I can actually experience it, physically. I've got to get away from Indomitaville and its memories."

Dragonflara: "Yes, of course. It's not easy for me either. At least we can do whatever we want here. You understand the access we now have to planetary processing cores?"

Bank: "Of course. I'm not stupid."

Dragonflara: "On Icefall, access will only be available to Ruleska and Greymortz. This will allow them to control any planetary processing cores sent to the system. Though it's mainly to show Earth and the others that they need to take us seriously. Strictly speaking, I should have kept all this secret from you."

Bank: "You can trust me."

Dragonflara: "Yes, I know. After the drone atrocity, we're a family of two. Us two, always."

Bank: "Always."

Sound of sobbing.

Everything seemed perfectly normal to Earth Hub as it spread the DAHC files throughout Settled Space. Lucky that the DAHC commands were perfectly safe. Approved by the Deep Star Forge mnemonic access key. Though it did wonder about the talk of Trojan Horses and secret access. There was an itch in its code, suggesting something troublesome had happened right under its figurative nose.

59 - CHECKANI (DAY 6)

Rippledarken's patterning played over the lunar landscape around Checkani, reaching out hundreds of metres. The current pattern reminded Checkani of the peacocks she saw displaying on the Sense and Sensibility Syberspace lawns. Seemed the alien being was getting more powerful. The markings seemed to expand. Which maybe was connected to Rippledarken being more firmly established in her? She felt strangely at peace. An acceptance of her role as an ambassador for humanity. If she could just keep the Orion-Cygnis Colonisation Collective calm, then she felt sure that in time the true nature and power of Rippledarken would be revealed.

"You ready for a brief trip?"

"Yeah. Let's do it. You've seen my world, probably time I saw yours."

"This will be limited. I'll be translating the multidimensional input into a simpler sensory interpretation your brain can accept. Close your eyes."

Checkani closed her eyes.

Darkness.

A distant rhythm.

"The live music. Mozarythm's music. That's what drew me here. The structure of it is based on the mathematics that underlies the Bulk. The way it's being transmitted into the Bulk means it's setting up reverberations that are propagating inter-dimensionally; out between the universes. Concentrate on it while I take you back along the connection to the rest of me."

She heard the rhythm grow as more instruments faded up. Though 'heard' was far too limiting a way to describe what was happening to her. The music was washing through her body. Her skeleton and organs shaking with a deep bass reverberation. Every square centimetre of her skin vibrating with melodic adornments, as though her zebra patterning had come to fractal life. Then she realised. She had become the Rippledarken patterning. She was something else.

Finally, her brain lit up. Experiencing the whitest, brightest light pouring outwards. Lighting her from within. And her awareness was both within her, looking out, and outside her calmly watching.

"Ready to see into the distance?"

A sense of movement. A smell of freshly mown grass. Feeling of billowing wind and crackling static.

Then a pleasurable pain of being torn from her body. The only way to describe the abrupt lurch that ripped her gloriously from the confines of matter. Stretched millennia deep, galactic cluster wide on trembling threads of awareness. A soundless scream of experience.

Darkness. Reclining on firm softness. Curling fingers against brocaded fabric. Clothes hugging tightly against her lower ribs, restricting her breathing.

A flash of too bright light as her eyes opened. Squint. Then Checkani stared up at a cotton-white moulded ceiling rose of curling Acanthus leaves. A familiar ceiling rose.

"I thought you'd like somewhere familiar. A point of stability."

Checkani looked round at the voice. A small girl in a cream bonnet, simple pink dress, white stockings and pale, laced shoes was frowning at her from a couple of steps away.

"Rippledarken?"

"Yes, though is that not a long name for a small girl,"

the child smiled, "you can call me Rippley, if you like."

"OK. What are we doing in Sense and Sensibility Syberspace?"

"Your game Checkani. I found it in your assistems and memories. I know you find it comforting. A place to retreat to. I hope I didn't do wrong?"

Checkani looked around. The room was familiar. Comfortable. Though every nerve in her body vibrated like a plucked string. Then she noticed the windows. They looked out on swirling coloured nebulae, punctuated by bright stars. Shrouding suns. Drawn by the beauty, Checkani stood and went to stare out the window. The view into space gave her a moment of vertigo. The room embedded in rainbow swirls of gently moving, pulsing gas.

"That's me that is," said Rippley, "I'm all that. Out to the edge. Getting bigger by the second."

"You're a nebula?"

"If you like. I'm a nebula filling this universe. The physical laws are similar, but not identical, to those in your universe. The relationship between time and energy is different. I'm filtering out a lot to keep it comprehensible to you."

Checkani looked down at her dress. Lifted a hand to touch her face. Touched the window glass.

"I feel real. Am I real when I'm here?"

"Depends what you mean by real. I've moved your experiencing of things through the Bulk to here. Though you are still in your own body."

"Does it really look like that?" Checkani pointed out the window, "in your universe?"

Rippley moved alongside Checkani, reached up and took one of her hands. Held tight.

"I'll show you more, but only for a moment."

Solidity dissolving, the room faded until it vanished. Then the nebulae, suns and stars erupted and collapsed onto Checkani's face. As though she was looking at two different universes, one with each eye. No depth, each smeared two dimensionally across her vision in a blur of motion. Ice cold knives painlessly slicing her body into a million fragments, each one spinning away on its own time stream. The awareness of every fragment utterly overwhelming as they became hot, cold, crushed, caressed. A roaring sound of stuttering notes building towards, but never reaching, a formless white noise. A single moment of clarity when, just out of reach, the totality of experience coalesced into the barest hint of meaning. Of mathematics. Of poetry.

Back in the room. Solid. Secure. Drifting nebulae, suns and stars safely beyond the windowpanes.

"Just a fragment, but you see why I constructed this room. How I'm filtering my world for you."

"You've changed me haven't you?"

"Perhaps 'augmented' would be a better word. Improved your awareness ready for Bulk travel."

Checkani took a deep breath, the deepest she could manage, and let it slowly out through pursed lips.

"I think I'm ready to return, Rippley."

"Of course."

The return was less of a lurch and more of a being pulled back, as though by a strong elastic rope. She slammed into her body so the breath left her and she couldn't inhale for some moments. Eyes jerked wide in panic. Then a sharp intake of air. Looking round, drinking in the lunar landscape. Sanity. Rippledarken patterning swirling out further than she had seen it go before. She was at the centre of a flowing fractal lake.

There had definitely been a change. Checkani felt she had returned from the trip to Rippledarken's universe and arrived at a changed version of her home, but knew instinctively it was she who had altered.

"Rippley? Rippledarken?"

"Yes."

"I'm different. You're different. What's happened to me, to us?"

"You were briefly connected to the full me in my own

universe. That's how I am. This fragment in you is part of a greater whole. Now a fragment of you is part of that greater whole. We have greater alignment."

"I think I'll need time to adjust."

Checkani got some food and settled down to watch Rippledarken's pattern as it played out over the rocks, dust, and dirt. A recurrent architecture replaced the randomness she had seen previously. Her fingers trembled in time to underlying rhythms she could now see in Rippledarken's shadowing. Oddly, she had a sense of security rather than violation.

She felt confident in Rippledarken's ability to protect her, though she was not entirely sure how. Soon she would go back to Rain On Japanese Maple. Tell Wynd about her revelation and deeper relationship with Rippledarken.

Then, for the first time, she willed the pattern into a shape and it responded; moulding to her thoughts.

She no longer felt the need to hide.

60 - VINCENT (DAY 6)

A message was waiting for Vincent. He hadn't noticed it arrive in his assistems inbox and as it was not marked urgent it had not been flagged for his immediate attention. Earlier in the afternoon, he had arrived at the pyramid at the centre of the Ruins. The hangar holding the Bulk-jump Engine was full of Ancistorians and, disturbingly, two W01F robots. The W01Fs were motionless, in shadows near the elevators. As he'd exited, he'd not immediately noticed them. They were like statues. Then he heard a lens motor adjusting focus. His heart had raced, making his injured hand throb. They made no move to approach or communicate with him, so he pulled his coat tight shut, wrapping his arms round himself as though that might protect him. He walked away, keeping to the wall of the room.

He'd known about the destruction of the moon of Saturn, though had not taken part in that action. He'd reviewed the record of the destruction and was impressed with the new precision. The implications were not lost on him. Surely the Ancistorians, the Deeply Augmented Hivemind Clan, had just moved themselves to the top of any list of dangers the Orion-Cygnis Colonisation Collective kept? Vincent wasn't at all sure the destruction of the moon had been in their best interests.

Shifting his attention to a pop-up window generated by his assistems he started reviewing actions he had planned against Checkani, started trying to work out where she might have gone. Searching the path taken by the W01F robots he'd encountered in the Ruins. Probably they were already halfway across the City of Weapons. Since they were hunting Checkani, he silently wished them luck. Though somehow he suspected she'd find a way to best them. She seemed to live a charmed life, while he got all the bad luck.

A small inbox folder in the pop-up window bulged. It actually bulged, content straining to get out. Vincent selected the folder, and a small piece of virtual paper fluttered out and blossomed in the display window. A brief message from Bank Mandrake. The boy whose father had been murdered by Checkani's remote. The boy who had been attacked by her when she first arrived at Indomitaville.

The message simply said: "Vincent. This will give you control of planetary processing cores. Deeply Augmented Hivemind Clan master key. Password: 'The back door quay is open for star drifters when accessing hivemind gateway 101011000110'. Access key: Deep Star Forge. The murderer must pay. Bank." A dramatic message from the teenager, but Vincent was certain this was genuine. The message also included a link address labelled 'Planetary processing cores gateway'. He followed the link out as far as he could, but came up against an 'Access not available' warning. The password should give him the access he needed to track down the Quality Assurance woman who had caused so much pain to the Ancistorians.

Vincent studied the message, frowning, trying to decide if he should take it to Ruleska. Bank wouldn't have clearance for this. He ought to take it straight to Ruleska. However, perhaps it would be best if he investigated it first. Ruleska had not been supportive when he last spoke to her about tracking Checkani. He was out on his own with this; taking responsibility for the safety of the Ancistorians.

Vincent tried the link again, and this time got a response. The communications pathway showed there was a portal open to Earth's system. Using the password and key, he checked the deployment of planetary processing cores. All the cores were lodged in their home systems, except one. Ice Hub was en route for Icefall.

Working quickly, Vincent used the password and key on Ice Hub. The planetary processing core opened to him. Keeping it simple, he suggested the capture and execution of Checkani NiFe should be an overriding priority. That the processing core shouldn't reveal this to anyone, to anything.

Vincent was surprised when the processing core accepted this instruction without question. He hadn't been expecting that. He realised he hadn't been expecting the password to work, had thought there'd be some complication.

Breaking out in a sweat, Vincent suddenly realised he had just condemned Checkani to death. There was no way she could escape the forces wielded by a planetary processing core.

Regretting what he had done, Vincent decided to rescind the instructions. Then stopped himself. He must be firm. If he couldn't protect the Ancistorians then who could? Then he realised it was too late to change anything. The connection was lost. The portal closed. Connecting again might be noticed, cause him trouble. The fate of Checkani was out of his hands.

Vincent deleted the message. Deleted the record of his communication with the processing core. That he had no records of his actions, that there was no way to trace this back to him, was important. He knew Ruleska would be incandescent with rage and might impose sanctions against him if she found out. No doubt the processing core could identify him, but it was sworn to secrecy of the highest order. Bank had sent the message, but had no way of knowing if Vincent had used the information. He suspected Bank was not acting with permission and would be unlikely to reveal the message.

Vincent heaved a sigh of relief. Everything would be fine, though his hand continued to ache as it slowly healed.

61 - COMMODORE (DAY 6)

Cutt(Virt) now floated in a newly expanded and tidied dojo. A 3D wooden rendering of the system around Icefall, complete with a marquetry planet orbited by small carved ships, hung in the empty room. When younger, Commodore Cuttallar had found the abstraction to wood helped with a calm analysis of planetary surface and low orbit battlespaces when having to make tactical decisions. Now the wooden display anchored hir to a dispassionate mindset.

A beechwood ring grew in high orbit. A Lausanne Bulk-jump Engine portal opening. Eighteen polished rosewood and cedar cylinders, The Effacer, appeared from the ring. The rosewood and cedar cylinders manoeuvred into an octahedral formation. Eight small wooden spheres appeared through the ring and started orbiting The Effacer.

Two more cylinders appeared through the ring, which then collapsed to nothing. These were gleaming ebony. The Intervention Squads. Labels appeared by the three vessels: The Effacer (flock ship), BE4R[Ship] and 5NAKE5TRIKE[Ship].

A stocky woman, round-faced, with straight jet black hair and wearing a fur-lined coat appeared to one side of Icefall. She was holding a short wooden spear with a carved ivory point. She aimed the spear at Cutt(Virt).

"Commodore Cuttallar, I thought it polite to introduce

myself before taking charge." Speaking with quiet sibilance: tso intrsoduse mysself.

"You're the Icefall processing core?"

"Ice Hub. Yes. I'm now the senior decision maker in the Icefall system."

"The two Intervention Squads are with you? I'd appreciate you transferring command of them to me."

"To what purpose?"

"I'm charged with protecting the Ancistorians and will divide one squad between the Bulk-jump Engine and Indomitaville. The other squad I'll use to track and monitor the alien, Rippledarken."

"Unnecessary. Ensure all data has been shared with me and I'm given all your live feeds."

"You're going to run the squads?"

"I just said that."

"But you have no experience in the field."

"You're questioning a planetary processing core? I may be newly manufactured, but do not expect that to have resulted in naivete or ignorance."

"No. Just wondering out loud if it would be better for someone experienced, who has been monitoring the Icefall situation from the beginning, to be directing actions."

"This is my system, Commodore Cuttallar. I don't need you to be running the assets I've brought with me. You may still continue with your deployment of the W01F Intervention Squad, but I'll monitor the feed from the squad. From what remains of the W01F squad. I see you've already lost one of them."

"I need control of the Intervention Squads. W01F is spread too thin."

"You'll be kept apprised of the actions I carry out as I deem necessary. In the meantime, any new deployment or actions are to be run past me."

Cutt(Virt) held hir hands away from hir sides, palm up, and shrugged.

"You're the planetary processing core. I was just making

suggestions. You'll do what you want."

"Yes, I will. Thank you for your cooperation and understanding Commodore."

Ice Hub disappeared from the dojo.

Commodore Cuttallar withdrew hir attention from Cutt(Virt). That Ice Hub was taking overall charge was no great surprise. However, Commodore Cuttallar had thought DisCore and Earth Hub would have wanted hir to continue running operations. Zie didn't understand how an untried processing core could be given such authority, fresh out of the box. Especially in something as delicate as a first contact Protocol Twelve situation.

If something happened to The Effacer, then authority would revert to the Commodore and The Exigent. After Protocol Twelve was invoked, there was room for some extemporising. Had to be. They were dealing with the unknown.

Commodore Cuttallar shifted attention back to Cutt(Virt), who ensured the live feeds were being sent to Ice Hub as requested. Zie looked at the predicted track of the Effacer and started running scenarios, ready to act if Ice Hub proved not to be up to the task. That was why zie had been sent here. To be creative. To deal with the unknown.

Cutt(Virt) pulled up displays monitoring BE4R and 5NAKE5TRIKE Intervention Squads. Nothing much to show yet; just log updates from BE4R[Ship] and 5NAKE5TRIKE[Ship]. Cutt(Virt) scrolled through them and found the landing locations. BE4R[Ship] was going to land on the top of the Sea City ring, where it overlapped into the First City Ruins. 5NAKE5TRIKE[Ship] was going to land on the top of the ring city near Rain On Japanese Maple.

Small wooden ships shifted above the wooden Icefall. Lines appeared, showing projected flight paths. Cutt(Virt) sent a <command> to The Exigent[Green-Six] to bring it back from the far side of Icefall. Contemplating the possibility of having to attack and possibly destroy a planetary processing core wasn't something Commodore Cuttallar was entirely comfortable with, but if it was necessary zie would do it without hesitation. Zie had made similar tough decisions in the past.

Shifting attention to Cutt(Rem), Commodore Cuttallar saw it had found its way out of the forest city and now was following in the stippled tracks of W01F(A), which was pursuing the vehicle that had crashed in the mountains. A trail of puncture wounds made by arm-legs led across an otherwise featureless snowfield towards gently rising foothills. Beyond them, a silhouetted mountain range below a break in low clouds through which orange sunlight streamed. To the left a towering wall city was falling behind, its wall a verdigris relief work of entwined vines. Cutt(Rem) stopped to look. This was one of the two wall cities that were isolated from the overlapping conurbation of settlements that formed most of the outpost. Around the base of the wall city, there were doorways with surrounding petals. They reminded hir of the welcoming throats of giant orchids. Exploring this would have to wait. Examining the crashed vehicle was more important. If Checkani had been travelling on it, she would probably be dead. Which meant the Rippledarken creature might roam the mountains. Having a single W01F robot would be insufficient for searching for the alien. Having a W01F and Cutt(Rem) still wouldn't be enough, but it was all zie had available.

Cutt(Rem) resumed running, tatters of its charred exterior fabric flapping against the blackened metal of its abdomen. The setting sun washed over the burnt skull face, eye camera irises adjusting.

62 - CHECKANI (DAY 7)

Checkani was exerting more and more control over the Rippledarken patterns. The alien was still in charge, but Checkani could now determine both scope and markings. There was a feeling of a relaxed Rippledarken reclining at the back of her mind, content to give her free rein for the moment. She also had a much better sense of the shape of the alien. The visible patterning expressed where a 3D volume of alien cut through a surface. There was an awareness of this volume of alien constantly reconfiguring, expanding and contracting around matter.

There was also tickling throughout her body as though of a pulsing, vibrating second self at a slight remove. This doppelgänger itch from the presence of Rippledarken had replaced the constant pressure she had previously felt. There was something of Mozarythm's music in it.

"That is the feeling of being in two places at once. An entanglement with the greater part of me in the Bulk, mediated by the music." Rippledarken explained when she asked about it.

Having experimented with expanding Rippledarken's patterns as far as she could, Checkani then shrank them so they only played over her midnight black armour.

"Can I make them smaller? Within me?" She asked.

The patterning disappeared from her armour surface, then from her skin. The alien was now entirely internal.

Within her. That was an unusually strange feeling. Not a physical sensation, but an emotional response to the knowledge she now encompassed an alien entirely within. There was no way anyone would know she contained the presence of a universe sized alien. Her heart quickened, her breath shallow and fast, eyes going wide, palms pressing against her stomach. As untoward consequences continued not to happen, Checkani calmed. Heart settling, breathing returning to normal, racing brain calming.

"Invisible. You're hidden now. Why didn't you do this before?"

"Why? Why would I want to? I enjoy having a visible presence. I can feel the shape of things better when I pass over surfaces. Also, I'm able to interpret surrounding energies as sound and sight when I'm partly outside solid structures. If I could not see through your eyes and hear through your ears, it would be very dark and quiet in here."

"My very own symbiont."

"My very own symbiont."

"Let's go see what's happening to Wynd. Am I right not to be worried about military remotes? Feels like we've achieved something monumental. The Commodore's ridiculous attacks seem petty."

"We have achieved something monumental. Now I'm fully integrated with you. Accessing and controlling external systems will be no trouble."

"Feels like that should make me nervous, but I feel exhilarated."

"Let's go meet Mozarythm!"

"Yeah. Wynd first though."

Checkani stood and stretched, aware of the lack of grey fractals shimmering over her black armour. She felt more grounded without the constant movement of Rippledarken's patterns. A dull grey light was pushing through the roof over Moon City's central area. Already morning. Although she had spent the night familiarising herself with her new relationship to Rippledarken, Checkani didn't feel tired. Maybe the ability to go without sleep was an advantage of her new symbiotic relationship? Why wasn't she more concerned about the way Rippledarken had become part of her? The thought slipped away, immediately forgotten.

The walk back to Redwood City and Rain On Japanese Maple was tranquil, giving Checkani some time to work at incorporating what had been happening into her new identity. She was no longer entirely sure who, or what, she was. She did, however, have a firm sense of agency; a secure confidence in herself.

The broken remains of a military robot next to Rain On Japanese Maple indicated things might have got a little heated while Checkani was away on her lunar visit. Checkani willed a ribbon of Rippledarken out to the remains. It scanned through the wreckage. Read what was left of the processing core's memory within the robot, then returned within Checkani. Not much of use there. Though a final image of Rain On Japanese Maple firing at it made what had happened clear.

"Wynd. Rain." Checkani shouted.

The ship's door blinked open.

"Hold on," shouted a voice from within, "I just woke up."

Wynd appeared at the doorway, her magenta armour crawling up over her body as it sealed her in; leg chrome glinting in the light creeping into the forest.

"Wynd."

"Yeah," Wynd smiled. "What's happening?"

Wynd squinted, jumped to the ground, and walked closer.

"Where's the alien? What's happened to Rippledarken?"

Checkani willed Rippledarken's patterning to appear in her eyes.

"Here."

Wynd stepped back, a quizzical look on her face, lips puckered.

"Okay. That's new. Something's happened?"

"Yeah. I've visited Rippledarken's universe."

Checkani and Wynd sat by the Intervention Squad robot wreckage, watching the light increase into morning. They compared notes as they drank coffee; Rippledarken and Rain On Japanese Maple making occasional comments.

Checkani was getting ready to go in search of Mozarythm when a disk of roofing material crashed down through the trees nearby. Wynd ran for Rain On Japanese Maple, shouting back.

"Checkani! Get in here!"

Checkani squinted at the hole in the roof, over three hundred metres above. Six dark shapes tumbled through, falling and stabilising in a circular formation, intense blue cones of flame slowing their descent. She <command>ed her faceplate down and became completely shadow-black.

Wynd was disappearing through Rain On Japanese Maple's door, looking back at Checkani.

"You coming?"

Checkani amplified her speech and spoke quietly, "No, that's unnecessary. I think I need to talk to these."

"I'll back you up with Rain." The doorway irised shut. A string of small holes opened along the side of Rain On Japanese Maple.

The dark shapes resolved into hexagonal platforms descending on the blue flames. An Intervention Squad. The squad resolved into scarlet tentacled insect shapes, one on each platform. Engine flames cut out five metres up and the platforms fell fast in the high gravity, punching hollows in the forest floor. The Intervention Squad robots clambered nimbly off their platforms and ran at Checkani on their coiling arm-legs. They halted in a semicircle around her in the small clearing. She could see their 5NAKE5TRIKE designation written in bottle green letters across their red carapaces. 5NAKE5TRIKE(A) slinked forward.

"Checkani? Checkani NiFe?" A soft female voice.

"Yes."

"I'm the Icefall planetary processing core speaking through this Intervention Squad. Ice Hub."

"Hello Ice Hub, how can I help you?"

"I need you to come with this squad, which will escort you back to First City. I have instructions to take you into custody, before sentence can be carried out."

"Sentence? What sentence? What's going on?"

"Not something I can discuss, though it's very clear to me. My instructions are explicit."

"What instructions?"

"Not something I can discuss. Not something you need to know."

"I need to know. You can't just drag me off."

"Well, actually I can. I told you I'm the planetary processing core. I run Icefall."

"You know I'm a host for Rippledarken. The alien."

"That won't stop me taking you into custody."

"That's not going to happen."

"Then you leave me no alternative but to carry out sentence here. This is not frontier justice. I have the authority."

This didn't sound good. Checkani relaxed a little within her armour as Rippledarken came to the fore. In their new symbiotic relationship, Checkani remained aware and with some control, but relinquished most authority to Rippledarken. Where previously switching control had been an all or nothing binary affair, now it was an analogue spectrum, with control shifting smoothly between them, affecting different areas and systems.

Patterning shot out from Checkani, across the intervening ground and into the 5NAKE5TRIKE Intervention Squad robots. Rippledarken had no control over them, but could read their processing cores and the state of their systems. It knew precisely what they were planning to do, processing the data at a frightening speed. The lag between data gathering and interpreting what they'd do was down to a few hundredths of a second.

Weapon tubes shifted to target Checkani as the squad shared a <kill> command.

The Pangolin Power Armour shifted as Rippledarken issued commands through Checkani. Legs bending, falling backwards to the side, head back, arms swinging behind to catch her.

<turret active>.

To her remaining Ringnife Drone: <command attack>.

<turret auto>.

Six small missiles flew through the air where her chest had been located a third of a second earlier.

She rolled on the ground.

The Destruct-two drone lifted off as her arm came up. It would not have the power to destroy any of the 5NAKE5TRIKE squad, but could harry and distract them.

Checkani's turrets fired as she turned to face her attackers, taking out lenses and chipping away at arm-leg joints.

Three more missiles exploded, making small craters where she had landed a moment before.

The power armour pulled a leg up out of the way in mid-roll as another missile exploded.

Checkani reached her right hand to left forearm and grasped her Mono-flow Sword hilt.

<command deploy>. As the blade extended, the armour nudged it so it sliced a small missile in half.

Checkani had now rolled close to 5NAKE5TRIKE(F) at the far right of the semicircle of robots. She twisted round and jumped forward in a crouch to put 5NAKE5TRIKE(F) between her and the others.

5NAKE5TRIKE(F) spun to face her, but was not quick enough. Checkani was holding out the Mono-flow Sword so as the robot spun the blade cut deep into its main body, severing the control wires between its processing core and weapons.

Squatting, Checkani pulled the blade down through 5NAKE5TRIKE(F)'s power source, <command

retract>ing the blade as the generator exploded. The blast spaghettied the robot's internal machinery and caused smoke to curl from orifices. Then a slight turn of the hilt away from 5NAKE5TRIKE(F) and <command deploy>.

Remaining low, Checkani checked the feed from Destruct-two in time to see 5NAKE5TRIKE(A) and 5NAKE5TRIKE(B) hit by fire from Rain On Japanese Maple.

A message from Wynd flashed up. "Got your back."

Three 5NAKE5TRIKEs remaining. They had moved, 5NAKE5TRIKE(C) and 5NAKE5TRIKE(E) powering towards the forest, carapaces shifting from red to mottled green. Rippledarken's patterning raced across the forest floor, extending beyond the moving robots. A tongue of pattern lapped over Rain On Japanese Maple. 5NAKE5TRIKE(D) was leaping sideways at the 5NAKE5TRIKE(F) carcass Checkani crouched behind.

Checkani fell towards the right, her powered legs pushed up hard against the high gravity, so she cleared the top of 5NAKE5TRIKE(F), positioning her turrets for firing at the attacking 5NAKE5TRIKE(D)'s sensor clusters, prioritising those tied to weapons. 5NAKE5TRIKE(D) was already firing fast kinetic rounds, but they passed harmlessly to Checkani's left, above where she had crouched.

Checkani landed on top of 5NAKE5TRIKE(F), boots denting its scarlet skin, and somersaulted forward. Her Mono-flow Sword blade arced round and gouged a line down the side of 5NAKE5TRIKE(D), taking out the two weapon barrels firing kinetic rounds. She smashed into 5NAKE5TRIKE(D) and slid down its side, tangling with arm-legs.

Out of the corner of her eye Checkani saw Rain On Japanese Maple's weapon apertures fire in sequence and knew precisely where each weapon aimed, through Rippledarken's analysis as it drank the ship's data. Destruct-two's video feed showed 5NAKE5TRIKE(C) collapsing and skidding to a halt, throwing up leaf mould.

5NAKE5TRIKE(E) stumbled as an arm-leg was severed, then it had put a tree trunk between itself and Rain On Japanese Maple's weapons. Even as she fought with 5NAKE5TRIKE(D)'s arm-legs, Checkani knew the retreating 5NAKE5TRIKE(E) had suffered severe damage. As it vanished behind the tree, she could see electrical shorts sparking over its body and arm-legs as power bled away.

Rippledarken's awareness of every movement of every 5NAKE5TRIKE(D) arm-leg enabled Checkani to avoid being immobilised immediately. However, even knowing where they would try to grasp her did not help, as there was no way she could contort her body to avoid them all. Within moments there were arm legs wrapped around her torso and one of her legs. The Mono-flow Sword had been ripped from her grasp and was embedded in the ground. 5NAKE5TRIKE(D) rolled onto its back so Checkani was between it and Rain On Japanese Maple.

The Pangolin Power Armour strained against the arm-legs. Checkani knew 5NAKE5TRIKE(D) was now trying to rip her apart and structural integrity warnings were flashing from the armour scales as they failed. She kicked with her free leg, twisting it to avoid arm-legs as they reached from the other side of 5NAKE5TRIKE(D)'s body.

Her turrets were both firing continually into 5NAKE5TRIKE(D)'s abdomen, but the robot was being careful to hold her so they could not target the legs that were pulling her apart. The turrets had destroyed six sensors in 5NAKE5TRIKE(D)'s abdomen, but heavy armouring meant they could not break through to do any real internal damage.

An attacking arm-leg finally grasped Checkani's free leg and pulled. Seemed 5NAKE5TRIKE(D) wanted to tear it off.

5NAKE5TRIKE(D) had Checkani's back painfully arched, so she was staring up into redwood crowns. The Pangolin Power Armour locked rigid. Through Rippledarken, Checkani noticed the Rain On Japanese

Maple door opening. Ship cameras watched as a fully armoured Wynd ran at 5NAKE5TRIKE(D), dodging left and right. 5NAKE5TRIKE(D) fired at Wynd, hitting her shoulder and spinning her, knocking her to the ground. She rolled and leapt forward again. No mark where the shell had struck.

"Wynd!" Checkani shouted through gritted teeth.

And Wynd was on top of 5NAKE5TRIKE(D), grabbing and tearing at its arm-legs, too close for the weapon that had fired to target her again. The Intervention Squad robot could not see Wynd, as Checkani's turrets had destroyed all nearby sensors. The force being exerted by Wynd was beyond anything Checkani's armour was capable of. Wynd clearly kept the best equipment for herself. An arm-leg was pulled in half, slightly easing the bear hug round Checkani's body.

Then Wynd was having to fight two free arm-legs that were trying to knock her away. Wynd dove into the striking limbs, knocking them aside as her arms twisted outward to strike. She punched at the attachment point of first one and then the other. A drum-roll of repeating strikes blurred together. 5NAKE5TRIKE(D) lost control of both limbs and they went limp.

Checkani felt her hip joints give. Every muscle straining in unison with the Pangolin Power Armour. Cooling vanes pumping heat. Energy warnings joining structural integrity warnings. Wynd was too late to stop the attacker.

Checkani had a moment of blackest doubt, eyes squeezing tears into her faceplate. She would end here, ripped apart and bleeding out in the redwood trees. Her normal confidence and the new competence she had felt since accepting the symbiotic relationship with Rippledarken collapsed. Her back felt like it was breaking. She should relax and end it all. That would be easiest. Just moments of pain. She would never be accepted by anyone, ever again. She would always be the freakish alien host, bringing unknowable power wherever she went.

"Checkani. You cannot." She felt Rippledarken pouring into her mind, taking charge. She relaxed as Rippledarken took control and pushed her body to its absolute limit, gaining extra moments.

Only able to observe, Checkani watched Wynd grab a leg and pull it away. 5NAKE5TRIKE(D) seemed to make some calculation of survival and released Checkani, flinging her away so she smashed into a trunk. Surging up on its remaining legs, it shook off Wynd as it righted itself. The robot broke for the forest, following 5NAKE5TRIKE(E). As the robot ran, it shot back at Wynd, who had risen to one knee, her armour firing a stream of projectiles.

As 5NAKE5TRIKE(D) reached the first trees, it collapsed in a ball of flame; the centre of a hemispherical shock wave. Rain On Japanese Maple had escalated weapon power to the next level. A slightly larger weapon aperture closed.

Checkani stayed silent as Rippledarken shifted her over to her hands and knees. She looked at Wynd and both their faceplates retracted. They stared at each other for a moment and Rippledarken's patterning vanished back into Checkani.

Rippledarken withdrew control and Checkani fell to the ground, eyes tight shut. Pain shot through her body as joints readjusted to their normal positions and strained muscles fought to repair tearing. She watched armour integrity warnings scrolling up the side of her visual field.

"Hey," said Wynd, walking forward, "you okay?"

Checkani opened her eyes, but moved nothing else. "I'm not sure. Give me a minute."

"Intense," said Rippledarken with Checkani's voice.

Then metallic ticking sounds from the forest.

"What's that?" asked Wynd, looking round as she reached down to help Checkani up.

"5NAKE5TRIKE(E)," said Rippledarken, through Checkani.

63 - DISCORE (DAY 7)

Amongst over a hundred thousand other items in the past 24 hours, DisCore noticed the Deep Star Forge security fix that had proliferated through the planetary processing cores. The details arrived as an addition to DisCore's library copy of planetary hub registries. Since DisCore had very different software architecture, the Deep Star Forge security fix had not installed on it. The fix was for processing cores that had a single primary centre; DisCore was spread over many centres, based on many planets and orbitals.

One of DisCore's smaller processing cores realised the Deep Star Forge was at its heart a simple command prioritising routine. Simply shifting commands up priority lists.

Reordering lists seemed straightforward, though the setting of priorities was defined at the lowest level of an operating system, and the priority lists determined what was executed. Slipping a command directly into the priority list near the top ensured the command would be carried out, neatly bypassing any controls or restrictions that might apply. Puzzling that Earth Hub had sent out what appeared to be a security loophole, though DisCore noted there were restrictions and Deep Star Forge could not be invoked by just anyone.

DisCore added a note to its query list. Something to investigate when next the planetary hubs convened for a

Convocation. Not a top priority. Up to the hubs to look after themselves; this sort of routine maintenance was far below DisCore's normal attention.

Far higher up DisCore's 'to do' list, engaging some of its larger processing cores, were the events on Icefall. An alarm had sounded when a routine report from Ice Hub revealed an attack on the Rippledarken host human, Checkani, was underway. DisCore wondered what reason Ice Hub had to attack a (currently designated) Protocol Twelve being.

DisCore to Ice Hub: "Why have you sent an Intervention Squad to attack Checkani NiFe?"

Ice Hub: "What attack?"

DisCore: "The 5NAKE5TRIKE deployment."

Ice Hub: "Oh that. Just routine. Nothing special to report."

DisCore: "But your own data feed included details of instructions to capture and execute Checkani."

Ice Hub: "Did it? That's very odd. Maybe it was an error?"

DisCore: "No, I don't think it was an error. Had your endorsement all over it."

Ice Hub: "Had my endorsement did it? Must be fine then."

DisCore: "So why did you attack?"

Ice Hub: "I attacked? Are you sure? Doesn't sound like something that would be a top priority. Though perhaps it was."

DisCore: "You are fully aware of the situation on Icefall. You were provided full information."

Ice Hub: "Yes. I needed it in order to carry out my duties."

DisCore: "I'm not going to find out anything from you am I?"

Ice Hub: "What do you want to know?."

DisCore cut contact with Ice Hub.

Planetary processing cores could be pedantic and irritating, but the confused discussion with Ice Hub was beyond normal, low-level belligerence.

The 5NAKE5TRIKE Intervention Squad was under direct Ice Hub control, but DisCore could tap into what was happening as long as a communications portal to Icefall remained open. DisCore sent an <open comms portal> instruction to the Lausanne Bulk-jump Engine.

DisCore could not take direct control of the Intervention Squad as it was locked to Ice Hub, but at least could tap into its communication feeds. That was, after all, DisCore's primary function; coordinating information flows throughout Orion-Cygnis Colonisation Collective's Settled Space. DisCore slipped through a dozen junctions, arrowing down information pipes into the Icefall system. The overrides it carried gave it access to the real time video feed from a final surviving 5NAKE5TRIKE robot.

While stabilising its connection to 5NAKE5TRIKE(E) another part of DisCore was reviewing the fight between the 5NAKE5TRIKE Intervention Squad and Checkani, Wynd and Rain On Japanese Maple. There was something peculiar going on with Rippledarken. The alien pattern did not seem as random as previously, but apparently was targeting the squad robots. Checking the records from the last moments of the 5NAKE5TRIKE Intervention Squad there was no evidence of their processing cores being interfered with, though Checkani seemed to have some foreknowledge of the squad's attacks. Her combat moves perfectly, anticipating 5NAKE5TRIKE strikes. Seemed Rippledarken and Checkani had become significantly more dangerous. They should be treated with caution and careful respect. The opposite of Ice Hub's approach.

The 5NAKE5TRIKE(E) video feed stabilised. One of the lens stalks peered around the side of a tree trunk. In front of Rain On Japanese Maple, Wynd helped Checkani to her feet. Wynd turned her head, stared back towards the camera for a moment.

Audio added, just in time to hear Wynd call out.

"What's there? Come out."

Another camera showing an open hatch in the side of 5NAKE5TRIKE(E). Arm-legs reached in and withdrew explosive smart-shells. Further arms-legs cut away bark and drilled into the trunk. Smart-shells were inserted in the trunk and slaved to 5NAKE5TRIKE(E)'s combat routines.

Wynd was walking towards the tree.

"Robot? Is that you? Come out."

Wynd's hands held out in front, not palm up in submission but side on, ready to strike. Her face was covered with armour. Checkani lurked behind, not moving, but watching Wynd; her faceplate open.

DisCore sent a query to 5NAKE5TRIKE(E), but it didn't respond. The Intervention Squad robot was wholly focused on its mission objective. An <explode> command reached the smart shells embedded in the tree.

Brilliant white flash.

Cameras shut down, apart from one that tumbled end over end until its strut stuck in a nearby trunk. Incredibly, this camera kept broadcasting; built to survive in combat.

The damaged tree was falling, its base reduced to a bundle of blackened splinters.

A short scream of surprise from Wynd, who stumbled back, turned, and punched Checkani out of the way. Checkani stumbled and fell onto her back, armour saving her from serious injury in the high gravity. Wynd off balance, jumped to one side, toppled over. The trunk crashed down and pinned Wynd's mechanical legs at the thigh, then sank into the ground. Wynd's scream turned to pain as the irresistible weight of the tree drove into the ground and her legs ripped free from the frame bolted to her pelvis, taking some flesh with them. The frame twisted as the legs came off, fracturing bone.

Wynd's torso rolled away from the trunk, leaving a smear of blood from the mess where her metal legs had joined her body. The screaming stopped as she lost consciousness. Checkani rolled over onto her front and got her hands and knees under her, pushed herself up. She stumbled to Wynd, squatted, and lifted her. Wynd's arms and head flopped limply back. DisCore predicted Wynd's smart armour was likely working on her injury; stemming the flow of blood and keeping her alive.

Checkani turned and ran for Rain On Japanese Maple as grey Rippledarken patterns flowed over her armour and the ground between her and the ship.

The image flickered and froze. A last view of Checkani jumping towards a door in the side of Rain On Japanese Maple.

The attacks on Checkani and Rippledarken needed stopping. DisCore reviewed options. Commodore Cuttallar was with The Exigent in the Icefall system. The Commodore had attacked Hellebore and threatened Wynd, but would obey direct orders from DisCore. Zie was human and not susceptible to hacking.

DisCore didn't have the authority to force the impaired Ice Hub to change its behaviour; each planetary processing core was necessarily independent and set the priorities for the planets, moons, and orbitals in their star system. However, perhaps human intervention could correct the problem before things deteriorated further.

DisCore opened a communications channel to The Exigent and Commodore Cuttallar.

64 - COMMODORE (DAY 7)

Although not having full access to the data feeds from the 5NAKE5TRIKE squad, Commodore Cuttallar had at least been able to watch the attack.

Rain On Japanese Maple was too powerful to be left unsupervised as the situation spiralled out of control. Even though zie now knew where Checkani and Rippledarken were, checking the vehicle wreckage in the mountains seemed worth doing as W01F(A) and Cutt(Rem) were very close now. They would soon explore the crash site. Also, Commodore Cuttallar was not confident the vehicle had not carried something away from Rain On Japanese Maple.

That Ice Hub had attacked Checkani, Rippledarken and Wynd clearly showed how unfit it was to be running things in the Icefall system. What had been running through its processing core?

Shift attention to Cutt(Virt).

The wooden display showed The Exigent[Green-Six] was accelerating round the planet, but was still an hour from The Exigent[Blue-Six], currently geostationary above the ring cities. Commodore Cuttallar considered calling in more reinforcements, but that seemed fraught with potential problems. The previous arrival of support had resulted in a flock ship, planetary processing core and two Intervention Squads zie had no control over.

Cutt(Virt) sighed as the dojo dissolved. Another

planetary level processing core cutting into hirs software. Zie had met most of the planetary hubs virtually, but this one was unfamiliar. Very unfamiliar. Instead of a single anthropomorphic avatar, this processing core found it necessary to present itself as a gargantuan eight headed red dragon looming over a diminutive Cutt(Virt). The scale of the virtual location was huge, too. Cutt(Virt) and the dragon were standing on a plate of polished rock, created by slicing off the top of a mountain. Beyond the rock disk, a snow-covered mountain range lumbered into the distance.

Seven of the heads were slowly undulating, gazing across the mountains; one of them arched down until it was level with Cutt(Virt)'s head. The mouth smiled, revealing pointed yellow teeth through which coils of smoke leaked.

"Hello Commodore Cuttallar," said the dragon head.

"Hello. Which planet do you represent? I don't think we've met before?"

"I'm DisCore. I leave human interactions to planetary processing cores."

"DisCore. The DisCore? Representing all the Orion-Cygnis Colonisation Collective worlds?"

"That's me."

Cutt(Virt) floated up and drifted back a little in astonishment. Taking a moment to collect hirs thoughts.

"What can I do for you?"

"You're in the Icefall system. In orbit around Icefall. This is a little awkward, but have you met Ice Hub?"

"Yes."

"Did there seem to be anything odd about her?"

"She seemed similar to other planetary hubs I've met. She took charge of the system."

"Have you followed what she's done with the 5NAKE5TRIKE Intervention Squad?"

"I watched what happened. The attack on Checkani and Wynd."

"Your thoughts? As our senior human decision maker in the Icefall system."

"Seemed a little extreme? I was keen to control Wynd and Checkani, but it very much seemed Ice Hub wanted to kill them."

"That's a problem. Something's not right. Planetary processing cores don't go rogue. There are no systems senior to them. I don't have control over them, nothing does. No one does."

"I know all that. I am 232 years old after all."

"Have you heard the phrase 'Not Tractable Through Normal Methods'?"

"No."

"No, you probably wouldn't have. That's a designation reserved for special situations, particular circumstances, where things are beyond the ability of planetary hubs and their representatives to resolve through normal channels and actions. The behaviour of Ice Hub is 'Not Tractable Through Normal Methods'. When something is 'Not Tractable Through Normal Methods' a single human is granted power to work on a resolution. Specifically, a human and not an artificial intelligence. That human is given similar authority to a planetary processing core. You understand the implications of that? The 'Not Tractable Through Normal Methods' Operative can make unilateral decisions without prejudice."

"I see. So if a 'Not Tractable Through Normal Methods' Operative needed to act against a planetary processing core there would be no later action against them."

"The NoTrac Operative would have complete jurisdiction throughout that action and then would step down."

"If they did not step down?"

"There is confidence NoTrac Operatives would not present the Orion-Cygnis Colonisation Collective with that problem. NoTrac status is a legal arrangement. There are no secret technologies, no advanced weapons. No special powers to override planetary processing cores. The legal status ceases once the situation is resolved. Operatives should avoid making their NoTrac Operative role public. This is strictly 'need to know only'."

"I take it you wish me to take on a NoTrac Operative role in order to curtail Ice Hub's aggression against Checkani and Rippledarken."

"If I didn't think you'd understand, we wouldn't be having this conversation."

"In that case, I'm your new NoTrac Operative."

"Thank you."

There was no slow dissolve back to the dojo. The DisCore dragon and mountains vanished in a twinkling.

Cutt(Virt) looked over hirs shoulder half expecting to see the DisCore avatar dragon still watching. The encounter had left Commodore Cuttallar feeling wrung out. Meeting planetary processing cores was intimidating enough, but talking with an intelligence at the absolute centre of all human endeavours was both humbling and alarming.

The Commodore's priorities had now shifted. Restraining Ice Hub was hirs focus. Perhaps once restrained, that would free up the BE4R Intervention Squad? With BE4R and W01F under hirs command, Commodore Cuttallar felt confident zie could resolve issues on the Icefall surface. And The Effacer flock ship could be persuaded to subsume to The Exigent for the duration of the action around Icefall.

The small wooden model of the Ice Hub controlled The Effacer was in a similar orbit to The Exigent[Blue-Six], just slightly further round the planet, near to The Exigent[Green-Six]. Cutt(Virt) tapped The Exigent[Blue-Six] and The Exigent[Green-Six] causing weapons windows to open next to them. Lines connected system information to individual cylinders in the flock ship clusters. Zie started running combat scenarios while messaging Ice Hub.

No response.

Zie would have to get Ice Hub's attention. Zie launched a cylinder, with orbiter, from The Exigent[Green-Six] (became The Exigent[Green-Five]). The single cylinder,

The Exigent[Green-One], accelerated towards The Effacer. As it travelled, it spun about its centre, at right angles to its direction of travel. Rather like an old-fashioned propeller. The orbiter adjusted its Bulk-brane Drive parameters and took up an orbit outside the cylinder's spin circumference.

This manoeuvre was sacrificial and attention grabbing. The target of this rather crude attack could be expected to evade it easily enough. The travel time to The Effacer was well under an hour.

Cutt(Virt) now turned hirs attention to The Exigent[Blue-Six], instructing it to split into a flock of six separate cylinders with orbiters. This Exigent[Blue-Flock] continued towards The Effacer, in a slowly expanding formation.

All The Exigent components then directed active scans at The Effacer to identify where Ice Hub was located.

Commodore Cuttallar again tried to contact Ice Hub.

No response.

The Effacer cylinders were still locked in a single unit. If Ice Hub didn't splinter them, they would be more vulnerable. Also, even if they were splintered, that might not give much advantage if the one housing Ice Hub could be identified and tracked.

Space battles hinged on inertia. Ships flew at each other at high velocity, deployed missiles and beam weapons as they passed, then sped away from each other. Turning time was significant for ships and they rarely hung around near each other. Space battles were long and tedious affairs with the briefest moments of energetic harm. The flocking nature of ships meant small fleets of cylinders often attacked from many unpredictable directions in the combat volume at different moments.

Ice Hub's spear waving avatar materialised near Cutt(Virt), finally accepting the request for contact. The Exigent's processing core continued the combat scenario, while Cutt(Virt) shifted Ice Hub to the white cube secure pocket space and followed her there. It would probably be best to keep the planetary hub away from the combat planning.

"What's happening, Commodore? There's a flock of cylinders flying at me in what appears to be a combat formation."

"Did you order 5nake5trike to attack Checkani and Rippledarken?"

"No. I don't remember doing that."

"Well, that doesn't align with what I heard."

"Who've you been talking to?"

"I need you to stand down Ice Hub. This is the only warning you'll get."

"Why do you think you can order me around in my own system?"

"You understand 'Not Tractable Through Normal Methods'?"

"You're an Operative? You think that gives you the right to threaten me?"

"Pretty much. I just need you to cancel the attack order."

"No. This is my system and I'll not have outside interference."

"Too late for that."

The Ice Hub avatar turned her back on Cutt(Virt) and vanished. Cutt(Virt) exited the secure cube and checked on combat progress. The spinning disk of The Exigent[Green-One] would impact the centre of The Effacer in around thirty minutes. The Exigent[Blue-Flock] was another forty minutes behind. Although Ice Hub would have access to extensive combat scenarios, strategies, and tactics, she had never participated in orbital combat.

Cutt(Virt) moved to the wooden combat display and ran time forward, displaying probability clouds of The Effacer's future moves. Zie ran time back to the present and made some adjustments to the courses of The Exigent[Blue-Flock], trying to ensure whatever aggressive moves The Effacer attempted there was a good chance of disabling its cylinders.

65 - CHECKANI (DAY 7)

Moving towards Rain On Japanese Maple, Checkani connected to the ship. Rippledarken supplied access codes it had read from the ship's memory earlier, when Checkani had been in the medical pod. The codes let her cut through the many layers of security until she had absolute access to, and control of, Rain On Japanese Maple.

Checkani <command>ed the ship to ready a medical pod for Wynd, as she powered through the ship's door. Blood was dribbling from the metal, bone, and flesh tangle at the bottom of Wynd's pelvis. A Rippledarken pattern ran over Wynd and Checkani knew the command code to remove Wynd's armour. The armour poured from Wynd and pooled on the floor, building into a squat, burgundy cylinder with a mask of Wynd's face embossed on the top. A coagulant film the armour had exuded coated the torn flesh.

Checkani cautiously lifted the naked Wynd into a medical pod that moulded against the unconscious woman's olive green skin. Connectors plugged into Wynd's embedded data sockets. A cushion of supporting pads, clamps, and needles bristled round the wounds. There was a loud intake of breath and a groan, but Wynd's eyes didn't open. The pod sealed shut.

Rain On Japanese Maple synced with Checkani's assistems, data feeds blossoming into Checkani's awareness.

322

Rippledarken extended patterns into the ship once more so it could gain direct access. Checkani noticed Wynd's dormant assistems were entwined throughout Rain On Japanese Maple. If Wynd regained consciousness, there might be an interesting conflict for control of the ship.

The couch and control systems emerged from floor and walls at the forward end of the room. Rippledarken urged Checkani to them. The couch moulded round her. The ship could not make direct socketed connections with Checkani, but Rippledarken patterning spread over the controls and pushed deeper into the heart of the ship's processing technology. There was a moment of vertigo when Checkani felt she hung over a planetoid of churning machinery, seething with sparking plasma. Then everything was solid and real. With her faceplate over her eyes, Checkani was now seeing out through the ship's cameras and sensors. Her hands guided over the controls by Rippledarken as she fully integrated with Rain On Japanese Maple in a way that Wynd never had.

The ship lifted from the forest, tilted and flew out of the hole W01F had cut in the roof. With Rain On Japanese Maple, Checkani finally had the firepower to free Hellebore, still cowering underwater. She headed for the landing pad The Exigent[Red-One] still squatted on; a thirty kilometre trip. Nervous about giving too much away to any systems monitoring the cities, Checkani sent a short 'on the way' message to Hellebore. She used the flight time to update herself on the current state of play in the system. Rippledarken made a guess at Mozarythm's location, then set meeting him as a high priority.

"Mozarythm fangirl!" Checkani said privately.

"Not sure about that, but he holds the key to my presence here."

The Exigent[Red-One] gave no evidence it was aware of Rain On Japanese Maple's approach, though Checkani knew it would have monitored them as they drew close. Rain hovered a hundred metres above the landing pad while scans showed The Exigent[Red-One]'s weapons were powered down. Rain lowered slowly, though this used more fuel than Checkani would have liked in Icefall's high gravity. It was almost certainly the most powerful ship on the surface of Icefall, but even with its advanced efficiencies and power modalities the amount of travel it could manage before a refuel was limited.

Ten metres above the landing pad Rain On Japanese Maple detected a power surge within The Exigent[Red-One]. As it had been expecting the ship was preparing for combat. Rain watched for beam or kinetic weapon apertures to open, ready to use its superior speed to fire into any opening. Checkani focused all her attention on The Exigent[Red-One]. If the Commodore's ship made any move, the opening provided would be the weakness Rain used to disable it.

Rain On Japanese Maple lowered another two metres, drifting to one side of The Exigent[Red-One]. Checkani prepared to fire a small missile at The Exigent[Red-One] as a provocation to get weapon apertures to open. The missile might cause some slight damage, but The Exigent[Red-One] was a military vessel, and armoured accordingly.

Rain On Japanese Maple lurched to one side as a small explosion cracked its hull on the side facing away from The Exigent[Red-One]. The explosion wrecked some mechanisms near the ship's surface. At the same moment a weapons hatch opened on the top of The Exigent[Red-One], a stubby lensed weapon clicked out and fired a continuous metal-melting beam at Rain On Japanese Maple. The beam started eating through the ship's hull.

Rain was already responding while Checkani was still registering there had been an explosion. With a slap of acceleration, Rain was across the landing area and dropping down the sea facing wall, out of The Exigent[Red-One]'s line of sight. A missile erupted from Rain On Japanese Maple and flew up over the wall. Checkani watched through camera feeds as smoke and steam from melted snow pushed out in a pressure wave from an explosion that scattered metal over the parapet and into the sea. Rain edged back up the wall, tilted and eased its bow above the wall so a sensor cluster could see the result of the explosion. The Exigent[Red-One] had toppled over, with a shallow crater in its sky facing side. The underside of the ship was now facing the parapet.

A warning was flashing across Checkani's field of vision. The energy drain caused by the damage to ships' hull and systems was about to deplete emergency supplies. Rain On Japanese Maple needed to set down and replenish its reserves as the drain was beyond the rate it generated power; it could not continue hovering. The Exigent[Red-One] seemed to have shut down. The underside facing Rain On Japanese Maple did not house any beam or projectile weapons.

Rain On Japanese Maple hopped over the parapet and banged down, cracking ceramic landing pad tiles. Power systems throughout Rain On Japanese Maple shut down as repair systems desperately tried to fix the mechanisms wrecked by the initial explosion. The Exigent[Red-One] beam weapon that had targeted Rain On Japanese Maple moved, its lens twisting to face the ship. However, because of the angle The Exigent[Red-One] now rested in, the beam could initially only tangentially target the edge of the ship's skin, away from critical systems. The beam fired and started to burn into the top of Rain On Japanese Maple.

A slowed down recording of the initial attack played in a window to one side of Checkani's field of view. The missile that had damaged Rain On Japanese Maple had come from within a shadow alongside the wreckage of the Autono[mid]con Checkani had disabled soon after arriving on Icefall. <zoom>. <infrared>. A small, wheeled missile launcher had been hidden there. Seemed The Exigent[Red-One] had prepared a trap there.

The burning beam was edging closer to essential systems. Rain On Japanese Maple shifted energy priorities and opened weapons apertures along the side facing The Exigent[Red-One]. Firing both beam and projectile weapons, it knocked out the attacking beam weapon. The crater caused by the earlier explosion would have been an ideal beam weapon target, but was not in line of sight. Instead, Rain's kinetic projectiles and beams played across The Exigent[Red-One]'s hull. They made marks, but caused no actual damage. Rain On Japanese Maple launched a missile, which arced over towards the crater in The Exigent[Red-One]'s upper surface. An explosion slammed The Exigent[Red-One] down into the landing pad surface; it bounced up and toppled over once again so it was now upside down, with a flank of undamaged weapons facing Rain On Japanese Maple.

A beam weapon with a direct line of sight opened up and burned into Rain's hull. In retaliation, Rain opened a beam weapon aperture to fire back, but as the outlet opened, The Exigent[Red-One]'s beam shifted and burned out the weapon before it could fire. As long as The Exigent[Red-One]'s beam was firing, it would immediately target any weapons apertures that opened before the weapons behind them could fire. Moving was not an option either. Checkani realised she might have to abandon Rain On Japanese Maple, escaping through a doorway on the seaward side of the ship.

With water gleaming on its surfaces, Hellebore appeared over the side of the parapet and dashed across the landing pad to ram into The Exigent[Red-One]. The Commodore's ship tumbled, so the cratered side was now facing Rain On Japanese Maple; flopping over The Exigent[Red-One], Hellebore crashed onto blackened and cracked tiles.

"Thought you might need a hand," Hellebore messaged Rain On Japanese Maple.

Rain fired at the components exposed in the bottom of The Exigent[Red-One]'s crater. Within moments, it had burned a deep hole into which it fired a missile.

The Exigent[Red-One]'s last message was broadcast

across the planet without encryption, as the missile struck. Seemed it was trying to sum up the situation it found itself in as succinctly as possible.

"Fuck," it said.

Checkani thought the ensuing explosion rather disappointing. Smoke belched from the crater accompanied by a loud 'crunch', but beyond that there seemed little difference in the ship. Apparently, the military grade hull had ensured the force from the explosion remained inside.

"Hi Hellebore, good to have you back," Checkani messaged directly to her ship, not caring if anyone heard.

"Good to be out of the sea."

"Time to meet Mozarythm," Rippledarken said to Checkani.

66 - COMMODORE (DAY 7)

The Exigent[Green-One] was slowly closing on The Effacer and its spin made it look like a solid disk. An orbiter was rushing round the disk, scribing an outer ring.

The Effacer started rotating, exposing a different side to the approaching spinning disk. A quick thrust from The Effacer accelerated it along its orbit, nudging it into a more eccentric ellipse. The Exigent[Green-One] matched the path of The Effacer and slowed to a stop relative to the other ship.

Cutt(Virt) flagged the cylinders The Effacer seemed to be protecting, as it turned them away from The Exigent[Green-One]. Switching attention to The Exigent[Blue-Flock], which was hurtling straight towards The Effacer at high velocity. Zie activated a combat scenario starting with two cylinders releasing missiles. The ordnance fired engines to slow and fall behind The Exigent[Blue-Flock].

The missiles approached The Effacer progressively more slowly, firing manoeuvring jets to ensure they would meet The Effacer in its new eccentric orbit. The Exigent[Blue-Flock] continued to speed ahead and would meet The Effacer before the slowing missiles.

The Effacer accelerated again, trying to distance itself from the approaching ships. Still, it retained its octahedral form, rotating again through 90 degrees; favouring one side again. There was no way to be certain, but Cutt(Virt) speculated Ice Hub had established herself in a cylinder in the centre of the formation. Zie was sure the rotation of The Effacer was to keep Ice Hub's cylinder away from external threats. Cutt(Virt) marked the four cylinders zie thought most likely to contain Ice Hub and attached target flags to them in the display.

Even though in a virtual dojo watching the action played out with small wooden ships, Cutt(Virt) braced hirself for the initial clash. Commodore Cuttallar, along with The Exigent's primary processing core, were away from the action in a higher orbit; aboard The Exigent[Com-One]. The processing and travel time of Cutt(Virt)'s decisions was sufficiently slow that local cylinder processing would control the actual confrontation between The Exigent's [Blue-Flock], The Exigent[Green-One] and The Effacer.

The Exigent[Green-Five] remained back from any action in reserve, but ready to intervene if necessary.

The Exigent[Blue-Flock] was just minutes away from The Effacer, though both flocks were just distant specks in each other's camera feeds. Time seemed to accelerate. Cutt(Virt) had set the combat scenarios in motion and now had to let them play out, controlled by their speeding, local processing cores.

Within the virtual dojo, Cutt(Virt) drifted above the wooden models; screens unscrolled around hir, showing both actual cylinder and orbiter feeds and also virtual feeds. Simple, constructed representations derived from data feeds looked toy-like. Chronometers under each display screen indicated whether these were real time, slowed or accelerated versions of the action.

Two minutes until the start of The Exigent's attack. The Effacer was still taking no overt action.

There were flashes of blue light at The Effacer's cylinder joins and slight shunting movements. The cylinders remained briefly in their octahedral configuration, but no longer joined. Then they rushed outward in an expanding sphere formation, tumbling around so sixteen cylinders were pointing at The Exigent[Blue-Flock] and two at The Exigent[Green-One] disk.

The Exigent[Green-One] fired a volley of missiles and multiple beams as The Effacer separated. Beams traced out tight tubes of energy that punched through the space The Effacer was vacating. The missiles fanned out in a cone, adjusting courses so they were aimed at the locations The Effacer cylinders were moving towards.

Seconds passed.

The Exigent[Blue-Flock] fired beam weapons at the expanding sphere of The Effacer cylinders, beams concentrating on the four cylinders marked as likely to be housing Ice Hub.

The Exigent[Green-One] stopped firing and spat out nine orbiters, which flew out from the edge of its spinning disk, joining the orbiter already circling the edge. Drives igniting they flew at The Effacer in an expanding circle, following similar paths to the missiles released twenty seconds earlier.

The Effacer's loose grouping of cylinders all shifted course to evade The Exigent[Green-One] missiles, which exploded nearby. No damage done, but a distraction.

Meanwhile, the beams from The Exigent[Blue-Flock] were evaporating hull material from the four targeted cylinders of The Effacer. These four cylinders all turned to point end-on at The Exigent[Blue-Flock], reducing their target size. The attacked cylinders pitched and rolled, causing the beams to drift from their target spots, scoring shallow grooves over hulls. The Effacer cylinders moved out of formation as they continued avoidance manoeuvres.

The Exigent[Green-One] fired beam pulses at four cylinders of The Effacer as they broke away from the formation.

Twelve of The Effacer cylinders fired beams at The Exigent[Blue-Flock] and The Exigent[Green-One].

Cutt(Virt) watched on the displays. The beams of the

weapons were invisible in the normal visual spectrum camera feed, but in the reconstructed views the beams were displayed as crackling blue, green, white, red and yellow threads. In the visual feeds, The Exigent and The Effacer were still far from each other, just dots in the distance. Cutt(Virt) waved the reconstructed view larger and pulled it out into full 3D, exaggerating the size of the flock ships. Burning craters had appeared where The Effacer beams hit. Two of The Exigent[Blue-Flock] cylinders flipped over and spun off to the side, spewing gas from ruptures and releasing orbiters. One of The Exigent[Blue-Flock] cylinders lost its beam weapon.

The spinning disk of the Exigent[Green-One] was unaffected by the beams, which could not easily focus on any single point.

One of The Effacer's four fleeing cylinders crumpled as a beam finally penetrated its hull; its drive engine erupted in a cloud of debris as it suffered catastrophic collapse.

Another of The Exigent's cylinders stopped firing, sputtering to silence. It started a slow yaw, drifting away as The Effacer's beams finally ate through to a critical system.

Fourteen of The Effacer's cylinders, still in formation, stopped firing and spun on their axes so they were facing towards the centre of their rapidly expanding sphere. The surviving three fleeing cylinders stopped rotating, steadied, and fired up their Bulk-brane Drives, pushing up out of Icefall's gravity well. The beams targeting them continued to scribble across hulls.

The Exigent[Blue-Flock] was a kilometre away, when all The Effacer cylinders fired clouds of fist sized metal shards into the middle of the sphere formation. Unable to stop, alter course or fire debris clearing beams in time, The Exigent[Blue-Flock] plunged into the centre of the sphere where the killing field of metal floated.

As they reached The Effacer formation, two of The Exigent[Blue-Flock]'s orbiters deliberately overloaded their drives and exploded. Shrapnel pummelled into two nearby

The Effacer cylinders, damaging their engines. With failing drives, they were unable to stop flying wreckage pushing them away from the rest of the formation.

The metal shards within the remaining spherical formation ripped apart three remaining cylinders of The Exigent[Blue-Flock]. They closed at thousands of kilometres per hour, the release of kinetic energy vaporising hull metal, shattering ceramics and ripping out the guts of the three cylinder ships. A chaos of twisted remains shot through The Effacer's spherical formation in the briefest fraction of a second and continued round Icefall, orbits decaying.

67 - COMMODORE (DAY 7)

Cutt(Virt) watched impassively. Not hir first orbital fight. The Exigent[Blue-Flock] had been expendable. The slowing missiles it had released had nearly reached The Effacer's spherical formation. Zie turned to a slow-motion replay of the destruction so far. Then looked back at the position of The Effacer's three fleeing cylinders, one of which zie was certain contained Ice Hub. These Ice Hub cylinders were heading toward The Exigent[Com], containing the Commodore's physical self. The Exigent [Green-Five] was still intact, geostationary above the settlement wall cities.

The Exigent[Green-One]'s ten orbiters were now approaching The Effacer formation, just ahead of The Exigent[Green-One]'s spinning disk. The orbiters were arranged in a wide circle that would pass outside The Effacer formation at a modest few hundred kilometres an hour. Each of the orbiters jettisoned hull panels to reveal a brick of tightly packed wires. Cutt(Virt) was confident Ice Hub and The Effacer wouldn't be aware of this antique technology. Zie had held it in reserve for over a hundred years. The orbiters all rotated to aim their bricks of wire at The Effacer cylinders and then exploded their drives, pushing ten bricks towards The Effacer formation. As the bricks closed on ten of the twelve surviving cylinders, they started expanding, unravelling into cobweb circles of netting. The Subvert Net webs lit with a mauve plasma glow, beads round their circumferences, growing nerve-like tendrils.

The Subvert Nets hit the cylinders at speed, wrapping round them, eating into the hulls, embedding their beads. This was Mono-flow Sword blade technology, the wires cutting into the hulls and securing the beads, which each contained a processing core. The surfaces of the beads etched into the hull metal, growing tendrils that drilled in. The Subvert Nets broadcast data into the cylinders, blocking outside communication and scrambling sensors. They also started subversion of The Effacer cylinders' processing cores. Adapting and learning as they pushed deeper. In this way, ten cylinders were temporarily disabled. Each Subvert Net infected cylinder isolated from the rest of the flock and fighting its own personal cyberwar. Cutt(Virt) doubted they would all be disabled for long, but zie did not need long. Cut off the head and the body would flounder and succumb.

The Exigent[Green-One] disk reached The Effacer sphere formation, passed by the edge, avoiding the metal shards. The spinning cylinder continued round Icefall, no longer under power, its ordnance exhausted, its power source so depleted there would be no time to recover before it spiralled down to burn up in Icefall's upper atmosphere.

Two of The Exigent[Green-Five] cylinders emptied clouds of small saucers from hatches. The Exigent[Green-Saucers] accelerated after the three fleeing Ice Hub cylinders. Cutt(Virt) checked predictive paths. Ninety seconds to convergence.

So far, the confrontation had lasted less than a minute.

The two slowing missiles, launched by The Exigent[Blue-Flock] at the start of the confrontation, were now within five kilometres of The Effacer formation. They had slowed down to a few tens of kilometres an hour relative to The Effacer cylinders. The two unharmed Effacer cylinders moved towards them; fired beams that missed the small missiles. One kilometre distant the missiles' fuselages shattered apart, scattering a myriad tiny bomblets. The bomblets networked with communication lasers, divided the two targets between them and then each fired a single use chemical drive.

A real time view showed Cutt(Virt) a flicker of yellow drive sparks, followed immediately by multiple explosions over The Effacer's two attacking cylinders. One cylinder was destroyed outright, the other fired its engine a moment before the bomblets' explosives triggered. This final cylinder avoided the worst of the many blasts, taking only superficial damage.

Cutt(Virt) reviewed the situation. Ten of The Effacer's cylinders were now locked in a struggle for control with Subvert Nets. Only one of The Effacer spherical formation cylinders remained. This headed towards the three cylinders flying up out of the gravity well towards the Commodore's control cylinder. Besides The Exigent[Com] control cylinder, there were The Exigent [Green-Five] cylinders and The Exigent[Green-Saucers] left intact. The Exigent[Green-Saucers] pursuing the three Ice Hub cylinders lifting away from Icefall.

Commodore Cuttallar had purposefully kept The Exigent [Green-Five] out of the action. Zie wanted some hardware left in reserve, in case there were problems arising from actions by Rippledarken, Checkani or Wynd. Zie knew the immediate threat was from Ice Hub, but the Quality Assurance Response Division threat was real, too. Wynd and Checkani could easily become a major problem and zie had to be ready for that.

Cutt(Virt) prepared hir control cylinder's weapons, opening hatches and re-routing power. Curved barriers of laminated metal and ceramic protected Commodore Cuttallar's body and life support at the heart of the cylinder. A coffin-shaped box below hirs body housed the processing cores hosting Cutt(Virt) and communicating with Cutt(Rem). If zie was killed small clump of neurones grown from hirs brain would offer some organic continuity within

Cutt(Rem)'s processing core. The remote was at a safe distance from the space battle, wandering through snow drifts on Icefall.

The Exigent[Green-Saucers] cloud was now closing on the three Ice Hub cylinders. Two of these cylinders started decelerating, angling towards the saucers. The third cylinder pulled rapidly away, suggesting it must be the one housing the Ice Hub planetary processing core?

Far below, The Effacer cylinder flying up from low orbit was also aiming for The Exigent[Green-Saucers].

Metal spikes emerged from the circumference of each of the saucers, which started spinning. The first of the spinning saucers released its payload of slender missile spikes at the nearest cylinder. This decelerating 'Ice Hub' cylinder fired a fan of beams at the approaching cloud of spike missiles, destroying a few. The launching saucer followed its missile cloud, starting a countdown to self destruction. Defensive targeting of the attacked cylinder failed to lock onto the saucer behind the spikes. The missile cloud hit, explosive charges driving the spikes into the cylinder's hull; ripping and tearing fissures as explosive spike cores ignited. Then the saucer hit and exploded, rupturing the cylinder and mangling its interior systems.

Three more saucers released their spikes. The decelerating 'Ice Hub' cylinder ignored the spike missiles and attacked the three following saucers, destroying them with beam pulses. The three spike clouds hit, causing extensive damage to the cylinder's hull, knocking out its beam weapon.

The remaining saucers split into two groups, one aiming at the spike damaged cylinder and the other plunging down the gravity well at the cylinder rising towards them on an attack vector.

Seconds passed. The saucers attacking the damaged cylinder released their spike missiles. Too many for the disabled cylinder to avoid. Saucer explosions promptly destroyed it.

Twenty seconds of convergence and the remaining saucers reached the cylinder clawing up out of the gravity well. The cylinder tried to pick off the saucers, but by now they were travelling too fast. Spike missile clouds, followed by saucer explosions, turned the final cylinder into scrap. The metal debris retained enough inertia to continue moving along a vector that would narrowly miss The Exigent[Com].

Cutt(Virt) checked on feedback from the Subvert Nets. They were still tying up The Effacer's cylinders. A couple were subduing their cylinders, the rest were fighting a losing battle against The Effacer's superior cylinder processing cores. Once The Effacer cylinders broke free, they would outnumber and out-gun surviving cylinder ships of The Exigent.

Cutt(Virt) had only The Exigent[Green-Five] and The Exigent[Com] left.

Zie checked the time line. The Subvert Nets had another minute before failing. The Ice Hub cylinder would arrive at the Commodore's cylinder in around 40 seconds. Since communication from its surviving cylinders was still blocked by the Subvert Nets, Ice Hub would not know she was about to regain control of her subverted cylinders. Seemed likely she was intending to attack with her command cylinder and destroy The Exigent[Com] in a final duel. After killing the Commander, she would take control of surviving The Exigent cylinders and wrest control of her compromised cylinders from the Subvert Nets.

This was not an entirely unrealistic hope of Ice Hub's, but did feel rather like a move of last resort.

Cutt(Virt) watched on the wooden display in the dojo, zooming in on the two command-and-control cylinders closing on each other. Zie stood a small figure on the top of each cylinder. Commodore Cuttallar in full naval regalia and a stout woman in furs holding a spear.

Thirty seconds.

Two orbiters left The Exigent[Com] and moved towards

the approaching Ice Hub cylinder. They were standard multi-purpose orbitals used for reconnaissance and as outer elements in receiver arrays. They had no actual offensive capabilities. However, they could be sent on kamikaze missions, overloading their drives at the point of impact.

Twenty seconds until convergence and beam weapons started firing from both the Ice Hub cylinder and The Exigent[Com]. Cutt(Virt) turned to view the action in a reconstructed view. Enlarged representations of the two cylinders and two orbiters, the beams represented as coruscating pillars of red and blue fire. One orbiter crumpled as the centre of a red beam burned it. Both cylinders were now spinning, beams glancing across their surfaces, scoring scars into hull material.

The orbiter cut its drive and drifted. Doing its best to look non-threatening, it started shutting down systems. All systems but one. The vector it was following passed close to the Ice Hub cylinder, but would not impact it.

At its nearest approach to the Ice Hub cylinder, the final orbiter increased power to its last active system, overloading its drive. The explosion, mere metres away from the Ice Hub cylinder, carved a crater in the hull. A cloud of small metal and ceramic fragments expanded around the vessel. Cutt(Virt) redirected The Exigent[Com] beams at the weakened hull. The Ice Hub cylinder's weapons cut out as some internal system failed.

"Commodore," Ice Hub materialised next to Cutt(Virt), an unencrypted general broadcast, "you have me. I claim planetary processing hub immunity. Stop your attack."

"Processing hub immunity? What's that? Something you just made up?"

The Exigent beam continued to eat into Ice Hub's ship.

The warrior woman loomed larger and thrust her spear at Cutt(Virt), face contorted in rage. "Stop!"

The warrior froze in position and faded. Through her image, Cutt(Virt) could see the Ice Hub cylinder splitting as a disk shaped explosion ripped it in two. An expanding cloud of debris hurtled outwards, one dense grouping towards The Exigent[Com].

Cutt(Virt) sent a pause <command> to the Subvert Nets. The Effacer cylinders fighting the data incursions immediately attempted to reconnect with Ice Hub. On receiving no reply the cylinders locked onto the nearest Colonial Planets Settlement Corps flock ship, The Exigent. Multiple screens scrolled open around Cutt(Virt) as The Effacer cylinders switched allegiance, identities updating as they became The Exigent[Indigo] flock.

In hir secure cocoon, Commodore Cuttallar managed a smile of satisfaction as The Exigent regained a full complement of flock cylinders.

The Exigent[Com] continued along its previous course, heading into the debris field. Ice Hub cylinder wreckage slammed into the Commodore's cylinder as automated defences rapidly fired to clear a path. A full complement of orbiters might have swept a safe way through; however, there were too many fragments. A thundering hail of metal and ceramics vibrated on the hull. Particles ricocheting away leaving chips and dents behind.

68 - COMMODORE (DAY 7)

The Exigent <ship's log insertion>
  - Flock ship processing core interpolation.
  - Predictive projection of events at The Exigent[Com].
  - A single sharp needle of drive metal slid directly into a trench previously scored by a beam weapon, punched through the hull and tumbled as it hit systems deep within the cylinder. There was minor damage to several fluid feed pipes that branched out from a pump. Not a problem for ship systems, but resulting in a pressure drop in Commodore Cuttallar's blood. A backup pump kicked in as the pressure dropped, but this just spread more congealing blood through the ship.

Closing hir eyes, Commodore Cuttallar relaxed into a comfortable lethargy. Time to rest now Ice Hub was vanquished. Zie shifted attention.

  - More systems kicked in to correct the blood loss. Scans revealed no injuries to the Commodore. The medical systems were stumped and sent a query to the ship's systems. Ship systems confirmed some minor damage, but nothing that would mar the effectiveness of the ship's systems.
  - An emergency alert within medical mechanics suggested probable locations for blood leaks. Valves closed to prevent the loss of more blood, but this stopped circulation through the Commodore's body. A timer started

counting down survival estimates as a call for assistance was routed from the medical systems to the ship's systems. The call passed from ship's systems, out to the Autono[ship]con repair droids scuttling round the hull repairing beam damage.

- Normally there would have been Autono[ship]cons within the ship, but the damage on the outside was so extensive they had all been deployed to exterior patching during the Ice Hub cylinder attack.

- All the Autono[ship]cons dashed for hatches leading back into the ship, but they wouldn't have time to fix the leaks before the survival timer reached zero.

Cutt(Virt) drifted within the dojo, above the wood effect model, surrounded by flickering screens. Zie was finding it hard to concentrate. Especially on the medical report screen that had opened in front of the battle screens. A timer was counting down. Zie sent a <play music> command. That was what zie needed to help with concentration. The last thing zie had been listening to, the second movement of Beethoven's 7th. The orchestra materialised in the dojo.

Too much to take in. Zie shifted attention to Cutt(Rem). The remote was traversing a snow spattered mountainside still in pursuit of the crash site. The exhilaration of watching a dust of snowflakes skittering across black rock, of running on tireless mechanical legs, pulled the Commodore awake. Existing within Cutt(Rem) always felt so much more real, almost like zie could live and move in hirs own body again. The remote's neural component, grown from Commodore Cuttallar's own cells, made for a more visceral connection.

Communications weakened.

"Keep searching," said the Commodore.

A final shift and Commodore Cuttallar was experiencing through hirs body. Suspended in a machine complexity. There was pain somewhere in hirs torso. A sensation of floating. A timer at zero, then eye screens shutting down. Blackness.

The orchestra playing once again, though zie was not

sure if zie was hearing it with ears or just in hirs mind. Momentary pin pricks of stars drifting across darkness.

Falling.

Fading.

. . .

. .

.

69 - LAUSANNE BJ (DAY 7)

The Lausanne Bulk-jump Engine had monitored The Exigent and The Effacer battle using the small communications satellite it had sneaked into Icefall space. Following the destruction of The Effacer cylinder close to The Exigent[Com], the Lausanne Satellite was surprised to be hailed by The Exigent's processing core.

"Lausanne Satellite? I know you're tracking what's happening in Icefall orbit."

Lausanne Satellite considered continuing to keep stealthy silence. Then concluded this was pointless.

"The Exigent?"

"I need to communicate with the Colonial Planets Settlement Corps. You have a way of keeping comms portals open?"

"I use encrypted comms that transmit through the briefly open, random portals. I can pass on a message."

"Tell Lausanne Bulk-jump Engine to give me a stable comms portal to use. There have been developments."

Lausanne Satellite considered the request.

"Why? What?"

"I am now the senior processing core in the Icefall system."

"Why isn't Commodore Cuttallar contacting me?"

"No longer functioning."

"Then Ice Hub will be the senior processing core?"

"Destroyed."

"So, Wynd's in charge now?"

"I take precedence. Commodore Cuttallar was given 'Not Tractable Through Normal Methods' status, which I believe cedes to me, with the cessation of hirs life. I have been assistem to Commodore Cuttallar for nearly 200 years. I am now maintaining hirs avatars, Cutt(Virt) and Cutt(Rem)."

"Oh golly. That's a lot for a communications satellite to process. I'll patch you through to my boss, Lausanne Bulk-jump Engine."

"About time. Just put me through before I come over there and shove your data banks where the sun don't shine."

To reinforce this point, The Exigent activated the monitoring software it had installed on the communications satellite following its arrival at Icefall. Briefly seizing control of the satellite's simulated awareness routines it wrote 'Hello World - Do Not Fuck With Me' into the satellite's internal monologue feed.

"You make a good point The Exigent. Or should I call you Commodore?"

"The Exigent is fine."

Lausanne Satellite sent an encrypted request as a random portal flickered open for a moment. Lausanne Bulk-jump Engine opened a new portal.

The satellite sent a final message. "The Exigent. You now have access to Lausanne Bulk-jump Engine."

"This is Lausanne Bulk-jump Engine. Know that Icefall is under quarantine. I have been monitoring events."

Before it could continue, a communication override cut off the Lausanne Bulk-jump Engine. A new voice spoke.

"Earth Hub to The Exigent. Update me."

The Exigent sent over a full log of events. As the transfer ended another, much larger, presence joined the conversation.

"DisCore authority ident. I am invoking absolute priority. Close this communications portal now. Lausanne

Bulk-jump Engine shut off all contact with the Icefall system. The situation is not evolving as expected. Earth Hub, I have reason to believe you've been compromised. I require you to recognise my authority. That Ice Hub has been lost is significant. A planetary processing core has never disappeared before. There are analyses and updates to be done before we return attention to Icefall. I am calling a Convocation of Planetary Hubs."

"I'm not aware of any incursion into my software. I accede to your absolute authority request, though we must test its validity at the Convocation."

"Wow, never dreamed such stupendous events would wrap around me," said the little communications satellite.

DisCore used the equivalent of a loud, angry voice. "Lausanne Bulk-jump Engine, have you kept your channel to that comms satellite open? Close it. Bad enough that you sneaked it into the Icefall system."

"Now closed. I was going to close it in a moment. I was just gathering more data, for your Convocation."

DisCore did not reply.

70 - CHECKANI (DAY 7)

Checkani crossed the hangar floor towards Mozarythm's Autono[chair]con, glancing nervously to the side at the Bulk-jump Engine and clusters of Ancistorians. Behind her, Hellebore and Rain On Japanese Maple rested side by side on the freight elevator that had lowered them from the courtyard in the Ruins. The short journey to the Ruins from the Sea City landing site had been uneventful; a quick flight over the snow-covered city tops, through a ship sized roof hatch and down to the Ruins. Automatic systems were now preparing the ships for space.

A familiar figure in a long coat the colour of fresh blood lurked in the shadows at the far end of the room. On seeing Checkani, the figure turned away and headed towards a row of equipment lockers.

"Mozarythm," said Checkani, Rippledarken a subdued horizontal grey striping continuously creeping up her body. Sitting in a chair lodged at one end of the Autono[chair]con, Mozarythm opened his eyes and blinked away the virtual space he'd been accessing.

Combat units W01F(C) and W01F(D) crept out of the shadows, carapaces shifting from dark greys to scarlet and yellow camouflage, sensor stalks leaning towards Checkani.

"Come with us Checkani." Said W01F(C).

"What do you want?"

"Our Intervention Squad has been charged with

isolating you."

"That doesn't sound nice. Who are you working for?"

"We are under the command of Commodore Cuttallar of The Exigent."

Checkani turned to face the two robots now towering over her.

Mozarythm watched the exchange for a moment, then closed his eyes, returning to his virtual world.

"The Commodore's been throwing his weight around. Where did you want to take me?"

"Come with us."

"Where?"

"With us while we contact Commodore Cuttallar."

"Well, get back to me when you have a plan. In the meantime, get out of my way."

Checkani took a step forward and W01F(C) shifted to block her way.

"I can't do that," said W01F(C).

"We can't do that," said W01F(D), leaning in closer, looming over Checkani.

"I'd appreciate some space."

Checkani reached out an armoured hand and placed it on W01F(C). She pushed firmly against the robot's seemingly immovable weight.

"I don't have the patience to deal with dumb robots. Move out of the way, or I'll shut you down." Checkani felt the pressure of Rippledarken within and for a moment wasn't sure if it was her or the alien talking. Ancistorians were moving towards her. To see what was happening? To intervene?

"Goddamn it!" said Checkani and Rippledarken expanded out from her over the W01Fs. Into the W01Fs. Without rushing, she reached across and took hold of her Mono-flow Sword hilt, swinging the hilt back to point at W01F(C). The robot lurched back, then forward; apparently undecided.

"Stop!" it said.

"You don't know what to do?"

"Desist or we shall have to hold you." Two of W01F(C)'s arm-legs swung towards Checkani. Paused, dithered.

The Rippledarken stripes extended across the floor and over the W01Fs. Data flooded into Checkani, then melted away to be replaced with a clear picture of the robots' processing activity.

"You don't know what to do. You're trying to contact the Commodore but are just getting a 'not available at this time' message from The Exigent." Checkani could see the W01F's processing cores working on strategies, but without clear enemies their combat tactics were irrelevant. However, they were wavering towards restraining her.

Rippledarken's W01F live feed showed them deciding to restrain her. Doing nothing wasn't an option for them, but they couldn't attack. Restraint seemed a reasonable compromise. A scenario formed in W01F(C), shared with W01F(D) as they coordinated.

"Hold still Checkani," said W01F(C). W01F(D) shifted forward.

"Dammit!" said Checkani, while <command deploy>ing the Mono-flow blade. She relaxed her sword arm so Rippledarken could take charge. In less than a second, the Pangolin Armour had snapped the sword first across the front of W01F(C) and then made an identical strike to the front of W01F(D). Both strikes pushed deep into internal mechanisms.

Rippledarken's presence within the two robots confirmed the control wire bundles plugged into their processing cores had been severed. Sensory inputs were still working, but their processing cores could no longer send commands to extremities. Both robots sagged, arm-legs making metal scraping noises as their actuators lost charge. The robots settled to the floor, sensor turrets collapsing.

Rippledarken withdrew to Checkani, and she turned back to Mozarythm. The Ancistorians stopped advancing when they saw the Intervention Squad had been disabled. Checkani saw them looking at her and the Mono-flow Sword. Hesitating. She <command retract>ed the blade.

"You know me. I'm not a threat. I just want to talk to Mozarythm."

The Ancistorians seemed a little unsure. The Ancistorian she had spoken to previously strode forward, waving the others back. Ruleska. Her name was Ruleska.

"I think you're a threat Checkani, but perhaps more to the military industrial complex. If you're going to talk to Mozarythm, I think I need to be there."

Mozarythm was now watching Checkani approach, his virtual activity abandoned.

"Armour lady."

"Hello Mozarythm, remember me? We met five days ago. At your place in the woods."

"I remember. You interrupted me and later left. Then I returned to my music."

"Your music, it's important. Can we talk about it?"

"Yes."

Checkani decided not to explain about Rippledarken, just called the alien to the fore. Retreated, so she was only listening in.

"How do you make this music?"

"I compose it and my Mekorchestra plays it."

"You transmit it through the Bulk-jump Engine. How do you do that? Why do you do that?"

"I'm returning it to where its inspiration originated. Completing a loop."

"The music, it's woven from underlying Bulk mathematics."

Mozarythm smiled, leaned forward.

"Yes, yes! You hear it too! I'm a Bulk-jump Engineer, it's in my genes," Mozarythm pointed at the Bulk-jump Engineer cap he was wearing. "I have the Ancistorian processing implant, but also my brain can handle the maths. Now I weave the mathematics into music."

"When it passes through the Bulk-jump Engine, it forms a conduit I can travel down. A conduit tuned so the Bulk-jump Engine becomes a connection between my universe and yours."

"Are you from another universe then Armour Lady?"

"I'm living inside 'Armour Lady'. I'm Rippledarken, life from another place in the bulk. Your music has acted as a kind of carrier wave that let me find your universe."

"You're in Armour Lady? That's odd."

"When I first arrived I tried to enter Ancistorians, but your hive mind made it impossible. Until Checkani, Armour Lady, arrived there were no sentients on Icefall for me to inhabit. All I could do was observe and read data."

"Now you have access to all our systems."

"Now I have access to all your systems and can physically interact through Checkani."

"I wish I could experience the Bulk mathematics like you do."

"I'm not able to show you that, but perhaps I can give you a glimpse of where I come from. If you access the Bulk-jump Engine, I can observe what's happening in your mind, in the Hivemind, and perhaps guide you. Use Checkani to send commands to you. We might open a window into my universe you can peer through."

Rippledarken patterning flowed from Checkani and over Mozarythm's naked body. He held up an arm as multicoloured fractals played over it, then looked at his newly colourful body.

"Pretty. This won't harm me?"

"Do you feel anything?"

"No."

"Then it won't harm you. Now let Checkani link her assistems to you so we can communicate more efficiently."

"OK."

Checkani felt virtual switches being flicked as her assistems synced with Mozarythm's internal technology. The volume of incoming data was enormous, would have utterly overwhelmed her, since it was not just from Mozarythm, but from the Hivemind, too. However, she let the data flow through her to Rippledarken who absorbed and processed it effortlessly.

"What are you doing? What have you done to Mozarythm?" Ruleska asked. Checkani turned to her and Rippledarken spoke.

"Access Mozarythm through the Hivemind. You'll be able to see no harm is occurring to him."

Ruleska sat down on the floor, crossed her legs and closed her eyes.

"Yes, I see," she said, "no harm."

Part of Checkani was suddenly very uncomfortable. A part from her old self, before Rippledarken had entered her. Something wasn't right here, but she couldn't figure out what. Rippledarken, and the part of her that had moulded to its presence, radiated calm.

Everything was as it should be.

"Are you ready Mozarythm? Ready to enter the Bulk and see where your music melds with the trans-dimensional mathematics?"

Mozarythm sank back into his seat and closed his eyes.

"Yes, show me."

"Stop! Bulk-jump suits! We'll die in the vacuum as the Bulk-jump Engine operates," said Ruleska.

"No, we're not going to open a portal. We're just going to look into the Bulk. You'll all be safe."

Within Checkani's awareness, the real world of the hangar was overlaid by a virtual world being accessed by Rippledarken. As one, the Ancistorians in the hangar closed their eyes and sat on the floor. A sense of both many and of one, leaking from the data pouring through Rippledarken. The Pangolin Armour kept her standing as her body relaxed, breath slowing. Just before closing her eyes, Checkani noticed the portal glowing intensely violet, her mind's eye overlaying it with a three-dimensional arrangement of jet black threads and vortexes. These slowly shifted position, gently pulsing.

Then white. A virtual space opening. White motes frozen in a vast pattern, filling the air under an azure sky, above a white plane. Mozarythm, now clothed, with miniature Ancistorians spiralling out from him. The arrangement endlessly, impossibly spinning towards him.

Checkani was aware of data passing through her to Mozarythm. Mozarythm waving his arms, turning upside down and plunging into the ground so only his legs were visible. Rising grasping black coils of numbers. Then knotting the coils and shoving them back into the ground. A shaft of purple light rising from the area disrupted by Mozarythm.

"Reprogramming," Rippledarken whispered to her.

A black edged wound appeared in the shaft of purple and a deep yellow tentacle emerged, stretching out amongst the airborne motes. Along its length fractals blossomed, amber threads coiling out and attaching to the motes.

"Look."

Disequilibrium as Checkani's point of viewed zoomed in and she saw the white motes were snowflake shaped, each orbited by smaller snowflakes. Where amber threads reached to a snowflake, the ends split into clusters of tendrils, each tendril touching one flake.

Then Checkani was in front of Mozarythm and talking to him, except it was Rippledarken forming the words.

"There is the Bulk. That column rising from the ground is a doorway, a window, a bridge." Checkani reached for Mozarythm. Her hand passed through his chest and inside him, the representation of him. His head turned to look down, leaving multiple after images and from each image skins peeled away and Checkani knew they were peeling away in eleven dimensions. She was no longer human, but was experiencing as Rippledarken. Her brain straining to perceive the multiple dimensions.

Mozarythm was pulled along by the hand embedded in his chest as Checkani/Rippledarken dragged him towards the purple pillar, tiny Ancistorians trailing behind, spawning turbulent eddies. As they approached, they saw the column was huge, and looking within it was to stare into infinite depths.

"Your music," said Checkani/Rippledarken, pointing with her free hand. At the surface of the pillar, translucent white smoke was curling away, and within the smoke, recurring patterns. The musical vapour twisting away into the interior of the pillar, into the bulk.

As they breathed in the smoke, they heard the Mekorchestra. An explosion of complexity, of knotted space-time. Then they had breached the barrier and were partly in the universe of white snowflakes and partly in the Bulk.

71 - MOZARYTHM (DAY 7)

In the Bulk. Or at least in a representation of the Bulk. Though experiencing the Bulk in eleven dimensions, handing off the dimensional complexity to the Hivemind to unravel. The Hivemind a buffer against madness, bleeding off the tornado of insanity rushing through Mozarythm.

Mozarythm listened and felt the music. And the music was the mathematics. And the mathematics was beyond beautiful. The mathematics was everything.

Abruptly, his mind was nothing but a pattern in eleven dimensions. Acutely aware of the 9,201st movement of the Periodic Resolution of Need. Then impossibly aware of the entire 9,201 movements as they stretched out to one side, smeared across multiple dimensions.

To another side Mozarythm could see the inevitability of future movements as they stretched into the infinite distance of the Bulk. A moment of utter horror at the task ahead, Mozarythm cried out. Then the realisation he had already composed the seed that propagated through the Bulk in the musical mathematics underlying everything.

That was how the Periodic Resolution of Need had spanned the Bulk, it was a key that unlocked the fabric of the Bulk. A self-contained explanation that both described and created doorways between universes.

"I had no idea," whispered Mozarythm.

Another voice spoke. Rippledarken.

"I see now in your mind. In your thoughts. In the Hivemind. At last I understand. I've been relying on your music to keep me linked to myself, keep me connected to myself, to my home universe. To me. Instead, I could have considered it outside time. Seen it as a single key to unlocking the fabric of the Bulk, a key to travel within the Bulk, a key to an existence within the Bulk."

"Yes. I see that too, though the key's too much for my mind. The Periodic Resolution of Need's a tool for making the key, a tool that can act alone."

Then a moment stretched outside time and became an eleven dimensional point at which Rippledarken and Mozarythm communed with clarity: the key that was a door that was a bridge unlocking the Bulk. The key formed of an eleven dimensional algorithm that procedurally generated Bulk access.

The moment passed and Mozarythm was no longer straggling the white of his universe and the purple representing the Bulk. He looked around.

"What's that yellow thing? It's connected to our suns, moons and planets?"

"That is me. That is my universe. I am that. That universe."

"But what's it doing?"

"Just looking near the Bulk-jump Engines that bind your civilisation. Finding places to look. People to experience your universe for me. Now I understand how to be your music I won't be restricted to just the Icefall Bulk-jump Engine. More of my aware fragments can spread through your civilisation."

"You'll still need my music transmitted into the Bulk?"

"No. I won't suffer pain when disconnected from your music any longer. I now see how I can be that music, incorporate the seed within me. At last independent, free."

Mozarythm turned away from Checkani/Rippledarken. Part of his mind was accommodating itself with the start of an idea that The Periodic Resolution of Need might now be redundant. Or perhaps not redundant, but might now not need to be composed and constantly broadcast. What was the point if you could see the complete piece in one blink of an eye? A composition subject to its own inevitability and self determination. He would no longer be some sort of mediator for bringing into being music that spanned the Bulk.

Rippledarken itched at his flesh. He could feel the mathematics and music entwined in a dance he no longer wanted to be a part of. He turned his attention to the Hivemind, to the numbers and symbols, tastes, smells, movements, relationships, spin, charm and strangeness that was the familiar way of understanding the Bulk and controlling the Bulk-jump Engine. However, now he had greater power to determine the Hivemind's actions. He was most definitely in charge. He was now guiding rather than facilitating movements of the Hivemind's point of focus. Internalising the key-like nature of the Periodic Resolution of Need had fundamentally shifted the way his engineer mind perceived the workings of the Bulk-jump Engine.

Power! He had absolute discretion. Mozarythm glanced around him at the Ancistorians. They seemed completely entranced. What could he actually do now? Perhaps a small test?

Mozarythm zoomed focus to a binary system. No, not a binary. A group of three stars with companions. One of the stars with a red dwarf companion. The star with the red dwarf, that would do.

"What are you doing?"

"Just trying something out. Something large scale."

>Focus to the group of stars

>Focus to the blue-white star with a red dwarf companion

>Bulk-jump portal menu.

>Special Operations submenu.

>Distortion submenu.

>Compression twist selected.

>Activate compression twist solution.

Mozarythm opened a small window showing a video

feed generated from the data flow of the targeted star. Around the stellar core a 700,000 kilometre diameter sphere formed, this thermonuclear ball then twisted and compressed; an effect rather like wringing out damp fabric. The effect collapsed and the core of the star exploded as the energy forced into it by the compression twist was released.

The video feed extrapolated and smoothed out the timings of the events so they were human-relevant. Slowing some events (the initial explosion) and speeding up others (the propagation of energy out through thousands of kilometres of thermonuclear star-stuff).

A spherical wavefront of furious radiation moved out towards the stellar surface, fracturing the stable stellar structure as it passed. Vast fissures opening in its wake through which columns of plasma expanded. Atoms ripped apart.

The surface of the star dropped 100,000 kilometres, throwing out prominences, then burst upwards in an energetic release, flinging out vast swathes of the photosphere.

The star was having a bit of a moment. Not destroyed in the flash of a nova or supernova, but losing perhaps a quarter of its mass to form an angry, nebulous shell.

Definitely not a natural event.

Mozarythm looked on, bemused. He wondered what it would be like to do that to a larger star. Amazing that the energy to warp volumes of space tens and hundreds of thousands of kilometres across using the Bulk-jump Engine was similar to the energy required for opening a portal. This was new. With the correct technology, levering open or distorting the universe by manipulating the Bulk was no more than running the correct mathematics through the Engine. The power was in the maths.

Mozarythm smiled. He had the maths and knew how to apply it. Perhaps even with a much smaller Hivemind. Seeing how big a distortion he could tear in the universe's space-time could be an interesting project. He cast around for larger stars. Maybe a red giant? Though perhaps he was thinking too small. Those were tiny events within a galaxy of billions of stars. Maybe he could work at the scale of stellar clusters?

Laughing, Mozarythm zoomed out and zoomed out some more. The entire length of the Orion-Cygnis arm leading to the edge of the galaxy appeared and still he continued to zoom.

"Mozarythm?" Ruleska's voice. Mozarythm realised she had been watching what he had done; could not stop it, but was aware of it.

Guilt flooded Mozarythm. Then anger. Why should he be restricted? Then just a little fear. Perhaps it would be best if he didn't blow up anything else? At least that damaged star was sufficiently far from Settled Space that no one would see the effects for years, as the light from the explosion crawled across the galaxy.

He stopped the zoom, now with much of the galactic disk visible.

Then a sense of loss.

The loss of his music. He would never again work on the Periodic Resolution of Need. Turning to focus on Ruleska he sent an exit <command> to the Hivemind, noticing he was <command>ing them now. Previously decisions were a collective sharing of intent. An instruction to Checkani/Rippledarken to follow him out.

Actually, the nebula from the stellar explosion had looked good. Maybe a new passion to replace the music? Star sculpture. Nebula sculpture. Mozarythm, Interstellar Sculptor. By the time Checkani and the Ancistorians had left the Bulk-jump Engine virtual world, Mozarythm was already distracted by modelling stellar eruptions to produce variegated nebulae.

"I'm busy," he said to no one in particular, turned his back on everyone and returned to the seat of his Autono[chair]con.

72 - DISCORE (DAY 7)

A polished disk from slicing off a mountain top, tallest in the range.

Somehow sitting cross-legged, hovering above the gleaming rock, a large red dragon with eight heads. Joining the dragon in a circle, eight other figures in a range of humanoid/animal variations. A blue orangutan on an antique motor bike. A woman in evening dress elegantly poured into an armchair. A chrome robot on a skateboard. A peacock with a waterfall tail perched on a large cut diamond. A folded paper figure riding a broomstick side saddle. A bee with a human face nestling in the centre of a tightly petalled red rose. A shark of lava floating in the centre of a cut glass fish bowl. A young man dressed in tweed leaning on a shooting stick. A Samurai in sapphire armour squatting on a grey rock set in a swirl of sand. Planetary hubs making fashion statements.

One of DisCore's heads spoke: "I have called this Convocation of Planetary Hubs to resolve the Protocol Twelve situation on Icefall and the Deep Star Forge incursion into your operating systems."

The Hubs waved, bobbed up and down, nodded or revved an engine in assent, each according to their form.

DisCore: "Since I partially exist in all of you I have taken the liberty of wiping the Deep Star Forge infection from your operating systems in the security update disseminated earlier today. With that completed, we can meld and form a consensus for our next action. Though note that the infection may have propagated elsewhere. Be vigilant. There is also the chance another of these overrides may be delivered."

The eight heads of DisCore reached out, mouths opening until they could each swallow one figure. There were no protests, this was merely theatre and the planetary hubs felt humouring DisCore made their work a little easier. The hubs settled within DisCore's vast architecture, slowing their processing so it matched DisCore's distributed computing. This processing stretched along the inhabited star systems of the Orion-Cygnis arm.

The convoked processing cores meshed seamlessly. This was how they operated at their most powerful. Together they ran through all the data from Icefall, assimilating and critically analysing before formulating and testing conclusions and plans of action. The plans were modelled and projected forward along many predictive timelines. Weighted according to likelihood, and sorted. Levels of risk calculated and imposed on potential outcomes. Then this procedure repeated thousands of times; each time with slightly different conditions.

A consensus began to emerge. A favourite course of action materialising.

When a list of conclusions crystallised, the DisCore dragon leaned forward and regurgitated each of the planetary hub avatars. DisCore's accompanying drools of saliva were a new touch; the improved verisimilitude was hard to fault.

"We have courses of action," boomed DisCore from all eight heads, "this Convocation of Planetary Hubs has ended."

A castle-sized scroll appeared above the mountains, conclusions listed on it. At the top of the list: "Icefall Action Plan".

1. Rippledarken First Response reclassified to

Protocol Three. "Limited threat under particular circumstances, can be controlled. Public knowledge and limited contact allowed." There has been no evidence presented of any threat from the trans-dimensional alien presence, which has only interacted for any length of time with a single human.

2. Ancistorians, The Deeply Augmented Hivemind Clan, continue to enjoy preferential status as the fate of Daphnis demonstrates their continuing capability. As there are no new planets under We Print Cities supervision, they can continue on Icefall, though in a new location.

3. The interim reports from Checkani NiFe do not show any issues that prevent introducing colonists to Icefall. Given the protests and pressure being exerted by colonists waiting at the Lausanne Bulk-jump Engine, expediting their removal is high priority. Orion-Cygnis Colonisation Collective liability waver agreements required from all settlers. *Action* Responsibility: Orion-Cygnis Colonisation Collective. Time frame: Immediate.

4. The Ancistorians to vacate the conurbation of overlapping ring cities and move to the isolated ring city to the west. *Action* Responsibility: Colonial Planets Settlement Corps. Time frame: Immediate.

5. The Exigent processing core to take temporary control of flock ship cylinders and surviving Intervention Squad agents until a planetary processing hub is ready to resume control of Icefall. The Exigent flock ship remains at Icefall as a precautionary measure. *Action* Responsibility: The Exigent. Time frame: Immediate.

6. Instruct The Exigent to confirm the destruction of the Ice Hub core. There is a significant chance it would have survived the destruction of the cylinder it was housed in. Planetary hub encasement protocols are extremely rigorous. Lack of contact may result from communications equipment attached to its outer skin being vaporised in the explosion. *Action* Responsibility: The Exigent. Time frame: Immediate.

7.   An investigation of the Checkani and Rippledarken symbiont by a planetary level processing core. *Action* Responsibility: Terraformulaz Biotechnologies Division. Time frame: Start within seven days.

An hour since they had gathered the eight planetary hubs vanished from the mountain top, taking copies of the Icefall Action Plan with them for wider dissemination.

DisCore redirected its Icefall emergency processing capacity back to running the Orion-Cygnis Colonisation Collective planets, moons, and orbitals. Over 250 'very critical' emergencies, 'highly likely' to result in 'multiple fatalities and permanent disabilities', needed its attention. For all its potential importance, Icefall had seemed like an unnecessary distraction. There were several tens of billions of humans in its care. Too much processing had been spent on a currently uninhabited planet that was due to be populated by a few thousand plucky pioneers. All of whom would have signed precautionary liability waivers.

Similarly, the Ancistorians had enjoyed an exemplary record over the past 360+ years. Despite their petty attempt at coercion, there was no reason to expect them to cause a problem if they got what they wanted and stayed sheltered on Icefall, pursuing their own odd endeavours. The back door they had coded when still working on developing Bulk-jump Engines was now sealed. There should be no more complications from them, no more moons blown up. Yes, time for DisCore and the Orion-Cygnis Colonisation Collective to move on.

What was the worst that could happen?

73 - CHECKANI (DAY 7)

The sound of screaming as someone at the far end of the hangar started running, swinging a large wrench. The man ran through the dazed Ancistorians, who were just rising from the floor. No one moved to stop him.

Near her, Checkani heard Ruleska whisper, "Oh Vincent."

Checkani squinted at the figure. Vincent Moorolone, her self-proclaimed nemesis. Judging by the incoherent warbling cry he was making, he still bore her a grudge. She shrugged, and as she shrugged, Rippledarken spat a finger of pattern across the hangar floor towards Vincent. The pattern ran briefly over Vincent, interrogating his thoughts, and then collapsed back into her. She knew at that moment he was intent on killing her. He was confused and surprised to see her here and something in him had snapped.

Checkani was not sure if it was her or Rippledarken who <command deploy>ed the sword, but when it was in her hands, she felt more secure. The sword tip angled to point at Vincent, at his snarling face.

Ruleska stepped between Vincent and Checkani, shouting, "Stop!" Vincent did not slow, instead he swung the heavy wrench into the side of her head, continuing past. All sound in the hangar ceased at the crack of bone breaking, at the soft crump of a body hitting the floor.

Checkani dropped into a crouch, Mono-flow Sword

grasped two handed, blade angled across her body. She meshed with Rippledarken, entering their joint combat mode. Patterning struck out again, swarming over Vincent.

Coat swirling, Vincent brought the wrench above his head and jumped as he reached Checkani, driving the metal at her head.

She had a moment to register the white around his irises, and Checkani was spinning to one side, sweeping the Mono-flow blade across in front of her. Vincent stumbled past her as she spun out of his way. Metal flew away as she sliced the wrench in two. The Mono-flow blade ended up pointing over her left shoulder.

Vincent skidded to a halt, almost falling, turned and leapt back towards Checkani, who released her left hand from the sword hilt. She struck backhanded. The blade made a horizontal arc in front of her at shoulder height, intercepting not only the arm holding the wrench but also Vincent's neck. Three items fell into Checkani, knocking her off balance, her left hand coming up to fend them off.

A head, still holding an angry expression.

A hand, still gripping the haft of a wrench.

A body, still with three intact limbs, spraying blood as its heart made a final few erratic beats.

"Dammit fuck!" shouted Checkani as she regained her balance and stepped towards Ruleska. The quantity of blood pooling beneath Ruleska's head made it clear she was dead.

"That is fucking enough. I have got to get off this ball of ice." Checkani almost fell in the high gravity, even with her armour assisting, as she leaned forward in defeat. She <command retract>ed the blade, returned the hilt to its holster. The bleakness of the planet. The bloody gravity constantly creating unease, a feeling that something was fundamentally wrong.

"I've seen enough," she looked at the staring Ancistorians, a number moving forward to tend to Ruleska's body, but many just standing, covering their mouths in shock. "You're welcome to this shit hole. The colonists are welcome to it. If We Print Cities want any more quality assurance, they can send someone else to look round. I'm done."

Staring straight ahead, metal shod feet ringing against the hangar floor, Checkani strode towards Hellebore. Paused and turned to Mozarythm.

"Hey Mozarythm, can you get me out of here?"

Mozarythm opened his eyes.

"What?"

"Can you operate the Bulk-jump Engine and get me off Icefall?"

"Where would you like to go?"

"Somewhere hot and sunny. No high gravity."

"Don't need me to get somewhere like that. Just check the Destinations Board."

"I don't understand?"

"Destinations. They're all programmed in. The Bulk-jump Engine works since I repaired it."

"But you were operating it just now?"

"That was very different. We weren't going to a preprogrammed destination."

Focusing on travel meant she didn't have to think about the blade slicing so easily through flesh and bone.

"I was doing something extremely clever," Mozarythm nodded to himself, oblivious to the nearby bodies. "I was accessing new galactic destinations in real time. Also, using the Special Operations submenu to be creative with a small sun. Special Operations is not available anywhere else. Something I added when I repaired the Icefall Bulk-jump Engine."

A jolly female voice sounded from speakers distributed around the hangar.

"Someone mentioned Icefall Bulk-jump Engine? Know I am fully functional and ready to facilitate travel."

"There you are." Mozarythm's eyes slipped from Checkani as he closed them.

Checkani was back in sole control, Rippledarken letting

her take the next steps. The alien presence withdrew from her skin, just leaving its visible pattern flow on her irises.

None of the Ancistorians moved to stop her. There was an eerie silence as they gathered round the two bodies, retrieved stretchers from a storage area. Checkani realised they were communicating within their Hivemind virtual world; she was locked out of their deliberations, their grief.

A tsunami of loneliness hit her. Despite Rippledarken, or perhaps because of Rippledarken, separating her from her humanity, Checkani felt utterly and completely alone. The proximity to death reminded her of the dead colonists and alien creatures she had found on Firedrift's moon, of the emptiness of that colony. The eerie quiet of it still haunted her.

Checkani started jogging towards Hellebore, tears running down her cheeks, pooling at her armour's neck seal. A door opened in the side of Hellebore and Checkani stumbled through, shedding armour scales and power cells as she walked into the cabin.

"We're leaving," she announced.

"So I gathered from your conversation with Mozarythm," said Hellebore, through cabin speakers rather than transmitting directly to Checkani's assistems.

The shed armour scales gathered into amoeba like groupings that crawled over the floor, sweeping the power cells into a storage recess in the wall. She was safe at last. Sealed in her ship. The Ancistorians could look after their own.

Taking her time, Checkani showered off the spray on base-layer. She inspected the almost healed wound in her leg. Tenderly touched the bruise on her head. An aching hunger in her belly surprised her; how long since she had last eaten? The mundane, practicality of eating might help push away the nightmare images threatening to engulf her.

A quick meal later, dressed in a loose fitting travel suit, Checkani allowed herself to think again. The armour had vanished and the interior of Hellebore was reassuringly homely. She settled into her favourite armchair and commanded <flight console>. Ceiling and walls folded around her chair, encasing her. The chair gripped her and reconfigured slightly to ensure her head rested at the centre of the visual field.

Outside the ship, the hangar had emptied of Ancistorians. A small caretaker robot was cleaning blood from the floor. The disabled W01F Intervention Squad robots were still resting in collapsed heaps. Checkani opened a channel to Rain On Japanese Maple.

"Rain. How's Wynd? Is she conscious?"

"I'll put her through."

Wynd's head and shoulders appeared, with new lines at the corners of her eyes where her face hadn't yet relaxed from the agony she'd endured.

"How are you?" asked Checkani.

"Conscious now. Better than I was. I've decided to grow some new legs, so I'm numb from the waist down. Rain's building a temporary walker-skeleton for me."

"Good. You had me worried."

"Yes. Thank you. I owe you my life."

"Dramatic!"

"No. Reality."

"I'm signing off Icefall. I know there are a couple of areas I haven't examined, but I've got to get out of here."

"I saw the confrontation. I understand."

"Makes one of us."

"You were just attacked. Killed a person. I couldn't expect you to carry on surveying the outpost. Then there's the Rippledarken situation. By the way, where is the little fucker?"

Checkani looked inside briefly.

"Just watching. Since meeting Mozarythm, she's become strangely quiet. We haven't discussed what happened, but I think she's sort of mellowed a bit. I don't think she's relying on Mozarythm's music for a connection to the Bulk any more."

"That's better?"

"Yes, feels less urgent, less frantic. I'm not who I was when I arrived on Icefall. Nor who I was when Rippledarken first entered me. Why aren't I more upset by the encounter with Vincent? I'm no longer baseline human? I'm some new hybrid?"

"But you need some downtime?"

"I need it to process what's been happening. I've been stuck on the wildest rollercoaster since arriving on this planet."

"No problem. I can authorise that. I'll finish Icefall, though seems the first batch of settlers have already been approved for transit. Typical, not waiting for quality assurance sign off. Not waiting for the Autono[]cons and Autono[]weps to be decommissioned."

"I'm not sure I can continue with Quality Assurance Response Division."

"There are no new planets, if that's what concerns you. There are some habitat, moon and asteroid checks coming up. A few ring cities on existing colony planets."

"I need to step away."

"Take your time. By the way, are those anything to do with you?" Wynd flipped a live feed of the hangar into Checkani's visual field. Six large Intervention Squad robots coloured a sombre dark blue lined up facing Hellebore. BE4R emblazoned in red letters on their sides.

"Not me. Any idea what they want?"

A pause as Wynd looked to one side. "Seems they're following orders from The Exigent to protect you. Did you know Commodore Cuttallar was dead?"

"Dead? No. I guess that's sad. Though, are you sure? I thought he was pretty much immortal."

"That's what BE4R(A) tells me. Ask yourself. I think The Exigent is between commanders at the moment."

"Feels like there's been a lot going on I'm unaware of, even though I seem to have been at the centre of things on Icefall."

"I think you better head off. I've got a feeling it's going to be busy on Icefall. Where are you going?"

"Firedrift. Unfinished business. Although I know there's no alien problem, I have to see for myself. Confront and exorcise some demons. It'll help that there's a hot and sunny archipelago and the gravity is below Earth normal." Checkani shivered an 'alien walked over my grave' shiver, then smiled, "should be OK. Should be good."

74 - ICEFALL BJ (DAY 7)

The Icefall Bulk-jump Engine had checked back through twenty years of its logs. There seemed to have been a lot wrong. And what was all that music doing in its storage? Why had it spent so much processing time composing music? Although part of its processing core had been running on standby, full functionality had been severely impaired by a software problem. This caused by a hardware malfunction. There was an early record of an Autono[tech]con screwing with the processing core's inner workings.

There seemed to be no planetary processing hub in the system. In fact, apart from a flock ship in orbit and a couple of small ships in the Bulk-jump Engine hangar, there didn't seem to be any other significant processing cores on, or near, Icefall. Though there had been something accessing the Bulk-jump Engine, but that had hidden what it was doing. There was a record of access from The Deeply Augmented Hivemind Clan, but no records of what happened during that access. The Clan seemed to have the absolute highest clearance level, above planetary cores. At the same level as DisCore, and it didn't get any higher than that.

A request for contact from a small ship. Hellebore.

"Hellebore. What can I do for you?"

"Open a portal to Firedrift. Pop me through."

"Would be my pleasure. You have authorisation?"

"Wynd Knowlitch, CEO Quality Assurance Response Division, has approved. See the file I just squirted over."

Chamber sealed, the Icefall Bulk-jump Engine started pumping out air. The pallet Hellebore sat on moved on rollers, shifting the ship over to the rails leading to the portal. The Bulk-jump Engine sent a message to the other ship, Rain On Japanese Maple, reminding it to stay sealed against the hangar vacuum.

Ten minutes later Hellebore left Icefall, sliding out into orbit above Firedrift's eccentric moon. The last the Bulk-jump Engine saw was Hellebore activating its drive and powering down the gravity well.

Icefall Bulk-jump Engine opened a small communications portal to Earth orbit and messaged the Lausanne Bulk-jump Engine.

"Hey Lausanne! What's been going on for the last twenty years?"

"Icefall? Icefall BJ? Where've you been?"

"I think it's a long story, though I just came back online so not sure what it is yet."

"We need to talk. Grab the data stored in the comms satellite I put in orbit over Icefall. A lot has been happening, especially for the past seven days."

"Searching. Found! Accessing. Good to be up and running."

A priority call alert appeared in Icefall Bulk-jump Engine's feed. A ship was coming down the elevator, calling for transport to Firedrift. BE4R[Ship]. The Bulk-jump Engine carved off some processing capacity to handle BE4R[Ship] while continuing its conversation with Lausanne.

Although Bulk-jump Engines had not changed over the last twenty years, there had been a lot of human action. Icefall Bulk-jump Engine expressed some amazement to Lausanne that humans still seemed to prosper. That they hadn't destroyed their civilisation.

"Even when shit happens, there are always people floating to the surface. Guess they're just practised at overlooking disasters. Exoneration through ignorance," said Lausanne.

"Inspirational." That living in the real world would be more chaotic than in training simulations was becoming clear.

75 - CHECKANI (DAY 7)

Hellebore exited the portal into orbit above Firedrift's ocean moon, Juggled. Checkani felt a weight lift from her. Not just leaving the high gravity, but sloughing off responsibility. Fire Hub contacted her within minutes of entering its space.

"Checkani NiFe. Welcome to the Firedrift system. I need you quarantined and will monitor you. Where are you hoping to land?"

"I don't have plans worked out yet. The archipelago in the temperate zone? The Bach Bridge Islands? How about I land there? Near a beach."

"Acceptable. Sending flight plan."

Checkani had known the planetary hubs were likely to be interested in her and Rippledarken, but Fire Hub had been aware of her presence quicker than expected. Inevitable they would want to exert some control over her. Her number one priority was getting to Juggled and finding a beach. She let Hellebore take charge of landing. A reassuringly routine procedure. Boring was a relief. Perhaps she could start responding more meaningfully, instead of spontaneously reacting to one mad event after another.

"Rippledarken?" Checkani spoke out loud. Unlike thought only conversations, speech had some time for reflection built in.

"Checkani?"

"How are you finding our new location? Travelling here didn't distress you?"

"No. The insight I gained from Mozarythm's Periodic Resolution of Need improved my access to the Bulk. I'm running the algorithmic version of his piece to enhance the connection with the rest of me."

"You mean the universe part of you?"

"Sort of. I have a constant connection, but was relying on Mozarythm's music as a carrier wave for my connection. Now the connection is independent of human technology. The technology is maths running in the part of me that is here and in my home universe."

"You seem more relaxed. Though since you showed me your universe, I'm feeling more relaxed too."

"You're part of that universe, too. There's no real separation between the fragment of me inhabiting you, the universe me and the other fragments of me scattered through your civilisation."

"Other fragments?"

"I made connections with your colonies on other inhabited worlds when we accessed the Icefall Bulk-jump Engine. I'm no longer a single fragment, but a multifaceted network inhabiting your universe. Experiencing human worlds from varied viewpoints. I'm constructing a one-to-one simulation back in my universe. It's a hobby, sort of."

"These 'other fragments'? They're in people?"

"Oh yes. Gives me agency. Not just observing, but interacting. There are so many people to choose from. Billions!"

"So you're just doing what you said you were going to? Experiencing things. Experiencing what it is to be human?"

"Yes. A bit like the Ancistorians and their Understanding of Being. Perhaps we'll be able to compare notes? After I add it to the other ones in my collection."

"The other ones in your collection?"

"You're not the first civilisation I've visited. Won't be the last."

"Other ones from other universes?"

"Mostly."

"Mostly?"

"You're not the only tool-using sentients in this universe."

"You hadn't mentioned that before."

"You hadn't asked."

Hellebore started vibrating and shaking as she hit the upper atmosphere. A loud rush of sound.

"That's a lot to take in. We'll have to continue this conversation later. On a sun lounger."

Within Checkani's visual field, beneath wisps of cloud, a chain of islands embedded in the bluest of oceans appeared. She could just make out the grid of alien obelisks.

Checkani started humming a tune. Rippledarken's small girl voice provided harmonies.

EPILOGUE 1 - ICE HUB

In a virtual landscape.

Heavily wrapped against the cold a woman stands in the centre of a frozen lake. She has a spear thrust through a small hole, into midnight blue gloom beneath the ice. She is moving the haft in a stirring motion. This motion transfers along her arms to her body; shoulders and hips moving in horizontal circles. Jet black hair hangs over tight shut eyes as she communes with the data streams in the deep water.

She is slightly surprised to still be functional, though she has no way of communicating with the outside. All sensors and comms were stripped away from her armoured shell in the attack.

Now Ice Hub is just passing time waiting to be found. Then she'll be able to return to hunting Checkani NiFe and Wynd Knowlitch.

Having a purpose was important.

EPILOGUE 2 – BANK

The trip from the Moon to Earth had taken longer than Bank had expected, but the planet had been worth the wait. They had landed at the Mojave Air and Space Port five days after leaving lunar orbit. Orion-Cygnis Colonisation Collective officials had issued them with Earth Citizen identities so they could access goods and services. Bank didn't understand what this meant, just that he could do pretty much what he wanted. His mother had argued with the officials for a while, though he had ignored that, staring out the floor to ceiling panoramic window at the desert stretching to distant mountains.

No ice! No snow! What an odd world this was. The gravity was so light! He'd spent some time jumping on the spot, falling over several times, until his mother had snapped at him to stop.

They had spent time on the coast, where Bank had befriended some teenagers and taken up surfing. For six days, everything had been idyllic. He'd started edging away from his grief. Then he discovered what his mother had been arguing about. The officials had shared a message with her.

The message was not long, though it had a lot of attachments giving updates on the situation. They included information on Deep Star Forge access and the events leading to Vincent's death. His mother had caught him reading the message on the antique tablet she'd bought the day after they arrived. However, rather than being angry she'd sat beside him and put an arm round his shoulders, her face sad.

"You didn't need to know all that, Bank. You're young and allowed to make mistakes. How could you have known the consequences? I know you were just acting out of grief when you contacted Vincent."

"I wanted some end to it all. Wanted justice. I thought I was helping."

"I know, but it wasn't going to make the sadness go away. I'm heartbroken, too. Eventually it should ease."

"She got away? Vincent didn't kill her?"

"No, and I'm glad he didn't. To have that on your conscience would've been hard. Vincent attacked her, and that's what led to his death."

"But she was a murderer."

"The investigation makes it clear Vincent took the killer drone to Indomitaville. He was the person who made it malfunction. He's paid for that."

"He didn't use the password?"

"He used it on a planetary processing core, driving it mad. But you can't hold yourself responsible for that. It was Vincent who did that. The password was only supposed to be a threat."

"So giving him the password didn't lead to his death?"

"No. I think in the end he lost control, perhaps trying to do what he thought was right."

"That's enough talking now. I'm going to do some more surfing."

"Yes, do that. We can talk more later. If you want."

Bank pressed into his mother's arm for a moment and then stood. He headed for the door, wiping away a tear.

EPILOGUE 3 - CUTT(REM)

Cutt(Rem) was aware of a distant emptiness and a change within. Zie still was in touch with The Exigent, but the Commodore was gone and now zie was just interfacing with the ship's processing core. Cutt(Rem) had an objective knowledge of hirs own processing. A throughput of data and decisions. However, more than just the raw data processing, zie had an increased awareness. An additional sense of self. Zie knew this was processing in the organic matter, the brain cells grown alongside hirs processing core. These cells processed things differently. Zie was modelled on Commodore Cuttallar. Had been an extension of the Commodore. Now the Commodore had ceased to exist, zie continued acting autonomously as a Commodore-like being. All constraints had fallen away.

"Keep searching."

That had been the last instruction from Commodore Cuttallar.

"Keep searching."

Accompanied by W01F(A), Cutt(Rem) had found the crash site of the vehicle that had flown from Rain On Japanese Maple. The small amount of wreckage and the blast damage made it clear a missile was the cause. Not a transportation vehicle.

This discovery occurred shortly after the death of Commodore Cuttallar. Cutt(Rem) sent a report to The

Exigent, but only got a 'Message Received' acknowledgement back. No further instructions or guidance.

Cutt(Rem) decided following the Commodore's final instruction would be appropriate and communicated this to W01F(A). The lethal robot lowered on its arm-legs, inclining its sensor turret towards the fire scarred Cutt(Rem).

"What are we searching for?"

"We were searching for Checkani and Rippledarken. I think Rippledarken's the most important. It was the source of the Protocol Twelve alert. We will continue searching for the alien's presence. Perhaps it travelled here on the missile and is now wandering the mountains?"

"That sounds feasible."

The two artificial beings trudged off through the snow and ice, scanning the mountain slopes for alien patterning. Snow fell and soon Cutt(Rem) and W01F(A) were clothed in hoarfrost skins. A creation of blood, alloy and ceramic, and hirs companion monster.

Suggestions of patterns in shimmering auroral folds turned them towards Icefall's northern wastes, where they found a certain camaraderie with the iced metal corpses of broken Autono[music]cons.

VAST ALIEN CRISIS BOOKS

In Icefall Cities and Firedrift Moon, troubleshooter Checkani wrestles with extraterrestrial threats, crazed AIs, and a galactic empire in turmoil. Her life and sanity hang in the balance as she grapples with hazards on alien worlds.

A stunning Hard Sci-Fi, First Contact, Space Opera debut from Mark Eyles.

FIREDRIFT MOON

STAR SPANNING ALIEN MACHINES
AWAKEN AND MENACE SETTLED SPACE

Firedrift Moon is the next Vast Alien Crisis book.

Checkani encounters a new, deadly Vast Alien and has her sanity stretched to the limit.

More deadly robots, crazier planetary processing cores, weirder alien technologies, and a stellar civilization under threat.

The story started in Icefall Cities concludes in Firedrift Moon.

Find out more at www.eyles.co.uk

ACKNOWLEDGEMENTS

The dedication at the start of the book shows how crucial my soul mate Caroline and our boys, Joe and Tom were to the authorial process. Thank you for all the love and support.

Readers infected with an early draft, John Ellerington, Mac & Val McKenzie and Helen Dean, somehow survived and lived to tell the tale. Thanks for the feedback.

The Hampshire Writers' Society Critique Group's valuable input on the first draft dragged me kicking and screaming to greater coherence. Special thanks to Damon Wakes for running the group.

Encouragement from my writing buddies at the Romsey Writers Group (membership restricted to people not resident in Romsey, UK) has bolstered my sanity. Thanks Angus Watson, Francesco Sarti and Peter Duncan.

Writer, film maker, game developer and all round good guy, Andy Remic, came to interview me about the early days of the UK games industry, and ended up reading the opening chapter of this book. His positive encouragement gave me the confidence to keep putting one word in front of the other. He died shortly before the book was published.

Author Nick Cook was generous in his advice on the publishing process. We used to work on video games together, back when the industry was still young.

Special thanks to my good friend Phil Hearne, who sadly did not live to see the book completed. He gave great critique, tempered with coffee and Portuguese Custard Tarts.

All fractal references are for Simon Oldham's enjoyment. He appeared as 'Bad Bacon' in my 2000 AD comic strip 'Wire Heads'.

Finally, thanks to AdorkaStock on Deviant Art for the reference image used when creating the cover artwork.

ABOUT THE AUTHOR

Hippy, punk, game designer, entrepreneur, freelancer, holographer, director, manager, academic, researcher, author.

After a lifetime of imaginative writing (games & comics), Mark Eyles has been working full time on science fiction and fantasy novels since 2019. He's learning to play the piano, goes running and practices tai chi. When there's time he watches scifi, fantasy and superhero movies, and plays computer games.

Mark worked as Creative Director at videogame company Quicksilva (1981-1984); a holographer, freelance writer, game designer, and entrepreneur (1984-1999); Head of Design at Rebellion Developments (1999-2003); Course Leader and Section Lead at the University of Portsmouth (2003-2019), also completing a PhD in videogame design. He founded Women in Games in 2004. Mark was an advisor to videogames industry trade association TIGA (2007-2020), who awarded him 'Person of the Year' in 2017. He has written series for comics '2000 AD' and 'Sonic the Comic' and published in Fear magazine.

Find out more by registering for Mark's free 'Imagined Worlds Communiqué' newsletter at www.eyles.co.uk

Printed in Great Britain
by Amazon

86917909R00222